THINKING
ANIMALS

PAUL SHEPARD

THINKING

Animals and the Development of Human Intelligence

ANIMALS

THE VIKING PRESS | New York

ACKNOWLEDGMENT
J. B. Lippincott Company: From *An Alphabestiary*
by John Ciardi. Copyright © 1965, 1966 by John Ciardi.
Reprinted by permission of J. B. Lippincott Company.

First published in 1978 by The Viking Press
625 Madison Avenue, New York, N.Y. 10022

Published simultaneously in Canada by
Penguin Books Canada Limited

LIBRARY OF CONGRESS CATALOGING IN PUBLICATION DATA
Shepard, Paul, 1925–
 Thinking animals.
 Includes bibliographical references and index.
 1. Animals and civilization. 2. Intellect.
I. Title.
QL85.S5   128′.3   77-10338
ISBN 0-670-70061-4

Printed in the United States of America
Set in Primer

For their stimulating presence, without which the ideas that follow would have remained unformed, this book is dedicated to *Buteo jamaicaicensis, Colaptes chrysoides, Eptesicus fuscus, Rana catesbeiana, Chaetura pelagica, Agkistrodon contortrix, Sceloporus undulatus, Bubo virginianus, Crotaphytus collaris, Coccyzus americanus, Scalopus aquaticus, Urocyon cinereoargenteus, Epiaeschna heros, Vanessa atalanta, Elaphus maximus, Butorides viresceus,. Cryptobrancus alleganiensis, Papilo marcellus, Actias luna, Oridatra zibethica, Equus burchelli, Bufo terrestris, Colinus virginianus, Archilochus colubris, Lycaenopsis argiolus, Lepomis megalotis, Terrapene carolina, Ursus americanus, Corvus brachyrhychos, Didelphis virginiana, Limenitis arthemis, Micropterus salmoides, Passer domesticus, Sylvagicus floridanus, Cercyonis pegala, Trionyx muticus. . . .*

Z is not for zebra, but for ZOOLOGY,
Since our effort herein has been to achieve
the inclusive view rather than any
particular stripe, we are firm on this point.

Habit has its own animals and will cling
to them, but perception concerns all beasts.

Therefore Zoology, which is the science
most like a looking glass, teaching us
resemblances, when we learn to face them.

—John Ciardi
From *An Alphabestiary*

CONTENTS

THINKING
ANIMALS

1 ON ANIMALS THINKING

Preparing the Soil for Thought

A world where people are beginning to crowd one another intolerably is a world too small for animals. Until recent centuries, big clusters of people were widely separated. In the towns some animals, such as pets, sparrows, and cockroaches, thrived, but the realm of the wild birds and mammals was between towns. Now the planet is becoming a city. Animals that once lived on farms or simply away from civilization soon will no longer find space. They use "our" air, land, food, and water. If that nonhuman life is to continue, it will be only because it is purposely included in the human designs on the Earth, because animals are more valuable than the resources they use. In a world of periodic starvation and widespread poverty, where wants are created daily by civilization itself, that will be a hard value to prove. A huge, well-fed human population, sustained by global manipulations of our island planet, cannot afford animals—not unless they are essential to us.

What necessity could this be? Technology is rapidly replacing animals as both workers and material substances. Research in medicine is increasing with tissues and cells rather than whole creatures. Our pleasures and our aesthetics can find alternatives. Oil, nuclear power, and solar energy make the man-animal partnerships of the past obsolete. In a Buckminster Fuller world there is no time, room, or need for creatures bigger than yeasts and bacteria. The great passion for human betterment is endless, repeating around the globe the theme of a world garden, green lawns, and plastic domes. After centuries the brutes and monsters that for so long contended with and haunted us have all been put down.

So it seems. Such is the myth of fossilfuelman. But there is a

1

profound, inescapable need for animals that is in all people everywhere, an urgent requirement for which no substitute exists. It is no vague, romantic, or intangible yearning, no simple sop to our loneliness or nostalgia for Paradise. It is as hard and unavoidable as the compounds of our inner chemistry. It is universal but poorly recognized. It is the peculiar way that animals are used in the growth and development of the human person, in those most priceless qualities which we lump together as "mind." It is the role of animal images and forms in the shaping of personality, identity, and social consciousness. Animals are among the first inhabitants of the mind's eye. They are basic to the development of speech and thought. Because of their part in the growth of consciousness, they are inseparable from a series of events in each human life, indispensable to our becoming human in the fullest sense.

This claim will seem extravagant and even offensive to some. At the center of our humanity is pride in our independence from animals and animality. We have bodies as they do, but we also have minds. We tell ourselves that minds can free us not only from the animal in us but also from the animals around us. In our mortal life this mind is the focus and the means of all we most prize, our hope for making something of ourselves, of rising above mere existence.

My thesis is that the mind and its organ, the brain, are in reality that part of us most dependent on the survival of animals. We are connected to animals not merely in the convenience of figures of speech—a zoological equivalent of "flowery speech"— but by sinews that link speech to rationality, insight, intuition, and consciousness. It is not the same as thinking *about* animals. The connection is in the act and nature of thought, the working of mind.

Animals themselves have brains and probably share some aspects of our mental experience. Our animal ancestors were in this way, as in others, intermediate between ourselves and other kinds of animals. Mind is a universal and very ancient dimension of life, widely shared in varying degree. But to claim that living animals are a necessary part of the mental growth of humans goes far beyond our casual, poetic sharing of a generalized quality. What follows is not so much about animals as about people; the ways people must use animals because animals evoked, during the long stretch of the past, our human capacity for minding. We cannot avoid the subject of the evolution of intelligence in order to understand its workings. Every child is committed to the use of animal images in the shaping of his own consciousness because thought arose in the past as an interaction between different animals and between people and animals.

It is customary in describing the evolution of intelligence to arrange the creatures in ascending order, and to find correlates of the details of the human brain in the different levels of animal life. But there is an emptiness to such an approach that cannot be avoided. It dumps us into the present as a unique fulfillment, the survivor of all the sunken hulks of the past. This kind of human thinking of evolving from animals turns the rest of the world of life into a vestigial zoo. Our frustration with this isolation from other life makes us resent its otherness. Our culture is hostile to the physical, material world. By their very presence the other creatures haunt us as beings we have evolved from; their being seems to affirm that our consciousness sets us free in an unprecedented cosmos, surrounded by ghosts, loosed from all guidelines, each of us a bundle of wandering thoughts.

But there is another way of understanding that evolution. What is to be known, even in our self-conscious distance from other life, is predicated by the nature of mind. Man is a unique combination of qualities and organs like those of other animals. They are the framework in which his thought is given and in which it works. This history of nature is the history of what to think, what conclusions the probing mind can arrive at, what questions it can raise. We do not graduate from animality but, in our most prized capacity, into it and through it.

The necessity of animals is psychological. Its roots are in the history of intelligence. That history is like a busy atelier of active, crucial figures and events. Among them are flowers, fruits, seeds, insects, soil, birds, primates, and other large mammals. From our view in the present, that arena of moving forms which makes up evolutionary time seems almost like a dance whose purpose and objective was ourselves.

But the evolution of mind is not like a great river of species, emptying only into us. It is a tangle that diverges instead of coming together. It is not a single great crescendo of emergence, but a pulsing or surging, separated by still pools of time. Its background is the era of reptiles, played out in vast swamps and low-lying forests of evergreen: conifers, horsetails, algae, mosses, and ferns. The flowering plants and mammals which were to revolutionize that world were at first a minor part of it. Then, amid worldwide volcanic activity related to collisions of the great tectonic plates bearing the drifting continents, whose bent edges were riddled with deep fractures and outpourings of molten materials, new upland habitats appeared, the climate was altered, and the world was dappled with the first blooms.

Gradually the flowers evoked and responded in their own evolution to a growing host of insects. The insects supervised flower pollination, engaging with them in alliances that would gradually spread color and deepen the organic blanket across the Earth for a hundred million years. This collaboration was probably the most fateful event in the history of mind. It created soil, the world of color, fruit, and the seed. Seeds, with their nutrient and energy-storing capacity, would eventually support whole families of primates and dynasties of large prey and predators, the mammalian herbivores and carnivores.

The plant-insect symbiosis gave birth to a true humus and soil, the most complex organic system in the world. Until then, the land was only freckled with life. Afterwards, the soil (and ooze at the bottom of lakes) became a skin, mediating the mineral and biological kingdoms. Intelligence is a fragile thing, and the soil was its nest, the flower its first encyclopedia, and the seed its source of power.

Because of flowers, a thin, sour, silent world was turned into a sweet nursery, and out of its microbial ferment came three quarters of the world's million species of animals, the insects, still being discovered at more than a thousand new species per year. We acknowledge (as grassland primates) the roots of our existence in their gift to the prairie community. Their marvelous perceptual systems involve the distinctions of color, odor, number, symmetry, and even sound. They are attuned to the pigments, oils, vitamins, and other special compounds of plants to a degree beyond our experience and understanding. They have exquisitely sensitive organs and behaviors that are phased and synchronized over life cycles that last as much as seventeen years. These complex cycles, mostly spent underground or inside plants, are keyed to the seasons and to other organisms. They are able to locate precisely what they need, care for their young, and communicate. Yet all this does not require or develop in them reflective thought or imagination. It is almost as though they are the secret chemical ingredients that make the prairie's thinking possible.

The soil was, and is, their main incubator, a placenta modulating the world's rawness, otherwise too wet or dry, hot or cold, too acid or too barren to dependably share out the compounds generated by decomposition. The diversity of flowering plants and the complexity of plant structure, especially of the flowers proper, and the vast array of insects associated with particular species are the foundation upon which the world's ecological stability rests. That stability is the forerunner of warm bodies, and only warm bodies have keen minds. Complex natural communities make complex bodies, make intelligence.

The most characteristic feature of such communities is their multiplicity. The variation of the flowering plants and of the parts of plant anatomy, especially flower and fruit parts, and the profusion of associated insects are like so many tributaries of the life stream. Such variety and diversity are not only the source of intelligence but the necessary subject of all thought, for the thing mind must do above all else is make distinctions and choices. Beyond that, benefiting from experience and communicating the decisions are marks of superior brains.

Diversity is relative, but there may be some yet undiscovered relationship between the number of kinds of things in a world and the possibilities open to intelligence. Why are there not ten times as many or ten times fewer animals than there are? Ecologist G. Evelyn Hutchinson has suggested that the number of terrestrial forms is the result of the number of food chains, that is, the routes that energy can flow within a natural community. The chains begin with plants. The question becomes one of the diversity, size, and complexity of plant species and their support, in turn, of specialized herbivores. Beyond that, diversity is limited by the number of links in food chains, usually about six. By the time F eats E, which ate D, which ate C, which ate the herbivore B, which ate the plant A, there is not enough energy left to pass on to a level G.

As for the relationship all this has to human intelligence, we anticipate a little from later chapters, but Anthony Wallace once observed that the number of kinship terms in folk cultures corresponded roughly with semantic spaces; that is, our ability to discriminate between stimuli, such as sound frequencies or colors. The number is indicated both from perceptual testing and lexicons or collections of names. The cognitive limit is said to be characterized by the 2^6 rule. Beyond about 64 the complexity of sets ceases to increase, giving way simply to the number of sets. Whether this rule of six binary dimensions is in any way associated with our taxonomies of animals has not been studied.

There is a physical as well as psychological aspect to natural complexity. Diversity is generally recognized as a stabilizing dimension. Rich communities of plants and animals fluctuate less in all ways than sparse ones. Nervous systems are delicate and complicated. No one yet knows how many kinds of plants and animals are needed to stabilize natural systems enough for any given level of brain complexity.

If mind, in this view of history, begins with insects, one still hopes not to slight the tribes of life that had previously come and gone, or the great families of fish, amphibians, and reptiles, some of whom remain, none of whom should be considered only as links in a chain connecting the beginnings of life to ourselves or seen as totally lacking in intelligence. Their orders, together with the precursors of the insects, the rich, unseen world of the invertebrates, and the ancestors of the first mammals need no apology.

So the era of intelligent life as *we* understand it was initiated at the end of a long geological peace. It went in five directions, all of them ultimately dependent on the concentrated packaging of the embryos and nutrients by the flowering plants.

One was the way of insects, masterpieces of finely tuned sensory systems with precise, pre-programmed muscle responses and elegant social unions. A second was the way of birds, eaters of seeds and insects, each of whose minds are conscious instruments of extraordinary visual and auditory integration for following instructions to move through a space defined by a map in the head. The third and the fourth are interrelated. They are the large mammals—the predators on the one hand and prey on the other. The dynamic of pursuit and escape is the great sculptor of brains. While this includes the dolphins and whales, as well as the elephants, we know less about the genesis of their psyches than we do about such terrestrial carnivores as the big cats and members of the wolf family or their prey—the deer, antelope, and other hoofed forms. Hunter and hunted are engaged in an upward, reciprocal spiral of consciousness with its constituents of stratagem and insight. (The small animals are predators or prey, too, but their skulls are too small for good brains; their size in relation to terrain and plants gives a different cast to their mobility; and their habits in the dark are more mechanical than tactical.) The final group is the primates, especially the monkeys and apes, those graceful, highly social fruit-munchers for whom experience forms a perceptual world. Zoologically, this is "our" group and the evolution of human intelligence is incomprehensible except in the primate framework. Unlike that of the apes, however, our past is ecologically intertwined with that of the large mammals of the open country. So it is to them and the clues from the grassland pre-predator system that we look first for intelligence in general and then for the special episodes in our own beginnings.

The grasses are central to this intricate history of the relationship among seeds, nervous systems, and minds, even though they themselves do not have bright blooms and pollinating insects. The story—our story—is one of the cycle of events relating flowers and mammals in grasslands, starting more than fifty million years ago.

The Post-Archaic World; or How Thinkers Started the Day with Cereals

Progressive intelligence is the evolutionary sharpening of mind due to the interplay between animals. Except among the primates, it is not so spectacular in forests as in open country. It is easy to imagine great trees and giant forests as the acme of plant evolution, but there is actually something about endless woods that is stultifying, and even relatively simple. Far more complex and elegant are the grasslands: the prairies, tundras, steppes, and savannas of the world. Trees are comparatively shallow beings and the earth beneath them a cool veneer. Wood and tree leaves are mostly cellulose and lignin, indigestible for most animals, materials that fungi and bacteria slowly recycle. In contrast, the prairie plants are high in pectin and protein, available in the whole tissue of the plant, substances rich in the compounds of life. The deep roots of grasses, interlaced across whole chunks of continents, penetrate, absorb, store, transport, deliver from bedrock to the bright surface, yet tunnel and build their own organic substances into the mineral substrate. They die and decompose as humus, processed by hordes of microbes into the world's richest soils. These soils support prairie and steppe habitats. We call them grasslands because we recognize that the grass seeds support large mammals. The term is botanically misleading. Although grasses are a conspicuous part, a typical modern prairie has only about 20 percent grasses and at least that many legumes and composites; that is, the nitrogen-fixing and conspicuous flowering forms. The remainder of the flora is a mix of hundreds of species, from algae to mosses to rare orchids. The vast flowering spectacle of the plains is not due to grasses, whose flowers are small and mostly independent of insects. But the whole community supports the perennial grasses, the grain-makers.

The grassland flora are the most advanced kinds of plants from the whole experimental laboratory of evolution, and they are accompanied by the most diverse and complex animals: the insects and vertebrates. It is the ultimate community of life, a chemistry so intricate that it remains, late in the twentieth century, mostly an enigma. The intelligence of mammals and insects and birds is the mind of the grassland. The brainy things exist by dint of their prairie home, which they pollinate, ventilate, disperse, fertilize, and crop.

Because of the energy they could store, seeds made big bodies and big brains possible. But at first it was only bigger bodies. The early millions of years of this history do not point toward more than minimal intelligence. The most ancient mammals seem to have been honed for size by evolution in the open, while their brains increased only enough to serve their greater mass. Such size changes in brain and body follow an allometric rule: the brain is enlarged at two thirds the rate of body enlargement. Brain efficiency makes up for the difference. Hence, big animals tend to have proportionately smaller brains and heads than little animals.

This two-thirds relationship between brain and body was typical of the ancestors of the grassland mammals for several hundred million years. As each new species emerged with more weight than its ancestors, it kept the conservative brain-body map. Meanwhile the prairie itself slowly grew in complexity, its soils deeper and reserves greater. The progenitors of the hoofed mammals appeared in the savannas among their massive, relatively sluggish cousins, the carnivores, crude by modern standards, committed to an uncomplicated search-and-destroy pattern.

Very slowly something quite different began. The fossil record of skull sizes shows emphasis on brains. This change foreshadowed the end of the simple rule of chance and strength for predator and prey. Unlike their archaic ancestors, these new forms began to develop brains beyond the minimum needed to coordinate bodies in fixed patterns and serve the mechanics of physiology. Sheer roulette of the open tablelands, in which eater happened onto his victim or prey happened not to be found, gave way to stalking and escaping.

Over the past one hundred million years four whole groups of such progressive mammals have come and, except for the last, gone. The record of disproportionately bigger brains is indisputable. It signifies an investment in brains as specialized adaptations by hunters and hunted with large bodies. The carnivore ceased searching at random and began to track, stalk, intercept, and coordinate. Instead of seeking the prey itself, the hunter would start by seeking signs of the prey. From largely automatic responses and reflexes the hunt shifted to persistence, combined sensory modalities, memory, experience, and skill. The older predators had simply searched, like the herbivores themselves roving through a world of scattered but abundant food. That strategy of search-and-find was associated with reflexive and mechanical patterns of attack, simple response chains. The techniques of the newer stalkers began to vary with the species hunted, to be aimed at selected individuals, and to take advantage of special features of the terrain, wind, and group interaction. Out of this progressive predation came hunting skills so highly timed and carefully coordinated that the old became leaders and the young had to be taught.

The prey, on the other hand, would not last long unless it could respond in its own capacity for stratagem. Indeed, the archaic forms did not last. Only a progressive prey could withstand the emphasis on intelligent assault. Being faster or bigger was not enough. Natural selection from the pressure of increasingly intelligent predators produced clever escape tactics. Recognition of differences in the behaviors of different predator species, insight into the body language of distant hunters, the employment of terrain or water as barriers, deliberately confusing the trail, decoying the pursuers from the more vulnerable individuals, complex group movements and defenses—these are only a few of the sorts of behaviors that emerged from the more flexible capacity for learning and the development of social integration by which the herbivores countered the tactics of the carnivores.

The ratio of brain to body size, or "encephalization quotient," among both predators and prey can be compared for the four series of grassland-inhabiting mammals.

MAMMAL GROUP	HERBIVORE	CARNIVORE
I (archaic)	.18	.44
II (60–30 million years ago)	.38	.61
III (30–13 million years ago)	.63	.76
IV (recent)	.95	1.10*

Notice that the hunter always has a relatively bigger brain than its prey. This must be so; the contest cannot be equal or the predator would die as a species. But too much success is also destructive. The predator must have an advantage but not reduce the prey too much. The result is an upward spiral of intelligence occurring over the ages among interacting big-bodied mammals, mostly in grasslands. The combination of circumstances, habitats, and interactions is essential to our understanding of mind. The animal groups to which it refers are the hoofed animals and the wolf and cat families.†

It is fair to ask at this point what this has to do with our intelligence, since we belong to none of these groups. The answer will be forthcoming. First, some further observation on this system of brains and plains.

Popular zoology often gives the impression of evolution running all-out in certain directions. The fifty million years of mutual honing and selection between prey and predators was never unqualified. Every mutation has its price, especially where brains and behavior are involved. Brains put heavy demands on nutrients, energy, and oxygen. They affect prenatal and postnatal life for both mother and offspring. The time committed to immaturity and growth, the delicacy and fragility of the brain itself, and the probabilities of going wrong by interfering with

* Table from Jerison. See Notes.
† A parallel process of the evolution of tactical social hunting and cunning escape in the open may also account for the intelligence of the marine mammals. It probably also accounts for the intelligence of many of the rodents.

other neural and behavioral systems, and of psychopathology all act conservatively to dampen increased braininess. Calculated choices do not necessarily lead to survival more often than spontaneous responses. The slow working toward better brains among the hunters and hunted was not isolated feedback, independent of the rest of the species' requirements; it had to be subordinated to the function of the whole animal and every aspect of its life. Only four or five orders of mammals among twenty have some species specialized in big brains: the primates, the two orders of hoofed animals, their terrestrial predators, and the marine mammals. For each group, or for each community of life, there seems to be a balance struck, like distribution along a normal curve, requiring or distributing other specializations that inevitably diminish intelligence. When all this is taken into account, and when we reflect on what a mess man is making of the planet, we can see the wisdom of the genes in a highly restrained commitment to flexible behavior.

In the popular image, evolution not only races along in certain directions, but sweeps all before it. For example, the anthropologist Pierre Teilhard de Chardin and his followers perceive the evolutionary emergence of mind as a kind of shell growing around the planet, a "noosphere." This gives the mistaken impression that all brains are growing. But there are not only more large-brained forms today than in the past, there are also more small-brained species. There seems to be some kind of ecological ratio at work, like taxpayers supporting the privileged. Insects, for all their sensitive ways, do not have the intellectual freedom to embarrass the community. Mind among the mammals moved toward the calculating consciousness for which part of the ecological price is a wide base of "traditional" animals with conservative brains.

You Think What You Eat

With these cautionary words about popular zoology, let us return to our theme: that mind advanced in the grasslands as sparks from the friction between two ecologically synchronized groups of mammals, the carnivores and herbivores. Predator and prey are the means of a dialogue that the prairie carries on with itself. Intelligence has been used as a catchall to include all the improved brain functions, but certain of its components were improved more than others.

The kind of intelligence favored by the interplay of smarter catchers and keener escapers is defined by attention—that aspect of mind carrying consciousness forward from one moment to the next. It ranges from a passive, free-floating awareness to a theta or slow-wave rhythm which is investigatory, and to a highly focused, active fixation. The range through these states is mediated by a brainstem structure, the limbic or arousal system, a network of tracts converging from sensory systems to integrating centers. From the more relaxed to the more vigorous levels, sensitivity to novelty is increased. The organism is more awake, more vigilant. Vigilance is that aspect of attention especially improved by progressive predator and prey. It is sensitive to signals from the surroundings. Prompted by these signals, ever more subtle with more vigilance, the processes of arousal and concentration give attention its tone and direction. Arousal is at first general, with a flooding of impulses in the brainstem, then gradually the activation is channeled. Thus we begin to concentrate, to hold consistent images.

A more proper meaning of intelligence is the way in which this keenly gleaned and alertly searched information is used in the context of previous experience. Consciousness links past attention to the present. It helps tie signs and possibilities together, past and present, manipulating the world by first attending to images from memory, causal chains, and the integration of details with perceived ends and purposes.

These elements of intelligence and consciousness come together in different styles in predator and prey. Herbivores and carnivores develop different kinds of attention, related to their lives of escaping or chasing. Arousal in herbivores or prey species produces adrenaline from the adrenal glands, which is fear-inducing. In predators, the substance produced is its reciprocal, norepinephrine, resulting in aggression. For both, arousal attunes the animal to what is ahead. Perhaps it is not forethought as we know it, but something like it, using past events as a gestalt for the hunter's anticipating. The predator is searchingly aggressive, inner-directed, toned by the sympathetic nervous system and the adrenal hormones, but aware in a sense closer to consciousness than, say, the reflexive snap of a hungry lizard at a passing beetle. The large mammal predator is working out a relationship between movement and food, sensitive to possibilities in cold trails and distant sounds, and yesterday's unforgotten lessons.

The herbivore-prey is of a different mind, as well as digestive system. Its mood of wariness rather than searching and its attitude of general expectancy instead of anticipating are silk-thin veils of tranquility over an explosive parasympathetic-tuned endocrine system.

The smattering of clinical language and technical terms to describe differences of mind in predator and prey may be helpful to some or seem unnecessarily scientific and detailed to others. I hope it conveys the idea that the differences are real and not impressionistic. The impressionist differences between predator and prey are grievously misleading when seen as a kind of viciousness versus sweetness. The polarity of predators and prey has nothing to do with the widespread sentimentality that projects meanness into carnivores and kindness into herbivores.

Indeed, the polarity is simply a convenience in a scale of characteristics. Like male and female, predator and prey share much more than they separately possess. Even so, rabbits, deer, and sparrows all have qualities in common which we recognize. The ferocity of the lion and the persistence of the wolf are not only part of their hunting behavior. In repose they do not become gazelle-like or rabbity. Their carnivore traits are whole-body, whole-life saturated. The differences between predator and prey are character differences in the deepest sense of the term— organically rooted effects on personality.

We can now move to ourselves and our place in the prairie dialogue. There is a third group of animals standing at various distances between the two polar extremes, sometimes carnivores, sometimes herbivores. They are omnivores, the versatile meat- and plant-eaters. They have their expectant side, a kind of fruit-minding, danger-watchfulness, an outward-turned, keen receptivity. At other times they stalk with a yet more flexible attention, subliminal, investigatory, and focused at different moments. The following table compares some omnivores to carnivores and herbivores.

I. CARNIVORE	II. HERBIVORE	III. OMNIVORE
hawk	sparrow	crow
mink	rabbit	raccoon
cougar	deer	bear
wolf	sheep	man

In terms of behavior and personality, this grouping is more important than genetic relationship. Psychologically, hawks and cats have more in common than hawks and sparrows. Bears, raccoons, crows, and foxes all possess qualities which we not only recognize but for which we feel affinity. They have flexibility, a readiness to try things, to meet the demands of the occasion. They are our omnivorousness speaking to us. Our fellow omnivores hold a special place in our thoughts though we may never have consciously classified them as such. What we count as intelligence, adaptability, and diversity are given generic shape by reality, not by us or our art.

Omnivorousness integrates the two poles of catching and escaping. Sometimes it is one, sometimes the other. The cunning, relentless stalker and the silent, cautious prey are in equilibrium. The characteristics are ecological, not social. Our herbivorousness is not in us that passive, loving, and tender feeling for others, nor is our carnivorousness the basis of savagery in our purely human relations. Lions and tigers have their socially tender side, while some of the interpersonal behavior of rabbits and sheep is exceeded nowhere in nature for its brutality.

The omnivore is not simply balancing two opposite tendencies, but integrating them in novel ways. It is a creative duality. For example, we might expect that the carnivore in us and other omnivores would dominate our relationships with other animals, while our plant affinities, our herbivorousness, would be the master shaper of our perception of all plants. But we are not so simple. Part of the strangeness of human experience and history is the capacity for directing the restless psychic force of the meat-mind upon the non-prey world, to experience forests and fields in some strange sense of pursuit and capture. Or is it our ability to attend to animals with the impressionistic, subliminal attention of the browsing consciousness? We can translate our ecological vision so that the carnivore in us makes new prey of the plant world and the herbivore in our heads creates environment from the animals. This psychology of omnivorousness may also make a new vision of one's own preyship, turning toward aggression by scrutiny rather than the knee jerk of flight.

That we feel these possibilities is in a sense our creatures informing us. To put into words what these feelings are is to name those inner beings. With Adam and Orpheus as the namers of creatures, we celebrate a mastery over our inner zoo which that naming seems to give us. Only when they are named and we can speak of them can the animals speak to us in this way, as the means of our reflection and discussion of the forms of our own transient emotion. By means of named images our own behavior becomes subject to our own consciousness.

In this way we come to the use of our ecology for thinking about our humanness. Other omnivores, however, do not seem to have come to this concern with the inner landscape. To see why, we must consider our primate nature.

What the Arboreal Eye Knows

Early in the chapter we said that the evolution of the terrestrial mind followed two streams. One was the grassland or savanna. The second was the tropical forest. Keeping in mind the importance of flowering plants in the evolution of insects and soil, which made complex terrestrial life possible, and the progressive refining of mind by cycles of predator and prey whose dances became less and less random encounters and more and more choreographed, there is yet another aspect to the growth of the psyche as we experience it. We have seen how larger bodies, more energy, more complexity, and more stability in the ecosystem are related to one another, but that relationship omits a peculiar sequence of events in mammalian evolution without which the biological anomaly of human thought is unthinkable.

The daytime or diurnal reptiles and amphibians whose behaviors have been studied have fixed connections between eyes and brains and muscles. Bodies are activated by just the right visual signals. For example, if the right-sized image moves across the retina of a hungry frog's eye, the frog reacts by eating it. If the image is not right, the "food" signal will never reach the frog's brain or trigger its food-catching movements. The filtering device is located in the eye, not the brain.

The same is true of reptiles and probably of that reptile-like ancestor of the earliest mammals, who were small ground-dwelling creatures at the time of the first flowers. The new plant communities opened up wider opportunities for all kinds of animals, among which were nocturnal beings. Some paleontologists think the early mammals were "driven" into the dark. This entailed a shift from vision to hearing and smell in obtaining information. Hearing gives distance, movement, and direction of another creature. This requires successive stimuli. Perceiving these signals as a pattern meant ordering them in time rather than visual space, translating them into the all-at-once of a spatial map.

Like the olfactory part of the brain, the auditory centers are located deep inside. That is, the stimuli go directly from the sensors to the brain for analysis and storing. Sniffing conveyed information about the environment close at hand for these ground-dwelling nocturnal forms.

Sound and smell were analyzed and integrated cortically, not sensorially—in the brain rather than in the sense organ. Though hearing and smell are not basically spatial, their temporal analysis creates a kind of analogue to space. Because we descended from these sniffers and smellers, the first step in human-like intelligence was the encephalizing or deep-brain elaboration of tissues for storing information. The perception of patterns from signals coming at intervals meant holding what had gone before, putting it into a spatial code. And it meant the reverse: calling and marking by scent were actions scattered through time by which the individual conveyed information about its location and movements.

The second step in this evolution was the further opening of new niches in the trees, made possible by elaboration of the flowering, fruiting plants in the tropics. After some fifty million years of mammalian life, opportunities arose for visual or day-time movement and food-finding. Night tree-climbers can scarcely go leaping about, nor can they find fruits as efficiently by random searching as they could by color vision.

When the primates emerged once again into the dawn or twilight from that long night passage of their earliest history, they had already at hand a deep-brain integrating and storing ability, created through the interaction of the senses other than vision. It related time to space, a time-binding capacity. The kind of temporary storage that made melodies from tones now occurred in vision. Holding of images would in time become the imagination. From the time of the reptile-like mammal ancestors to the era of the higher primates, the old reptilian retinal vision system had given way to the primacy of audition for creating nocturnal space, and it was replaced in turn by a new kind of vision organized in the brain instead of the retina, based on time-coding like that of sound. A perceptual visual world was created in which distance could mean time or space, and those events distant in time were remembered as mental images in the space of the mind's eye. The visual world became, as it were, constant or continuous rather than an illuminated field punctuated by the right signals.

The integration of sounds over time into a recognized pattern was discovered independently by the birds, and the neural structures to do this are an important reason for their relatively large brains.

The primates redefined the whole idea of the stimulus. It ceased to be simply a releaser and became entrained in sets, patterned as objects making a perceptual world, subject to autonomous re-presentation or recall. This recall of images establishes an imaged past and imagined future framing the present. This capacity for the visual presentation of objects from the past to one's self and the way it sensitizes us to a stream of time is not a general capacity. Consciousness is a very highly specialized mode of modeling and learning, dependent on specific brain elements and functions.

In sum, the evolutionary sequence was: (1) hearing replaced vision as a distance sense when mammals became nocturnal; (2) this required a capacity to translate successive signals into spatial maps, to perceive sequences of sounds as wholes and to re-hear or re-cognize them simultaneously in space; and (3) with re-emergence into daylight activity and vision, the same kind of temporal encoding of visual imagery, creating a continuous visual world of objects. Our reptilian ancestor's hearing analyzer was deep in its head, its vision analyzer in the eye itself. Its descendants became night creatures, centering their attention on hearing. When, much later, as primates, they emerged once again to live in daylight, their new visual analyzer was connected to the deep-brain hearing centers. Like the primates, the marine mammals also renewed their visual emphasis, using the deep centers of a powerful, time-integrated, auditory heritage. If this use of the old hearing-smelling apparatus for linking visual images into a continuous visual world—with a recalled (re-viewed) past and an imag-inary future—is the foundation of mammalian consciousness rather than the old "hand and eye" theory, it becomes easier to comprehend how the dolphins may have achieved their high intelligence without hands.

The interim of early mammalian evolution in the dark may have made later brain enlargement possible by the advantage it gave to body-temperature regulation. Keeping warm without sunlight may have been initially a physical or behavioral adaptation, but out of it came the warm, constant internal environment, or "warm-bloodedness," necessary to higher brain activity.

The progressive brain repacking by which terrestrial predators and prey honed their respective intelligences on the whetstone of each other's strategies, and the enlargement of brain centers for visual time-binding among the primates were the sources of the increase of certain brain tracts, of reticular clusters of neurons, specific interconnections, and of brain cell and intercellular glial mass in areas governing these behaviors. We can now see that they were essential to our past and they made possible the even more unusual steps that followed.

Speech as the Summons to Images

Man is a primate, the beneficiary of the shift of the deep mid-brain, nose-ear information storage into a time-binding visual coding process. The primates use this special kind of attention for learning and communication, even for consciousness. Man's special form of communication is speech. Like brains, speech did not emerge as a blank check to be drawn against the future. It was the outcome of something, not just practice or need, but a set of selective events in human prehistory.

Since none of the other primates has speech, it apparently arose in the protohuman line after that line had separated from other primates. Our prehuman ancestors lived in semi-open country and they shifted from primate omnivorousness in which their protein was acquired from such things as insects, nestling birds, eggs, and crayfish toward the hunting/gathering omnivorousness of root-digging, grain-foraging, and large-mammal hunting.

What is the correlation between speech and this shift in ecology? It is unlikely that hunting alone was the selective force in the evolution of speech and its brain centers (at the confluence of three lobes: temporal, parietal, and frontal). There are many animal hunters who are extremely efficient and highly evolved, but none has speech except man. Nor is speech simply an accessory to the neural needs of a warm body, of learning, of hands, upright stance, or even tools. Yet somehow language is related to them all.

The clue to language is in the nature of the *primate* hunter. Consider what happened when the typical predator attention system was joined to the incessant communicative turmoil and total self-absorption in the group. Few other kinds of vertebrate terrestrial animals even approach the monkeys and apes in the intensity and subtlety of personal interaction impelled by a sound-linked visual intelligence. From birth to death the primate is swept by currents of taking and yielding, rank-order anxiety, expression and response, play, learning, all the relentless commitment of the social contract. It often seems manic, the nuances of posture and intention more like chemical reactions than intermittent signals made across space. Everything in its life—food, enemies, weather, danger, movement in space—is experienced through a social screen. Intelligence is wrapped in a social skin. Self-assessment is a perpetual concern: in relation to parents, siblings, competitors, and mates. A tenuous, vibrant personal status is the nucleus at the heart of all primate experience and action.

The non-primate predators also interact, reproduce, protect, and nourish. But primate food is at hand, like that of most herbivores. Feeding is almost incidental to social interactions. Many large carnivores are social, and yet the hunt focuses their attention away from themselves. From their persistent search, energized tracking and interception to the rush of pursuit and kill, their attention is on another species. The intelligent predator learns from experience, and the strategy of the hunt itself is a tactical whole needing attention to past and future: what is ahead, some image of a prey perhaps yet unseen, and a sense of continuity. Here the predator and primate cross trails, both have temporal concerns, a kind of protohistorical sense, a forward and backward looking. They are deeply different: one haunted by social identity, the other engrossed with the mystery of movable feasts; one fixated on relationships with its kindred, the other absorbed in its symbiotic beings.

What happens when you cross the two types of attention? What hybrid emerges from the mixing of the furiously solipsistic world of the primate with the rage of pursuit of the other—political stratagems and ecological tactics? Obviously, such a combination cannot be simply additive. We might expect a fusion centered on some integrating factor not found either in the primates or among true carnivores, and we might expect novelties of attention.

For example, our hypothetical new breed would extend primate intraspecies perception into the hunt. That is, the hunt would not only take on social implications, but the prey might themselves be seen in a social relationship to the hunter, as subjects as well as objects. Or the social contract might also be transformed: personal relations seen as having ecological dimensions, so that the role of the individual emerges as an analogy to the niche of the species.

The common ground of time-binding in this new form of consciousness could provide the basis for a new dual sense of genealogy. When the time sense is applied to the social stream, we create kinship. But when it is applied to other species, we create natural history. Our new primate hunter experiences both, and more. He becomes aware of a natural history or theory of origins of his own species. He begins to apply the idea of kinship obligations to the interplay of other species. Although he heeded the dangers of life, the primate ancestor had only one set of relationships uppermost in his thought: relations with his fellows. Likewise, pure predators have their social side but are defined by rapt attention to other kinds. Now, our novel hunter-primate not only experiences both kinds of perception but can apprehend them as alternative expressions of a transcendent theme. Or, by applying kin-thought to his ecology and eco-thought to his society, he doubles the modes of knowing relatedness from two to four. Natural history is articulated in a tale of origins or mythology, and thus does the explanation of one's kinship in an interspecies framework spring from the mixture of the primate's inward and the hunter's outward attention.

And the new integrating element? Speech is its instrument, music its deeper expression. Anthropologists debate whether speech or song came first, as though one were the parent of the other. One may be, yet the two functions are automatically separated in left and right lobes of the cerebrum and may have had separate roles in the synthesis of primate and carnivore attention: one the voice of social harmony expressed in chant and dance, the primate fixation on social relations whose frictions threaten the cooperative necessities of the hunt; the other the voice of history, telling of myth by which clan and totem poetically incorporate the animals into society. Music is acoustic and is, like other sound stimuli, integrated temporally. Speech is linear and analytic. Only insofar as it is chanted or rhetorical (and it is therefore sung) does it constitute whole melodic patterns. It is almost as though we do not trust the temporal integration of our vision that evolved in association with the old ear-mind of the nocturnal mammals squeaking under the leaves of some Mesozoic forest floor. The smell-brain, ear-brain structures may automatically make our visual experience into a continuous flow, but what of the visual images that we call up from memory or imagination before the mind's eye? What's to keep them from seeming fragmented and disjointed? They need another sound overlay, arising, like the images, from within.

In this sense poetry and music connect past, present, and future. They symbolize continuity and persistence through time. What the primate group suffers most, introverted upon its own scuffling for rank and power, where the whole of the life cycle is given to repositioning, is discontinuity. From the outside it is clearly patterned, but from the inside (and I speak as a primate) life is uncertainty, endless change, jockeying, betrayal, emotional storms, coalitions forming and breaking, ephemeral sexuality, and the lifelong wheel of growing and aging. For the human primate, song and dance counterbalance this shifting unpredictability and inconstancy. They affirm the solidarity of community over generations by articulated time-binding. Traditional music confirms the resistance of values to the erosions of human frailty. Because it does raise us above the level of individual experience, it evokes the idea of an enduring entity of which we are part. Because of it we can see the human parallel to the nonhuman species, for we can see their continuity or natural history from the outside.

Of course music does other things, too. It makes anthems. It is an archetypal frame upon which a particular group makes its own phrasing, a biological form for conveying the melodic arrangements symbolizing cohesion within a given culture. It confirms the reality of history not only universally, but directly for its members. Indeed, it serves in this way at specific points in maturation. The lullaby is a transitional connection for the infant in a world sensorially fragmented. Tunes are imprinted on the adolescent so profoundly that each generation grows into maturity nostalgic for the music of its youth. What today separates generations is precisely the process that connects those generations in traditional societies for whom there are no fashions in song or tunesmiths who manufacture new melodies.

This sentimental attachment to imprinted music extends even to our perception of the song of birds. Birds become identified with place and the particular mix of bird song of a locality evokes "home" in a way that no other assemblage of sounds can. Perhaps human singing was, in its beginnings, modeled after that of birds. But more likely there existed in human evolution a dynamic between the two, not in the sense that they serve the same purposes, but that birds were one of those nonhuman beings whose use by man was to reflect one of his own abilities, to objectify and make more visible a trait so that it could be given a name and become available to thought. We sing and birds sing, but only we think about song.

Unlike music, which establishes connectedness and flow in a disjointed and episodic world, speech penetrates and dissects. Its first objects were external things, animals in particular, and they were the first parts of a whole.

According to anthropologist Grover S. Krantz, a threshold of brain size at about 750 cubic centimeters (a little more than half the size of the average human brain) is necessary to contain all the circuits and substance required for speech. This size in prehumans could have been achieved by adding one additional round of cell divisions in embryonic growth to a chimpanzee-sized brain, and it would add slightly to the gestation time. Communication without true speech, that is, without the use of phonemes and morphemes, which distinguish it from a call system, might already have been rather advanced, as we see it now among the apes. A brain of this size already makes a very substantial mind possible, and the crossing into verbal representation would certainly not be like going from a shadowy world of reflexive animality into a reflective sunshine of humanity. The beginning of speech was no great breakthrough; it was a modest specialization that required perhaps as much as six or seven million years to lead on to those elaborations of conceptual thought which were associated with a very slow advance in brain size. Since brains also enlarge with body size, it is possible that, early in the evolution of our genus, *Homo,* only adults could speak, and the onset of speech in the individual coincided with puberty or sexual maturity rather than early childhood.

One may imagine speech in its primitive beginnings to have been entirely practical, a labeling of useful objects and acts. But it is just as likely to have been entirely composed of poetic terms with multiple meanings, what we now call metaphors, words connecting unlike things and events. To speak poetry is to illuminate and give meaning from intuition. Today, in our species, poetry and analogy are the special obsession of young adults and adolescents, perhaps because speech first appeared at puberty in our distant ancestors. Its evolution extended its practice to the years of childhood. Thus, the emergence of language and sex, at first synchronized in the life cycle, was gradually divided and separated; more precisely, the poetic part of language and the reproductive part of sexuality were initiated at puberty while the infantile and oedipal components of sexuality and the empirical vocabulary learning both shifted to the earlier years. Poetic speech was reserved for puberty, preceded by years of vocabulary learning.

The schedule of language acquisition in the individual, as we now see it, is profoundly divided into literal meaning in childhood and literal-plus-metaphorical in adulthood. Abstract usage is preceded by ten years or so of vocabulary, cataloging, and taxonomy. This separation probably did not exist in the early evolution of speech but has emerged after a long evolution of language-using behavior during which all the phases of individual growth have become more sharply differentiated. That part of the young brain combining signals from vision, sound, and touch in the inferior parietal lobule physically matures, or becomes myelinated, with the end of childhood. Names pass through a part of it, the Wernicke's area, like beasts entering Noah's Ark and, with the transitional period of puberty, the door closes on the real world, that is, on the raw materials from which a cosmos is to be created. The bridge connecting the wholly tangible past with the adult consciousness is the abstracting, poetic, metaphorical period of adolescence. The adolescent "discovers" that all those tangible things, even the creatures, signify something beyond themselves. All help to secure the polarity between the self and nonself. The poetry which the older *Homo erectus* spoke but did not recognize as such became a synthesis not only of self and world, but also of past and present, inside and outside. Naming and classifying connected the old intuitive mind consciously with the animal world that brought it into existence. Before knowledge there was wisdom, and before facts, knowledge.

Such a view stands the old order of existence from primitive to philosophical on its ear and contradicts a premise of modern education: that wisdom emerges from the contemplation of facts or data.

Language is a coding device for recall. What is recalled is attached to an image. No one knows the exact form in which millions of sense data are stored, but we do know that words retrieve some of them and that a visual picture is presented from memory, resembling that which was first offered by sight.

It is quite possible that sounds—words, even—produce mental images for educated chimpanzees. What chimpanzees cannot do is speak, transmit images by words, or construct more elaborate scenarios of visual play by speech. What the chimpanzees and other primates never needed was a vast storehouse of objects, a dictionary of otherness. What wolves and tigers had was a storehouse of diverse images—but as releasers rather than image-objects. There was no need for them to formulate models or scenarios about the world. The driving reason for those scenarios is knowledge of the self, and that was the compelling force among primates. What carnivores lacked was social fullness, one that approached the invention of abstract symbols for social categories. The carnivores had the species interest, the available symbols, but didn't need them. The human primate-omnivore brought them home to social thought.

Hypotheses about the self could not be made in terms of the self. The self is not so easily perceived as an object; it is too fluid and close. Nor can it be easily represented. Some kind of stand-in is needed, disintegrating the person and isolating traits, making them accessible to speech and thought, and thereby to new syntheses. Complex ecosystems contained enough diversity to model the complex human individual many times over. But how was it to be got at and on what levels did it contain components that might serve as suitable analogies?

The Zoology of the Self

The most conspicuous order in nature is species membership. But how do we recognize the consistent differences that separate kinds and the similarities by which different individuals are related? All birds have wings and beaks—where do we go from there? The answer is that particular parts must be seen apart from the whole. It requires the dis-integration of individuals and the naming of those part-groups abstracted from the whole animal and whole species. Such taking apart in thought may have been preceded by taking apart in reality. It is a primate possibility because of hands; monkeys often peel and otherwise dismember the fruit they eat. But the real takers-apart of animals are the meat-eaters.

Categories are composed not only of similar entities or creatures, but similar parts. By noticing types of organs—legs, necks, livers—as well as types of animals, we give a new dimension to the imagination. Indeed, one cannot be done without the other. It extends the idea of breaking down and putting together. It enlarges the probing and scanning of the body features. Language, for mankind, directs and codes that scanning and, in speech, makes the labels that evoke similar images at the same time in different heads.

Making categories is done by classifying things or ideas with common properties as types and then repeating the operation among the types themselves. In this way the higher groupings emerge—genus, family, order, and so on. The categories are storage markers and retrieving handles. They are attention-directors, too. There is an openendedness about this approach to objects because one is never sure at first what detail may be crucial. The hunter does not know where, for certain, to look. All details are potentially significant. In this way, visual forms become objects, composed of parts, themselves in a field, not just signals or releasers, but figures in a ground.

A group or set of things with common elements is denoted by a name. It is a concept with its clutch of shared qualities recalled by the name. It is just our ability to single out similar constituents of objects or events, to group and name them, that is cognition, the source of reason. The name can become a substitute for the recollection of the experience, a term that encapsulates the past.

Something happens when our attention is directed to this verbal code that is parallel to the hunt—searching, comparing, selecting, ordering, integrating.

The scrutinized object is surrounded by silently perceived data, just as the fovea centralis of the eye, the point of visual acuity, is surrounded by peripheral vision. Recollected images and the concept for which they serve as symbols move through larger contexts, whole communities of thought. Life is a hunt or search. One can only tell (or understand, or communicate) about the first hunt by mastering the second. One recapitulates in the linear sounds of speech the spatial events by which things are chased into order. When the events are retold, visual images march across an inner landscape. Television did not invent instant replay.

While it cannot be proven that language initially arose as an instrument for the dissection of the human personality as a means of comprehending the self, by an intensely social primate moving into a hunting ecology, it is a more interesting theory than many others, which simply take its advantage for granted. As self-consciousness was facilitated by consciousness of the diversity of the world, our barely speaking ancestor found in animals the tangible objects he needed to embody otherwise slippery ideas.

For all animals the perceptual world is composed of a limited number of signals—some inherently recognized, some learned—which serve as releasers for behavior. In speech the word becomes a releaser that triggers an image, flashing it before the mind's eye, trailing the emotions and circumstances of something past. These images are recruited from whole animals, and parts of wholes, such as "leg" or "head," and even actions. Traits—like sluggishness, joy, nocturnality, deceit—could be dealt with in the same way so long as they could be attached to an image, an animal. The different animals not only represented usable images for social categories and sensed experience, but evoked further thought about them. The ecology of the lion produced an ecology of thought. Its anger, hunger, or motherhood bore peripheral messages. These analogical images carried whole trains of connection.

Many kinds of animals learn, but few are taught. Except for man, little comes from a transmitted heritage, and even that is given by example—the migratory routes among geese, hunting techniques in tigers, or wolves, for instance. The kind of learning that culture carries, however, is born on the symbolic vehicle of speech which, among other things, denotes intangible qualities, invisible events (as in the past or at a distance), spatial relations, personality traits, spiritual forces, and the whole adjectival realm of description. To the early humans and to the young human mind, these things are not perceptible; they are imageless. They cannot easily be seen in the self or even in other people. They are discoverable only as they inhere in other creatures. Friskiness, hunger, and patience can be seen respectively in pups, the searching coyote, or the waiting hawk atop a tree. Such uses of animals as various parts of speech continue now in an enormous variety of forms. A few of these are:

to buffalo	to be mulish
to bug	to have a cowlick
to hound	to be dog tired
to bulldog	to give a bear hug
to bullshit	to be mousey
to outfox	to be kittenish
to skunk	to be a horse's ass
to grouse	to play leapfrog
to hawk	to play possum
to crab	to turn turtle
to badger	to make a pig of yourself
to flounder	to get his goat
to goose	to be chicken (hearted)
to parrot	to make a monkey of
to rat	to put on the dog
to duck	to duck an issue
to lionize	to coon apples
to rail	to tomcat around
to chicken out	to lark about
to dog it	busy as a bee
to wolf your food	in a pig's eye
to worm your way	a lounge lizard
to clam up	cock and bull story
to crow about	quiet as a mouse
to horse around	cold turkey
to ram home	bull in a china shop
to fish around	cat got your tongue
to bull your way	

Some of these are new, some old. Anyone can make such a list. The point is not that they persist in the language from some distant time, but that they are so rich a part of language. Joseph D. Clark's *Beastly Folklore* is a collection of about five thousand of these phrases. The above examples are grouped to show that the animal term can be a noun, verb, adverb, or adjective. Not included is the simple labeling of someone as a "hawk" or a "dove"; derived terms applied directly to people, like "feline" or "dogged"; or exclamations such as "Rats!"

After perhaps as much as five hundred thousand years of human speech, it is not surprising that these terms are generally regarded only as colorful choices of wording, colloquial custom, or poetic metaphor. On the other hand, if language did begin in this way, then we could expect this animalizing to be part of its deeper structure, or of the mental apparatus that lies beneath language. If this is the case, then the intense drive of the child to learn animal names and actions may be very old and persistent, even necessary in some way to the development of speech.*

To summarize briefly what has been said: Speech is the means by which human intelligence developed beyond that of the apes. It was the instrument by which images could be retrieved from memory and communicated, images that made the classification of other life possible. Classification, in turn, is that order-finding analysis by which the objective world could be used to reflect the many-sided experience of being human.

Bringing time into consciousness also required tangible objects. The season, the weather, the cycle of life, the beginning, the flow of events were manifest in the coming and going and seasonal behaviors of beings other than man.

Carved and engraved animal figures could be used to transmit such ideas. A drawing or carved figure is a communal source of images synthesizing new thought. Language is a good analyzer but poor synthesizer. Its left-brain virtues fasten consciousness in linear spurts that excel in part-naming but work as wholes only because words elicit pictures and song. Art makes use of pictures directly.

Hunting evolved through three stages before man: goal-directed persistence, such as the crayfish following a scent

---

* There are some cases of autistic children whose recovery is initiated by giving them a pet; that is, they first speak by speaking to or about the animal.

through the water; interception tracking, such as the falcon aiming ahead of the flying duck; and interception by configuration, such as the wolf waiting at a rocky pass for migrating caribou. In a further—human—stage, the experience does not have to be that of the tracker himself, but a "real" experience communicated in advance. Thus do we approach reason and insight, foreshadowed in the problem-solving capacities of omnivores such as monkeys, bears, raccoons, and crows, but limited by their inability to disassemble the world and store it with words as handles and the arts as whole-makers, and the images that words summon.

For such minding, the world is infinitely rich in clues. Nature, as Elizabeth Sewell wrote in her beautiful book, *The Orphic Voice*, becomes a language, hieroglyphic in its mystery, but subject to the scanning of the hunter's eye and the vigilance of the primate ego.

We now come back for a few moments to the grasslands and the cereal world with which the chapter began. The upward spiraling of intelligence evoked in each other by predators and prey in open country made them fit tutors for our prairie advent. They were an example of the benefit of prairie hunting and escaping. Man the primate came into this milieu of mind-making after it had matured for millions of years. The pre-humans who ventured into it brought a brain that was already unusual. Even the oldest known primate, *Tetonius homunculus*, whose fossil bones are fifty-five million years old, had an encephalographic quotient of .68; that is, a brain much larger than ordinary mammalian proportions. But none of the primates in forests or primate herbivores in open country evolved a brain beyond speech-threshold size, except the one meat-eater and hunter of large mammals.

Among the routes to intelligence already mentioned (insects, birds, forest primates, and grassland large mammals), only man is both primate and open-country carnivore. Man was plugged in to the running dance of wolf and deer. His primate psychology was not simply glossed over by his predatorship but synthesized with it. If one draws lines from chimpanzee, baboon, and wolf, their point of convergence would shadow forth a kind of glimmer of ourselves. Other primates or carnivorous mammals may be able to summon images to the mind's eye and even hold them there, but probably cannot hitch abstract qualities to visual figures or yoke them to arbitrary verbal signals.

What makes the human experience different is not simply primate origins or hunting past, but the shaping of the envisioning mind by the auditory brain, cradling imagination in time. Because of it visual thought is stretched in past and future. Like the images conjured in the head, objects seen in the terrain are never only momentary. Everything seems to take a place in memory and in anticipation as well as in the instant, a gliding triple reality. Like the linear flow of words, which is the harness of those images, objects are part of an ongoing world. The past and future are a story told, a left-brain evocation of right-brain images, order and meaning-giving.

Art as the Collective Imagery of Animal Form

This recall of the past as a series of images is a public as well as a private experience. It is made public by art, especially a tactile form. The worldwide body of "primitive" art, the petroglyphs, lines cut in stone, read by eye or finger tracing their course, is such a flowing, left-brain form. Drawings or pictographs are right-brain, all-at-once messages heard by the eye. Sculpture and carved objects combine and synthesize the two, but may also be the ancestral mode, the first art, from which the etchings in stone or bone and the drawings on stone or bark are specialized developments.

This biology of art is most clearly seen in some of its oldest surviving expressions, the fabulous, worldwide cave painting and etching which span more than twenty-five thousand years. These cave and rock-shelter sanctuaries were the antecedents of temples, where the significant passages of human life were ceremonially represented. The figures in them, however, are mostly animals, a fact that misleads the modern viewer into thinking they are about animals. They are fossil forms of thought in which the act of imaging and symbolizing is embedded in its maternal substance, the hunt.

The drawings are virtually all large animals, hoofed and hunter, arranged in groups or individuals in significant combinations according to their kind, carefully positioned on walls, ceilings, or floors, distributed in a pattern throughout the sanctuary. Few of the drawings represent animals in motion. They are, like the visual images of memory itself, and like dream figures, stills.

Their connection to a flow of events in mythical time must have been given by narration as men confronted the animal pictures. Like recollections from the personal past of our individual childhoods, they are static. Like the sleeper who scans his memory for the vestiges of his dream thoughts as though they were illustrations in a book, the cave artist presents visual images to the impressionable eyes of youthful initiates, for whom they will become the visual traces of their collective memories, not only of those awesome moments in the cave but of the time of creation and tribal beginnings. The cave drawings are in turn related to an even older body of carved objects carried into the sanctuaries as models. Recalled words and melodies echo in this cavern from wall to wall, like our voices in our own heads. Sounds in caves reverberate laterally as though entering from the ears. The old earth temples—and the newer—are the social ear. One crawls in to become part of a sense organ to receive messages that help explain images already there. The cave is an externalization of the head, which is in fact experienced as internal space—dark, image-laden labyrinths where we become conscious of our own thoughts, memories, history.

Numerous studies and students of this art concur that these thousands of figures are not just about animals, but that they signify special aspects of human life around which society was organized: marriage rules, kinship and genealogical descent, clan membership, tribal origins, the mores and myths of self-conscious beings, or at least the public instruments for asserting and affirming what is central to people. They are the tools of a cognitive and communicative process, a part of language below speech, a universal means related to thought itself. As shared and mutually stored images to which song, dance, or recitation may have been attached, they were figures of mystery except to the initiated.

Again, why formulate such central questions in the form of animals? The answer is many-sided and is not only that thought evolved in the contemplation of animals. There is also the otherness about them which shakes us loose from ourselves, helping us to separate what is transient and personal from what endures. That about ourselves which survives us has a kind of otherness, a public aspect, part of a whole detached from individuals. Being like us and yet different, the animals manifest that invisible otherness. It is not just singular "spirit" or "soul," but as many-formed as animals themselves. Art historians have puzzled why

there are so few images of men in these paintings, but we can
see that the human image only reflects the puzzle of the singular
and universal mixed in the one. In the animals there is a sly
dissection coming between it and ourselves, a separation from
which we can re-cognize those slippery abstractions.

The hunters of this transcendent otherness, whose primate
blessing and curse was the relentless need to know themselves,
created an art which isolated in animals constituents of the self.
The cave sanctuary, like the modern temple, is a communal altar
for the ceremonial attachment of collective images to myth. But
religious thought is never only an explanation of the outer universe. Abbreviated and stylized as icons, beautiful mnemonic
instruments of recall, these animal figures troop across the dark
earth-cranium like ordered thought, the fauna of our complex
self and selves.

The cave sanctuaries were probably used for facilitating passages, personal steps in certain crucial phases of individual development and, at the same time, formal social affirmation of that
progress. Personality growth is marked by times of transition,
intermediary stages when the individual is betwixt and between.
For these episodes parents or tutors provide a special class of
devices which, like a rope thrown to a floundering swimmer, connect the old self at one end and his new self at the other. These
devices are known to psychiatry as "transitional objects." The
animal images in the cave sanctuaries are transitional objects
used to help the adolescent make a major step toward maturity.
The cave ceremonies were a continuation of good mothering
practices, one of the many steps by which personal identity
moves from mastery of body schema toward an increasingly complex awareness of the self in the cosmos. The animals are symbols of social structure as well as recognizable species that are
met with in daily life. The cave images encode a dual system in
which the ecology of animals parallels the society of humans.
The terrible otherness of the animals is thus approached. The
drawn figures and the rituals attending them are a lifeline connecting the fragile human community with the bewildering ebul-
lience and hidden purposes of the whole of life. In their position-
ing and arrangement, the mammal figures represent the human
groups or clans. The animals to which they refer live in an
orderly world, a visible ecosystem. Transposed to the cave walls,
they bring an aura of coherence and meaning to that which they

symbolize—the human community. To the eyes of the beholder they assert, with all the force of their uncanny and ravishing setting, that the human social order is part of a meaningful universe.

In its dark depth the night sky is similar to our eyes to the cavern ceiling. Like those irregular rock surfaces the spectacle of stars seems at first formless and chaotic. But it is far too large a part of the world to accept as randomly structured. Simple familiarity with its consistent patterns, even spiritualizing of the star points, has not been enough. We discern or make there organic figures. Of the forty-eight Ptolemaic constellations, all but a few are seen as organic and twenty-five are named for animals. Of the twenty-two added in the seventeenth century, nineteen had animal names. Needless to say, the choices and dispositions are arbitrary. There is nothing intrinsically animal-like (or man-like) about them, and the particular configurations seem almost playfully imposed on the stars. But it is clearly animals, and to a lesser extent our bodies and the things we make, to which we turn in order to give shape to such a haphazard spectacle.

The panoply of celestial figures contrived to give order to the sky occupies that dark vault like the figures seen in caves—not the painted ones, but the natural cracks, surfaces, and forms of the rock to which the painters responded by using them in combination with their art. Just as all tourist caves today are peopled with figures of the imagination, guided by the suggestive notions of a leader, perhaps Paleolithic men found in the unmodified rock what they did in the sky for centuries before they gilded those rocks with art.

The use of the imagined animal figures as an organizing nexus for subterranean amorphous rock and for the speckled night sky is also found in the daytime sky and the terrain. The attribution of creature names and likenesses to passing clouds, presumed in our civilized world to be the frivolity of children's play or poetic fancy, may be instead an important passage, a working of existential confidence, the finding of meaningful transformations in the endlessly shifting forms. On the Earth's surface, colossal prehistoric earthworks, mostly in animal form, are widely found in the Americas. Some in Peru are more than a mile long. In Ohio earth sculptures form clusters occupying more than a hundred acres. Very few of them can be seen by a normal observer on the ground. Anthropologist Marlene Dobkin de Rios has developed the theory that they were designed for viewing during out-of-body trances, when the individual feels himself rising out of his own body and flying or floating upwards. Whatever their ritual function or mechanics of access, such designs give form to the landscape and imply a general unifying principle underlying its seeming randomness, organizing the terrain in the truest sense.

It seems at first like childish tricks, deluding one's self and others into seeing all those fantastic animals where reality tells us is nothing but the haphazard erosion of limestone surfaces or the coincident view of distant suns. Most of those who painted the caves and made the earthworks are gone, but the Australian aborigines and Kalahari bushmen who still live with cave or rock-shelter art are anything but simpletons. They know rock from flesh; nobody is fooled about it. The "trick" is not some personi-fying pathetic fallacy, nor bemused, indulgent dreaming. Our modern fancy and travelers' appetite may reduce the cave figures to triviality, but that is because we think of them as spectacle and decoration.

For us the human will—the same imperious will that now creates everything around us—is our god. To it everything seems to come from within. The world is only a stage where we act out those scenarios that suit us. How could the ambience of nature be part of our physiology? How could ecology have anything to do with mind in such a view?

But another truth is that the unordered head with which we begin life has some properties of the raw rock and maze of celes-tial lights. We are aware of things flitting across. Our own ideas move at first through the velvet cranial spaces as unpredictably as the passage of herons or the brief flash of a startled deer at twilight. As we get to know them, we learn that their movements are not random and that they exist even when we cannot see them. If only we could hold them for a few moments and study their marvelous symmetry. . . .

In this way birds become ideas. They flit through conscious-ness, connecting with this twig and that branch, are attended to momentarily, and in a flash are gone. Birds are not like ideas—that is a literary simile. They are ideas. They are, each in its kind, bits of different qualities for which words heighten awareness and give control over recall. Birds are not metaphors, those analo-gies chosen by the private artist seeking unique expression. We do not apply this significance to the birds; it has emerged over

an immense time of minding birds and being endowed with mind
by them.

We may think of birds as externalizing a mental process, but
it would be more accurate to say that the idea is our inward
occasion of the bird's presence. Apart from the bird itself, what
of the habitat through which it moves, and to which it returns
unseen? If all creatures are possible ideas, relationships, emotions, feelings, the habitat is for us the outward form of the whole
space of the mind. Its visible extent is like our conscious experience and its unseen distance like the unconscious. A bird flying
across the sky is an idea coming from the unseen of the precon-
scious and disappearing again into the realm of dreams.

We have surrounded ourselves with geometrized, humanized
landscapes cut from an ancient wilderness. Most of the animals
are tame. Our man-made landscapes are caricatures of the rational mind, the external extension of civilized thought. Here
and there in them we have put little lessons in meaning, intended
to relieve the terrain made by the implacable economics of the
state and detritus of our mastery. These are gardens, and garden
style is a continuing expression of the changing idea of the universe. In medieval Europe it was a distant, perfect Paradise, a
stark contrast to the sullied and soiled nature that had fallen with
Adam. For the Renaissance in Italy it was a private domain, com-
plexly ordered like aristocratic society. In Isaac Newton's day it
was shaped by the laws of cosmic geometry, a vast mathematical
diagram. And for romantic England it was a dream of pastoral
peace in which the tame and wild worlds merged at the boundaries. But such formal statements are few. The countryside everywhere is an embodiment of the cultural perspective, economic
imperatives, and historical preoccupations of its modern human
occupants.

It is easy to misinterpret the point in this. The terrain is not
something we dream up; no mind-is-all solipsism is intended.
What is perceived is not "our" creation. The older Berkeleyan and
the modern existentialist would have us believe that the world
is the product of human imagination. Having discovered psychology, we proceeded to try to make it the only reality. What is
meant here is something more mutually and functionally inter-
dependent between mind and terrain, an organic relationship between the environment and the unconscious, the visible space
and the conscious, the ideas and the creatures. In the forest

visible space was sharply limited; in the prairie things opened up
and we awoke.

Inner and outer terrains vary, just as do the choice of animals
as analogues of qualities. The man-made domestic landscape is
the extension of those deliberate and intensive acts of domination
with castrated and corralled animals. But they are only a few
thousand years old and are not the environment in which the
terrain of human thought emerged, with its peaks of achievement, depressions, streams of ideas, areas and fields of work, its
paths and information pools.

The man-made habitat and domestic animals are related to
each other just as wilderness is related to wild animals. If the
mind discovers structure in nature because its own structure is
a product of the order of nature, then such comparison is not a
discovery or an original insight, but is inevitable. We know that
the brain has a projection area to which the visual tracts lead
in the occipital lobe, which has real space in neural tissue,
where the firing of neurons in some sense duplicates the three-
dimensional space perceived by the eye. Things move through the
brain as they do through the field of vision, giving off sounds,
reflected light, and odors that carry into the distance. As geo-
psychist Dewey Moore says, "Any of the aspects of intelligence
we have are developed from modeling or association with the
environment. As we look at nature we always unconsciously
recognize the source of our mental function. That feeling of
'experiencing the wilderness' from which we have come is an
operational definition of the basis for nature mysticism."

The individual may project his psychic events into the external
world, fastening his unconscious thoughts symbolically onto
objects there, but only because those external forms shaped his
psyche in the first place. The inner and outer counterparts have
living as well as past meaning, a continuing, necessary relationship. As primates we are obliged by our nature to persistently
examine the social contract, but not only in the field of action as
other primates do. The leap in mind that made us human was
a result of the synthesis of that inward scrutiny with an external
means, the carnivore's scrutiny of other animals. That redirection
of attention to the nonhuman never lost its social context. Consciousness for us signifies duality, the poetry of marriage and
diet, the rules of eating and kinship, the rites of food-sharing and
exogamy, the adventure of hunting and courting, the figures of

love and death. Through language, common terms appear for relatedness (sex and nutrition), history (genealogy and the animal life cycle), membership (clan and species), individuality (personality and species behavior), role (gender and age and niche), drawing simultaneously from within the society and from the ecology without. Each of these is incomplete without the other.

Of a generation reared on introspection, analysis, dream study, and group dynamics, exploring the affluence produced by the drive of its Faustian drive modeled after the Creator whose prominent feature is His will, the inheritors of Jewish inward vision and Greek narcissism, little else could be expected than a loss of ecological roots of mind. The roles of flowers, pollinating insects, soil, seeds and cereals, fruits, the grasslands, the ballets of predator and prey, the intense interpersonality of monkeys and apes are all foreign to that overriding premise of thought—that human identity is a matter of mirrors and self-determination. Our reflections on how the mind works must now carry us beyond ourselves, pursuing the nature of thought as the thought of nature.

2 | THE MENTAL MENAGERIE

The human brain is an evolutionary experiment made possible by primate society and predator ecology. Its most unique feature is the opening of mind and thought to the whole of experience. Its dual origin combines the interiority and social purposes of monkeydom with the attention to otherness of carnivores. The strategy by which natural selection created such a brain was the infantilizing of the individual—that is, the extension of immaturity and specialization of the psychological processes of development.

An imaginary, magisterial overseer of all animal life, looking at brains, might characterize them as screening and shunning devices for translating incoming data into action. They are not generally intended, he might say, to create whole models of the world or to suggest its profusion and complexity to consciousness. An animal needs an efficient, coordinated relay system hooked to sensors at one end and to glands and muscles at the other. Improvements of such an organ would increase its sensitivity to specific stimuli and thus modulate behavior more delicately. While there could be some advantage to storing information, there would be little in removing those filters which admit only usable input and screen out a flood of unusable stimuli. For most mammals it is enough for the brain to administer the body's internal complexity and adjust to one's fellows, foods, enemies, and habitat without building a world picture.

Braininess was not intended, our magistrate might add, to replace all the other means by which a species keeps in equilibrium with its natural environment.

As any trip to the zoo will show, however, evolution seems to try everything. An exception to the limited role for brains is found where cunning has high priority, where there is challenge and competition. There is no advantage to cunning creatures without cunning protagonists. No need for a highly intelligent predator if his food is all bumbling sluggards or predictable automatons. No point in having intelligent deer if the wolves are mere random searchers. There is no point in sniffing political nuance or craftily imposing one's will except in a society rich in graded and complex relationships and fine shades of dominance.

But even among those animals with their progressive, predator-prey intelligence, new limitations would appear. At how many removes could information remain pertinent? Whether to cross an open field or to skirt it was not a problem for the old archaic forms with brains prewired for such decisions. But for the new brains, seeking insight from a whole new range of experience, how would they know when they had enough or what they should attend to? A single lifetime was too short a period in which to answer this question. The kind of information needed could be got only from the pooled experience of others. The limited utility of personal experience is that death is a poor teacher. What one needed was a view into the possibilities beyond personal horizons.

This is the level at which the predator-prey and primate brains reached their limits. The wolf and caribou and all other modern hoofed animals and their pursuers, as well as the monkeys and apes, were admirably advanced beyond their duller ancestors. They were a great experiment that worked. But the new experiment was limited without a means of encapsulating units of experience and referring to them. There was no way to label, package, store, retrieve, and transmit these data bundles between individuals except by acting as example. The hunter-hunted mammals and the socially dominant/subordinate primates could not otherwise benefit from the past or each other's experience. This probably just made hunting tactics or social jockeying more efficient, a more flexible integration of their respective main concerns.

The breakthrough required speech. Today one can imagine all sorts of advantages in the human departure from the primate social frenzy and the preoccupation with catch-or-escape. But all the benefits reflect the bias of retrospect. Speech has enabled us to solve problems, think philosophically, know love, consider the stars, make art, cherish ideas, keep history. The trouble is that none explains why or how our prehuman ancestor should have developed the capacity for attending to the irrelevant as well as the relevant, with its almost certain danger of making wrong decisions. There is a sense in which speech and the perceptual world of objects put a barrier between ourselves and the world which was not there before. The image-world could be an illusion-world.

For a time some anthropologists proposed that the early pre-humans were "forced" into the human realm because of weakness and vulnerability. But the Reject Ape theory of human evolution conflicts with everything we know about the history of life and of species evolution. No creature lives without a home; none is kicked out (of the forest) and wanders nicheless and nomadic; none is unadapted to the environment in which it lives. And the evidence now is, in any case, that our ancestors, like ourselves, were never fragile or at the mercy of other animals.*

This is related to another troublesome side of the evolution of the human psyche. Opponents of the theory of evolution have argued for a century that such marvelous organs as the human eye could not have come slowly into existence by natural selection because any imperfection in it would render it inoperable, like taking a part out of a fine watch. Whatever our theory about the larger brains and other organs of human emergence, they must somehow be shown to have worked at all stages. A century of comparative anatomy of eyes has shown convincingly (to biologists, at least) that eyes, as seen in different species, represent varying degrees of resolving power, binocularity, light/dark adaptation, conjugated movement, optical brain specialization, and so on. Speech, however primitive, must have "always" worked. Trying to imagine how it worked early in its evolution without reference to other aspects of the emergence of our species is a mind-boggling, paralyzing game.

It is like the millipede in Robert Frost's poem who fell down when the toad asked him how he managed to move each of his legs in harmony with the others; or like the golfing ploy suggested by "gamesman" Stephen Potter in which one gained advantage by showing the opponent a picture of the human body with all of its muscles labeled.

The enlargement of human attention from a small, genetically determined segment of the surroundings to the whole of it was surely achieved slowly and by degrees, probably beginning with

---

* With the qualifications that our hunter-gatherer forebears ventured into open country and, like all social predators, developed group defenses against other carnivores.

an intelligence very similar to that of a chimpanzee. In the "opening up of the call system," anthropologists have speculated that primate calls had the potential for becoming words, and words are the labeling instrument by which an enormously complicated world could be systematically presented to the mind without collapsing it into chaos. Words very likely were applied to tangible objects with some common element before they were applied to abstract things. From the beginning, words probably evoked fleeting mental images similar to the visual experience of the objects they represented.

Language and Taxonomy

In short, the evolution of the noun opened a door beyond the point to which primates and predation had brought the brain. As a word spoken to the self the noun evokes a surrogate image; as a sound it communicates that image to another. A system of purely additive nouns and images runs into the thousands before it even begins to make landscapes of the mind possible that simulate an ongoing visual reality. This could still work so long as the nouns refer to physical objects. But for ideas and concepts it rapidly becomes rootless and full of hot air. Name alone creates perceptual objects, but no pattern for storing, ordering, or retrieving them.

The inception of language required some kind of hypothesis about world interrelationships from its beginning. But, in a sense, the question never came up, because the first words were nouns for human individuals and kinds of animals who already signified systems. They were members of a family group system or a natural group system, the most conspicuous orderly patterns already available.

Consciousness, according to Harry Jerison, the author of *The Evolution of the Brain and Intelligence,* is the ability to summon images. To do so requires that they be named. Naming is not arbitrary, but follows a logic of similarity. It is a sequence of alternatives, of simple binary choices. For example:

1. A thing is alive or not alive.
2. If alive, it moves about or is anchored in place.
3. If it moves it has four legs or it does not.
4. If it has four legs it has fur or is covered with something else.

5. If it has fur it is small and lives in trees or is otherwise.
6. If it lives in trees it has a furry tail and scampers or
   does not.
7. If it has a furry tale it is uniformly gray, not brown or
   reddish.

At each of the alternatives to these seven steps one may be led
to other series. If it does not have four legs it may have wings, in
which case one shifts to a different set of alternatives. The procedure is familiar to anyone who has ever used a plant or animal
key. At each step a name is given that includes all the creatures
in the succeeding choices. At number 4 above, if it is covered
with fur it is a mammal, and all the choices to which numbers 5,
6, or 7 can lead are mammals. Classification is therefore binary
and hierarchic.

As the social sciences attended to human differences while the
natural sciences studied the species themselves, the relationship
of human cognition to the species system has been left out. In
the example given above, the name given at number 7 is the
Gray Squirrel. Individual gray squirrels differ in detail—which
is a source of wonder and cause for reflection in itself—but
there is a clear separation between gray squirrels and other species of squirrels, just as there is a clear gap between mammals
and birds and between the alternatives at all other levels of the
hierarchy. The pondering on variations in the theme "Gray Squirrel" is not a child's task, but his task is to think the sequence
in its simplest, most streamlined form for every creature he
encounters. Elaborations, contradictions, unclassifiables all come
later.

Descent and kinship form a master model. The *visible* difference between different species of birds, for instance, is in part
due to the evolution of adaptive size and structure, but also in
part to distinct features that make it easy for the birds themselves
to know their own kind at a glance. Crows and ravens differ
because they are adapted to different ecological niches, but also
because they themselves must keep identities clear. If birds were
nose- rather than eye-oriented, their appearances might not
clearly separate kinds. It is fortunate for us that they are visual
and this may even have been crucial for our own intelligence,
insofar as it depends on categorization. We also use the mammals

for models of classification. They are not primarily visual but, luckily, are so few in kinds that we can easily see the differences, even though they are based almost entirely on function in food chains and other ecological systems. Like the birds, the butterflies are, as Adolf Portmann says, "designed to be seen" and recognized by one another, and therefore serve as compelling yet discrete species to our eyes.

The child does not learn a key, "one-two-three," but exercises its logic and gets names from the nearest person at hand and then says the names aloud and speaks them back to a listener. The clarity and constancy of distinction between birds or squirrels is the most important feature of the system, even though the child will spend much of the rest of his life coping with exceptions. The terms that he learns are like stepping-stones, which are provided by his culture. But the species to which they refer are not a human creation. From the standpoint of his developing mind, they are the supreme gift. They are the only system of external reality which can serve him in this way.

Classifying by arranging things in binary pairs or opposites is our way of thought, its utility confirmed by the physical reality of species. Dividing everything into opposites is the most logical way of coping with an extended, chaotic world—like that of the child. "The fairy tale," says Bruno Bettelheim, "suggests not only isolating and separating the disparate and confusing aspects of the child's experience with opposites, but projecting these onto different figures."

To use such a key does not require a formal understanding of its logic, which is tacit. Its structure was not invented by institutional science. It is human logic, inseparable from cognition itself. It is the way each of us brings order into his world, however carelessly or with whatever contradictions we exercise it.

It is innately human, and yet it does not operate in a social vacuum. The details of anatomy or behavior by which such distinctions are made differ among different groups of people. The names of the animal groups, or taxa, are part of a particular language, which is part of a culture. As anthropologists are quick to assert, the cultural variations for classifying are very great. Indeed, much of anthropology has been preoccupied with those differences. The universality of this taxonomic sorting process lies at the root of our humanity and our consciousness, our ability to name and recall, to review experience, to plan, to investigate, to imagine. While its style and content are endowed by our particular group, the process itself is intrinsic to every child.

In building up and employing this model, the individual may learn a great deal about animals, but it is unlikely that this was ever the primary function or "purpose" of such a laborious and difficult activity. It is not even clear that this activity improves our efficiency as material users of nature. The requirements of hunting and gathering were never that difficult, as thousands of other species, no better physically endowed than ourselves, will attest. As a naturalist, I do not doubt that natural selection is the agency by which thought came into being and grew, and therefore had some benefit in terms of the early human niche and in terms of the advantage that some offspring had over others. But that advantage may have operated at several removes from the actual causes of death or of the differential success in leaving one's genes in the living stream.

In any case, the logic that the child exercises as the core of the maturing skills of intelligence is certainly not applied by him to daily needs. The whole of his capacity for insight is involved. Its application is not only to animals and plants, but to his interpersonal life, to the elements material and immaterial of the cultus, to the realm of man-made things, and to nature in its broadest sense.

The vast preponderance of the Earth's surface is *not* made up of such pellucid memberships and discontinuities as the species system. The terrain, the weather, the land forms, the sky are distressingly continuous and blended. The total physical space occupied by conspicuous plants and animals is extremely small, but the total perceptual space that they occupy cannot be underestimated. It can be truly said that we are "naturally" interested in nonhuman life, but that is not simply because it is alive like us or because it is useful, but because creatures are consistent in their likenesses and differences, members of species and patterns among species linking them into larger orders. That is exactly the instrument that conceptualizing required in order to store the world's diversity into word-images that did not simply pile up like objects at the city dump.

Words are themselves abstractions, but there is a difference between words that stand for a discrete object and those that refer to things intangible and invisible. Abstract category-making must have been the second step in truly human cognition, made possible because of speech on the one hand and a tangible model on the other. The opening-out of attention to the world at large would have otherwise been a fruitless experiment in sensory flooding and psychological overloading. Language is itself a coding system, but the coding system apparently needed an objective schema in order to work.

Apart from the design limitations of a data bank system without hierarchic classification, one may, however, still ask, "Why animals?" What the prehuman hunter-gatherer primate was doing was bringing the mental organ to bear on his two principal concerns: the social drama and the food quest. Relationships in both realms were bound up with kinship—simply in the sense of birth and family as the source of closeness and the basis of grouping. It is not surprising that language should have brought food and family into an electric conjunction that would permanently mark the conception of each with qualities of the other. What we eat—the animals—are descended one from another and related, one species to another, just as the infant is related to the mother, whose nipple he "eats." Here is the oral-centeredness of the infant as described by psychoanalysis, where eating and kinship are one, its symbols uniting the maternal with the nonhuman through the instrument of speech. Eating or being eaten are the shaping constraints on the lives of all predators and prey, but, except for man the predator, none of them ever got around to the practice of engulfing the world in order to project it, of interiorizing the environment before it can be found out there.

The social and ecological aspects of life were the real polarity stamped upon the world of thought. Language administered the dualities of experience: inside and outside, male and female, social and ecological. Category-making is the result of a sequence of binary choices by which classification and taxonomy are carried on. One term, like a family name, was the means for recalling its members. Those early members of our kind were internalizing the species system as an instrument by which ideas could be stored in memory, retrieved, presented to the self and others, sorted, retried, and manipulated. As primate hunters, men probed the guts and muscles of birds and mammals, noticing the orderly arrangement of the organs and the unity in diversity of patterns reflecting the species themselves. A monkey-like herbivore with no real interest in the insides of animals bequeathed to its meat-eating descendants a flair for social nuance which they might employ in thinking about the relationship of the liver to the gall bladder, as well as the crow to the raven.

To the question, "Why animals?", we might tentatively answer that only animals have living organs inside which make up the whole like a small community. They are related to corresponding parts in other animals like species in a genus since all mammals have livers, lungs, heart, blood, and so on. They are related to the body like members of a social hierarchy. The society of the insides confirms objectively what consciousness, thought, introspection, and dreaming tell us subjectively: that there is an orderly arrangement within and without, that the beings within have a life of their own which in some inscrutable way is a transformation of the life without. Language clumps these inner and outer domains and makes their parts and the relationships of parts memorable. It presents details to consciousness by linking to them an architecture of sounds. Speech is composed of a limited number of vocal elements, but their combinations enable us to inventory the world and explore the imagination by using a code modeled by the species system, the touchstone of the intangible and abstract.

The Vocal Obligations of Infancy

At this point the reader may feel that there may be some validity in what had been said, but that it all belongs to the very distant past. As a guess about things that may have happened long ago in prehuman evolution it is all right, but, beyond that, so what? The universal membership of plants and animals in species and the membership of groups of species in higher orders may have been the key that unlocked Pandora's Box, releasing the natural world potentially into human mental grasp as a means of analyzing and sharing ideas. But, having achieved that breakthrough in perception and intelligence, the whole matter would seem to be as distant from us as the Trojan wars.

The seeming irrelevance of these events to the present is due largely to our tendency to think that an organ is independent of its origin. Our analytical habit of thought confuses the products of evolution with inventions, with made objects. We take the brain as given and try to think what we can do with it in the same way we think about an electric generator. The genius of our creative and inventive style is itself seen as an invention, like the machine or the idiosyncratic piece of art. But the organic realm and evolutionary process is not like that. Instead of the means and ends, there are only means. What we achieved as hunter-primates was a means of learning. We did not graduate from thinking-animal classification to thinking philosophy, but adopted it as the mode of individual development.

It might seem from this that the purpose of the human brain is not to ponder the universe but to think about the relationship of oaks to elms or about why a leaping legion of bullfrogs may be grouped as kindred. In the light of our many needs for clear thinking, those ends would indeed be disappointing. Fortunately that is not the case, and there is a difference between thinking about something and the use of that something as means of further thought. No doubt an important part of human thought, past and present, takes Nature as its object, but the use of natural order as an instrument of thought is a very different matter.

For the individual the process is not a culmination of his powers but a part of the developmental process. In many ways, the evolution of *Homo sapiens* seems to have freed him from the rigidities of animal behavior, to have enlarged his freedom— a point widely celebrated in modern humanism. But that freedom is specific. It is part of some organic processes which are not free and over which we have little control. Freedom is the understanding and affirmation of one's limitations, such as the developmental procession of each individual life.

Human ontogeny is the most complex of any we know. It is spread across more years and is so vulnerable that it has built into it periods of mending that can, to a degree, heal the inevitable errors of infancy. This genetically blueprinted timetable of needs, behaviors, and dependencies begins before we are born and lasts at least a quarter century—perhaps for life. The overwhelming evidence from studies of nurturing and nutrition, physical growth, sibling relationships, play, learning, and other maturational processes emphasizes the biological unfolding of episodes. Theories of what it means to be human have come a long way from the view espoused by John Locke that the mind begins as a blank sheet and the body as a bit of new clay. When the hunter-primate emerged from the blinders of the older lock-and-key vision, that new human sensibility to the multiplicity of the world did not free man from the physical world but increased his dependence on it by extending his perceptual needs. The new mind had a prodigious appetite for visible species. Its development sets off the phases of individual growth more distinctly, giving each its own environmental requirements.

One of the most astonishing aspects of language is its ties to the personal calendar, for primary language-learning is scheduled to be basically complete in the individual by the age of four. Yet the kind and amount of communication in speech done by four-year-olds hardly seems to demand language at all. We are likely to assume too quickly that the more talking we do the better. We adults live under a verbal waterfall and are seldom dried out by silence. Whatever could evolution have been thinking of, to rig our personal timetables so as to put words into the mouths of babes? The unfolding process, starting with the yearling, is as tightly regimented as a fire drill: cooing, lallation, babbling, single nouns, adverbs, conjunctions, all in their time as though a Chinese scroll were unrolled bit by bit at the striking of a gong.

In the nineteenth century, biologists were fond of chanting, "Ontogeny recapitulates Phylogeny," a ritual way of asserting that individual embryological development was first invertebrate, then fish and amphibian-like, followed by quadrupedal mammalian and finally monkey-like features, a minute simulation of the whole evolutionary series of our ancestry. The idea was adopted by some anthropologists and other social scientists who thought they could see each child transiting the stages of human history from primitive hunters through simple pastoralists and planters on their way to urban adulthood.

The old chant had to be revised, however, when closer examination revealed that the human embryo was never a fish, but something like a fish embryo. As for children passing through the stages of primitive man, what they really went through was a phase resembling that of hunters' children.

The corrected chant, "Ontogeny recapitulates Ontogeny," didn't seem quite so catchy as the old one, but it was more to the point. When we apply it to the emergence of speech in the child, we get a clue as to what evolution had in mind—that, from its very beginning in human prehistory, perhaps two million years ago, speech in childhood, even though derived from sound communication among adults, had to do with the development of thought in the human suckling.

It is generally recognized in psychiatry that the more profound pathologies are traceable to the patient's childhood. The deeper the character flaw, the earlier it began in the individual's past. Although somewhat too sweeping to be exactly true, this generalization inversely says that normal adult behavior of the healthy individual has infantile antecedents. The earliness of language in the individual life span speaks to its depth in the matrix of adult behavior, and is evidence of its place in the life of the unconscious. Nothing so superficial and adult as philosophy, science, political ideas, theology, aesthetic theory, or literature is the purpose of language beginnings, though speech makes them all possible later in life.

What evolution had in mind was as much characteristic of the two-to-four age group as drinking milk. Before it could become communication, speech was the crucial agency of the developing rationality. It provided an "external" link between the sound brain, with its age-old ability to make sense of sequential input, and the newer visual perception that gave a Big Picture, at which the primates excelled.

Speech is the means by which category-making could proceed, a series of symbols for things that could be pyramided and stacked in memory by classifying. If memory was analogous to a great vault whose records are hidden from view, at least some of its spaces were accessible to the waking mind directly through the speech apparatus and its neural connections. The cognitive process is, of course, far more than naming, categorizing, and recalling, but they are basic to cognition. The meaning of words is straightforward for the child. The subtleties of symbolism, serendipities of insight, and the permutations of thought are of great value, but they are only potential for the individual if he has a proper infancy of mundane name-learning.

As surely as he "learns"* to walk, the two-year-old begins to

---

* The "wolf-children" literature is one of those jokes like patent medicine cure-alls, for which there are always buyers. The lost infant raised by animals is represented as still crawling at the age of eight or ten, since it never had humans to "teach" it to walk. Since the only way you could keep a normal child from beginning to walk would be to tie it down, the evidence for the wolf-child's animal past seems logical only to those who have assumed uncritically that a child must have human adult supervision in the initiation of walking.

demand the names of things. By vocal imitation and repetition, he begins a compulsive collecting of kinds that will go on for a decade. The process has that inexorable quality of the growth of plant tendrils and one can almost feel the neural cells putting out synapses like rows of garden bulbs putting down rootlets that organize the soil spaces beneath them. No imaginary animals at this age are of interest unless there are pictures. The lust for seeing the creature is as strong as that for naming it. Imagining is obviously something that does need practice, a skill which, like much of our behaving, from walking to religious speculation, is initiated by genetic timers but achieved through practice.

We can now return to the question of "So what?" Except as a description of prehuman evolution, why should we care about the relation of the mind to the external world of animals? The answer has at least three parts.

First, what evolved in man was not intelligence, but a developmental process. The process, like the embryology of the eye, is prefigured by a genetic program but not completed by it. If a patch is put over the eye of a newborn animal, it fails to develop those final nerve connections in the absence of light and the creature remains blind, even after the patch is removed. If children do not learn the names of visual images early in life (because of congenital lack of sight), they may do so later, after restoration by surgery, only with enormous difficulty or not at all. The permanently blind substitute tactile schemata for images, but must associate them also with a spoken terminology. The blind and deaf must learn a tactile language or lose the capacity for intelligent thought with which they are born. Helen Keller's autobiography speaks of the enormous importance to her of the "discovery" that everything has a name.

The use of the natural species system as the model of universal coherence was not a catalyst that set in motion, once and for all, the abstracting and ordering human mind. It became, rather, a part of the process for each individual. It was incorporated as a necessary ingredient, like light shining on the eye of the newborn. From the standpoint of the developing brain, an assembly, say, of horse-like animals—donkeys, tarpans, zebras, asses, and other groups of their odd-toed relatives (the Perissodactyla)—is as essential as blood, stable temperature, moisture, and tissue nutrients in its growth.

Second, what natural selection did was not produce a higher cognitive instrument that could assimilate an infinitely complex world like a stomach digesting meat, but instead a linking device. Timed to the appropriate stage of individual development, this device, coordinated with speech, visual consciousness, and instinctual drive behavior, took an imprint of order from the orderliness of natural creation. The clever brain employed the existing composition of plants and animals of the ecosystem itself as a master model. To have done it differently would have involved vastly more information storage of DNA and cumbersome connections and tissues. The price was that it had to become part of the ontogeny of each individual, to be done again with each new human life. But that had its advantages, too, perhaps even a saving grace.

Third, by not fixing the order-making independent of the actual surroundings, the system was highly adaptable to both differences of environment and human cultures. Apart from its cognition function, speech lent itself from the beginning to this differentiation of human groups and the in-focusing and cohesion that are part of belonging and loyalty. For consciousness newly opened up to the world's enormity, otherness, and diversity, membership took on not only new intellectual dimensions but new emotional intensity. For a frog or a cat, that otherness is largely invisible. When the world was taken as an object of thought, the breaking of those protective filters by the hunter-primates required new kinds of protection. If the world's diversity was not to be a maddening chaos, order-giving proclivities were necessary. One of these was, perhaps, the extension of belonging, beyond the resident group to other groups whose connections were a reflection of the organization of nature and whose instrument was a common language.

From an ecological point of view, basing the cognitive process on learning to classify real species instead of a totally self-winding model enabled our ancestors to spread out across the world. The ecosystems they invaded were already occupied by different groups of plants and animals. They moved into lacustrine basins, river valleys, tundra, desert scrubland, spruce-moose communities, cold steppes, and so on across the continents. A main purpose of thought is to make sense of one's environment, ecological as well as social. Suppose the primate hunter had evolved a set of fixed relationships to certain species during protohuman inhabitation of tropical savannas. Such brain machinery might be maladaptive in equatorial rain forests or on high plateaus. Moreover, half the species of large animals present during the early evolution of our genus, *Homo,* when all this began, have since become extinct and their places taken by newer forms with different behaviors. With a fixed, autonomous minding, unrelated in its genesis to personal experience in the natural world, human thought would have been cut loose from the reflex system of the older primates only to flounder in an alien, changing world. There would have ceased to be any connection between idea and reality or means of testing the rationality of a plan or the significance of an idea. Grouping and categorizing is not something done by children simply because their biology requires it, but because the real animal world of each child is to be his concrete model of reality.

It is this notion of coding our ideas to the visible order that leads to the next consideration: that every child should have to initiate his cognitive training by reference to the images and names of real creatures trains his attention. The laboratory science teacher, the naturalist guide, and the art critic struggle to make people look carefully, to see what is there, to scrutinize what they have already glanced at. The taxonomic job into which the small child plunges like a fledgling penguin leaping into the Antarctic Sea is not one of mere recognition but of intense examination.

Reflexively, visual animals need only a simple signal for recognition: A robin defends its territory not against another robin but against a red patch—cloth, feathers, any material—as long as it is about the right size and has two legs. People still behave this way in the use of emblems, insignia, logos, icons, and other simple signals, as well as toward a host of innate releasers. But the quest of the ordering mind was toward the thousands of forms that had no given meaning, and the quest of each new human mind is a renewal of that open-ended venture toward the meaning of meaning.

As Roger Fry, the art historian, once pointed out, emblemizing things reduces their visual demands; it has just the opposite effect of the rigorous visual work required to discover precisely those details which all oak leaves or all finches have in common and the other details in which each kind differs. The individual differences, to which primates are by nature supersensitive among their own kind, attract the knowing eye. Butchers, ethologists, still-life painters, veterinarians, and zoo-keepers extend to members of other species that attention to "character" which surgeons, portrait painters, psychiatrists, and others attend within the species. What all these people are doing is confirming the shared traits by discerning the particular, struggling against the tendency to tag and thereafter not to see but merely, as Fry said, to glance at the tags around them.

Such is the pitfall of taxonomy as an end in itself. Does it draw and focus the attention of an eye looking to see how the individuals depart from the norms of the tribe and so speak silently about the peculiarities of the particular environment and the scars of history, or does it become an exercise in overlooking? Is this not the same paradox that confronts democracy with its concern for the individual, which a manipulating power can transform into mass-man? Isn't it the same set of alternatives among the giant redwoods of which one version is that if you've "Seen one redwood you've seen 'em all"? *

We have wandered away from the child, but my point is that the differences in these two positions grow directly from early experience and from our categorizing capacities. Taxonomy is not a two-edged sword. It has a sharp front and a blunt back. It is incisive and opens things to their inner order, or it merely names. It is either the most exciting or the dullest subject in the whole realm of the arts and sciences. It is either a Russian novel or the telephone book. It is the instinctive approach to the world by every human child, the key to a lifelong series of ever more elegant refinements in perception of the mystery of life, slicing surprisingly across the conventional perception, a key that makes the intelligence—or it is monotonous rote that dulls instead of educates. It is employed to enlarge our individual human power because our species knows that the natural world holds clues to meaning, and life, an eternal hunt among kinds. Without the assumption of the hunt, we lock ourselves in our primate half by creating a world of mirrors.

The widespread observation among anthropologists that tribal peoples throughout the world develop elaborate taxonomies of the natural world was recognized by Claude Lévi-Strauss as a

* A remark, possibly apocryphal, attributed to Ronald Reagan, then Governor of California.

universal inquiry into order. Nature's differentiating features are more important than content—that is, the purpose was not utilitarian, aimed only at exploitation and use of creatures for food and raw materials. The natural realm can be classified not only by its species but by classes of anatomical parts. Dual sets of features form grids that elaborate combinations. In this way, he says, a universal flow of events and beings is sectioned and made intelligible.

"There are probably no human societies," says Lévi-Strauss, "which have not made a very extensive inventory of their zoological and botanical environment and described it in specific terms." Such terminologies often run into the thousands. The lexical systems include species and higher groupings, organs, body parts, diseases, habitats, modes of travel, and virtually any and all characteristics by which one can compare kinds of living forms. It was his genius to see beyond the order-giving symbolic function of these systems in themselves to the sets of oppositions generated when two such series were envisioned on the axes of a grid, and to proceed in *The Savage Mind* and elsewhere to examine human social structure and mythology as they are influenced by men making social analogies to these arrays of natural forms.

As Lévi-Strauss was careful to point out, "the savage mind" is not only a property of savages, but an aspect of all human minds. Among those human groups not yet buried in their own effluvia he found "a consuming symbolic ambition such as humanity has never again seen rivaled." His concern was the mature expression of a "passage between images and ideas." In discussing the way in which nature is used as the language of the internal logic of an invented myth, he emphasizes the purpose and the innovative composition of the myth, and he understates the inexorable taxonomic training in the young.

He has observed that, of the hundreds of creature kinds and thousands of categories known to any of the hunting/gathering, planting, or pastoral people, only a few score have practical use. He emphasizes their use in art and myth. But for either use only a few dozen are eaten, worn, or depicted as clan totems. Something is missing from his observation that, for instance, the Dogon of Mali recognize and classify hundreds of kinds of organisms, use them in a vast system of correspondences to man, and employ them in the construction of epic stories. That missing element is their psychological use in the development of cognition in children. What is omitted is the possibility that the taxonomic enterprise has very different functions at different ages of individual development, a sequential or ontogenetic sequence of related purposes.

The animal totem, because of anthropologists like Lévi-Strauss, has ceased to be disdained in social theory as a magic idol to which childish savages bowed in superstitious worship. It is now seen as a conceptual tool. Like other conceptual tools, it did not spring finished into the human head, nor is it simply inculcated in the young. It emerges in the maturing of the brain's own timetable, nourished by cultural care. These taxonomic enterprises, to borrow a phrase from Gregory Bateson, are personal "steps toward an ecology of mind."

Parallel to the games of childhood that create muscular skills, the name game is focused in the years two to twelve. Language, its means, serves different functions in this age group than in adults. In the decade of childhood the quintessence of taxonomy —speech applied to species as the ultimate manifestation of reality—is its literalness. The successive binomial choices call attention, and fix by rote, the names of existing animals and plants. Taxonomy is unambiguous. It has no multiple meaning for the child or juvenile, no poetry. The mode of mythical and totemic thought that lies ahead is not foreseen by the individual. The society keeps it hidden. Thus does the secrecy of initiation reveal itself not to be arbitrary and exclusive, but the true purpose of cult concealment may be the protective nurturing of the uncommitted and immature.

Like the rooms in a house that may be used for different purposes, the mytho-poetic meaning of the species system rests on an utterly banal foundation that has no metaphor. The child-mason stacks rocks whose surfaces no more tell him what is to come than does his infantile sexuality reveal mature love.

The naked realism in which all things are what they seem, and in which they seem to be ends rather than means, is part of that halcyon Paradise that every youth must lose. All its creatures are pure. The luster of creation is perfect and nothing seems concealed.

A Fauna as Home

The intensity of this primordial radiance is focused upon a particular set of animals. The imprinting of a particular group of animals has its significance as "the originals." The question was posed earlier: Why should each child have to develop the order-making, classifying process by studying the kinds of creatures instead of receiving it as an automatic, built-in mode of behavior? It was suggested that there must be something crucial in knowing the particular group of creatures that belong to one's personal youth. Its sentimental and nostalgic value is that it means home. The heartache of being a stranger in a strange land is the uncanny displacement of its creatures. To the displaced person the whole arrangement is there, the landscape with its plant and animal inhabitants, yet all are unfamiliar in kind. Immigrants to a new country often find that they are never able to accept this slightly skewed creation as the real one, and that is due to the branding effect of the singular truth of one's first fauna.

Not only does the original set bond the individual to place by rootedness of images, but perhaps the purpose of this fixation is to protect reality from the intellectual abuses to which we put the species system as adults. The human primate is a shameless exploiter of this system by analogy. A lifelong builder of fantasy castles, myths, metaphors, symbols, parables, and caricatures might very easily mix up the original order with his homological creations and confuse the derivatives with the original. Nature is in constant danger of becoming a paradigm or some other abstraction. Intoxicated by his own mind, the human animal may need to be reminded by that first deep imprint that animal drawings are not animals and that there is a concrete reality which he did not invent, whose velvet glove will deliver the final verdict on the validity of his imagination.

Concealed Creatures

All animals are prompted by their own nervous system to seek those signals in nature that will trigger feeding or fleeing or mating. Like his ancestors and animal kindred, man too seeks such sensible figures. For him, however, they can mean not only a meal or danger, but clues, indirect signs, all of which are parts of a puzzle. In loosening the locked-in meanings of fixed signal/response behavior, our species did not escape nature and its constraints, but turned the whole of it into a language. Like any good carnivorous predator, man continued to separate figure from ground, searching out the living forms in the terrain. But the child of two to twelve is only incidentally looking for animals to kill or to run from. He is not yet ready to divine from them a social parallel or ritual omen, but only to prepare his thinking.

Evidence for this is seen in an unusual experiment reported in *Science* magazine in which the subject was given a brief glimpse of the drawing of a tree, some of whose contours formed the profile of a duck. Asked to describe what he saw, the observer revealed that he was not conscious of the duck outline. He was then told to describe a dramatic scene or tell a story. The details of the story include a highly improbable number of references to feathers, nests, flight, ponds, and other phenomena related to ducks. The examiners concluded that the duck had been perceived subliminally or unconsciously. The conclusions of the researchers went no further. But the implication is inescapable that this perceptual activity goes on all the time, that, as adults, we see creatures to which we do not attend, and that we weave them continuously into the flow of thought, from which they shed telltale signs into our conscious life.

A curious aspect of these "embedded figures" is that people suffering from some forms of schizophrenia are especially keen at spotting them. Schizophrenics tend to withdraw from the world, to dichotomize it irreparably. Some make ingenious neologisms or new words for parts of their separate, lost reality. They have an aura of overheated existentialism and seem to represent the breaking point of a culture overdependent on left-brain functions, unable to put their masses of data together into wholes. They are at the opposite pole from the traditional, rhetorical, polemic society that can get overcharged with structure and starved for information, whose psychosis is to run amok rather than to withdraw.

One is reminded of color-blind artillery spotters who can better see camouflaged enemy gun installations than spotters with normal vision. When a pathology makes some organic function such as these more efficient, we might wonder if some opposing

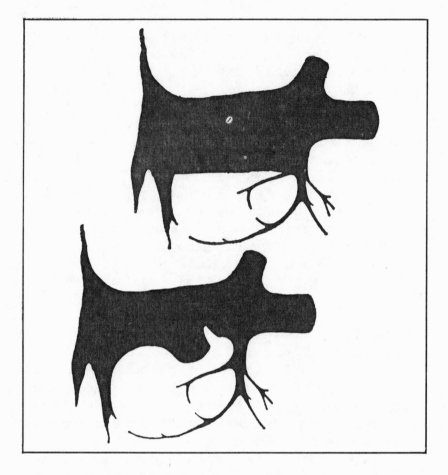

The hidden-figure experiment. When seen for a fraction of a second, the picture evoked feather, nest, and other bird or duck references in stories made up by the subjects, who did not consciously see the "hidden" duck. (From Science 151:837, 1966)

function is impaired. The advantage of color vision is that objects intended to be seen (such as flowers and fruits, eye color and stoplights) are more easily located and attended to at the price of seeing the whole, of which those objects are but a small part. We are eternally caught in a bind—to see parts or to see wholes. Discerning cryptic patterns in a maze of lines may be less advantageous to an "open-minded" species than recognizing wholes. The tests with the concealed duck figure suggest that we keep both abilities, but as healthy individuals we relegate the perception of subordinate forms to the unconscious in order that we may perceive overall design. Perhaps there is a set of triggers or templates in the unconscious that fit animal forms and that communicate mood and motivation to the searcher or hunter by saying, "Keep the big picture in mind if you must, but *keep looking,* there is a duck there," or, alternatively, "Of course you see the duck, but file it away where it won't interfere with your sense of the whole."

The researchers did not say why they chose a duck and not a shaving mug. If this were an isolated instance in psychological research we might dismiss it as an accident. But the use of the animal figure is widespread in intelligence tests, personality studies, psychological therapy, and perceptual research. The whole realm of visual figure use in psychology, especially in the study of children, is shot through with animals. In a recent book summarizing thousands of tests in which children were offered pictures from which they were to make up stories, Mary Haworth outlines her theory of clinical interpretations, sorting out the symbolic meanings in terms of the child's relationships to other people. The most extraordinary aspect of all such studies is that the researchers never raise the question of the reason for using animals at all, except to say that children "identify more readily" with animals and that animals offer better disguises for the people whom they "represent."

One could say, perhaps unfairly, that psychology traditionally addresses itself to aspects of human behavior related to personal experience and not to species experience. Its professional heritage, though now changing, regarded as unfashionable that about ourselves which cannot be modified by therapy. That children are interested in animals seems self-evident, one of those assumptions that betrays credulity, one of those "givens" which in the past has not aroused the curiosity of psychologists.

A whole subdiscipline, based on the Rorschach test, in which the subject interprets bilateral "ink blots" is another example. The blots are usually seen as animals, but the journals, books, and papers on Rorschach theory devote little attention to the most fundamental question that it raises. That otherwise meaningless shapes are perceived as the bodies of organisms is simply accepted, perhaps regarded as innate or due to conditioned experience, but it is not seen as evidence in the genesis of thought itself. To the question, "Why do we use animal pictures to elicit information about a child's relationship to parents, siblings, friends, strangers, old people, or babies?" it merely begs the issue to say, "Why, because animal figures have 'high stimulus value' or 'symbolic proximity,'" or that "In dreams and imagination humans are symbolically represented by animals."

We must go beyond the explanation that assumes that the child chooses animals as surrogates in the same spirit that writers choose metaphors, or the alternative, that it is an innate mechanism invented by fairies at the boundary between the id and the ego. No ex post facto explanation after the evolution of brains or the growth of each individual brain will do. We do not come into the world with brains that we learn to use any more than our distant forefathers evolved brains and then learned to be intelligent. Brain and thought process evolved together and they develop together.

Animal Protagonists

Literary studies have also dealt with the presence of animals, but, like the psychologists, the analysts of contemporary literature usually seem to assume that their use is arbitrary. In *Animal Land*, for example, Margaret Blount's examination of the animals in children's stories, the author faces up to the question, asking why so many stories are about animals if their purpose is to shape the child's understanding of people. Her answer, however, is simple literary relativism: Some authors are so inclined. And, she adds, the animal stories signify a return to Paradise or Eden. The answer is undoubtedly right so far as it goes, but her first response starts at the wrong end. While it is true that some writers write about animals and some do not, *all* children tell and listen to stories about them. Blount's book is about children's stories, but her reference to Paradise would seem to apply better to adults than to children.

As for stories as such, convergent theories come from anthropology and psychiatry. A recent anthropological view is that stories establish cultural moods or attitudes and formulate ideas of a general order of existence. Life is very complicated even for adults, and children are excluded from much of the information that enables adults to make sense of things. Stories remedy this by clothing in simple, dramatic episodes the mood or cultural mode of thought. They convey the gist of what is valued and what is tabooed. The story is a kind of code about how a culture explains things, its choice of reference points. It is both attention-directing and programming, a sort of inventory of things loved and feared in which the actions of the fictional beings themselves illuminate the relationships between motives and events. Finally, stories convey a traditional set of figures that will bear religious symbolism later in life. The psychiatric view of the function of fairy tales, recently given eloquent voice in Bruno Bettelheim's *The Uses of Enchantment,* is centered on the child's "existential dilemma." By simplifying inescapable human situations—limitation, Oedipus, sibling rivalry, separation, danger, and all the other anxieties and uncertainties inherent in the unfolding of every life and personality development—the fairy tale both externalizes and reassures. The main differences between the two is that the anthropologists tend to emphasize cultural content and the problems of group coherence while the psychiatrists tend to see the difficulties arising from the individual's unconscious fears, which are generated by the loss of his fetal omniscience and the equally frustrating internal problems of ego formation in the child. They have in common the belief that storytelling serves the inevitable steps of growth essential in normal development.

If it seems strange that animal figures should be chosen to simplify human relations, we must realize that the strangeness comes largely from our adult attitudes in a culture that emphasizes the gap between the human and nonhuman. The demand by children for animals in these stories and the silent affirmation of this wisdom by the consenting adult suggest that their purpose endures even in conflict with the prevailing mood of modern society, which rewards heroic, eccentric art and which places contemporary human problems in political perspective. The industrial and technological mood is away from animals and toward machines.

If one were trying to guess how to invent such a complicated thinking being as a human from parts inherited from the hyper-social primates, it might seem more logical to develop each individual first socially and then ecologically. Indeed, such a view of human development is widely held. Born an animal and made human by culture and experience, the argument runs, the infant and child live in a social cocoon, taking a playful interest in the nonhuman, but they are shaped from a kind of vegetative, glandular blobness primarily by human example and instruction, and thereafter project these social perceptions onto nature as a whole. The shaping of consciousness is set in a human context, growing from intense mother/child interactions through layers of parental, family, and communal cultural surroundings, outward toward the nonhuman, which it reaches at the end of a long maturing process.

But the truth is that no such simple progression to the more distant animal world occurs. There is an early, intense embryonic and maternal relationship that is more organic and more chemical than personal. The first decade of life is characterized by an oscillating harmonic between attention to the human *and* to the nonhuman, in which the latter is seen both as an end in itself and as an instrument in human socialization.

The very small child does not distinguish types of other beings from roles. He is sorting out consistency of form and behavior in general. At first all the characters in the world exist only dimly in their own right, for they are primarily the figures of *his* imagination and dreams. From lullabys and Mother Goose in his early years to fairy tales and animal stories later on, he does not need to learn that each member of the cast means something to him personally. Childhood fears are at first vague and unshaped: separation anxiety, oral greed, loneliness, fear of the dark, sibling rivalry, oedipal dilemmas, self-worth, dependencies, incompetence, smallness—these and their solutions can be given concrete representation in the stories. As members of a cast they can be handled, or at least be seen as subject to the coherence of the play, which can even have a good outcome.

The growing child quickly learns to separate people from four-legged animals, to perceive general types in fish, birds, and insects. For a decade his principal task is to refine these differentiations. He is gaining an ecological education, but, equally important, he is gaining the forms of an inner as well as outer taxonomy, the threads from which the whole tapestry of his feelings are prefigured.

Mother Goose, the animal fable, the fairy tale, and the myth differ from one another in the nature of the communication. Some deal with human social relations, some with moral precautions, some with psychic dilemmas of the personality. But all use animals because their variety of form offers holding ground for otherwise intractable and transient experiences.

This is not to say that the content of such tales and rhymes is always good, for they can be badly used—to repress, to frighten, to impose rigid moral order. The whole process can be perverted. Unresolved fears, given the forms of animals, attach themselves to the real creatures. The adult whose phobias are triggered by a spider, snake, or bat had failed to cope with the inner problems for which these animals once served as objective vessels and will hate real snakes and bats. The unconscious has remained chaotic and the world becomes a jungle. Monsters too have a real place in the child's fantasy: They signify the danger of inner ambiguity, of things run together. The psychologically arrested adult will fear them in the real woods and fields.

Thus we learn two lessons early in life: There is no limit to the degree by which inner and outer fauna can be differentiated; each kind of animal is sticky and will carry some train of connections. And no matter how long we live or how intelligent we become, this rule continues to apply. Books like J. R. R. Tolkien's *Lord of the Rings* in the 1960s and Richard Adams' *Watership Down* in the 1970s are examples of this continuing process for adult readers. One moves from Goosey Gander and Chicken Little through the Three Bears to dragons and orcs and societies of rabbits as complex as a Dickens novel along the frontier of one's uncertainties. These stories constrain the slippery parts of reality by temporarily harnessing them to the net of animal systematics and ecology.

Many of these, from simple small-child ditties like the "Three Little Pigs" to the preadolescent dramatized natural history of otters, wolves, and eagles, are ostensibly only about animals. But the inner voice with which we translate them to ourselves denies this. The central organizing process by which we begin to think depends from the beginning of our lives on these animal instruments that make our mental lives possible. It is not only that each species occupies a taxonomic space that serves to model categorizing, but each is framed in relationship to others by behavior and personality. These animal nouns carry the whole of the verb and adjectival world with them.

This connection-building between animals and qualities is done partly in sleep. Why are animals in dreams? Freudian psychology holds them to be part of the body of symbols acceptable to the dreaming mind by which otherwise repressed ideas are allowed to ascend to thought. But why should the mind use animals and not something else? What makes them universally suitable for representing repulsive people, fearful feelings, contradictory attitudes, or danger? The unconscious is that stratum of memory to which much of our early experience descends, not only as fact, but to be organized. The cataloging system is in some mysterious but dynamic way an extension of the dominant logical classificatory system available to us as children: the system of creatures. There are also systems of things (people are symbolized in dreams by machines or houses or stones) and systems of heroic figures, but they are apparently not as satisfactory for certain kinds of symbols. Perhaps it is a matter of access, the more formal animal classification being more precise and efficient as a storing, retrieving, and coupling device. Perhaps the animal image links more easily into other, conscious analogical systems: the fairy tale, myth, fable, or folktale. For the child, action can replace understanding, and animals are characterized by their actions. The will, ideas, feelings all seem to "move" us and are imaged as things that move.

Animals are like an infinite company of sign-bearers. By the time the child is eleven years old we may give him a book on the life of the salmon, written by an ichthyologist, which carries the National Academy of Science's stamp of approval, but the child can no more read it like a computer storing information than he can fly. For the preadolescent there is no such thing as purely natural history. Science fairs, natural history books, academic courses, and other extensions of scientific objectivity grant him a formal mode for his public demeanor, but the sensory channels into his brain can never be completely unhinged from that system of analogies and homologies that is the stuff of his perception.

The Intellectual Abuse of Animals

At the other extreme, the modern literary child's enmeshment in a warm and cozy world of little furry creatures is often sentimental. Since the purpose of animal stories is to bear cultural loads (and to bare cultural lodes), they can be made to shape the responding mind, to create and tone moral and conceptual frameworks. One reaction to human callousness is to hide it, to minimize the disagreeable—masking death and pain, padding the child's not-so-tender mind in the same way that female adolescents in middle class society were "protected" in the past from those facts of life for which their constitution was believed too weak. That animals live by eating other creatures, that more than 50 percent of the newborn will not live a year, that predators are good and necessary are incompatible with the sentimental cloak that characterizes the nineteenth- and twentieth-century animal story, the Walt Disney view.*

Thinking animals make possible an unlimited means of self-understanding and of appreciating the qualities of others in minute detail. But animal images can be misused to protect the person from unwelcome reality, too. Examples of such abuse of the animal tale that panders to the overprotective attitudes of parents are Hans Christian Andersen's "The Ugly Duckling" and Richard Bach's *Jonathan Livingston Seagull.*

Both are idealized from the Adlerian-Watsonian psychology of the self as the willful fabricator of one's own nature. "The Ugly Duckling" encourages the child to think that his problems are due to the fault of others and that he can be transformed by the unfolding of his superior destiny. In the popular book on the sea gull, the young bird is led to reject not only the qualities of his own kind before he can know them, but to aspire beyond all limitations and to repudiate the idea of kind. Both lead to the belief that the given world is only dross upon which the correcting and striving of the ego or the intrinsic superiority of the self will make a better reality. Because of their mangling of inner truth and the outer world, they can lead their readers in time only to deep resentment and rejection of the world.

The error of the sugared view is to assume that the correlation between interspecies behavior and interpersonal behavior is literal, merely scaled up or down. For example, in hiding the killing of some animals by others we suppose we are simply reducing the volume of violent death and that the child will be less inclined to solve his personal and social problems by resorting to murder or war. What actually happens is much more complicated and is likely to have the opposite results than those which we wish. Since death is a fundamental component in the

---

* That Disney films often show the predator as necessary to biological systems does not change their essential conceit—that at best predators are necessary evils. Sympathy is always with the prey, which usually escapes in the depicted episodes.

cycle of animal life, it cannot be abolished; it can only be censored. Knowing it is there, but deprived of all those strands of connectedness by which death helps hold a comprehensible world together, the child is likely to become obsessed, misinformed, and guilty. The whole transformational process by which animal food chains are assimilated as social analogies between people may break down. Shielded from killing among animals (seen as struggle for power, increase in disorder), as well as from any understanding of war in human society, the child may even reverse the order-making analogical series as an adult by "explaining" nature according to his social and political comprehension of war.

The human analogy of the repudiation of death can be seen in the "historicizing" of predation. One yearns for the escape of the innocent rabbit from the wily fox in the same context with which we seek the protection of peoples from tyrannical persecution or slaughter by aggressors. The Bible sees the fall of man and the fall of nature as joint consequences of Evil. It asserts that before the fall there was no predation, no killing, no meat-eating by animals of one another, between men and animals, or among men. Deprivation of death and monsters in the tales he is told give the child's inner monsters or his nascent affirmation of death no outer connection. Denied as real in the shared fantasy of myth or fairy tale, they can only be repressed by the child who rejects the messages from his intuitive grasp, his unconscious, and his own observations of the world. The cycle of his anxiety is perpetuated across generations. If an adult is convinced that predation in nature is the analogical equivalent of murder and war, he will translate this attitude in his telling of fairy tales and fables. A falseness of outer reality leads to falsification of the inner. The child is not ideologically convinced but perverted by the mechanics of his own perception, and an individual psychopathic trap is laid that will favor an ideological expression when he becomes a young adult. As an adult he will perpetuate the process on his own children.*

In Bruno Bettelheim's analysis of the role of animals in fairy stories, the problems of the id ("animal nature" or "instinctive

---

* Such a cycle would seem on its face difficult to break. But the infantile characteristics of adolescent behavior are the signs of an inward regression that make early experience accessible. For a few months there is a kind of insect metamorphosis allowing deep tissues of thought to be renewed.

drive" in each of us) are often represented as animals. Our task is to master and to overcome these forces. One might suppose from this that animals represent only the dangerous and troublesome aspects of the psyche, to be replaced by more humanistic symbols as we become mature. But Bettelheim assures us that this is not the case. The wolf does indeed represent our unconscious asocial tendencies, but the owl and dove signify wisdom and love. More important, the animal is not only the gross beast, but the vital potential for renewal and transformation. Like the body, it is our fundamental resource, that from which new energy and new beginnings come.

Organs as Creatures

Small children are as deeply curious about the insides of things as they are about kinds of creatures. Indeed, naming parts is a sort of general framework for this behavior, whether it is among creatures or within their bodies. As long as the child is uninhibited by adult disapproval or repugnance for squishy things, he is a keen student of insides, which are a kind of fauna. His own body is also a collection of soft parts, and he connects his perception of the insides of other creatures to his own insides, and his primary apprehension of both orders is through taxonomy. But the connection is not simply one of parallel patterns. The terrain contains creatures whose bodies are, in turn, landscapes —that is, a terrain of body parts. Creatures are geographies within geographies. They are like social entities within larger groups, all giving meaning and definition to the spaces they occupy. The arrangement of internal anatomy is as much a part of it as the names of the organs.

In time, the adult comes to think of the total community of life in a meaningful space. Euclidian/Newtonian space, as Jean Piaget has shown, becomes conscious as a normal part of late childhood, and our culture strongly encourages that view of space as fixed by geometry. But long before he has images of such rigidly proportioned and mathematically definable volumes, the child is alert to an Einsteinian inner world governed by the relativity of species and the skewing of proportion by feeling. The sensuousness of eating, defecating, or pain such as toothaches or stomachaches modify the "size" of body parts. This variability is confirmed by seeing how small the stomach of a lizard can be and how big the stomach of a caribou. The variations on a theme are very similar, psychologically, to the systems of difference in similarity by which taxonomy proceeds to sort out species. In spite of their differences in different animals, stomachs are all a kind of being. The hundreds of organs, bones, blood vessels, muscles, and other anatomical entities have likenesses across the boundaries of species. Indeed, each of the types of organs is a kind of species. This grouping of like parts from different kinds of animals is complementary to that which separates by conventional species and family, for it reunites them at new integrative levels. In a sense it brings together what species-naming has put apart, dissecting each kind of creature in order to form new families of parts.

But before we leave the subject of space, there is more to be said of the body's insides than that its parts form categories corresponding to those of other bodies. There is strong evidence that, as the child becomes increasingly aware of the diversity and spatial extent of his own body, he is simultaneously growing in sensitivity to the terrain. What we call landscape, but which might more usefully be understood as habitat, has boundaries (based on experience), like a skin, structure, parts, dynamic qualities, and even analogous features to the human body: streams like blood, vegetation like hair, caves like body openings, and so on.

In the modern world we are inclined to regard those analogies as poetic and to credit fantasy with a play of language that is entertaining, aesthetic, and somewhat frivolous. We have a catch-all term, "anthropomorphism,"* for analogies like that between the earth and the torso, or in which animals seem to behave as though they had plans, ideas, or feelings that are human. No doubt there are many literary applications of such ideas and expressions of them in the visual arts that are arbitrarily used by the artist. Like conventions they become hackneyed with overuse.

* Anthropomorphism is an overworked and misused word anyway. Literally, it means "the doctrine of ape- and monkey-like forms," since it refers to anthropoids, which are the primates except for its most primitive group, the prosimians. In our neo-Cartesian culture, to anthropomorphize is to endow an animal with bogus humanity. Apart from its weakness in this sense, the term has a destructive effect on understanding, for it closes the door on the common processes in men and animals by simply declaring them illusionary. One anthropologist criticized the work of another on apes as "too anthropomorphic," which is like calling a study of fruit trees "too arboreal."

In novels in the early thirties, for instance, Stella Gibbons and Aldous Huxley made fun of the terrain-body analogy in *Cold Comfort Farm* and *Antic Hay*.

The Dialogue of Inside-Outside

Any idea can be trivialized, but the abuse of the body/earth analogy may be not so much a matter of repetition as of a kind of disabled perception. The child seeks underlying schemata in the diversity of things. There is a kind of reciprocity in which terrain and body ramify and support each other. The young's taxonomic tools are commonly employed in an analytic way in the left-brain speech and naming centers, while the opposite right-brain integrates spatial wholes, both bodily and geographic.

For the child the common ground is not poetic at all, but a functional economy in which parallel images are handled, as it were, with a single set of mental tools. But their differences are as important as their similarities, for what is ultimately sought is not blending, but differences between them in spite of outward commonality.

When a good poet calls an adult's attention by way of a metaphor, it is to evoke our capacity for feedback between the members of a homology, and the next step of discovering diversity in unity. When a bad poet does so, one thing is simply defined in terms of the other and we are left with a bad pun that simply lumps things together and tends to isolate us from our own inner past.

The inner past is a progressive detailing going on simultaneously, creating vision on either side of our body-boundary, our skin, inside and outside. Graphically, the sequence is represented in the diagram on page 70.

At the center of each figure is the mind's eye, looking outward at the space of the world and inward at the body parts. It is, so to speak, a single eye whose healthy function depends on its looking at our inner visceral landscape and at the bright countryside in rapid order.

At stage 1 the detail on either side is limited and sparse. As vision grows, the graphic lines extend. Details increase in density, inside and outside, always named. This process of the further resolution continues with age in stages 2 and 3, as new things,

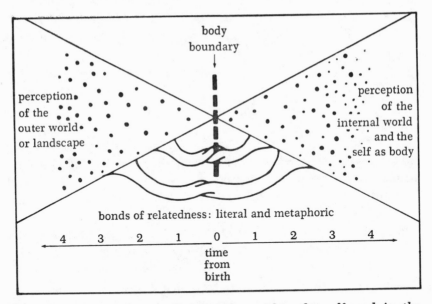

The density of things and definitions within the self and in the environment increase proportionally and simultaneously. As the individual ages, the inner and outer worlds are pushed farther apart, however, unless their relationship is progressively affirmed by concepts and intuitions of relatedness.

events, actions are recognized along with the spatial networks they form.

A danger in this is that the things discovered are increasingly far apart from the skin boundary, which separates. Something more is necessary, which must relate and integrate the increasing detail on the two sides; otherwise they become first separate, then isolated, and finally alienated realms. Without some kind of developing bonds of such relatedness, the inner and outer realities become exclusive, as the skin gets to be more like a barrier than like a transmitter. Such connecting bonds work like the world currents of air or its magnetic fields, giving the poles definition by their relationship to each other.

No doubt the theory here is too simple and the diagram too primitive. But there is evidence from the study of the pictures children draw of an equilibrium of parts inside and outside. Those with a weak sense of the origins of bodily sensation and of the location of body parts have an equally impoverished concept of the proportions, appearance, and diversity of the objects and events in the outer world. When there is no firm boundary between inner and outer, the child slips toward schizophrenia; when the body boundary rigidifies, he perceives himself encased in a protective shell and is neurotically frightened by threats to penetrate it.

In pretending in play to be different creatures, the child is preparing to accept his own inevitable transformations. He will move through a series of changes as he grows up that alter his appearance, feelings, relationship to others, and quality of his experience so dramatically that he can be likened to different beings. Myths and folktales on the theme of transformation are based on the plasticity of his changing body image. This sequence of selves follows an orderly growth pattern. The location of inside and outside, the places where bodily sensations arise, the outlining of the body with one's hands, tension where skin is stretched over bone joints, reflected images, observation of other bodies, living and dead, as containers, the rise and fall of libidinal energy around body openings—these are but a few of the experiences that contribute to the development of a phantom figure in our own minds, the body image. These formative events are enhanced in childhood by getting out of one's skin vicariously, mimicking animals, dressing up or masquerading. The capacity to go in and out of one's skin subjectively helps him resist the overhardening of the maturing image. The idea of what we are can get too brittle and our identity-making, utterly dependent on the body image, mediates between the hard and soft exterior. The imaginary transformations of childhood pretending, the dramatic mimicry in dance, games, and ceremony are an essential ingredient in this slow molding, keeping it from setting too hard too quickly, preventing it from becoming a shell.

And what has all this to do with animals? The child's first and most powerful attention to the surroundings, apart from his human family, is riveted upon animals. They constitute the inhabitants—the details. It is their names which give access to the model for order that can be understood internally as anatomical arrangement. Their movement in the terrain makes traces which are a network of lines giving space depth and interconnectedness. A land with no creatures running across it, flying over it, hopping, slithering, or walking is a static, two-dimensional, dead world. Great herds in motion across open land and vast flocks of waterfowl are among the most exhilarating sights on earth and imbue the setting and scene with special significance.

The interior terrain also has its creatures with their own kinds of movement, and most of our internal organs have the same shimmering, organic vitality. Seen in the newly opened body, the organs are clearly palpitating, vibrant beings. They compare to similar organs in the bodies of the animals, hence constitute the living animal. We eat those corresponding parts of the animals; they travel down our throats and occupy us and meet our muscles and livers with the gift of life and in part pass on through us. When we eat the brain of an animal we initiate a kind of courtship resulting in a mating of its brain and ours. This conception of brains as a species is one of those little wavy lines in the diagram on page 70 that connect inside and outside. In being eaten, the tissue enters through an opening in the skin, the mouth, which is where the word "brain" seems to come from. It is a taste and a texture and a smell as well as—or as part of—an image.

Eating different animals joins us in a kind of unity with them. But there are always parts that we do not eat, and this exclusion prevents unity from becoming identity. A total melting coalescence would bring everything together in a kind of lump, making the world poorer, not richer, in kinds.

Of course, plants play a further role in this. They remind us that our organs can be alive, though stationary. They create the points of reference and habitat through which movement takes on significance. Like animals, they pass into us from the outside, and the words that are their names pass out into the world. That their internal anatomy does not correspond to our own is a lesson in otherness, perhaps a more advanced kind; a lesson for older minds, a more subtle kingdom in the mental menagerie.

By now everyone has heard of brain asymmetry, that peculiarity found in the heads of people and birds in which right and left cerebral hemispheres develop differently during the third to eighth year of life (in man). The so-called "split brain" consists of a left "propositional" set of centers and their association tracts, which function in analysis, mathematics, and speech, while the right "appositional" junctions of brain lobes are the center for the perception of the body, space, and music, and may be said to be synthesis-directed in the sense of making wholes. There is as much as a 30 percent difference in the volumes of the two areas.

The growth of these two areas marks off childhood, and the maturing or myelinations of their neurons correspond in one side to the learning of faunal nomenclature and vocabulary. Simultaneously, on the other side, there is an imprinting of place, a human juvenile home range, which will be the original model for the idea of "home terrain." This division of brain is the primary model and organ of the perceptual disjunction of reality. One attends progressively throughout life to distinctions that separate and make a diverse world and to clues that keep it whole.

This bilateral structure—the split brain—is not totally divided but is joined by a tissue bridge (the *corpus callosum*). In a sense these two halves are not doing different things, but working in different directions along a single axis from a common center toward a richer perceptual world. Indeed, the differences in function tend to be largely quantitative, as the work of one side can be assumed by the other if the brain is injured early in life.

This view of the world as having a dual aspect, progressively fine-grained and yet variable and increasingly organized, is not, therefore, an invention of philosophers but a description of the way the mind works. Education is the means by which parents and society facilitate this activity. The system of plant and animal species is the most conspicuous place for it to start, the archetype of all such two-part order-making throughout life.

There is a curious relationship between taxonomic procedure and the structure of myth. The latter is composed of "intuitively selected pairs of opposed elements. These binary opponents are the basis of our elaborate structure of symmetries and isomorphisms which frequently repeat themselves as they undergo various logical transformations." In short, the mythical tale begins with a dual set and goes on to play with the two parts in a fictional story. In both identifying animals and hearing stories, the child is singularly demanding and is happy with repetition. It seems that the use we make of our classifying is a first step in myth-making, which in turn amplifies and extends that initial dividing and opposing of things into sets of opposing pair members.

The myth may refer to animal totems, give directions for growing up, deal with social and ecological problems, incorporate historical events, or rationalize taboos. But it contains an information code whose basic form is binary, like that of animal classification or taxonomic keys. It relays a mode of thought from one domain (animal identification) to another (human affairs), and establishes a framework for thought and feeling within the culture.

Stages in the maturing of both brains are undoubtedly inte- grated with other parts of normal growth or ontogeny. The way in which the polar system divides attention probably creates some competition between analysis and synthesis that different per- sonalities resolve in different measure. In clinical experiments in which the subject is exposed competitively to speech and music at the same time, music, the pattern synthesis, dominates. Cog- nitive order-making has priority over getting more details. Facts are useless without theory, figures are lost without a ground, information is dross without a plan. The dominance of music over visual data is even more pronounced, related perhaps to the more complex pathways between ear and brain than eye and brain, and to the evolutionary antecedence of hearing as a deep- brain complex, already working when our ancestral primates were just coming out of the dark of nocturnal existence.

Even within the right-side or synthesis brain, music is the most important input. This is the reason why no picture ever became a national anthem. Singing and song is unifying for us and for our perception of birds, whose songs are the anthems of their respective races, as we have seen. Human song may even have evolved from the avian example as prehuman groups moved toward group consciousness and cultural diversity. Man-made music may be the first music heard by human infants (or fetuses), but in much of the world bird melody is still available during many hours of each day during the first year of life and we should not discount its importance out of hand.

Deeply attuned to his mother's lullaby, the infant surely can- not miss the similarity of melodic phrasing and repetitive chorus- ing. No one who has cared for babies can doubt the importance of the lullaby. Can we afford to ignore the possible significance of bird music? To what extent might the social purposes of human song for the infant be paralleled by ecological purposes of birdsong?

If one takes song as being produced by air moving across the ligaments of the human larynx or bird syrinx, we can speak of sung music as the patterned movement of air over surfaces. We are all familiar with the literary imagery of the "song of the wind in the pines" and the haunting voice-like effects of desert and plains winds. One thinks of titles such as Joseph Wood Krutch's *Voice of the Desert* or Guy Murchie's *Song of the Sky*. Lying on the ground at night in a Mexican wilderness, I have been filled with a sense that the hills around me seemed to be humming, and yet I knew it was not the calls of insects. The celestial "music of the spheres" is the hackneyed expression of a widespread notion of a pervasive harmony, to which our Earth and we ourselves presumably contribute.

These musical landscapes have in common a joyousness that is more immediate than the satisfactions from pictorial landscapes, the more staid pleasures of scenery. I know of no other mode by which a sense of the goodness, order, and purposefulness of life is so clearly perceived. It may seem rash to credit birdsong as the first integrating experience. But why should not the idea of a joyous cosmos come to us unbidden from a singer "up there" unseen, an evocation of the first iridescent pleasure of sheer being? Rachel Carson's widely read book of the 1960s, *Silent Spring*, was only ostensibly about the death of birds from insecticide poisoning. Surely she referred to all those larger rhythms in which our first and most dear sense of coherence is sheltered.

Most of this chapter has been devoted to the human use of animal species and body organs as external models of the internal structure of things. By anchoring itself to the natural typing of species and to the groupings of species, the mind keeps its hold on reality. Every growing child reveals the human commitment to ecological and anatomical structure as the means by which his intellectual capacity develops. But taking to pieces is only the first step in cognition; nor is it the only aspect of thought for which the nonhuman world provides both the evolutionary stimulus and developmental instrument. Synthesis and integration must follow or accompany the anatomizing words that dissect the world. The body and the terrain are external counterparts to the fragmenting process. The interplay or symbiosis between species enacts the relatedness of parts and kinds, as though the exercise of putting wholes together were itself being demonstrated for us. Finally, we communicate this integrating reality to ourselves in music and poetry, and the archetype of it is found among those harbingers of thought, the birds.

3 | AMBIGUOUS ANIMALS

So far we have considered the natural species system as the model of concrete diversity and order. In nature animals do not grade smoothly from one kind to another, but form distinct groups of very similar individuals. Between species there is a gap that the animals themselves—and we—can recognize. We are order-making creatures and the natural world is a fit place for brains that grow by observing the adherence to kind and the clustering of kinds into groups.

The world of ideas and social relations, however, is full of fuzziness. Our feelings, ethics, and morality are often gray with twilight areas and fleeting incongruity. Coping with such shifting concepts is an endless task, but we have confidence that behind the uncertainty the world is coherent—our optimism resting in the dependable reality of the master set of types, the species.

Although we expect our abstract ideas to need constant clarifying and defining, we become agitated when the creatures seem not to fit the taxonomic system. Such incompatible animals shock us. The degree of our upset indicates that something more is disturbed than the plan of animal classification. Exceptions to the system threaten not only animal order but our basic model for order; more than that, those anomalies signify intrusion, some active principle of derangement and tumult, alarming forces of disorder and evil, much worse than flawed classification.

People are so touchy about this foundation to a meaningful existence that ambiguity even in well-known animals sets off an anxious reaction. Even small details of an animal that remind us of some other form trigger our alarm. The ambiguity can arise in a number of ways: physically, like the dubious sexuality of the mule; behaviorally, like a flying horse in one's dreams; or even in habitat, such as the tiny "horses" living in the sea. Parallel to and part of this is a corresponding disturbance of language. The names of the animals or of their traits are loaded with tension. Like the animal, the terms may be obscene and are regulated by formal precautions or prohibitions—in short, by

76

taboo. Even such familiar terms of abuse as "rat," dog," or "pig" are far more insulting than merely calling someone an animal, as they refer to an aspect of those animals that is unclear and therefore dangerous or dirty.

The Margins of Our Attention

That some aspects of an animal are equivocal while others seem perfectly normal reminds us that we actually think of animals as combinations of parts or traits. The animal figure is like a powerful magnet, drawing the child's attention. As he devours it with his eyes, he asks for and says its name. Both innately and by prompting, he learns to look for those traits by which it can be defined. He learns to scrutinize parts and to think of them separately. In this way we all become morphologists and anatomists very early. We see, for example, not only that birds have wings, but also the length of corresponding wing feathers or colorations of the equivalent body parts. In very similar forms we work from an abstract common model to which we add or remove those particular parts. They become psychologically detachable; each can exist in its own right, as much a part of the class "legs" or "wings" as it is a member of a species. The process of dissecting things and regrouping them by imagination leads to plural definitions for every species. Each animal is a combination of parts, but not only of physical form and appearance. We also "assemble" them by what they do, where they live, how they are related to each other and to people. By defining animals along a number of axes, sets of variables become available that can be used as grids for comparisons. Most of them are less precise than the anatomical features.

Many societies classify animals according to their proximity to the human dwelling. From those at the hearth or about the household, outward to adjacent yards or pens, in stockades and barnyards, pastures and fields, to woodlots and distant, wild places, the animal kingdom has been dispersed through the centuries according to the patterns established by the village or farmstead and those surrounding zones of reduced intensity of human use. Distance from the hearth is synonymous with wildness. Distance from the hearth is also related to edibility; not only whether animals are eaten, but which parts of each kind of animal, under what circumstance, and by whom.

Edibility and spatial distribution are seldom neat and tidy definitions. The cat and rat live in human dwellings but are not completely tame. Horses are not quite pets, nor are they quite wild. The free rabbit is game, and yet not very wild, and lives unusually close to human precincts for a hunted animal. The fox is game but quite wild, a meat-eater itself. Otters are both aquatic and terrestrial. Stags are like antlered cattle. Pigs share human food, are pet-like, yet in many places are kept only to be killed.

In each case the tension created may be expressed in any of several ways: where or how the animal is kept or hunted or eaten. In France the horse is edible, in England not. The rabbit hops alternatively between field and kitchen garden and is both cuddly and demonic. It bears a streak of lunacy that almost seems to signify its schizophrenia. Its notorious reproductivity, promiscuity, and harebrained behavior are keyed to the moon and the seasons. It was formally called a "coney," from *cuniculus*, from which also comes "cunt," and the Playboy bunny is at least as old as the eighteenth-century "cunny house." For centuries rabbit skin was made into underwear. When tabooed animals can be so closely associated with such heavily stressed areas as the body openings, the interdictions relating it to language are greatly intensified. The rabbit's transitional status is further signified by calling males and females "bucks" and "does," by the figure of the egg-laying rabbit at Easter, and by the humanizing of the animal in stories and pictures.

In some places the fox is even more intensely circumscribed by prohibitions and by impact on the language related to it. Its hunting is yoked to a whole body of special terms and formalities, intense feelings, and elaborate protocol. They are expressed in language where the fox hunt is ritualized by formal calls, meals, songs, toasts, buglings, and the inversion of fox to "dog," dogs to "hounds," the fox's head to "mask," and the tail to "brush."

The folk customs for speaking of and treating ambiguous animals would fill a whole set of encyclopedias. The theme that runs through most of these traditional uses is that the animal's name and related words are often terms of disparagement or description and are tension-creating in themselves. Terms referring to them are often correlated with tabooed aspects of the human body, such as "ass," "cock," "beaver," or with tabooed areas of social behavior, such as "bitch" or "slut." Except in slaughterhouse cultures, their killing is regulated by strict rules in both the slaughter shed and the field.

Even in societies that kill their animals commercially, some of the linguistic rites continue. One aspect of the rituals of the slaughter of large mammals is that, after death, their flesh is given a name en masse. Terms like venison, beef, pork, and mutton replace the names of the animals. This may be in part because the family does not eat a whole pig or cow at a sitting, or because in celebrations the meat from many carcasses is indiscriminately mixed and the different cuts separated. Flesh terms emotionally neutralize and formally deny the animals' individuality and so bring about blurring between themselves and persons. Thus we rear "beef on the hoof" or "porkers." In contrast, small mammals and birds are consumed as a whole. One does not eat rabbit steak or chops. The only anatomical distinctions are in terms of familiar parts: legs, breasts, wings. Evidence that the precaution in the use of animals is a result of the relationship of vagueness to a larger sense of general disorder is seen in Jewish customs.

Biblical dietary laws relate holiness to order, which is God's blessing. When the blessing is not there, barrenness, confusion, and the opportunity for evil follow. Conformity to type is felt to be moral as well as comprehensible. Hybrids are abominated, suggesting a breakdown of sexual law. In Leviticus, in the Old Testament, we find that all creeping forms (without legs) are unclean and inedible. So are the pig, camel, and marine shellfish. The logic is based on the Book of Genesis. At the time of Creation the parts of the world were made separately, each in its turn—water, earth, and air. The creatures, although created afterward, are appropriate to and defined by one or another of these divisions of the world. Their organs of movement—wings, fins, or feet—betoken their place in these habitats. Among the four-legged land beings closest to man are his cattle, which are defined as cloven-hoofed and cud-chewing. Exceptions to any of these categories are "unclean." Though of the earth, snakes have no legs; the aquatic shrimp and clam have no fins; the camel has a cud but no cloven hoof; the pig a hoof but no cud. Each offends the integrity of Creation, the order of which is acknowledged in dietary laws.

Historically speaking, the original explanation of their unclean status is not clear. The reasons may not have been those that were rationalized from the Bible. The camel, for example, was detested by the village people and small farmers of ancient Palestine and Egypt. It was kept and bred by Arab traders and warriors who, for centuries, were their opponents and enemies. Nothing about the camel made it suitable for the farmer, and it is from his perspective rather than that of the soldier and merchant that most of the Old Testament was written. The Arabs do not find the camel anomalous, but rather see it as a model of those finer divisions of reality that train the perception. That is, they have a whole vocabulary of camel terms and phrases. Whether the Hebrews' categories of normal animals antedated Genesis or followed from it cannot be determined. Every society develops by custom its own set of definitions of the normal and abnormal. Once established, the rules are conserved because their logic is explained as the order of Creation itself, not merely from usage or utility.

The anxiety induced by exceptions to such order is psychological and personal, while the reasons given are formal and cultural. Taboo restricts the human relationship to the animal to compensate for its ambiguity. Such rituals reaffirm the animal's exceptional status as well as acknowledge the true order. Some are dietary, the more common are linguistic. Special terms, sometimes euphemisms, are applied to such animals. Not only phrases of abuse and obscenity, but the terms of a joking relationship develop because humor is often a means of controlling tension generated by ambiguity. The cat is profoundly dual, being domestic and placid but having a dark, wild side so threatening in its antithesis to human order that the Church has periodically considered it to be diabolical.

Even the ordinary naming of animals seems to follow widespread but little recognized rules that are derived from their classification. Species living close to human habitation tend to have short names, those more distant, longer, as in cat and catamount. The reason for this is usually not obvious. The explanation is not so evident in English, but in the Germanic and Latin roots of English it makes more sense, as the syllables are descriptive. The unfamiliar form is "put together" from verbal parts. In the example of the catamount, a colloquialism rather than another tongue reveals it to be short for "cat-a-mountain."

In the European languages there are probably additional practices also in the giving of proper names to each animal of which people are not normally conscious. Procedures for naming those individual animals not kept to be eaten, such as pets or draft animals, is based on unspoken rules derived from the place of the animal on a grid of intersecting definitions. In Western Europe and America the underlying logic of the rules for naming uses two criteria: whether the animal is "human" or "inhuman," that is, whether it has society or not, and whether it is a subject or an object. From these four possible combinations Claude Lévi-Strauss explains proper names and gives examples as follows:

1. Birds are subjects in their own society, parallel to man, and can be given Christian names, since they are sufficiently unlike us in form.
2. Racehorses are subjects in an eccentric society, so individualized that they must have nondescriptive names.
3. Dogs are lowly subjects in our society, and may be given stage names.
4. Cattle are objects in our society, and are named descriptively.

From these rules one expects to find a parrot called George, a racehorse called Island Fury, a dog called Carlos, Beppo, or Fido, and a cow named White Blossom.

That such customs exist does not necessarily mean that the anthropological explanation is correct. Anyone who has hunted with dogs knows how impractical it would be to have to call them if they were named Archer's Delight, and how confusing it could be among the hunters themselves if fifteen or twenty hounds had Christian names. Their one- or two-syllable names can be shouted clearly, perhaps for some of the same reasons that old-time actors had such names.

Whatever the underlying logic, animal-naming customs, like all kinds of traditions, are eroding. Pets with Christian names are not uncommon, especially among the "questioning" sectors of society. What disturbs us about this may not be only that it abjures old ways, but that it diminishes the information conveyed by the name. Extra explanations are sometimes necessary. Arriving as a guest, one must laboriously explain that "Fred" is a dog and will not need a place at the table or a bed. A member of my own family had the embarrassment of calling his own lost dog,

"Hopi," in the middle of the Hopi reservation in Arizona. A more serious effect may be the confusion to which this invites the owner himself, as it implies that the dog is human, that it "supposes," or "imagines," or "misses" somebody, or "is jealous of," or "knows that. . . ." Superficially, this reduces the gap between man and dog and makes a better "friend" of the pet. But the difference between human and animal that it denies is real and its otherness may be hidden from himself by the pet owner for whom it becomes threatening or sinister. This fear of that which is unlike oneself has a way of sliding back into the relationship. On college campuses, for example, the conspicuous outpouring of affection for pets disappears when vacation time arrives and the animals are cruelly abandoned. To the outraged citizenry who want to know how students could be so heartless when they claim to love animals, the answer is that they have not loved them in such a way as to acknowledge their un-humanity and therefore their desperate dependence. After all, one goes gaily off from friends at such times without worrying whether or not they can feed themselves.

One of the inherent dangers of pet-keeping seems to be that we will attempt, unwittingly perhaps, to neutralize the tensions arising from the ambiguities of such a relationship. We tend to think of tensions and anxiety as symptoms of sickness. But the stresses that arise from the variables of animal definition—anatomical similarities, the friend-enemy or wild-tame series, edibility and inedibility—are created intentionally, though perhaps unconsciously, to improve or elaborate definition and meaning. By hedging the murky areas about with taboo and linguistic obscenity, we call attention to the beauty and integrity of an orderly creation. In traditional societies the logic behind the taboo may be explained in myth. But even when such poetic interpretations are lost in time, there is a strong motive for keeping the rituals because this hidden logic relates a purposeful world to animal categories.

For each of us this personal aspect arises as part of our normal curiosity. The first question about an animal is always, "What is it?" (to be said aloud and the answer repeated back), and the next is, "What does it do?" and "Where does it live?" The bounds of all such classifications are, however, meant to be crossed, for it is in its transgression of some particular classification that each animal obtains a charisma. Crossing boundaries is, after all, in the nature of transformations. Without them nothing would happen. The human life span is marked by a series of passages in which the individual moves ceremonially from status to status. The animals, too, move through stages of being. One thing is eaten by and becomes another. The purpose of an elaborate classification is not so much to make nature static as it is to locate thresholds. The anxiety induced in us is our own device for generating attention. Although directed to animals, it is the means of preparing intellectual tools for perception of the human drama, an education in self-consciousness and in the art of thought.

Imaginary Combination Animals

While there is ambiguity in the natural species because of the multiple ways we define them, society needs more forceful images of incongruity in order to make that danger clear and to stimulate analytic thought. So it creates an imaginary fauna whose juxtaposed anatomies are intensely compelling. In our Western tradition the medieval bestiary includes many such inventions, such as unicorns, griffins, and dragons. Such hybrids are portentous, freakish, and marvelous; they disrupt our thoughts with their appalling insolence and force us to look and think. These multiple creatures may defy classification or bridge it. They may signify new order or new chaos, but they are always demanding and puzzling.

Occasionally nature plays a trick on art, or imitates art, if you prefer, by producing real animals that appear to be concoctions. To medieval Europeans giraffes and elephants seemed no less extraordinary than krakens or dragons. To northerners the exotic camel and the imaginary griffin were both regarded as inhabitants of distant lands and were described in terms of discordant parts. The camel is that beast said by those to whom it was strange to have been a horse put together by a committee. Everyone knows the parable of the blind men giving different descriptions of an elephant, depending on which part they felt. But consider how strange it would seem for someone to describe a cat as having the legs of a dog, the tail of a monkey, the whiskers of a sea lion, and the head of an owl. This tendency to see the novel creature as an assembly of parts from other animals is a clue to an important developmental effect in the perception of animals in the growing individual.

To the infant all animals are more or less alike. His ability to "tell" one from another (the question, "Can you tell what kind it is?" means "Can you identify its species?" and "Can you speak its name?") develops concurrently with his ability to dissect the animals in thought, to compare parts, and to see that the differences are in specific parts. For the child in the middle years of growth—from about six to ten—all animals have the fascinating and demanding compositional effect that such mongrel prodigies as cockatrices and wyverns had for medieval European adults. New creatures are surprising combinations of the old, not necessarily portentous or threatening for the child, but delightful new games of assembly. All creatures are equally real and magnetic: pets, zoo animals, creatures of film and storybook, those of nursery rhyme and bedtime story. Out of the two physical taxonomies he learns—creature kinds and part kinds—comes the delight of mix and match, a fine madness that only a species of hunter-butchers could have invented. Every animal for the child is "made up"; none is more synthetic than another, biological or mythological; Dr. Seuss's fantastic animals become part of a child's permanent faunal kingdom as readily as any robin or mouse.

Synchronized with the maturation of the nervous system, there is a locking-in process of the particular fauna of the first ten to twelve years. This idyllic period of innocent openness ends because of its own intrinsic timetable. A few individuals keep it longer than others, some for life, but for most it ends as puberty approaches. By adolescence the system is complete. Some gatekeeper of the maturing psyche has said, "There are no more regular kinds. Your fauna is assembled. They are the real animals. Any new creatures that you encounter in the future are either distortions, signifying some terrible malady at the root of life, or fabrications representing some parallel fabrication of ideas, not to be presumed as flesh."

For the adult, novel animals are aberrant forms of something else. They tend to threaten rather than enlarge the taxonomy, to be repulsive assemblies of uncongenial parts: amalgams, crosses, hybrids, bastards, chimeras. Adults have little room left in the mental menagerie. We are like zookeepers with no more stalls, fretting about the new arrivals or anomalies and denying them as normal kinds. As any set of children's books shows, no creature is too fantastic for the juvenile bestiary; as adult science fiction shows, any beast defying familiar classification threatens the rules of existing order, embodying a malignancy of that order, portending an evil or supernatural reality. In the language of ethology, an *imprinting* has occurred in the child, an irreversible learning synchronized with the learner's age.

Our nostalgia for childhood sometimes leads us to lament that joyful time when every creature shone with new creation, and we are inclined to blame our dull adult senses, the preoccupations of daily life, or simply blindness and cynicism for our loss of child-like joy in animals. But the filling up of animal taxonomies is a purposeful stage of thought. It does not close because adults lose their imagination, but because the young adult is turning to a new stage in thinking animals, one that will be administered by the culture in more abstract ways than the straightforward training of the child by the parent in animal names. The new types of creatures not of flesh and blood are for nourishing thought about society and the cosmos. Only by closing off the natural can these forms seem sufficiently strange and exceptional to alert the individual to their special status.

This separation of the fantastic animal from the mundane animal is thwarted by familiarity. The image can only be bizarre and epicene if it is new. An example of the collapse of the singular novelty of such creatures as dragons can be seen in Europe in the last three centuries. Animals that were once part of the adult mythology of Europeans, for example, are now found in children's books. In our culture there has been a progressive sifting downward of special symbolic animals into the realm of the natural. One explanation is that adults today are less child-like than those of the past. But this is not so.

In reality we have taken the dragon out of its context of mature instrument for dissecting thought and placed it in the realm of fauna. However imaginary, it has become familiar and accepted as one kind of animal. Robert Graves makes a distinction between legendary and mythical animals based on whether they are believed to exist or known to be symbolic. For example, he points out how the chimera, unicorn, and phoenix, which in ancient times were known to be pictographs representing complex astronomical concepts, were mistaken by medieval men as zoological species. This sliding of symbolic forms into literal reality, or from mythical to legendary, happens in cultural exchange, sometimes when the meanings are deliberately misread, but more often by ignorance of the original concept. The same kind of error can happen within a society when religious images become secularized, or when symbolic tales are told to children.*

If a people wants to prevent this demythologizing of species images, it withholds them from the young. The cult has secret "work" for its tales and pictures of fantastic beasts within the logic of a social and religious body. It can only evoke the child-like intensity of a "new idea" for the cult if it does not become commonplace to the child. It must be revealed under auspicious circumstances to serve the purposes of the new adult.

Such esoteric lore is traditionally transmitted in a series of ceremonies and clan rites administered by elders or priests and hidden from the uninitiated. Concocted animals are widespread in both archaeological and anthropological study. They are associated with sacred places, which supports the theory that they are used on occasions of great importance to the society and the person. Anthropologist Mary Douglas has observed that the young initiates in traditional cultures are confronted by such symbolic figures of animals and charged with special dietary rules related to animals at a time when they are themselves, both physiologically and socially, in a transitional state and therefore between classifications, or dual in category. The drawings and doodles of adolescents, who are intensely sensitive to identity questions at this time, are typically of ambivalent animals and man/animal combinations. Misfit animals and adolescents are not simply skewed in the order of creation, but are poised between realms, like tadpoles metamorphosing. The pubertal youth understands what it means to be marginal, for he himself is neither child nor adult, not fully male or female, not even fully human. The brotherhood of candidates is a comity, temporarily apart from the human order. The lines of their ontogeny and ontology—development and identity—have intersected, a state in part produced by their own intrinsic physical and mental calendars. On the threshold of becoming new beings, they are especially sensitive to ideas of purpose and social order, and to poetry and metaphor.

* Symbolic not in the sense of the unconscious of Freud or Jung, but in the sense of conscious representations.

For a time they are regarded as socially ambiguous and ritually unclean or impure. They have a special relationship to their instructors, but are otherwise incomplete and without definition. The rites by which their transitional nonbeing is made incarnate often employs ambiguous animal figures. Society is not simply acknowledging change; it is forcing the neophyte to think about his identity. The mixed animal is no accident from the standpoint of the cult. It is a lesson in analysis derived from the animal species model of clarity and signifying the abomination of the mixed state.

The candidate will, through the rest of his life, be committed to an ongoing search and resolution of his own identity—with respect to kin and group, life as a whole, and the cosmos. He will undertake new meditations on his own structure and parts. Gruesome and fascinating animal mixtures will always be part of his training, sometimes his own projection, his intellectual cadaver. He will learn to separate in order to make new abstractions, and to imagine new relationships between the forms which as a child he had learned by rote and the entities which they represent symbolically.

The details of the grotesque animal image are not a haphazard mixture from various animals. The culture presents a precisely contrived monster. The dragon which St. George slew was no arbitrary beast. Its actual composition varied over the centuries as it suited the needs of the time and place for defining the elements of evil. Assembled creatures are profoundly connected to transformation and the threat it contains for the old order. They are present in dreams and in ceremony, instruments for renovation and recognition. From the empirical childhood creatures to animal symbols in maturity, there is a necessary disruption by which one generates the other. Nowhere in this cycle is the relationship *to animals* the principal purpose, but rather it develops the capacity for perceiving and generating order. First there is a comprehension of ways of being in which inner states and qualities are yoked to real creatures; then there is the creation of fantastic animals to evoke special spiritual states. According to anthropologist Victor Turner, these combined animals used for instruction are a special case of the body as the prime example of order, even for abstract thought. Bodies, he says, are "symbolic templates for the communication of *gnosis,* the mystical knowledge of how things came to be as they are." But human bodies alone are too limited in scope to carry this power of microcosmic analogy far enough, and they contradict the process of externalizing and representation by which things in us become visible. The otherness within us is too close for scrutiny. Animal combinations evoke contemplation of structure and relationship, forcing us to look at constituents. The spiritual and power-giving images that we shape as the prime sources and movers cannot have ordinary form. They are brought into consciousness poetically, and their actions are described as bizarre parallels to familiar things. The punning or metaphorical age is adolescence, when the individual is predisposed to probe in this way. Religious instruction usually includes what is shown, what is said, and what is done. Passive observation alone is never a good teacher. Hence the importance of doing, of the ceremonial acts. The motif for these exercises is derived from infancy; that is, they are communicated through analogies to early experience: to eating, feelings of omniscience, family relationships, the naming of things, and bodily comfort or discomfort. Virtually all adult actions bear in some form unconscious memory or mnemonics of these things. The adolescent is notoriously infantile and regressive, yet speculative, idealistic, dreaming, and poetic. He instinctively goes back to early experience and primal forms to find structure for all that is to be newly revealed, the cult secrets and descriptions of world-wonder that every religion gives.

This use of animal combinations raises interesting questions about the animals that surround us today. In modern societies secular "creative" (i.e., idiosyncratic) artists manipulate or make up these high-pressure images for sensation alone, subverting their traditional cultural purposes. The artist benefits from the vicarious thrill for purely sensory ends, both his own and his client's. In livestock- and pet-breeding we create new strains by carefully hybridizing old, inbred lines. In racehorses or beef cattle we diligently dismember parental stock by selective breeding in order to recombine desirable parts in their descendants. We create novel individuals and breeds at will. We loosen up their correspondence to species type. If you ask ten people to imagine the chicken, you will get divergent views on its size, color, length of comb, and other details. Breeds are equivalent to natural races, the race being a geographical form of a species. That a species varies over its whole range is not visible to normal individual experience; it is rather a museum or scientific problem. But in shattering the parental form into breeds, we bring the gradations of race before us. In the modern world, where the ordinary person sees relatively few kinds of wild things, breed-making is one of our compensations. It keeps the world diverse and we treat breeds in our thought as though they were species. The difficulty arising from this is that breeds readily cross and intermix while species do not. The seeming inconstancy and indefiniteness of the world may be but one of the consequences. In traditional agriculture such experimental outbreeding was rare. Empirical practice built up desirable strains over centuries of inbreeding. Outcrossing was considered dangerous to the purity of the line and regarded as a form of corruption. The hybrid was despised. The combinational figures in art deliberately tapped that revulsion to instruct the neophyte in cognitive abstraction, an instrument for analogical and analytical thought, a raising of an intellectual fever.

Multiplex animals are the deliberate and inadvertent creations that have drastic effects because of our basic sense of the world as a balance of unity and diversity. Ambiguity, or a threat to the animal species model of a consistent, heterogenous world, arises in several ways. First, we are predisposed as the mind matures to regard any new kind of animal as ambiguous after the age of puberty. Second, all the secondary ways in which we try to classify animals—beyond the physical species system—contain graduated traits, so that some forms are always found at the edges of categories. Third, we deliberately create such combinational "mythical" or "imaginary" beasts in order to represent specific ambiguities. And, finally, we create them in the flesh when we fracture domestic animals into breeds. All of these are confusing or enlightening, depending on how the culture uses them. All are dangerous or inspiring, frightening or exhilarating. Through its control of language, image, rules, and ceremonies, society directs these strong emotions and vague disquiets to its own ends, especially as a means of enlarging its own inner dialogue on the order and meaning of the cosmos.

Heads and Tails

Among the figures etched in the walls of the great temples of ancient Egypt are votive spirits represented by men with the heads of jackals, hawks, and baboons. Outside rests the sphinx. Around the world the archaeological record teems with other such hybrids: Sorcerers depicted in Paleolithic cave art, votive figures from Indian temples with human bodies and animal heads, Pan, the classical woodland demigod with his goat's hindquarters, mermaids from the sea, and on and on. This horde of half-human beings is deeply related to the mundane fauna, the familiar "real" animals, and, at its other pole, to our concept of ourselves as human. Christianity regards such beings as the devil-gods of superstitious heathens, but for a thousand years was itself deeply committed to the idea of the angel as a combination of man and bird, though it was never said to be that. Christians inherited from the Jews the representation of major prophets as animal-headed people. Perhaps no culture allows its half-human spirit-beings to be so labeled, since that misconstrues their meaning. It is only the secular mind that so profanes these special creatures into a kind of man-animal incest and makes freaks of them.

Not only did the Church take its angels seriously, but it arranged them into orders and classes—seraphim, cherubim, thrones, dominions, virtues, powers, principalities, archangels, and angels—all fitted into their respective habitats at different levels in the space from Earth to Heaven. Thus did animal taxonomy provide a model and the conjoined man-animal image draw attention to constituents of our mortal and immortal being, to degrees of virtue and goodness, and the relation of Heaven and Earth.

Angelic differentiation was a leading intellectual concern for centuries and was probed and articulated by the use of a heavenly host. It dealt not only with the spatial arrangement of Heaven, but the relation of humankind to the celestial hierarchy. Similar man/animal spirits are found in world religions in general.

One function of such combinational figures is to shock our visual conventions and teach the separation and relatedness of man and animal. We live in a lifelong tension between our humanity and our animality. At one extreme we lose our kinship with the near-human and our roots in natural creation. At the other is the fear of regression to the animal state and loss of human status. A balance is symbolized in customs of diet and costume as well as figures and images. In tribal societies groups who observe eating laws in which certain edible parts are rejected as food are complemented by other groups who do eat them but regard still other parts as unclean. Eating is assimilation beyond just contemplation, a merger at the level of tissues and cells. Anthropologists have observed that some parts of an animal not eaten by a people are worn as ornaments. Efficiency leaves the physiologically indigestible parts, such as skulls, beaks, feet, teeth, claws, and skins, to be fashioned, among other things, into headdresses. Witness the wearing of furs and feathers in our own time.

The point of this winding theme is that parts are worn, signifying association. It is a kind of paradox in which instructors or priests don fragments of animals, thereby themselves becoming dual beings, though the purpose of their ritual cannot be simply becoming the animal. That would most suitably be done by joining its flesh to ours by total consummation. The purpose of animal-headed figures involves a special access to perceptions by which human identity is both preserved and enhanced. It is a drastic fusion forcing distinctions in spite of connectedness.

In part the difference refers to head functions as opposed to body functions. The animal head implies wisdom and leadership, mood and personality. The natural order of creation has always been seen as the work of a creator in relationship to whom different animals stood in special ways. It is as though the goose or stork had wisdom of the secrets of migration, butterflies of metamorphosis, and cats of hunting. Since the theoretical separation of animate from inanimate and rational from instinctive behavior at the close of the Middle Ages, this abstraction of special knowledge as an animal icon has diminished.

The logic of representing specific aspects of the animal mind has a history and distribution much older and wider than the Egyptian zoomorphs, the Hindus with their elephant/man, Ganesha, the Minoans with their legends of the Minotaur, for they remind us of the mask and its ceremonies, dating back to the beginnings of mankind. The famous man/beast figure of Trois Frères cave in southern France has equivalents around the world, as old as cavemen, as recent as last Halloween.

It is tempting to speak of them all as "the putting on of an animal identity," but I do not think that ritual imitation of an animal was done simply to make contact with a magic center of power. Their purpose was in the perceptual growth of the observer. The animal-masked man is a temporary merger or transitional state in which the consciousness of the participant or observer is raised toward some special principle or action beyond the everyday life for which words alone are insufficient.

A plains Indian wearing a bison skull in a ceremony may represent the buffalo in a rite simulating desired events; but he is evoking qualities and dimensions of life that the buffalo "knows" best but which can be shared with man. The buffalo-man is a centering nucleus around which some part of plains life makes sense when seen as a shared domain.

Domesticating cattle—bringing them into human society—sounds like a simple economic fact. But its consequences go far beyond the use of meat or milk or skins, control of breeding and convenience. In becoming oriented to their keepers, the cattle were changed, genetically and by conditioning, and the changes made them, by behavior as well as proximity, part of the continuum of the human family. The diminished differences between people and cattle and their intensified social responsiveness were desirable from an economic point of view, and yet created tensions. All those typically human preoccupations with social identity lapped over into the similarity/difference and ranking of cattle and other domestic forms. Like the formal relationships among people in a society, the place of cattle was assimilated and signified in the ritual arts.

From very early times priest-kingship in ancient Mesopotamia and Egypt was associated with sacred bulls. The pre-agricultural societies of men and cattle are very different. The cattle are an association of harems, tyrannically dominated by hierarchies of bulls. Human societies are basically extended family groups in which leadership is tacitly acknowledged rather than taken by force. But the conditions of village agriculture, with its territoriality, accumulation of food and wealth, and caste systems was incompatible with the old hunting system of democratic councils. Men had for thousands of years used animals as a means of pondering their own existence and with the rise of civilization the cattle offered a more appropriate model for the new chiefdoms. The earliest farmers may indeed have killed their own kings in order to keep the celestial cycles of renewal symbolically moving, but the sacred regicide gradually gave way to substitutes: the king's own son or some other relative; and later on, animals, particularly bulls. The drama of the sacrificial bull was written and rewritten for five thousand years.

In one form the Phoenicians and Carthaginians sacrificed children to the god Moloch by roasting them in the bronze image of a bull-headed man. How we got from bulls to bull-headed men is not clear, but probably as an expression of that combining thrust of man and "his" animals in domestication itself. The struggle among bulls was not simply a model for the organization of human power politics. Bulls did not remain at a distance, physically or perceptually, as they would have in totemic cultures of the Paleolithic. Having been brought into the society of which they were also a kind of prototype, they became objects and weapons within the game. In any case, the devourer of children was the ancestor of the Minotaur, the offspring of a bull and Pasiphäe, the wife of King Minos, who in turn was descended from Zeus and Europa, a mating in which Zeus appears as a bull. The ceremonial bull-slaughter and the ceremonial slaughter of children sacrificed to bull-gods, as the Athenian youths were killed for the Minotaur every eight years, appears to be one of those episodes in the culturizing of cattle, symbolizing a hard reality of the life of all herdsmen—that they must make many sacrifices to keep the integrity and wisdom of a pastoral heritage where the well-being of all is joined to that of the cattle. When, according to the myth, Minos' daughter, Ariadne, helped Theseus slay the Minotaur and escape the Labyrinth, human sacrifice ended. The ceremonial bullfights depicted in the murals of the royal palace at Knossos on the island of Crete are said to link the old bull-worship to the modern bullfight. So the enigma continues and perhaps the matador is an expiatory sacrifice by the crowd, continuing the conciliation of a noble species now reduced to slavery and debased a thousand ways every day. Our distant ancestors spent a half million years admiring the fine points of the old aurochs, the cow's wild ancestors, but kept that relationship both practical and poetic. When we took the aurochs into our homes and cow sheds, we deprived the animal of its otherness and double-crossed ourselves. Instead of dancing the auroch, we began dancing with it. Dancing it had opened our minds to ourselves, but dancing with it, we could not avoid the logic that somehow its subordination to us was balanced by a reverse authority. The shamanic figure that temporarily combined the human and bull in a penetrating way was eroded by the figure of the bull-man demon as a realization, the master of the fascinating, profitable, dangerous, and monstrous kinship with cows. The myth of the Minotaur deals with problems raised about human identity in a pastoral society doting on its cattle. The sexuality of man and cattle is a crucial element. Their overlap evokes a tale about a queen's sodomy and the conception of a monster in which the imagination contacts the precincts of cattleness and its deep wisdom, its price and its pure bovine being which so enraptures all cattle-keeping peoples. The Minoans were directed by the story to contemplate bovine and human traits in the light of each other, and encouraged to break free from the tyrannical hold that bull adulation and worship had for their peasant ancestors. Gymnastic sporting with the bull, a form of ceremonial derring-do among Minoan youths, may have been risky, but it has a more urbane, sophisticated play about it than the grisly sacrifices to a carnivorous monster, a sacrifice that in reality may have been more psychic than physical, but no less of a burden to bear.

No doubt the bull-man "stands for" something both in the way that scholars use the term and in the way that such creatures are explained by psychiatrists of the personality. But these explanations often overlook the domestic reality, that these images are the outcome of centuries of interaction between real men and real cattle and the animals are used as a particular cultural expression of totemic education. The image of the man-animal combination was a cognitive instrument whose meanings in a particular society could only be fully understood in the light of the details of the socioecology of man and cow, especially the taboos and values indicated by dietary laws, the spatial arrangements of stock-keeping, and the cow-related terms in the language.

Central to the problems with which the man-bull figures grapple is keeping man and cattle sufficiently separate in cultures where they live too close together. The image confronts ambivalence directly, as it were, by embodying it. Lurking in the penumbral cave, the Minotaur lives at the boundary of two realities, shadowless like all dawn and dusk animals. Moonlight is a dangerous twilight zone, neither daylight nor dark, when all kinds of marginal creatures stalk or fly or writhe about. Such ambivalent forms include the human vampires and other unfortunates who turn into their destructive phase according to lunar cycles, victims of an enchantment that is agonizing for everyone concerned. Other versions of this genre, which often as not are presided over by a witch, include those beauty-and-the-beast dramas in which the good and pure woman alone can subdue the vicious passions of human animality and the poor beast either goes down to captivity and death or is transformed back again and freed from the curse. These images ask the observer to dissect the beast figure, to see its good and evil components. The struggle between good and evil, animality and humanity, their war within us, is our Manichaean heritage. It is a duality too simpleminded about our insides and equally crude about the world of nature, where it gets its effigies. Recent fiction and film have depicted the wolf-man garbed as a Victorian gentleman, periodically convulsed with furry face. The Victorian prudery is a kind of ultimate rendition of the gross Christian peasant view of the body as a battleground. The real wolf, too, is just as maligned as human nature. We now know a lot about wolves that we had forgotten.

Only the most unreconstructed dualist thinks that real wolves have a hidden human side that combats their animality. The wolf has no human side at all but is totally wolf, and much of wolfishness is beautiful, intelligent, tender, and interesting.* Only when we reaffirm this goodness of wolves as part of the wolf and cease to blame the badness in people on nonhumanity can the combinational man-animal figures be seen for what they are, instruments of correlation and illumination, tools of social consciousness and philosophical speculation rather than fragmenting and divisive judgments or excuses for our fallen angelhood.

When Renaissance engravers illustrated the Greek myths they often depicted Actaeon, who was turned into a stag for watching Artemis bathing and then torn to pieces by his hounds, as having a human body and a stag's head, and Chloe, who was turned into a beech to save her from hounds, as a human torso with branches. Putting aside frivolous allusions to the first "stag party" or why ladies were said to have limbs instead of legs, the use of such images is not to suggest that either of them looked like that. The story does not say that they were turned into part stag or part beech tree. The artist has provided stills—which is the way we remember scenes, even of action—that represent transformation. Had they continued to be human, but with qualities that could be signified by another species, they would presumably be repre-

---

* But we do not need a new conservationist sentimentality misrepresenting the wolf. The wolf *can* be dangerous to people and, in any case, is aggressive, ferocious, relentless, and cunning.

sented by human-headed, animal-bodied forms. Instead, they cease to be human at all, but the human torso marks that particular tree and stag for us, the spectators.

Two distinct possibilities seem to emerge from the long history and wide range of animal-headed, human torsos. The first is found among those people for whom there are no domestic animals and where the joining of the realm of animal and man is always dangerous. Among these peoples the distinction between nature and culture is fundamental. The killing and eating of an animal, and its incorporation into us, are a typical crossing of the boundary and are attended with ritual. For example, anthropologist Stuart Marks describes a whole series of rituals related to the hunting and eating of the elephant by the Bisa of Africa. These include an invocation of ancestral spirits, a ceremony to return the slain animal's spirit to the bush composed of a series of songs, butchering procedures, reincorporation rites, and placation rites taking place over a period of days. Adornment with animal parts is codified by custom and strong taboo, and the use of animal headdresses and masks is the extreme formal occasion of bringing together what must be conceptualized as separate in order to clarify that conception. There is for such peoples no casual fraternizing with animals, no animal friends, no fortuitous use of them of any kind. All such social interactions are part of dream-time, the deep symbolism of the unconscious and of that beginning in time when myth was reality and therefore full of tension and special significance.

The second is found among animal-keeping people, for whom distinctions between the animal and human realms are not basic to an orderly universe, and for whom the animals are indeed brothers, lovers, and slaves. Certain of the animals are gods and demons with special powers. In such cases an individual elephant or bull is intended, not the whole species, and this creates a problem in the representation of the figure, for we do not normally perceive animals as individuals. In order to show the demon-jackal as having the particular individuality of the sort we recognize in people, it is represented as part human. The beast is not really believed to be part man and part animal, but wholly animal. Its image as a man-animal monster attaches our normal openness of individuality for other people to an animal and at the same time creates that awe of disjunction we feel for all ambiguous forms—an awe that religious training can turn into reverence.

The human-headed, animal-bodied hybrid puts the dialogue of parts and wholes into a different form than the animal-headed figure. There is a variety of such creatures in medieval bestiaries: the sphinx, mermaid, Medusa, centaurs, and satyrs. The perceptual task, which focuses and forces reflection and loosens up our categorical rationality, is essentially like that of all amalgams. But where the animal head implied the working of order, the personality, a kind of thought or powers by which spiritual principles spoke through animals, the animal-bodied figures seem to take the human order as given and to call attention to a different aspect of the sharing—the wisdom (or curse) of its animal vigor. Christians are likely to be reminded of the "mere" animality, like a penalty attached to the human visage, but the animal body has other, more positive, significance.

In the figure of Pan, the woodland goat-god, secular Renaissance painters, accepting the medieval orthodox view that in Pan human animality was materialized, reversed the Church's condemnation and rediscovered in Pan the verve, spontaneity, and joy of life that were inseparable from sexuality. By the time of George Bernard Shaw and D. H. Lawrence, Pan was restored to a wholly admirable cluster of principles, sex and all, which sprang from the vitality of the body and not the calculating mind, or, more exactly, from the unconscious wisdom of the body.

What Pan or centaurs and mermaids meant explicitly to the ancient Greeks was known to them in detail, but in general concerned the embodiment of experience rather than en-mindment of it. It seems focused on the agency and expression of being instead of its theory or its perception. It seems to say to the observer, "Suppose that you yourself (known by your face) were given the parts of a fish or a goat or a lion. See this picture of such a person. Reflect on that while I tell you this story. Once there was . . ." and you will then know the reality of the goatness in you.

This is very different from saying, as the shaman with the animal mask might, "There is a whole other way of knowing which is the way of the falcon or the bison or the bull. I shall dance it and you will realize that you do know it, that your consciousness and thoughts are like and unlike those of the bison."

It is necessary that we urban people keep in mind that the above are detached and theoretical views. For peoples of the world who live among a diversity of animals and who see the complexity of animal lives, there is no general theory about the compound image. It is a means. We may talk, somewhat wistfully perhaps, of the kind of thing that happens, for the real value is realized by those who have a good knowledge of the sea, or of livestock, or of falcons and the hunt, and who obtain by the conglomerate figure an instrument for taking an oblique view of their own lives.

Monsters

We use the word "monster" to mean any frightening animal, especially if it is unusually large. But the more exact meaning refers to those beings that do not fit ordinary classification. Just how many types of such non-types there are depends on your style of taxonomy. Scientific classification is divided into "lumpers" and "splitters." The lumpers reduce the number of categories and simplify the naming systems, while the splitters are forever dividing existing groups into subordinate classes. Experts in a highly specialized field tend to be splitters, whereas the general theorists prefer lumping in order to produce symmetry. Teratology, the study of monsters, is no exception. Monster devotees are inclined to see an enormous variety of monsters in the world. However, a general table of categories might produce no more than a dozen. Most of them fall into the following seven types:

1. Accidents of scale, a disproportionate of part size or "deformity."
2. Multiplication of parts, such as the many-headed Scylla.
3. Inordinate size. A mouse is not a monster, but a mouse-sized housefly is.
4. Transformational demons, which take different form at will, like the demon-woman or witch who can assume the form of a cat.
5. Combinational animals, like the dragon, made from parts of various animals.

6. Man/animal mixtures, such as the sphinx or Medusa.
7. Man/machine combinations, from Dr. Frankenstein's creature to the Bionic Man.

Obviously it is possible to combine types: the werewolf is a man/animal combination with a repressive transformation compulsion; Dracula is a man-bat altering nightly from comatose to conscious; the Cyclops is a one-eyed giant. Most of them are symbols of chaos or evil, either in nature or in ourselves, and are therefore augurs or portents, which is the definition of the Latin word "monstrum" from which the English word comes. The slightly alien is often more disturbing than the totally bizarre. The repulsiveness of apes, for example, is in part due to their similarity to human form. All monsters are profoundly affective, and therefore lend themselves so well to dramatic instruction.

To combine the definitions, monsters are unfamiliar aliens with certain exaggerated features, belonging to no common category. All vertebrate animals have a basic body plan from which skewing can produce distorted shapes. But the perception of deformity requires a pre-existing standard of conformity, a sense of what is normal. For each of us a bestiary of the normal has been imprinted by about the age of twelve. From there on we are especially sensitive to the tacit assumption that the new are illicit mixtures or gruesome distortions of the old. The logic of monsters is this deformity.

A badly deformed individual from birth is regarded as a "freak of nature." In all cases such unusual individuals, human or animal, are disturbing for reasons we sometimes find difficult or embarrassing to identify. One is puzzled in part by the way our attention is held. We stare and become "rubberneckers" and we pay to see a circus sideshow. Our society has a rich mythological basis in stories of congenitally deformed or crippled individuals who have a tender, sensitive nature or a loyal, normal friend. The friend treats the cripple humanely and compassionately ignores the defect. The message of these stories seems to be that "beneath" the ugliness are human virtues and needs.

The compelling quality of such stories is a measure of our compulsive attention to monsters, human and animal. The stories often hint at but do not tell us why we are entranced and repulsed by such individuals. They are not only unfamiliar and not part of the natural order, but frightening. They signify chaos in a system of kinds. Legends of enchanted children and deformed babies are rich in diabolical spells and curses. Often these are directed at the unborn. It is not only the seed or embryo, but the whole process of generation itself that is injured or threatened.

Of all the world's disorders, that afflicting the spawning of life is the most terrifying. A current example is the public anxiety about drug-induced or radiation-caused fetal deformity. The Gothic north and other deep-forest people and wetlanders of the world are familiar with legendary monsters who represent the turgid threat of swampish fecundity when it threatens the dry order of the city. The hordes of demons attacking St. Jerome in Grünewald's seventeenth-century paintings are part of a genre that have appeared in swampish scenes in Western art for a thousand years. The details of Jerome's appalling torture reveal a widespread characteristic of monsters as the embodiment of generative evil. Of the scores of hideous creatures shown there, all the forms and parts are derived from familiar creatures. Many are insect-like in their Gothic detail.

Insects and spiders threaten our efforts to make order by placing things in a habitat interspace. As boundary inhabitants, they offend the necessity of clear distinction. These animals live in cracks that are zones of separation, or under things, the surfaces between places. The flying insects swarm around our heads, near the body orifices, which are themselves marginal areas. Parasites on human and animal bodies seem like indeterminate forms, neither internal nor external, neither part of us nor free. Insects crawl, which is betwixt walking and swimming. Miniatures in art are simplifications of the original, so they direct and aid our perception. But the reduced scale of insects is contradicted by their bizarre detail. Worse still, they are so consistent in these insults to familiarity of form and specificity of habitat, yet so numerous in kind that they suggest a seething, secret world of transformations, menacing in fecundity and frightening in their metamorphoses. Out of scale, they live at the margin of the mesocosm where we live, the most dangerous boundary of all.

Educated on the images of real animals, we seem incapable of imagining creatures other than those reassembled from familiar biological morphology. In a sense, it could be argued that evolution has already imagined more kinds than we could, and, since they provide the components of thought, we can only reuse them in secondary ways. From exaggerated insects and microbes to sea-serpent snakes and squids to King Kong apes we seem unable to surmount given variety and its hold on the imagination.

Boundary forms, exaggerated size, and fearful transformations are prime modes of monster-making. Another is our deep pre-occupation with mobility or motility. There is a strong sense from early childhood for how-they-move and how-we-move. This may in part account for our fear of snakes, of vultures, and of horrors of the sea, such as man-eating sharks. Long before and even during the time we were hunters, our kind were prey, and in childhood games we still train our bodies in the delightful excitement of evading, hiding, and escape. In swampy places and in water we are slow and relatively helpless, and our nightmares of being unable to run may come from that collective past when we were the hunted.

Or perhaps it is not the power to invent, but the efficacy of interpretation that is limited. In the science fiction of interplanetary travel there are radical animate fictional possibilities. The real limitation may be the means by which invented creatures can be significant. Life forms without bilateral or radial symmetry, without a definite ectoderm, not covered by scales, skin, fur, feathers, or shell, without division into head, tail, back, and belly, without either flying, swimming, crawling, digging, or walking appendages, without internal organ systems or differentiated tissues, without apparent sense organs, not supported by the intake of materials, that do not reproduce their own kind, have no family or social integration, do not conform in engineering and form to the constraints of the surrounding medium, gravity, or body/surface ratios—may be possible. But the fictionist who invents them must invent a world in which they make sense. That is the rub. For us they are meaningless.

Animal parts are "masks" of environmental factors. All physical and behavioral details are solutions to the problems of support, motility, energy dispersal, heat exchange, heredity packaging, and communication, all of which we share with animals. Yet all are abstractions: There is no physically identifiable object we call "motility." There are only legs and wings and fins. The idea of wingedness forces us to detach them from birds. By reconstructing them with inappropriate anatomy, we make such monsters as harpies, vampires, dragons, Toth, and other demons whose purpose is to connect the human (head) with wings and therefore to consider the air as habitation for a body whose other details are still terrestrial, and we heighten our sensitivity to part and place, form and function.

By introducing disorder into the system of our thought in such hideous and contradictory anatomical mosaics and disproportions, we contact our deeper anxiety about a consistent and predictable world. Or they remind us of the supernatural and miraculous. Angels focus our attention on the relationship between zones or fields of play and widen our sensibility, our consideration of super order.

Stories involving shapeless beings, ectoplasmic creatures, disembodied spirits, and organisms of "pure mind" tend to be unsatisfactory in folktale, ghost story, or intergalactic drama unless they are somehow materialized. In such stories we are usually told that they "manifest themselves" or "take the form of." Their creature-image is essential to our suspension of disbelief. The voice from the sky, the disembodied cry, the moans of "spirits" draw our attention, but are without an image. When we say, on the other hand, "Listen to the gargoyle!" or "There's Uncle Harry's ghost!" we immediately "see" the creature.

In Mary Chase's play, *Harvey*, a friendly demon, or pooka, is visible only to the protagonist, not to other characters or to the audience. This intolerable situation is relieved when the being is made imaginary for the audience by being described as a giant rabbit.* The creature is a man-animal combination in that we are told that it talks and wears clothes. Being seven feet tall, it is indeed a monster. But why a rabbit? The answer to that lies within the context of the story, particularly the personality of its host. In the play the rabbit-goblin has chosen for a time to accompany Elwood P. Dowd, who is one of those mild and reflective and therefore subordinate individuals in an aggressive society who is obviously crazy with the kind of purity of insight that this society finds intolerable. Real rabbits are everywhere the animal most intimately connected with the moon, being "loony," that madness of the March hare. In all the folktales the rabbit is artless—its very face bespeaks its harebrained stare. The rabbit is the opposite of the clever fox and its candor is as plain as the

* And in some productions by the appearance of the actual figure in the lobby at the play's end.

moon's orb, a relentless, naive single-mindedness that borders on vacancy.

Distancing ourselves from the complacent, prudish, and over-fed middle class requires more than criticism or ironic comment from another human. In the play it comes from outside ourselves, from the rabbit-demon, whose placid domesticity and mild hip-pity-hop conformity contrasts to its wild love dances in the full moon. The very presence of a two-hundred-pound rabbit compels its dissection (and its shadow in us) as though it were a giant Pleistocene ground sloth whose parts are omens to its Paleolithic hunter-butchers.

Monsters are often giants. They are, in the language of ethology, "super-normal sign stimuli," that is, exaggerated signals that multiply our normal reactions. More than that, their image is not intended as an end: Harvey's purpose is not to engross us with the study of rabbits. That knowledge it assumes we already have. Indeed, that is what miniatures are for, to reduce the unessential and encourage synthesis and appreciation of wholeness. Miniatures live in our right-brain, from which they may troop, projected in large, each in its completeness, into the left-brain for naming and dissecting. But monsters are left-brained inhabitants, intended for analysis. The culture synthesizes man/animal monsters out of fragments of its experience as the only means of saying certain things, sounds heard by the observer as he demolishes the incongruous carcass.

The Diabolical Ape

As though unwilling to allow us to invent the worst of monsters, grotesque travesties of ourselves, nature (or evolution, if you prefer) has provided us with such a negative image that may be perceived as having either man's face and an animal body or the other way around. Such is the ape. It is at once the most insulting, degrading, obscene of creatures and yet the most intelligent, complex, and informative member of the animal kingdom. The tension between these two aspects is indicated by our laughter—that uniquely human convulsion of air arising from the contradictions of our own thought.

Had Charles Darwin concluded that men were most closely related to and descended from raccoons or elephants, things might have gone more smoothly for his theory in its first cen-tury.* It is clear that we already feared the worst, however, and that the storm which broke over the theory released great pressures that had been building for centuries, having less to do with intellectual disagreement or even with the Bible than we suppose, and more to do with our native unease about borderline creatures, especially when we are just across the line.

The blatant incarnation of human/animal could be ambiguous-good or anomalous-bad. Hindus, Japanese, Malaysians, lacking centuries of Western cultural bias with respect to "animality," and apehood in particular, resolved the similarity of man and ape as a family matter, and elevated certain monkeys or apes to sacred status and welcomed them into the temples. They found other monsters. But the monkey-haters par excellence were exemplified in the nineteenth century by the provincial English bishops,† guilt-ridden by the virtual voyeurism of watching monkeys, and in the twentieth century by neo-humanists,‡ who are equally ashamed of riveting the mind's eye, if not the eye, upon the monkey.

The apes (a term often used to include all tailless primates) were the worst. Even Aristotle had remarked on their grotesque caricaturization of men, making them the first hypocrites. The Christians in their time considered that no animal should be without a tail, the absence of which, with their humanoid body, revealed apes to be arrogant pretenders. The Christians had already been revolted by Egyptian simiology, and the worship of apes was the very stamp of the heathen in "the land of darkness." Today the Abominable Snowman and Bigfoot live at the snowy and sylvan limits of human life, themselves outlandish imitators of humans.

The upright posture, taillessness, humanoid face, good hands, and large size of the ape made it impossible not to perceive these animals as a strange race of degenerate man, not only by Christians. There is a tradition among North American Indians of an exploratory expedition before the Europeans came that took a party

* As a joke the editor of a literary journal recently promulgated in the "Letters to the Editor" section "evidence" that we had mistaken the evolutionary materials and apes were actually descended from man. But jokes betray anxieties, and, in this case, wishful thinking, if not for the editor, then for his readers. Modern literary humanism has never forgiven Darwin for shattering the classical/Christian illusion of human separatism.
† Otherwise known as The Primates.
‡ Or prima donnas.

far south. There they encountered "little men" in the trees. Being men of strong stomach but nonetheless reasonable, these hardy adventurers from the plains knew they had reached the end of things and so turned and went back to what would become Kansas.

Being neither Protestants nor intellectuals, the Indians probably were not contemptuous, just careful. Judged by the standards of human reason, as it came to be defined in neo-Classical terms, the monkey is a mockery indeed, the perfect conglomerate of the human potentiality sullied by animal appetite. Like the devil trying to be God, the ape trying to be human is a figure of evil.

Everything about the ape helped make it diabolical. It looked and acted like a depraved man or monstrous hybrid. It was an object of divine disfavor which imitated man as Satan mimicked God. Like the satyr, the ape was an exemplification of unrestrained animal appetites—if not the Devil or his viceroy, then his victim, appearing in Romanesque iconography as a fallen being. Keeping apes, knowing them better, didn't help; the smarter they appeared, the more contempt they generated.

The ape appears in church architecture with wings, the personification of vice, an aggressive, terrifying demon. Biologically and psychologically, it was an unwelcome bridge to man from the animals. It resembled the furry wild man of Germanic myth. In European folktales unfortunate people changed into apes. Associated pictorially with Adam and Eve as an apple-eating embodiment of carnal desire and the weakness of the female, the ape is related to Eve as Eve was to Adam. The parody of the amorous simian couple appears in the late Middle Ages, the male with a tail, the female without. The ape is an associate of Orpheus, whom it imitates as a musician.

The Renaissance, in its secular way, was slightly more sympathetic to apes. Chained, the ape represented natural man in civilization's fetters, the nut-eater, more fool than sinner. It became associated with the goat and owl in parodies of human foibles. In mockeries of man's pretensions, it was sculpted or painted in a whole series of imitation: cooking, at battle, hunting, in alchemy, at the dance. The droll ape emerged, a burlesque of human folly and vanity.

As a tree-dweller, the ape is would-be bird, the model of hopeless ambition. Associated with ape lore is a tradition of failed parenthood and abuse of the young, probably based on observations of stressed captives. Since the fifteenth century the ape has been associated with Dame Folly who, riding an ass, was said "to lead apes in hell" as a euphemism for adultery. So, from sinner and pretender, the ape became a fool and jester, prankster and thief. Riding a bear, it was part of a parody on courtly love, signified by its apple-eating and mirror-gazing. Rape by ape, marriage with apes, kidnap by apes became familiar themes. Less enmeshed in theology but still impersonating and imitating man, who was made in God's image, the ape was for cynics synonymous with art which, as Boccaccio said, is the "ape of nature" and the "nature of the ape."

This brief synopsis of twenty-five hundred years of the ape in civilization shows it to be persistently ugly, bad-tempered, ghastly, an exaggerated imitation of man, but ambivalent in its pathetic and hopeless human yearning. Sometimes the ape is portrayed as a victim, sometimes as the embodiment of human weakness, at others as a demon or ancillary of the Devil. Whatever the interpretation, its jangling impact on us is inherent in its duality. It needles us because the ape is uncomfortably close as an animal and disgustingly far away as a human. The ape and human images are a set of imperfect oppositions, an instrument for self-analysis.

No other human/animal combination renders the human and animal parts so dissectible, and the ape's behavior epitomizes our own failure to integrate our human and animal aspects, and, by parallel, our limited success in harmonizing our human and spiritual sides.

What made the situation worse was that the apparent perversity of the ape was exaggerated because of observations of captives who were probably demented by the conditions of their captivity, with all the bizarre forms of scatological obsession, sexual perversion, stereotyped motions, parental failure, aggression, and other symptoms of psychopathology common to apes and men in chains or cages.

In the Middle Ages apes become so laden with the moralistic and symbolic layers that even their fetters signified subdued carnality. What the ape "stood for," however, is not what is most important, despite the vast literature on ape symbolism. The significance of the ape is deeper than the myths of any particular culture. In this sense there is nothing symbolic about the monstrousness of the ape. King Kong will always live. Its value for dissection into abstract qualities is due to the structure of perception itself. That some people cherish apes as sacred and others abhor them as evil reminds us how close are the sinister and the numinous, notable among these ambiguous beings whose special status is not created but only explained by culture.

Monsters and Social Stress

At the other extreme from the ape, a natural animal, are fictitious amalgamations from the parts of various animals. The two are the ends of a series, naturalistic at one end and fictional or stylized at the other. Walter Abell, an art historian, looking at etched and sculptured figures in churches and on archaeological objects from northwestern Europe, found a consistent trend in the degree of malevolence of these beasts in history. In general the oldest monsters were the largest and most terrifying. As with Grendel in *Beowulf*, the very sight of them was paralyzing. Whenever they appear in combat with men, the latter are devoured. Even great heroes struggle desperately in a losing battle against them.

Teutonic, Vandal, and Norse mythology are crowded with hideous, carnivorous bipeds whom no man could withstand, save him who was pure in heart and hedged about with charms, prayers, and amulets. In time the monsters weaken and the heroes wax. The struggle becomes more evenly balanced. Beginning with the Neolithic, when men were beset by demons so awful that they are repressed from consciousness and appear only in dreams and other symbolic forms; followed by the Dark Ages, with its fiends and firedrakes, ravaging phantasmagoria and the ghastly creatures of *Beowulf*; then the Romanesque period with its Teutonic hero-dragon stories, the grim and ferocious beasts shown on church facades and portals; the Gothic era, with grotesque gargoyles and chimeras, often incumbent and subdued by bishops; and finally by the fifteenth century the vestiges—ornamental, whimsical, comic remains in balustrades and buttresses.

Abell saw that the less the animal resembled any one known

species, the more intense its effect. As the general stress of life decreased and men became more secure, the monsters became less abstract and more naturalistic.

Abell's thesis is that this change in the size and horror of the monster diminishes as society gains control over its own destiny and the forces of death and destruction, security from invasion, natural catastrophe, famine and disease are slowly overcome— in short, as modern civilization emerges. Finally, the monsters are reduced to that uncanny zoo of small figures whose hideous ancestors occupied central panels on portals and lintels, squeezed by ridicule to the more joking places on the decorative fringes and garden nooks.

Abell sees these animal figures as symbolic of uncontrollable features of the environment in much the same way that psychiatrists speak of animal symbols for unconscious elements of the personality.

The correlation of declining monsters with civilized progress and security is problematic. The fourteenth and fifteenth centuries, where he ends his series with impotent demons, saw the worst of the black plague, witch-hunting, perennial wars, and religious intolerance. Nor is it as certain as it once seemed that the primitive men of a hundred centuries ago lived lives of unremittent terror, besieged by animals so ferocious that they could scarcely be represented at all.

His theory of progression from terrifying to friendly, correlated with representations ranging from abstract to naturalistic, may be valid without requiring a historical sequence, or may even be seen as ranging from negative to positive. Perhaps any society at any time uses animal images in various ways, ranging from familiar to monstrous according to the need. Fantastic animals need not represent the powers of evil but a great intensity of being, the emotional dimension of an intense intellectual demand.

As a symbol of chaos, the monster may be exploited by religious authority. For thousands of years the myths of Eurasia and the Near East told of demon-dogs—the Sumerian Asag, Babylonian Tiamat, Greek Typhen—the containment of which preserved the world. The myths were basically cyclic. From time to time the heralds of chaos broke loose and the story told of the hero who slew them or returned them to their chains, often deep in a mountain. When Zoroastrianism, Christianity, and Judaism conceived history as a single linear episode, such monsters of chaos as Gog and Magog became the evil of the final Apocalypse, even as the Antichrist, which would be defeated once and for all. But in describing them, the cult always conveys information about the causes of chaos—which is to say that they can never be used only to inspire terror, but also to prefigure its nature. The widespread image of the dog-devil must have to do not only with the psychiatric function of the dog in childhood dreams, but also with the origin and security of domestication and the home itself, the foundation upon which agricultural civilization was built. In times of great stress—famine, war, pestilence—the dogs of the towns ran in packs and turned on the people. The horror of man's best friend becoming the devourer of his children is not only terrible in itself but evokes all the tensions of tabooed proximity and collapsing definitions. Far more hideous to the domestic society than the image of wild intruders was the evil inverse of the good and unfamiliar. Like the tyrant who fears his slaves, the keeper of domestic animals has his deepest source of fear within his own walls.

The Living Coded Messages

The monster or other ambiguous animal does not simply "stand for" something. In a sense it is put together like an organ transplant in modern biology in which a leg or an eye from one individual is grafted onto another. Unlike clinical therapy, this is not done to restore an injured whole, but to create disturbing wholes. In medicine the organ to be grafted should come from as closely related an individual as possible to reduce its likelihood of being rejected. In the making of cultural chimeras or man/animal mélanges, the parts come from radically different kinds whose fusion is at first disconcerting. The apparent incoherence of such a creature triggers our deep psychic alarm system because it turns on two or more different schema-image data chunks at once, one for each kind of animal.

But alarm does not yet mean fear, only arousal. Our response to such images has just begun. Our unconscious recall raises more than the independent files on "man" and "bull" when we are presented with a Minotaur, for connected with each is a whole field of information and meaning. These realms come forward, juxtaposed, into some scanning station of the mind, trailing long threads of perceptual experience, connotations from the character of cattle, pastoral scenes, the intricacies of the cave, comparison and admiration of bulls and their duality with oxen or with cows; and on the other hand a similar mnemonic farrago for "humanity."

Then a play of pattern-finding begins, open to suggestions from "the outside." It "works" in the sense of fermentation. Analogies, points of contact, illuminations, realignments, helped along by music, pictures, shrines, dance. The combination feeds back into the separate schemata for men and for bulls. New insight emerges to which our mentors have pointed. It affects that filtering and appraising activity in which feelings and actions about people will henceforth bear subliminal bullish influences as well as formal acknowledgment. The Minotaur becomes an image and a word for public rhetorical purposes and for private coding. A new chunk has been created, a recall signal whose image shimmers with the poetic substance of a new creation.

Such new forms vary in abstraction, that is, the level of anatomy conjoined to make the ambiguous figure. For example, the mermaid is a head-tail combination of woman and bony (higher) fish. But in the griffin are the shoulders lion or eagle? The farther we get from species anatomy toward mammalian fur, or vertebrate body, the more fundamental the animal reference. The more abstract amalgamation seeks, as Abell observed, to get at more basic and therefore enduring qualities. The monsters of Hieronymus Bosch, the fifteenth-century Flemish painter, of hell and paradise, are not only heterogenous chimera but amalgams at the level of bilaterality, terrestriality, backboned biomorphs, the level simply of wings or skin-cover or anterior-posterior. This level of abstraction is a desperate kind of monster-mongering, far deeper than mere familiar species-grafting.

These raw tissue and bone matings of scales, feathers, eyes, and anuses, of which terrifying specters are the extremes, are instruments of probing and searching, devices that can bring conflicting parts of reality together in a search for pattern. They do not merely signify times of social stress in the society, for they are always present, marking those areas of incongruity and disorder which are the most strenuous intellectual tasks.

At one time the vast post-glacial, primeval forest of Europe was the frontier of human settlement, physically the limits of occupation and psychologically the outpost of creation. Its monsters and hybrids are all beasts of the forest, whose pale descendants come to us in mere fairy tales from the Brothers Grimm or impotent gargoyles spurting water in a garden pool. One of its last remnants is the Bigfoot of the Pacific Northwest.

At another time or for another people the sea was the unknown, and fabulous marine animals were the tools for transforming the sea into a perceptual world, degraded in its time to moralistic bestiaries, ship figureheads, museum freaks, or the tutelary animals of romantic fiction.

More recently our frontiers have been focused on distant planets, and again our imagination has provided us with embodiments which like the architecture of hallucinations, never exceed but only juxtapose and combine and recombine from what we know, as a probe for the possible.

To a degree we remain primitive men: We do not see creatures wholly separate from their environments. All things are produced by a conflux of forces, are "made" by the world, and therefore convey something about that world. The Leviathan and the Loch Ness Monster are symptoms of events or processes extending far beyond themselves, events that threaten because they are bound to intrude on the present world.

This is not just a figure of speech or metaphoric intrusion. Human monsters—elves, gnomes, dwarfs, titans, joined twins, thalidomide infants, cretins, individuals with extra heads or limbs, tumors, harelip or third eye—are recognized by us as products of genetic accident or some other disturbance in the reproductive cycle. The germ-forming organs can be diet, illness, or exposure to radiation. Medicine bears out our intuitive sense that discordant forces affecting a whole section of reality can be revealed in individual deformity.

But monsters all have the potential for being inordinately good as well as bad. Attila the Hun was a dwarf, but so was the Buddha figure. The monster is always exceptional but not necessarily evil. When monsters appear there is some change in the fabric of things. Or, when we wish to give objective shape to a new idea or new danger, we create fantastic shapes from old, familiar parts. They serve this purpose like dream images and have "a strange and horrible appearance of reality."

Every age has its monsters. For Malory and the late medieval Europeans they were dragons, monstrous vultures, demons, and fiends. For us there are vestigial creatures of the deep, germs, outer-space beings or abominable snowmen. The specters of one period are seen as simple fictions in the next. They are as essential to the human thought system as conventional animals. They vary to fit the need, like grammar, and are related to the biological species as language is to linguistic deep structure. A revealing phrase from *Beowulf* in the eighth century is "twilight-spoiler" for the dragon. As a transitional creature, neither wholly this nor that, it shares the edge of the day with bats, goatsuckers, and owls. Grendel, the man-eater from the same tale, lived in the twilight of a cave under water.

Monsters are part of the critical period, the mental furniture of adolescence. Most of their impact stems from childhood fixations on the forms of danger. Society or art exploits the adolescent's regressive mood, those infantile fears of oral aggression and of helpless separation. They are evoked and enhanced by art, mobilized by images of appalling conglomerate beasts that transcend the animal categories of childhood and the logic of kind. As synthesized beings rather than biological species, dragons and other monsters lock into the adolescent receptivity to abstraction. If the monster movies of today are full of junior high school youths, it is because they are ripe for a new kind of danger and surprise of the abstract, ready to imagine and to symbolize. All this in the modern world has been removed from religious control and given to commercial story-spinners for entertainment.

Ambiguous animals are, then, intermediary code figures for different parts of our experience. As man/animal combinations they are images of the duality or multiplicity of self and other. Evolutionary theory tells us that we are all composed of disparate stages of the past. We are a mixture of all those forms in our descent. Civilized man has yearned for centuries for a different reality. Our dispersed animality is impossible to envisage as separate from our true human self. We have from time to time made the brain, the hand, the "noble countenance," or the pineal gland the sole human component, leaving the rest to animal heritage. Each of these has been eroded in turn by new knowledge. To assign our pure humanity to voice or abstract qualities doesn't work because our minds don't work that way. Imagery is essential.

To overcome this dispersal of our otherness requires not that we arbitrarily assign it to parts of the body, but that we consolidate it in the figures of animals and create explicitly conjoined images. In a sense we separate in order to bring together. The monkey is a very distressing animal because it looks like a botch of the combinational form, merely a more animal-like human or human-like animal in an all-body, general way.

To go one step farther, we dissect the animal and human bodies in order to regroup them into ambivalent wholes in turn to make new dissections. These latter are not anatomical at all, but newly joined portions of the overlapping aspects of each. They are the patterns of connectedness that allow us cognitively to come to grips with the reality of a diffused otherness.

After that one can no longer say in truth, "It is the animal in me that . . .," or "The humane thing to do . . . ," but one realizes instead that the unique self, or man in us, is conditioned by the other in us. The self and the other are realities, but only in the sense of occasion, not of sensible parts. What is truly at the heart of my selfhood, as an individual and as a member of a species, is the way in which I affirm and acknowledge beings and other kinds, momentarily assimilating parts of them to make new wholes to digest and truly increase my self-awareness.

This process is related to but different from that special class of things which the theory of Transitional Objects describes as intermediaries between the self and not-self. The T.O. is regarded by psychiatrists as essential to critical stages of the infant's perception of his own independent existence. Anxiety that may accompany the dawning discovery that other people and objects are separate from the self and more or less undependable is allayed by an attachment to certain of those objects. They are transitional in that they are seen as attached to one's own being and yet not attached. Thus the "security blanket" perceived by the child as an external object over which there is still control is partly his own creation.

These special objects serve to dampen the grief of early isolation, a link to the Other by an attachment to special pieces of it that continue for a while to be at one end, as it were, ourselves. While the person in us is getting accustomed to the idea of multiple realities, the Transitional Object serves as a temporary emotional umbilicus to the unity of prenatal existence.

The T.O. does not have the grafted appearance of two unlike things stuck together. Its dual qualities are dispersed throughout.

Because of this it would probably not be appropriate to call the combinational animals Transitional Objects in the psychiatric sense.

Much of our infantile and early childhood experience leaves unconscious memories, mnemonic trances and outlines. These include the human face, the mother-image, the "rising" and "setting" sun or moon, the alternation of day and night, and the passing of materials into and out of the body. Such imprints of experience are models of perceptual events to which some later experiences fit as homologies, that is, are seen as new expressions of familiar forms. Our sensitivity to them is acute and our emotional response intense. The impact of ambiguous animals reaches our conscious experience from deep layers of the past, our early intuitions of natural order. Life is a continuous awakening in which the past prefigures the future. We advance as persons toward a maturity measured by our responsiveness to and affirmation of a life that is transitory, limited, and mysterious.

In modern culture we think of a monster as a fictitious but exciting danger, uncannily fascinating. But the real danger of the monster is not that it awakens our old forgotten fears of being eaten by large beasts, though it may tap those vestigial worries. The real source of danger, often unrealized, is that its incongruity will remain unresolved. The conjoining of unlike beings is a fragment of temporary disorder, part of an uncomprehended net of relationships. Mostly we attend to the parts of the world that have meaning for us, but we know at another level of our being that much of the universe is temporarily inexplicable. We must believe that it does have systematic structure. Some of it will always be beyond our understanding, but some of it may be found out by playing with and rearranging parts. The message to ourselves in the form of animal combinations is to attend to and even manufacture seemingly discordant figures from reality, knowing that they have harmonious if hidden coherence, not so much as new entities but as familiar chunks in unexpected arrangements. We postulate that somehow they are related by composing them into a single body because the body is for each of us the irrefutable and final model for wholeness.

4 | IMITATING ANIMALS: THE CAST OF CHARACTERS

One of the traits of modern society under widespread reform is its conventions for classifying people. The young, in particular, object to the catchbins of race and sex, to typing people as liberals, capitalists, WASPS, hippies, or criminally insane. The criticism is justly based on the repressive effects of such labels and is supported by social theory. And yet the dream that there are as many kinds of people as there are people does not go down easily.

Sliding through professions and geography, minimizing race and class, the yearning for androgyny and psychological environmentalism are all unsatisfying because they neglect or deny the category-making nature of cognition itself. The fashionable ideal that everyone should be free of imposed definition in order to be whatever he wants, to choose and change identity in spite of the accidents of birth, and to define self according to ideology and personal taste is very appealing, though in some grievously frustrating way appallingly inadequate and wrong.

The adolescent, caught between the modern world's chronic shortage of order and the chic psychology of identity by assertion, is on queasy ground. The ideal conflicts with the thrust of his mental development, which is to distinguish, define, and classify. The central task of his first twelve years is to develop his powers of discrimination, linking them to speech, and to master the art of conceptualizing and abstracting by searching out the commonalities and differences among plants and animals—traits given, not chosen.

At the same time, a second activity is going on, also based on the classification and observation of animals. It is part of play, and, like most play, has its purposes apart from the simple joy of exercise. This is the mimicry of the nonhuman, the imitation of animals. Identifying creatures and playing at being them are contingent and overlapping. Learning names is both a mental exercise and a collection of information. The animals are known as much by what they do as how they look. Imitation of them involves similarities in their behavior and ours in which they become the bearers of certain traits. The child can see, hear, smell, or touch the animals themselves, or at least their pictures or other representations. They can be manipulated and dramatically enacted.

By contrast, the intangible "things" of inner experience—the qualities, moods, and feelings of people and animals—have no physical substance. By themselves sadness, innocence, cunning, mother love, tenacity, and loyalty are elusive. They loom and subside, submerged in the human personality amid a thousand other affects. They are not only difficult to isolate, recognize, and name, but even to be conscious of. The child goes from naming physical beings that are visible and touchable to learning those slippery qualities and states by linking the two, making one a kind of emblem of the other.

In order to do this the child must think of the behavior of an animal as one of its parts. Just as he becomes increasingly aware of the differentiation of his own bodily detail, he grows in sensitivity to the physical composition of the animal.

The *Just So Stories* by Rudyard Kipling are extraordinary examples of this activity in modern literature. In tales telling how the leopard got its spots, the camel its hump, the elephant its trunk, the rhino its skin, attention is fixed on a single constitutive part. The listener or reader dissects the creature in his mind's eye; he participates in a kind of gnostic butchering or dismembering that allows corresponding pieces of different animals to be compared. Kipling's incantatory language, focus on a trait of a species, explanatory and dramatic format, and vivisection place his stories squarely in the tradition of the hunting mind and the genesis of human thought.

In the stories some crucial action is associated with each trait. From this it is not difficult to see that what an animal does also constitutes his being. The next step is to apply this particularizing to behaviors and to emotions and motives. It is achieved by the insight connecting feelings and action, an empathy for the animal felt in one's self.

Thus we attend to types of creatures as the models of consistent actions. Unlike people, who seem to be bear-like one minute and cow-like the next, each kind of creature has some one notable characteristic from among those fugitive components and experiences of which we were previously unconscious.

The nursery rhymes of Mother Goose and traditional bedtime stories are essentially a training ground for the group-wide recognition of these traits. These stories, rhymes, and songs are part of a world-wide tradition of animal signs. Such ditties do not necessarily follow years of learning names, but coincide with it, identifying both the fox and foxiness, pig and gluttony, hen and hysteria, Mary's lamb and loyalty, Miss Muffet's spider and audacity, and so on.

Traits of behavior and names of feelings are an elementary lesson in abstractions given access and visibility by connecting them with particular animals. Those story and picture creatures are immersed in mutual relationships. The web of attitudes and sentiment forming family bonds and the network of relationships between families are modeled in the animal stories in all societies. That there are some human figures scattered among the animals does not seem odd to children. It lubricates the perceptual glide back and forth and induces the listener to associate these animal components of behavior with equivalent behaviors in people.

The stories presenting such traits are composed of dramatic scenes. It is typical of oral traditions that the scene and rhetorical dialogue are given. There are crucial lines ("The sky is falling!" cried Chicken Little), since the basic structure of rhetorical tradition is not a script but a series of scenes, most of which are easy to imagine as pictorial stills. Once we are shown illustrations of these scenes, our recollections are of these pictures. Children do not invent new scenes for familiar stories; indeed, they resist the introduction of new materials into old stories and get upset when scenes do not come in their proper order.

From physical traits, then behaviors, and on to whole chunks of familiar action, the animal is a kind of handle for abstractions. "Before men can find these traits clearly in themselves," says Suzanne Langer, "they can see them typified in animals." As children get older the stories they hear are increasingly interlarded with human figures. That is, human mothers and fathers appear in such tales quite early, then brothers and sisters, neighbors, friends, maidens and swains, soldiers and politicians. The repertoire of human passions and actions is slowly enlarged and repeated, clarified by its incarnation in specific animals, then transferred back to people and to the listening self.

This back and forth between animal and human is experienced by the listener not only in terms of himself and the animal, but in his observation of others and the animal. There is a kind of assignment of animality, for instance, that comes to Daddy from the story of Goldilocks. Daddy's bigness, gruffness, and protectiveness are clarified by the story and are ready to become part of daddiness everywhere, as the child becomes the man. If a real human daddy is small with a high voice and rather timid, it is no matter, for he will be endowed with a magic mantle of hearty guardianship.

But only listening to stories is not enough. Even when he tries to sit still and listen, the child is not a passive learner. He is never objective. His rapt attention as the story unfolds is accompanied by emotion and wriggling and action. The child wants to act it, to learn it in the muscle, to feel the motion of the protagonists as well as the emotion. Even the early lessons can no more be learned by unalloyed watching than a rat can learn a maze by observing it from a distance. Perhaps this is one reason for the wide concern over marathon television-watching by small children. The television tube locks the observer into immobility, in contrast to the heard story, which allows him freedom to move about and opportunity to practice his own image-making.

All kinds of fragments, taken from such stories, are spontaneously woven into play and informal games. The feeling is reconstituted with the act: the stealthy approach, the fear of pursuit, the chafing under unfair dictum, the defiance, the assurance of vindication, the generous giving. In a sense they are called forth by emulation and empathy, spoken or unspoken reference to the animal, transferred to little scenes with stuffed toys or puppets or to moments of romping with parents or companions.

This playing is part of the larger psychological phenomenon of acting-out in which expression in general is displayed and assimilated by what one does. Certainly no child needs an animal model to be jealous, lonely, affectionate, or frightened. But he does need an animal story to externalize and make concrete those experiences, to separate them by attaching each to an animal, to get words for them from his creature-taxonomy; and by recognizing them outwardly to know them as shared reality, and to enact them, to make them happen, and thereby master them. Gruffness is not simply learned from hearing about Poppa Bear, but by imitating Poppa Bear and thereby being awakened to that Daddy in one's self. It is incorporated into a germinating concept of the father, starting with stories and extended by pretending. Of course it is important to know that fathers are also tender and protective. But those other components use other images. Real father bears are not tender toward cubs. An early awakening to gruffness in the father may be a first step toward a healthy development of the boy-child's oedipal sensibility.

But why not, one might ask—since it is only a story and we can make stories go any way we want—tell a story about a tender daddy bear? The objective is to isolate qualities in specific animals that can be emulated, which is the reason for one-dimensional bears at this stage. If children learn different qualities for bears, play among themselves that refers to the bear will be confusing. Or, if the roles of Poppa and Mama Bear change according to the whim of the storyteller, making the bears an androgynous bear pair in which traits are disassociated from sex, the animal remains as ambiguous as the child is about himself. The teller may convey some sense of a tiny society, but the purpose of these animal stories for children is not to model society, only to establish individually the diversity of traits that make up the society of the self.

The stories not only serve as a vehicle for the incremental growth of individual self-consciousness, but enlarge an awareness of the reality of animals, the acceptance of a given reality and our affirmation of it as a good creation. Admittedly, it is asserted in such stories that bears talk and wear clothes; the story does not communicate natural history. The small child is not ready for details about wild bears; he knows from an early age that the tale, however captivating, is pretend. But somewhere in the background of all bear stories is the figure of the real bear. Somehow the real bear has a connection to the humanized bear of the bedtime story. One cannot change the little fiction without affecting that other image, the integrity of the real bear, though knowledge of it is still extremely limited in the small child. There are parallels in the natural and fictitious histories, consistent differences, accepted discrepancies. Exactly how these relate to one another will emerge as we proceed with our examination of childhood animals.

The Drama of the Animal

Small children play at imitating animals. The growth of such play to whole scenarios, which are learned by repetition, is characteristic of older children. Mimicking animals according to their generally accepted habits may have been the first game that people ever played, just as it is among the first games that children play. "Game" is a form of the word *gamen* or haunch. That the played game and the hunted game animal are the same word suggests the animal origin or psychological meaning of games. The idea of "rules of behavior" is first perceived as a code of consistent traits in animals by which identity is verified and, in the hunt, as the constraints on the hunt and conditions of success.

Generally, arguments based on word origins and similarities are more dazzling than informative. Yet play means both histrionics and childhood frolic. It is what we do in games. Game is both an athletic competition or other ritualized competition and the object of the hunt. The idea that rules are first perceived as a reliable trait or quality of the game animal, given, not invented, relates play to the hunt, though these linguistic connections may be fortuitous. The first drama is ritual mimicry. Play has its origins in the dramatic imitation of animals, first in exciting emotional states and bodily postures and movements, and then increasingly in more patterned games analogous to the rules of behavior that characterize animals.

In childhood games involving the role-playing emulation of animals, the action is an assertion about attributes or qualities. One thing is being affirmed of another. In a special tag played on the snow-covered ice of a pond, for example, the game of "Fox and Geese," circular paths are created by tramping the snow, usually in the form of concentric circles connected from a center by radiating lines. These become the running lanes from which players cannot deviate (the trail-following rules of the "game"). All the players are Geese except one, the Fox, who must catch a Goose. When he does the victim becomes the Fox. Games of tag are all predator-prey emulations.

This affirmation of qualities by the figure of the animal is a form of predication. Predication is the "saying one thing of another," in this case, the human taking of animal identity. Its structure is similar to scores of other such games that project upon the human participant one or a series of kinds of animals. In imitating their behavior the players discover and learn to control those forces within themselves. In the "Fox and Geese" a transformation takes place when the prey is caught and becomes the Fox. The Fox is of course not an It but a Who. "Who is It?" is the question in tag. Before we are debauched by the idea that flesh is a bland continuum (mutton instead of sheep, roast instead of leg), a Thing rather than a Who, consummation changes us into *who* one is eaten by, not *what* one eats.

As he takes various parts in such a game, the participant has game-animals briefly predicated upon him and paraded before him. One's attention is consumed for the moment in the animal which has taken him, that is, whose shape he invades. Anthropologist James Fernandez believes that such games are part of normal growth, events by which the self and then the society are more fully realized. He speaks of the young child as inchoate or incomplete. Creature-mimicking brings the person into the animal, with whom he is for a few moments enjoined. A certain trait of the animal contacts a corresponding part of the human self and awakens it. Some of the inchoateness is blown away by recognition, and the lesson is repeated again and again in the drama of the play with a series of animals. Taking animal shape, and thereby taking the point of view of the animal, converts a latent property into an active one; it gives the child an exercise in redirecting his thought inward at something that his naive self first apprehends as "out there." One becomes the object of the self and, in mastering that object, one becomes more of a subject to the self.

The self is not all that is still vague to the child. It is also the "you" and the "we." Playing at animal parts, the child is momentarily absorbed by the being he mimics. The Other possesses him, and yet it is he who assimilates the animal. This ephemeral loss of the self and recovery of the larger self is witnessed by the other players. Each child sees the qualities successively constituting the others and the clustering of traits by which pronouns are coaxed from simple second- or third-person references and given further definition.

The rules of such games and the particular animals chosen are provincial and traditional. Culture makes use of whatever animals are familiar. The one criterion must be that the creature is familiar enough to mimic and that it is appropriately cast, that there is a verifiable correlation of some kind between these persuasive performances and the real creature as seen in nature or known in folktale.

This use of animal behavior as a means for knowing one's own creature feelings and subjective behaviors ranges from horseplay and bear hugs with parents through leapfrog, copycat, and general monkeyshines, to extemporaneous dramas recapitulating scenes from familiar animal stories, to organized games with ritualized moves and standard formats. The child briefly but repeatedly scrutinizes and experiences some aspect of the animal as himself, then puts it off or trades it for another.

In looking at the eight-year-old's enactment of "Fox and Geese," we might say that a process of sign-making is taking place. Animal images are appropriated from conventional knowledge about them and from their biological forms. Such conventional images are signs or icons. The child is given in the form of the game a procedure for exploring the sign value (sign-ification or significance) of the particular creatures as objects, which then can become an objective part of the self.

There is nothing conscious about this linking of domains, no purpose to which the child is deliberately directed either by society or by himself. The whole of animal predication in play is largely an unconscious device both for the child and for the adult who has no objective knowledge of what it achieved. It is an empirical accumulation which, completing itself, enables the young person as adolescent to go on to the next step in the ecology of human thought development. It produces a mosaic of the self, a habit of perception and an attitude. One has acquired steps toward an identity that defines the self as structured without alienating it from nature.

There are two steps in the process of animal predication. One is the bringing of two unlike things together. However different the animal and child may be, the proximity of opposites places them in touch. The child reaches the animal that he imitates. This is the principle of contiguity or metonymic association. The second step is metaphoric. Certain details of these touching but unlike forms have similarities, sometimes unexpected echoes or parallels.

Children know that animals are very unlike us. That difference is alienating unless there is some energy exerted to counter it.

Resemblance is hidden in that unlikeness and extracted by the act of momentary unification, which is the subjective feeling of imitating. Only by forcing ourselves to see one thing as another do we bring some curiously redundant element into view. It is as though a figure were made visible in a jumble of lines by holding against it a transparent film with a master outline. Bringing the two together reveals a similar design hidden in unlike patterns. Imitating the animal is taking literally for a moment what is poetic in order to discover its existence in us, and more important, to make it our own as part of a shared domain. The remainder of the alien figure can be then matched against other master outlines to dissect still other traits. Some parts of the puzzle of the self can never be matched by animal predication and remain mysterious and perhaps uniquely ours. Thus does the participant-observer emerge with a new mastery of definitive qualities, appreciation of inner and outer multiplicity, and of intuitions of the duality of nature and culture, having a cultural game as the means of obtaining mastery of the natural or given.

There is no illusion or sentimentalizing in this, whereby an animal becomes human or is endowed with man-like qualities or personified; nor is the person brutalized. He is in the process of defining a relationship by discovering likeness and unlikeness. In such predication people have taken human shape by acknowledging their own otherness in the limited likeness.

This sorting out of parts by predication of the animal upon its naive human mimic does not end with an assortment of terms as though something had been disassembled or butchered and left around on the ground. The metaphor of the animal rescues the person from fragmentation. The figure of the whole creature from which some element of feeling has become recognizable is itself a message. The animal confirms that parts have a place, that we too have more to gain than analysis of pieces. Making concrete what is otherwise abstract is only a step toward our swallowing them into concepts of new totality.

The consequences go well beyond this self-identity, or even the definition of others. It clarifies the differences as well as the shared quality between the self and the other. Putting off the Fox is just as illuminating as putting it on, for it establishes the Fox also as a subject of whom I become aware, for if I have to imitate it I cannot be it, and we know that it too participates in the partial assimilation of other identities, by eating rather than imitating them. We learn that real foxes and geese are separate beings when we learn their names, but we learn from these games that they are not isolated, their strangeness from each other is balanced by their connectedness when one assimilates the other.

While the benefits are directly to the self by enlarging personal consciousness of the diversity of the self, this predication is essential to the subsequent participation in society at large. Going from one creature to another is a kind of movement. As we age and are initiated into the cults and rituals of adult society, the secrets of sex and obligations of marriage, we advise or tutor, beget children, lead or follow, conciliate, direct or submit, council and oppose, we move through positions in a kind of social space or game. Many of these actions and their affects we have already met and identified in childhood by linking our human domain briefly with a kind of nonhuman expert in each of those respective experiences.

Predication is at the heart of all social life. Sets of behaviors and feelings relate people. For the child, puzzling out human groupings, it is a kind of pronominal obsession, the means of making sense of endless transformation of *me*, *you*, *he*, and *they*. These pronouns are close to the center of reality in our daily lives. The world of this shifting reference is a task that never ends. The who-are-you, who-are-they, who-am-I that the child seeks is a game in which the classifying of moods, emotions, and other subjective states is achieved by experiencing an inner empathy for "species" of behaviors.

The idea of "metaphor" seems too arbitrary and literary a concept for this primordial predication as a way that children obtain thought. But we can see that it lies at the root of all inquiry, a beginning that becomes a flexible tool in the hands of adults— more like the "creative" imagination with which we usually associate metaphor. In language, being or being called an animal becomes a vehicle for adornment or disparagement. But between the childhood play at being animal and the discursive poetry of animal allusion is a series of intermediate steps. Taking animal shape is the first suspension of disbelief, the basis of all scenarios of ritual participation, liturgical rites, and even indulgence in one's role in history and myth.

Totemic Culture

The use of animals in childhood as the heralds of thought and self-knowledge is universal. It accounts for the fascination animals have for all children, a kind of mental food, at first an orderly mechanics of ideal organization and grouping, and then the separation and representation of qualities and traits, and at the same time protagonists of folktales and fairy tales that externalize elements of the child's inner life and give him the means of coping with the conflicts and uncertainties of the developing personality. All these are "found" in the animal world. Finally, as childhood draws to a close, the use of animals for self-actualizing moves to a new phase.

This new kind of attention to the species system awakens with adolescence. While furthering the lifelong goals of identity resolution, it shifts its emphasis to the social group and to a logic as well as personal definition. It grows from the impulse to symbolic thought which demarcates the adolescent from the juvenile as a phase in the calendar of growth. This feeling for poetry and hidden meaning is typical of the budding adult. His interest in the double meaning of language and metaphor in art opens abruptly, like a spectacular bloom on some drab green vine of juvenile literalism. As a flower requires pollen for fruition, this one also requires fertilizing. Myth, transmitted by art, is the culture's gift to the adolescent, its ministration of his adolescent karma. Animals play an important role in this, but that role differs radically in societies which live by hunting and foraging from all other kinds of human community. This division has its origin historically in the rise of agriculture. A convenient way of describing the two modes, both derived from the child-hold uses of animals, or totemic thought, is *totemic culture* and *domestic culture*.

The core of totemic culture is a set of myths or stories about creation. These tales of how things came to be as they are narrate events in the first society of beings, the ancestral ones, which includes some humans and a variety of other creatures, all speaking and behaving as though they belonged to a single sociopolitical unit. This fictitious community is the given model for human society to know what is more real and most important. Its different species correspond to human groupings, its actions and inter-actions portray in disguised form all human interrelations.

Many totemic cultures subdivide the tribe not only into local bands but into fraternities or clans that cut across the bands. Each of these secret clubs is dedicated to a totemic animal, plant, or some other natural object, of which it is guardian, interpreter, and representative. An animal is usually the totemic patron of such clans and the members are keepers of its secrets, serving as mediators between it and other clans. Membership is deter-mined differently in different tribes, often dictated by gender and parentage, but in some cases by omens or dreams.

In most totemic cultures the individual is initiated at puberty into the adult society of the band and/or membership in a clan. The ceremonies of initiation are often complicated, composed partly of highly focused ritual acts and partly of extended periods of training, during which the novice is in the care of tutors and undergoes a sequence of inculcations and trials. Full adult status may take months or even years. In some American Indian groups adult status is itself divided into degrees. Individuals may grad-uate progressively as they get older, learning the more esoteric medicine until some among them become leaders or elders of the tribe. Thus the lore of such groups is not a single bundle passed over to its new members, but a lifelong program of learning and responsibility. While the details of these secrets differ widely, animals continue to be exceedingly important symbols in their ritual uses and in the wisdom of translating their actions into the framework of human society.

Since non-totemic peoples are not concerned with the lifelong pondering of wild animals, in both natural behavior and its sym-bolic meaning, they cannot easily grasp the quality and sophisti-cation of such thought, and tend to look on it as simple animism. To domestic cultures the study of animals as a guide to human action seems to reverse the accepted order of value. For them no such poetic reading of a separate ecological realm exists, for all the animals of any importance have been incorporated into human society, which must then find some other model for con-crete reality.

The totemic cultural system not only allows but also encour-ages very complex intellectual exploration coupled with poetic deduction. For the child playing "Fox and Geese" there is no sym-bolism: "I am the fox stalking you" is not a symbolic statement or point of departure for reflection. Later, the young adult becomes aware of its symbolic possibilities, its amphiboly of action and sound. He can see in it a form of relationship that appears frequently in human society. In totemic societies the sacred myths are such a beginning point, infinitely richer than games. In them much of the religious liturgy is the assertion of one thing by another—that is, strings of predication—or scenes using animal imagery but always having "higher" meaning. This may include the portrayal of animals in dance, the use of animal masks, or the use of animal names in special ways.

Since non-totemic cultures are all descended in history from totemic cultures, they continue to have many such animal allusions. Even the ascetic and rather completely humanized systems of Judaism and Christianity have a surprising amount of animal symbolism. Christ is still "the lamb" and Moses was represented for a thousand years as having horns like a young bull. More often animals represent demonic powers or the least spiritual aspects of humans. Most of the "world religions" are actually other-world and man-centered, and a case can be made that the decay of the planet as a beautiful and habitable place is in part due to value systems that scorn plants and animals and have little regard for their integrity and otherness. It is not surprising that their missionaries and wandering priests were horrified by "pagan" ceremonies, mistaking animal masks and skins for deities in whose names the superstitious tribesmen worshiped degenerate animal appetites or used animal magic in their lust for power.

In recent years we have learned to be more sympathetic toward ceremonies that we do not understand, and know that all human worship has common objectives, such as the linking of spiritual and mundane realms and the affirmation and clarification of the people's identity and their relationship to their god. The critical moments of religious rites are not initiated by the participants but are led by special individuals—shamans, priests, visionaries—who can "leap to other domains" for "movement" and thereby impel followers to a reorganization of their existence by acting out the sign images or beings of those domains. In his games of mimicking animals, the child obtained thought, the idea of rules of action, the capacity to recognize what had been formless and to incorporate it as part of the self. In the ceremonies by which his adult status is recognized, the candidate extends his sense of those early experiences of play-drama as a symbolic intuition, an extension of thought into the timeless and invisible, a feeling for the dual meaning of all his actions. Life is a mimicry of the myth of origins and of the first beings. The adult discovers society to be a projection of the society of the creatures. The plurality of the social and spiritual realms are then to him an extension of the plurality of all life. New multiple predictions are performed both for and by him, revealing and persuading. The creatures in the myths are no longer unequivocal leopards or sheep or eagles, but allusive and catachrestical. Once he has experienced this duality of the zoological realm, no animal can ever be quite the same to him again. Even if it does not figure in the sacred lore of the group, it has that potential to signify something. Animals are the concrete prey available to thought for grasping the difficult and unknown, their interrelationship a frame of reference, thought-scantlings among towering concepts. The ecology of creatures is the model for the "society" of abstract ideas.

Among totemic peoples, the formal use of animals as clan emblems establishes each member of society on firm ground. The system of behavior into which the member is incorporated prescribes relationships and duties between the members of these groups, and their obligations of a more comprehensive and ecological sort: arrangements of dwellings, dietary laws, dress, seasonal ceremonies, and so on.

That their rules of life are adopted by the emerging adult under the auspices of a plant or animal sign seems, on the face of it, arbitrary and rather pointless. But when we remember that the foundations of personal mental life have been shaped by species taxonomy as a cognitive tool, and that games of animal mimicry were the instrument for conceptualizing human qualities, it seems logical to extend it toward further growth—that is, social maturity.

Belonging to a group having an animal emblem in order to learn social protocol doesn't seem to challenge the imagination very much. But the social contract, even in the most "primitive" society, is constantly being resolved. Life is penetrated by unprecedented situations, society is made up of complex, fallible, inconsistent, and individually unique human beings. Nothing works perfectly or exactly fits protocol. There is error, incompetence, eccentricity, genius, and the array of interpersonal conflict, alliance, loyalty, and change found everywhere in humankind. Because of this, decisions are seldom a matter of simple conformity. Many adjustments, solutions, and responses to complex individual and group circumstances are unique. The arrival of outsiders with novel behavior, complicated legal questions, disasters, contradictions in the customs, inconsistencies in myth or theory all add to the need for careful, sometimes abstract, logical insight, creative imagination, and wisdom. Not all are life-or-death matters, but for small-group societies such decisions seem important, even though any number of solutions may be actually possible.

What has all this to do with totemic commitment? Everybody in a clan society is affiliated with such a group. The relationship between clans is defined by selected details of the relationship between their totemic animals according to a myth; that is, a rhetorical story about the totem animals in the beginning of time. If not the myths, then observations of the creatures themselves give clues, to be poetically translated from ecological relations to their social analogies, to all the problems or circumstances of the interrelationships of those humans who are pledged by their clan identity to the mythic structure.

As every child has learned, each creature not only has a predominant character, but the whole of his behavior is in harmony with other animals. The animal totems of the two members of a dispute, for example, are not appealed to as sources of power but as related to each other either through myth or biology so as to evoke ideas and parallel logic for resolving the conflict. The logic is a kind of thought-wedge. The clues may range from details in myth to study of the animals' entrails, fur, or parasites, even to its most subtle responses to the environment and interactions with others. Modern urban people cannot appreciate the subtlety of such study because they so seldom watch or examine animals and are generally ignorant of the remarkable complexity and delicacy of nonhuman life. The crucial point of this sign-reading is that there is seldom a literal interpretation. Eating, fleeing, rising-earlier-than, living underground, migrating, or howling do not imply those behaviors among people to the totemic watcher, but are merely indicators.

To the pragmatism of the juvenile mind the fox is a virtual embodiment of cunning, as though it were condensed by God in order to furnish man with an image of that particular bent. The logic of the adult, however, is to trace outward from that spirit in all of its ramifications and contradictions. The task of the adolescent is to apprehend the metaphoric parallel. He is between the taxonomy of childhood and the wisdom of the tribal elder.

For the child (to age five), recognition of the fox as distinct from the wolf; for the juvenile (to age twelve), the abstraction of foxiness into the social realm; and for the adolescent, the perception of fox-wolf relations as analogies to human situations, a means to discover connections, causal relations, interdependencies, change and transformation, uses and influences: a paradigm for making social decisions. It is as though Nature had thought of the ecological food chain, fox-rabbit-clover, as a stimulus for man to think through the relationships in a kin group, and in so doing to realize the possibilities for social action and cultural forms.

According to the prophet of this vision of totemic thought, Claude Lévi-Strauss, Nature for the mature human mind is a system of connected ideas, a language, represented by the species and their attributes. It relates the abstract to the concrete by using real creatures as sign-images bearing messages and ideas. It starts with a straightforward classification and progresses to symbolic classification, begins in observation of natural history and derives a way of thinking and explaining human social interactions. It does not copy nature; adults do not imitate animals. It is a homology between parallel series—species and human societies—in which the latter is rationalized by references to Nature, a medium translated by myth, using epic tales, music, and the other arts.

Adornment and Animality

To speak of myth is to risk losing the modern reader who has no special interest in the past. But it is used here to mean virtually any traditional story about the past that a society finds instructive. It belongs not only to tribal peoples without written records, but to modern peoples as well, a mode of condensing wisdom in a tale. That stories about animals would be taken seriously by adults seems primitive, but, even though we do not live in totemic cultures, we are deeply committed to the animal tale and motif. It is inseparable from the generic mode of thought and imagination that Lévi-Strauss has called "the savage mind," meaning this aspect of all human intuition and reason.

Art may have begun and continues to serve as the means by which the gap between the natural order and the human order is bridged. It made sign-images from animals, exploring human social differences by scrutinizing sets of relationships among animals. Objects and acts linking the two are necessary. Such, for example, is the animal headdress worn by the priest or shaman in ritual conjoining of human and nonhuman.

His role is still seen around the world among preliterate people and among literate civilizations in various modified forms. All such theatricals involve the observer with the performer in a momentary identity, a kind of predication. It is exhibitionistic. It reveals the self—human motives, the irony of our inner contradictions, or some secret we have kept from ourselves. When an eighteenth-century New England cult received the divine message to do as they pleased, they threw off their clothes and ran about giving animal calls. As an alternative to putting on masks or animal skins, throwing off one's clothes is said to be a way of revealing not what we suppose to be our humanity, but what underlies it.

"This is not something we can do easily," says Leszek Kolakowski, speaking of the striptease, "and yet it appears to us as our 'own truth'; behind it lurks the individual's experience as a masked animal who cannot get rid of the feeling of discontent imposed by civilized dress. The exhibitionist projection springs from the wish to destroy the strict taboo which forbids us to reveal our true identity as animals to ourselves. . . . This assumes that we 'must' return, so to speak, to the animal world—at least a certain part of us; at the same time it also presupposes that this animality is a secret, and civilization's ascetic discipline serves to prevent our giving away the secret."

Human nudity, he says, is our "shameful secret." Therefore spectator nudity is a sadistic form of our search for truth. As civilized beings we are both clothed and curious about our alien naturalness. Both are part of our identity. We are ambivalent. This double impetus, says Kolakowski, causes our oscillation between projection and alienation, between the realities of animality and civilization.

Kolakowski might have gone one step further in his searching study of this equivocation as the source of the desire to see the striptease. That we are a naked ape is only shameful within a limited religious tradition. Our undress also reminds us of the symbolism of dress. The reciprocal to consciousness of natural nakedness is awareness of deliberate costuming. We are invited to examine the meaning of our bodies, therefore the language of our clothing, and by implication, the language of all plumage and pelage. Clothes are not only a cover for embarrassment. Conceptually, we do not differentiate between the nakedness of birds beneath their feathers and our own. A pile of plucked songbirds is nearly as hard to sort and identify as a roomful of naked people. In traditional societies, even in Europe until recently, dress indicated gender, status, and role. The striptease watcher may be troubled subconsciously by modern dress in which personal taste replaces social codes. Dress more than before conveys idiosyncratic information, making every man his own species. Perhaps this frustrating deterioration of plumage patterning makes the alienated modern man seek underneath the clothing for messages that he previously got from it. In a society where clothes drive us apart, naked bodies confirm our relationship to one another. Anyone who has seen baby birds in the nest knows that they, not their parents, are naked. In a sense, man is the only naked animal. The secret revealed by the striptease may not be that we are animals, but that we are all human, contradicting the class differences premised on the idea that "at heart" we are not alike, or overcoming the confusion produced by current eccentric individuality in dress.

What is the relationship between the ritual animal mask, by which we disguise our humanity, and clothing, which according to Kolakowski, is the means of hiding our animality? The animality revealed by nudity is one that transcends human individuality and returns the individual to the species skin, the badge of the naked ape. When we shed our clothes we abandon the artificial skin that identifies our class or publicizes our fantasies.

The animal masks, however, do not deal with a general animality, as our nudity does, but with an aspect of being human that is obscured by fine clothes and reconfirms at a deeper level the diversity of individuality.

Some evidence for this is found in early Greek drama, in which a chorus wearing animal disguises delivered an ode to the audience during an intermission. According to a student of this subject, G. M. Sifakis, "In the whole prehistory of drama there is perhaps no other point of more general agreement than the importance of the theriomorphic choruses (i.e., choruses of men dressed as animals or riding animals), represented on Attic vases of the sixth and early fifth century, as evidence for the origins of comedy."

These Greek choruses of men with animal disguises are a kind of halfway point between myths of animal ancestors and the modern, "purely" human drama. Those plays were not original or realistic, but rhetorical and redundant, the stories old, plots legendary, characters types rather than individuals. In these things they were typical of all folktales.

But the animal-chorus interlude in the play, or parabasis, was not intertwined with the story. The chorus was an intermediary, reminding the audience that it was seeing the action, for it addressed the audience directly, discussing the action as fellow observers. The audience accepted the performance as a kind of game in which it participated, says Sifakis, and the chorus was alternately part of the audience and members of the cast, inviting the audience to reflect on its own ambivalent status, preventing them from lapsing into the child-like, passive role of spellbound listener, and forcing them to step back from that involvement and discuss the action. Indeed, the choral ode to the audience was not only on the play before them, but on public affairs that were touched by the story. Sometimes, instead of addressing the audience, the birds and frogs in Aristophanes' plays addressed the gods.

Only in the role of participants in the play were the masks worn; when speaking aside, the chorus dropped their masks or outer costumes. The changing of viewpoints (technically "empirrhematic syzygy") that the audience was being coaxed to do in their thought was embodied by the chorus. It was as though the actors said, "Put off your animal immersion in the action, the mask of your unreflecting being; beneath it is a detached self which is human; the action is creature, but its consideration is your human privilege." Or perhaps, "Draw back a moment from that Dionysian ecstasy and see how in our social drama we differ, like species—like sirens, centaurs, satyrs, maenads, and amazons."

These choruses of transitional beings had entered comedy from older traditions of street-begging. The beggars wore animal masks and often formed processions, each begging "in the name of" his creature. Animal masks were common, too, in festival masquerades and in solo mimetic animal dances. Our Valentine's Day is derived from All (April) Fools' Day when, each spring, the animals speak and choose mates. The Valentine sweetheart syndrome is a recent, sentimental expression of traditional rites linking man and animal mating, an ancient representation of human difference and the diversity of individual experience by different species. It is apparent from these fragments of the past that parallel realities, a far older idea, are enduring elements of human consciousness. In every society an increasingly more detached and self-conscious attitude is possible where intermediary or ambiguous forms widen the space between the spectator and the drama and between elements of the spectator's own selfhood, but in their own wholeness help protect the observer from schizophrenia, or splitting.

In the battle scenes of Aristophanes, in Archippos' *Fishes* and Krates's *Beasts*, the chorus not only steps out of its animal masks, but speaks about itself, its disguises, nature, and deeds. In some plays a character stands in special relation to the chorus or members of it. This suggests a relationship between men and other species of a different kind, relating man to animals, making two series one, incorporation of the natural system by the social, a philosophy of hierarchic continuity suggesting domestic culture rather than one of the juxtaposition of human and nonhuman as societies with special parallels, as in totemic culture.

The putting on and off of animal masks to signify the polymorphism of human reality and experience raises questions about costume and the origin of clothing. The idea that "clothes make the man" has possibilities that go beyond the emblems of social class. Mael, the myopic missionary monk in Anatole France's *Penguin Island,* discovered an island of little beings whom he mistook for people and baptized, thereby entraining them in Christian orthodoxy. Ordered to make the best of his error, he insisted that they cover their nakedness, of which they had been previously unaware. Once clothed, the penguins, who had never before given much heed to each other's bodies, became intensely curious about what was underneath. The females, observed by enraptured males, moved with a new undulating gait, so that the wearing of clothes virtually created a preoccupation with sex.*

If clothes preceded voyeurism, why did men originally put on clothes? Anthropologists have from time to time suggested that clothing was practical—a way of keeping warm or of transporting a skin as a reserve food supply or signifying power. It seems also that clothing is a special case of the universal phenomenon of body adornment. The vast preponderance of materials used this way are actually parts of plants and animals or imitations of their designs, as in tattooing. Although it is playful and personal as all art, adornment signifies belonging or group identity.

The conspicuous traits by which people are defined—age, sex, rank—are not enough. The human psyche demands finer partitions, more to work with. Commitment, status, and identity are given by the total structure of personal appearance. Mutilations, masks, hair styles, and jewelry complement or exaggerate such things as sexual dimorphism, physical signs of age, and other intrinsic marks of membership. Clothing is the principal cultural correlate of physical differentiation. Since it is made (or was, until recently) from plant and animal materials, it has a built-in connection to the differences between species.

The exact content of the language of dress in any traditional society is hidden from outsiders. Strangers find the nuances of local dress amusing or irritating gibberish, as they do the spoken dialects. Within the group, of course, dress is significant in the smallest detail. When she studied the Swazi of southeast Africa, anthropologist Hilda Kuper found that, like most peoples, the men and women normally dressed differently. The men wore skins from wild animals, the women from domestic animals that had been killed in sacrifices to the ancestors. Clothing from combinations of wild and tame had special significance in a gradation of political power. Just as there are everyday languages and special languages for ceremony, so do costumes differ. Like sacred rhetoric, "Sunday" dress is felt to say something formally. In an annual ritual of Swazi kingship, the skins and feathers of different animal species are worn by men of different ranks,

* Why was France's satire told with penguins instead of people? He could rely on the totemic perspective of the reader, who would comprehend his criticism of Christians as troops of uncritical, mindless, nincompoop followers. Why go into lengthy description when the penguin conveys that artless mentality in a word?

again with subtle combinations. The wild forms are felt to be vital, beautiful, and sometimes destructive. A few are ritually central and represent the main conventions and ideas. But other species are peripheral or intermediate. They serve as probes and connectors in which the flux of cosmic powers is made concrete.

Costume, covering special parts of the body with prescribed furs, feathers, hides, signifies for the Swazi both the order of the universe and the social order. It is the visible link. The basic categorical themes are male/female and royal/nonroyal, with many degrees and qualifications, particularly in headgear. It is the idea made visible and embodied by men in the Swazi ritual dances. Keyed to the appropriate patterns and colors and seasonal plumage, the animal parts are much more than static emblems. The subtlety of intellectual and philosophical thought is therefore keyed to a great knowledge of animal lore and attention to finer differences, not only between species but within them. Some animals are especially important as transitional, such as the otter and the ox. They too are represented, mediating between the king's social and religious functions. They are worn in combinations by him who transcends civil rules and contradictions but who is yet controlled by the people. Every detail, says Kuper, is part of the "messages relayed through animals used in costume."

The perceptual surprise of entering the skins of an animal (or, for that matter, the fibers of a plant) is central everywhere to society. In dressing in skins one goes into the animal. It is just the opposite of the idea that the eaten animal enters the self. These transfigurations—to be entered by the animal, to enter the animal—are reciprocal ways of discovering and affirming a relationship to that animal, shared by a group who mutually and simultaneously share the rituals of dressing and eating.

This dance of transformations is a part of lifelong identity resolution. The wearing of alternate skins, the fragments of animals that are not eaten, was the inception of clothing wearing, and it continues to express an outward and public language of social quality space or identity. The small child's love of costume and the preadolescent's preoccupation with peer conformity of dress are also indicative. The antinomian movement in the United States and Europe in the 1960s, the hippie movement, symptomized identity crisis in a sociey lacking serious adolescent initiation rites and the guiding role of a mature cultus. It was a crisis of the meaning of categories: youth, sex, race, class, work, and ideology. But there is no escaping the demands of membership by the adolescent psyche. Beads, hair length, and blue jeans signified a fraternity, however provisional, which in turn opened into an exploration of clothing. The games of fantastic clothing ranged from togas and Elizabethan jackets through frontier skins, Victorian peasant gowns, and Oriental shirts. It was an era, quipped one observer, when clothing became costume and costumes became clothing. That is, the conventional gray-flannel body mask was itself challenged and reduced to frivolous adornment. The antinomians objected to the rigidified roles represented by clothing. Having rejected those roles, they proceeded to search for roles by trying on costumes. Only in a class society where the animal and plant tissues used to cover parts of the human body referred to groups without roots in natural models of reality could this have happened.

The hippie's reversion to childhood fun by dressing up in other people's clothes loosened up styles in general for a time, but had no lasting effects. Later the "flower children" either reverted to the conventions of general society or adopted the costumes of their group as a new convention—long hair, milkmaid gowns, and blue-collar work clothes. At thirty the latter are still so clothed, putting on the badges of their revolt when they rise from bed in the morning.

That modern clothing is a substitute for animal skins is only partly true. In a sense nothing has been substituted. If we do not go into the skins of cows or into the fibers of cotton, we enter filaments of "synthetics" from petroleum or coal. What could more clearly identify the fossilfuelman than his duds made from the exhumation and exploitation of plants and animals long dead? Even when we have gone to the other extreme from hunting "for to get a rabbit skin to wrap my baby bunting in" and are making our garments from molecular carbon taken from the air, we will not have escaped the ritual of costume: the expropriation of nonhuman, concrete reality as a second skin used in its various forms to signify social clumps.

It is appropriate that laboratory foods and clothes appear together. If "clothes make the man" and "you are what you eat," then identity, like nutrition, will be grasped (with difficulty) not from animal species perceived as a model for society, but from molecules behaving that way. The myths of such an era will not be about legendary hunters but about Nobel prize-winners in chemistry or czars of the petrochemical industry. As a metaphor of the well-ordered world of compounds, such a society will be a more lonely world, our alienation from both plants and animals signified by the absence of a living mesocosm. The molecules, as such, are invisible and inaudible.

When the Greek chorus removes some of its garments and directs its ode to the audience, something like the skinning of a game animal has taken place. The play is itself an organic whole; it has a structure and a life span. When a great game animal lies dead, the hunters gather around, knowing that its interior is a variation on a theme and its organs will tell a story and must be examined and pondered. The play is a haruspex, the game a visceral book. Taking off their masks is the transformation of participant, which all playgoers feel. When the chorus steps out of the action on stage, it says in effect, "The animal is open. It is time to observe."

The chorus has been replaced in the modern world by the critic. The critic is a dissector, an anatomist (not to say, butcher). Critics like to attend "openings." When Joseph Wood Krutch and Brooks Atkinson, two widely known critics from New York, retired, they went west and began writing about nature. An academic friend once remarked to me that he couldn't understand how Krutch could "strip himself" so. At the time I thought the remark merely intellectual hubris, but I now see that he had missed the point. Neither gave up openings. Atkinson later wrote a "review" of the Grand Canyon called "The World's Greatest Opening." Unfortunately, their protectionist bias drove a wedge between bird-watching and bird-butchering, a dichotomy that is one of the great failings of modern life. Neither Atkinson nor Krutch was able to appreciate the body cavity of animals as a dramatic opening, which would have greatly enhanced their enjoyment of nature. Krutch, of course, would whirl in his grave at such an idea, for he was much opposed to hunting.

Dramatic performance is the essence of all games: the play of children imitating animals according to the rules of characteristic behavior, and the play of adults that refers to hidden structures, its revelation represented by unmasking. Good make-believe is never escapist. Instead it frees us to be alternatively participant and spectator, to learn something about the structure of "the game" that we did not know, and it enables us to reflect on our identity, personal and social.

Until man began skinning animals it probably did not occur to him that we "wear" our own skins. What he found inside of different creatures was surprisingly similar, yet, as variations on themes beneath that similarity lay new regions of inner difference. The deeper systems of differences in beings superficially alike are therefore represented by the masks, or among animals by the markings on their feathers and fur.

Intimations of this conception were seen by ancient man in the play of the wild game, the dramatic life of animals. But its significance cannot be grasped by the individual all at once. Childhood is a training ground, a first step in which gaming the play means tracking the different animals' images into consciousness. Thus does it become possible, in the discovery of the parallels in unlike things at puberty, to compose society as subgroups with animal images and to probe the mysteries of human character with that instrument.

Animals embody every quality found in the human personality. In the whole range of human temperament and character there is nothing unique, nothing not found as some aspect of another species. It is the only other place they are found. What men do that may be unique or is at least unusual is to know this. Man is capable, to a limited degree and with great effort, of stepping out of the stream of events for a moment, even of his skin, and looking at the whole fauna and flora as a composite of his own possibilities.

By "possibilities" is not meant another bouquet to humanistic autonomy or another claim that all things are possible and that man can be whatever he chooses. "Possibilities" is a reference to the total context of living phenomena within which the human species has its own forms and limitations. This is why recognition of limitations is the essential step in achieving the freedom implicit in intelligence; it increasingly identifies one's kind of being to one's self. It goes beyond this defining and narrowing of our species sense to a widening within that frame. The same faunal realm within which humanity is but one point among many provides a patterned model for discovering and allocating the positions and quality spaces within society.

In human societies not committed to the maximizing of harvest, mainly the living groups of hunter/gatherer peoples, the use of this species model for perceiving society is explicit: In most such societies everyone is initiated into a clan membership with a natural totem. This relationship to other members of their clan and those in other clans is predicated on the ecological and mythological fabric relating the totemic animals and plants to each other.

Such societies are committed to a painstaking accumulation of information about those particular species and the web of natural connections that interconnect them and illuminate their interaction with the landscape, seasons, skies, and time. The ideas of relations that these suggest are good to think, allowing as they do for difference but overcoming discontinuity. Among themselves each kind of wild creature has a lineage, behavior, and social life, a cryptogram of order within the clan group, and ecological connections that can be translated as social.

In his cryptic style, Lévi-Strauss says this "culturizes a false nature truly," meaning that the different species are held ficti- tiously to behave as though they were members of a social group with its own domestic relations, marriages, and language. Thus bears "talk" to salmon in a myth, dramatizing an episode in the history of the world and establishing certain prototypical human rules of behavior. But there is nothing false about the keen scouting of these animals that forever turns up clues which appear in the stories or can be used in contemplation of their significance.

Insofar as there are indeed interactions between bears and salmon that are mythologized as something communicated or spoken, those ecological relationships are largely in terms of one eating the other. Systems of creatures eating and being eaten, food chains or food webs are therefore the prototypes of com- munication. It is not surprising that among preagricultural peo- ples the giving of food is itself part of the language between kin, clan, and tribal groups, a practice standardized or formalized symbolically in ceremonial ways.

Thus there is a flow of food-giving and -receiving that remains central to all human life everywhere, structured primarily after the model of the flow of energy in the easily visible part of the ecosystem, usually as avian or mammalian predator/prey sys- tems.

Anthropologists have long observed that man is the only primate who shares food. (The other food-sharers are all carnivores, or share only the meat part of an omnivorous diet. It seems likely that man began to share food as he began to hunt.) Since the flow of meat is along explicit lines, it is an assertion about relationships. In such systems the meat is not so much a gift as a due. The obligation is in both the giver and the receiver who is obliged to accept. There is no storing up of debits, no gratitude in the usual sense, though there is clearly a keen satisfaction and a recognition of the hunter's skill and reliability.

In this way wild game provides the vocabulary of a language by which intergroup and kinship relationships are expressed. These bonds are acknowledged in other ways, too, but meat-giving may be the oldest, the primordial form of sharing par excellence.

Food-sharing in early man was a major step toward role-making within the group. By enabling them to live without hunting, it meant the survival of the old, who could be living encyclopedias and history books on tribal custom. It allowed for the care of pregnant females and therefore the specialization of sexual roles in the food quest; the female gathering, the male hunting. It allowed for extended dependence of the immature, a pivot on which the whole cycle of specialized learning periods in infancy, childhood, and adolescence came to exist. If everyone had to gather his own food, as among all other primates, human society could never have come into existence or continued to work.

Food-sharing is, then, a rich and triumphant discourse, connected ceremonially as well as informally with each category of person—age, sex, gender, and role—and with the rites of passage in which the individual moves in and out of such groups.

Thus do certain selected wild creatures come to symbolize the categories and gradations in human groups. Wearing their skins, carving their bones, and above all celebrating by feasting or fasting—all are expressions of the language of an imaginary animal society, based poetically on real animal behavior. The system of creatures, or ecology, is a cosmic touchstone by which a people confirm their own destiny, cement mutual relations, identify roles, and make decisions.

The Lele, a Contemporary Totemic Culture

Such a system of animals that are right for thinking, in groups not committed to accumulating material objects, is seen in the Lele of Africa. For them the forest is the source and foundation. They are far more intensely communal than agricultural and urban peoples. The structure of their society is a relatively delicate web of obligations, the existence of which is premised on nonintervention from the outside.

Among the Lele, hunting is the most prestigious activity, though it is minor in terms of total caloric needs. But hunting puts the people intimately in touch with the forest. The pangolin, that ambiguous scaled mammal who is their supreme symbolic totem, manifests the meaning of life. It has the scales of a fish, four legs, climbs trees, and bears a single young. It neither attacks nor flees when approached. Its ambiguity is hypostatized in its duality, for the pangolin is unified in spite of its contradictions. The human dualities of inside and outside, ideal and real, male and female, nature and culture are transcended by the rituals of the pangolin, just as the pangolin transcends its own diversity.

The Lele are committed intellectually to the continuing exploration of these oppositions of the private and collective nature of man, and they see the endless separation and division of social structure, kinship, sex, and personality as in need of such wholeness. The polarity reflected in the village and the forest— everywhere among them, says anthropologist Roy Willis, has the "double imprint of disjunction and unity."

Oneness achieved through complex integration—that is the central ideal of which the forest itself is the ultimate model. Animal classification is a diligent vocation, the concrete example and instrument of analyzing an orderly world. There is a wild equivalent to the collective structure of society, whose cognitive boundaries are formed by category discriminations. The Lele find a lack of clear typing and consistency in domestic animals, for which they are held in low esteem as anomalous.

The centrality of the wild forest is supreme. Mythological, spiritual, and ceremonial life involves prolonged initiation, subordination of the material aspects of the economy, extended bachelorhood, midlife polygyny, gerontocracy, and small-scale political life. The Lele disdain the outside world on account of its individualism, trade, and material uses of the land that destroy the fragile existence of a social homology to the delicate ecological equilibrium of the climax forest.

The secrets of that forest are comparable to the secret innerness of communal feeling, so the forest is a kind of ground of being. The diversity of this world is regarded as superficial. Before the hunt, says Willis, there is a ritual confession of negative thoughts and feelings, hence they "know the secrets of their own hearts" of which forest spirits are the images.

Healing power brings them into contact with a higher state of being rather than increasing the power of the patient or seeking sorcery to counteract the sickness. The Lele avoid outside influences and have developed no cultural resistance or ideological protection from intrusion. By controlling a very few elements of Lele society, missionaries and traders quickly bring about the collapse of this system. The Lele's regulation of the young females is crucial, as formal dietary prohibitions are central to the linkage of animal and human realms.

A full understanding of the differences between the Lele and other hunting/gathering peoples must await examination of the effects of animal domestication on human thought. But their life is devoted to a subtle and extremely difficult intellectual challenge that begins with analogy between the lavish diversity of natural history and the structure of human personality and behavior, and proceeds to formulate society on the model of one of the most complex ecosystems on earth, the tropical forest. Nor does Lele philosophical ambition end with analogy of the infinitely complex natural and cultural system, but proceeds to fashion a unity centered in the forest that affirms man as a relatively humble component of the whole.

To speak of the Lele and their creation of a society modeled on the elegant structure of the great forest as vulnerable and fragile may be misleading. Its destruction in the face of missionaries, traders, political aggression, and economic subversion does not mean that it is inferior or obsolescent. History is a continuing record of superior human creations doomed by organized invasion and by exclusive monomaniacal ideologies. One could choose additional examples from around the world. However different such totemic cultures appear to ethnologists, they have a common characteristic that separates them clearly from the maximizing economies. They share a deep commitment to the native wild fauna and the hunt. That commitment is qualitative, not quantitative, as the bulk of their food is obtained by gathering or by horticultural gardening. It is typical of such peoples that the vegetative foods are hoarded—that is, gathered into the household and used there. Wild meat, on the other hand, is distributed according to a social protocol, the language of their social relationships.

The marriage rules of the Lele and other hunters are exogamous; they require that a woman marry out of her clan or residential membership. This has led Lévi-Strauss to speak of exogamy as a communication. Since both women and meat constitute connectedness and continuity between groups, they tend to have symbolic reciprocity. Thus do genes flowing through marriage, the special nutrient qualities of protein flowing through food gift, and common language demarcate and integrate the larger tribal units and subunits.

The consequences of marriage are lines of descent or kinship that are routinely affirmed by meat distribution. Wild animals are both the emblems of the clans and the sources of the meat. They are, then, for such peoples, the ultimate points of reference and identity, the background like a known constellation of stars (which are also named to represent fauna) from which human society emerges.

While there are plant totems, they tend to appear in societies more deeply committed to food storage, accumulation of goods and property, and the money economies and exploitative philosophy that are the subject of the next chapter.

The Game of Dividing and Dividing the Game

Why are animals initially chosen among hunter-gatherers for supreme symbolic functions? Human thought grows by the assertion of a duality that divides and subdivides everything, and classifies it. This polarizing is relevant to animals because they are both within us and outside. Human rationality (the real and ideal) and all human societies take their shape from this disjunction, with its inherent potential for reunification given by example in nature.

Animals are the key to intellectual comprehension and involvement of the whole being in both nature and culture. The purpose of discovering cognitive opposites is not to resolve and reunify by rejecting, but by precipitating new wholes. Animals are self-acting, while plants are not conspicuously so.

For people, animals are more clearly metonymic (contiguous or next to us in actual relationships or in physical space) and metaphoric (distant in kind but having more parallels to human form and behavior). They are close to man and yet strange to him, so they tease his thought about himself and about the non-human in himself as well as without. Because their lives are full of events and adventures like man's, they have an existential or circumstantial daily existence. At the same time, because different species have characteristic habits, they are normative. They have, one might say, both freedom and commitment.

All of these characteristics tell us why animals are the most appropriate instruments in the development of human thought but not why they are universally chosen, or why, in the modern world, they continue to be the supreme instruments by which the processes of perception and cognition grow in each person.

As for the hunting peoples, who build on this a totemic culture, the essential point is that the myths from which totem emblems are taken are fictions and individual assignments to clan membership follows rules devised by society. Beneath these inventions is the assumption that all people are born human, all of a kind. Tribal myths are tales of creatures interacting as though they too were basically alike. The divisions within the tribe are playlets in which all agree to believe. Such a culture is not the source of the problem raised at the start of this chapter—treating people of different groups as different in kind, or *pseudospecies*. Such is the way that domestic culture twisted totemic thought, where the differences between human groups were not derived from playlets or games of supposing, but were declared to be the nature of things. Instead of clans, people were classified by caste or class because of their work. The work took as its essence secret techniques to be protected at all costs from outsiders, like the bean seeds that subsistence farmers keep among their own village so that the superior strain won't be lost to their competitors. Such inbred societies consider group differences, like seed differences, or the differences between shoemaking and the priesthood, to be inherent. Dissipation or exchange of their secrets produces only a wasteful hybridity. The cruelty of classifying people is not in the recognition of difference, but in the model of exclusiveness, competition, and isolation to which the domestic world committed it.

The example of the Lele as a totemic culture people would, a few decades ago, have been regarded essentially as a piece of exotica, a curio of primitive behavior perhaps common to savages but good only for cocktail chatter among ourselves. That misconception is rapidly coming to an end.

For a great many reasons it has become evident in recent decades that the great myth of industrial man is that he can take his destiny in his own hands, and this myth finds its concrete confirmation in the things he builds. The heroes are the engineers and their political counterparts. What is now happening to that myth is not so much its demise as a renovation of its rules. The constraints within which it operates are changing.

The change is centered primarily on the discovery of how conservative our species really is, not only physically, but behaviorally and intellectually. We have not changed much, even in hundreds of millennia. Written history has made mankind conscious of the waxing and waning of economic and political systems, the wars and ideologies of states and nations. The social sciences endlessly explore the diversity and disjunction of cultures. The posture of detachment of history and analysis is itself an expression of relativism and rootlessness. But there are some signs of self-correction. Influenced by a recovery of biological perspective, there is a stronger sense of humanity as a species. In the past, what was common to all mankind was scorned as "mere," as in merely vegetative functions or merely physical characteristics, assumed to be more a burden than a heritage of value. What recently seems to be a kind of radicalism, as represented in the books by Desmond Morris, Robert Ardrey, Edward O. Wilson, Robin Fox, Clifford Geertz, and Konrad Lorenz, is only radical in its departure from a fragmentizing, alienating hubris that has dominated much of civilized philosophy and underlies its hierarchic rigidity and maximizing goals.

The new view is not radical, but conservative because it returns us to those aspects of being human that the ideology of industrial states, consumerism, and wealth accumulation cannot alter, but merely, as industrial cultures, give diverse or pathological expression to rather than viable reality. It links us not only to the horizontal present but to mankind of the past, reaching far back beyond recorded history. In connecting us to our origins it does not espouse a regression, but recovers our sense and joy of those archaic elements in us. "The savage mind," says Lévi-Strauss, is not the relic of some half-formed, half-human state. It is that most essential part of *our* minds. Because it is concerned with plants and animals and their transformation by art as primary acts of human thought, we have treated it as we have all wild things—made a museum of it, conserved it in sample enclaves. So we have viewed people like the Lele, in whom that essential connection between mind and nature is undistorted by domestic thought, as vestiges, and we have put them on reservations. We no longer recognize the organic role of that connection. Institutionalized, its fauna has been relegated to the galleries of our unconscious or to the frivolities of aesthetic zoo-keeping.

In the same way that poetry has become eccentric and isolated, housed between book covers, animals are kept in cages or parks that prevent them from interacting or their substances from flowing into human tissue. Art has been torn from its ceremonial formalities in the same way that animals are carried out of their habitats. There is no hunting in the national parks, no dancing in Lascaux, no dismemberment of mammals in the National Gallery, and no prayers in the Museum of Natural History.

Still, women do not marry their brothers, children eagerly search out animals, the creature/figure flourishes in popular culture and folk societies, game is killed and eaten, and games are played. The animal at the center of our being abides.

5 | PRETENDING THAT ANIMALS ARE PEOPLE: THE CHARACTER OF CASTE

G. B. Harrison, a Shakespearean scholar, once said, "A good department of English should include a diversity of creatures, like a good zoo, which is incomplete without its lion, giraffe, hippopotamus, and giant sloth, not omitting the indigenous fauna such as the viper and the skunk, who usually are also unbidden species in the collection. Personality is far more important for a teacher than an assortment of degrees and diplomas."

When we think of the teachers we have known, we immediately recognize their places in such a bestiary. Indeed, we can find such types everywhere in society. Classifying personality traits as types of animals is to us a familiar form of satire. Such parody is a modern expression of the blending of people and animals that has haunted the search for human identity since the first sheep, goats, and dogs came to live with man. Domestication added a new twist to the ancient puzzle that arose with consciousness itself—the relationship of man and animal.

It remains a problem for educated modern minds, for we now live almost totally among domesticated, tamed, and captive animals. In effect, we complicated the significance of animals for ourselves by getting too close to them. We added to the difficulty by lying to ourselves about the mentality of primitive peoples, in whom the elegant poetics of animals is still viable. As long as we were blind to the intelligence of tribal people, we were unable to see how the keeping of animals had affected us, how domestication profoundly redirected human reason.

The nineteenth-century view was that primitives, like children and other illiterates, were unable to make clear distinctions between humans and animals. Their intense interest in animals

148

was seen as itself animal. We assumed that they imitated, worshiped, and made sacrifices to beasts in an emotional, instinctive, and unreflecting manner ruled by their passions and reflexes, with only the vaguest conception of the self or society.

But our new image of pre-industrial people raises some questions that have not yet been faced. If savages are intellectual, rational, complex, and subtle in their logic, sensitive to the nuances among animals and men, confronting the question of relatedness with equal or better resources than ourselves, it follows that a mature philosophy is as likely to come from Australian aborigines or the Paleolithic cave art of France as from the classical Greeks. Cultural totemism, for example, makes sophisticated distinctions between human and animal realms, enhanced by a balance of respect for the human and the Other. Nature is seen as an endless drama signifying what needs to be known, and the scrutiny of the order of nature is a perennial exercise in logic. Totemic culture assumes the separateness of animals, not their participation in the household, in their confinement, herding, or treatment as fellows. Once that boundary of separateness is crossed the whole system of man/animal relationships is transformed. Instead of living independent but mysteriously compelling lives, the chosen species are fitted into the social web; they become companions or subhuman property, though they may still be admired and watched with keen interest.

The domestic animal is wrapped in emotional bonds, social roles (the tokenship of wealth and status), and enmeshed in a legal framework. Now as a *member* of human society, the animal can no longer represent the outside or be the totemic emblem of clan membership. Human society has shifted its model for identity and social differentiation away from natural species and toward vocation and the products of labor.

Animal captives and slaves are both members and property, beings and objects. As incompetent humans, they rank low in the social system. Sometimes loved and protected, at other times abused, they are essentially wards with amusing, boring, or profitable aspects. The transfer from a wild fauna, a parallel reality, to one of symbiotic relationships with people, locked into the kindred rituals and economic values, profoundly alters the animals and their keepers.

This shift reverberates throughout human thought. It is as though animal imagery, like a herd of Arctic caribou, had migrated to a different place in the human mind. The purpose of natural creation seems to change. Instead of being part of an infinitely subtle and complex net of ecological relations and behaviors, the nonhuman life is shorn of extraneous connections, becomes a possession to be ranked in the economics of accumulation and exchange, wealth and power. The leap from hunting/gathering, or cynegetic life to freeway fossilfuelman and his bestiary of professors is a long one. Intermediate cultures exist, herdsmen and villagers for whom the wild is not far from home. Many Third World people live in mixed heritages in which remnants of an ancestral totemic culture are meshed with a class structure, just as their occasional hunting and foraging is fitted into the outlines of agriculture routines.

Examples from the Thais, Nuer, and Balinese

An example of such a people for whom creatures are both "good to eat and good to think" are the Thais. The metaphor of diet and marriage is given physical expression through the manipulation of animals and their locations so that edibility, marriageability, and distance form a series of opposing elements. The order of creation is reflected by room arrangement in dwellings, house position in the village, the bounds of the village proper, the limits of cultivated land, and the fastnesses beyond. The houses, grouped in fenced compounds, are built on stilts. Their rooms are arranged according to the compass as a reflection of "a scale of social distance" and are built at different floor levels. The location of the sleeping rooms is especially prescribed, reflecting the sexual concerns of the society.

Domestic animals are kept below the house, their pens also arranged in a special order. Killing and eating the domestic buffalo and ox correspond to marriage and sex and are carefully ritualized in details that silently and symbolically correspond. The Thai word for "marriage" is *kin daung*, combining words for "eat" and for "female genitalia." Animals with social affinity to man are the domestic animals. Among them the ox is high or positive, being civilized by his castration. The dog, being a scrounging nonworker and scavenger, is low or negative. The wild animals are seen in a parallel but not a constituent relationship to the structure of human society. Monkeys, however, are perceived as degenerate humans, and the most feared and awful are the creatures of the remotest forest and wildest places.

Dietary laws apply across the whole of animal life. Anomalous forms are taboo for eating, such as those members of a class with exceptional properties like the wolf or owl, unaffiliated forms that enter the human enclave like the toad or crow, and those that seem to be at the border of the domestic and wild orders like the house lizard.

To the Thais the world of nature is a reflection of a moral universe, a parallel to the rules out of which the whole of kinship and social distinction arise. At the same time the two worlds overlap, for monkeys and domestic animals belong not only to that analogous natural system, but to the family system, and to the system of foods. Dietary laws are among the first and most obvious that children confront. In their relative position in edibility, the animals become a primer for other relationships.

Another example of a culture intermediate between totemic and domestic is the Nuer, an African people materially and psychologically fixated on cattle. As pastoralists they have invaded and restructured grassland ecosystems using the domestic animal, much as domestication is a restructuring of the totemic aspects of the psyche. The similarity of their lives to other herdsmen around the world is not simply one of externals but a way of understanding, a style of self-realization.

True to totemism, the Nuer retain attention to the nonhuman and even a commitment to a supreme symbolic animal, the ox. But it is a tribal rather than a clan commitment, and other animals are not taken as the emblems of component parts of the tribe. As we have seen, the Lele hunters' pangolin, a scaled mammal, symbolizes the transcendence of that physical incongruity, and thus it represents the communal subordination of individuality and the unity of all things in the forest itself. But the pastoral Nuer are more interested in a masterly selfhood, an inner-directed transcendence. Life is an endless pursuit of grazing advantage by means of individual political acumen.

The Nuer are much concerned with grazing rights, and thus with social maneuvering and strategies of competition. Territorial rights through male initiative is the core of ideological life. Although they are keen observers of all animals, the Nuer are detached about them, seeing the wild as a distant mirror of human society, not as an oracle but a shadow. Their society is a denatured totemic clanship in which that parallel of the animal and man has ceased to be a key to human order and is instead an echo. Cattle are the chosen creatures, and with them, says anthropologist Roy Willis, the Nuer "have the closest possible physical interdependence." There is no detachment about cattle. The Nuer have a vast language of description for cattle. Every person has a spear-name and an ox-name, the latter taken from a characteristic of one of his animals. Hence there is a "double linguistic association of men and oxen," and a Nuer genealogy sounds like the inventory of a kraal, begun by a renowned ancestor who was born as a "twin" to a cow and who started both a new herd and new human lineage. Cattle are the source of most disputes, the wealth for buying brides, the substance used in compensation, and sacrificial objects. All social relationships are defined in terms of cattle, which are a kind of "bovine idiom" and the exemplar of a "bovine esthetic" is at the heart of all beauty. This "cattle-obsessed human society" sees the cow as the connecting link between nature and culture, while the two remain otherwise separate and parallel.

To the Nuer the sun rises and sets on their stock, which are linked to human society economically, emotionally, and intellectually. They are the means of life, the source of song and affection, and in the classification of their color and horns there is a schematic order relating man and nature. Cattle mediate man's integration with the cosmos. The Nuer man is epitomized in the lone herdsman singing of his ox, his girl, and his kinsmen. The rest of nature and of mankind exists apart, in parallel but innocuous realms, physically separated from him by the space necessary to keep hoofed animals.

The Nuer hunt little and have few dietary prohibitions. The world is a set of balanced oppositions between heaven and earth, spirit and creation, man-cattle and wild nature. Conjunction between members of these oppositions is seen as accidental and unusual. Twins have great spiritual significance for this reason. While the human and bovine societies are recognized as dual, their unity is overriding, which is ritualized when a sacrificial ox dies in place of a man. This shift from plurality to unity, and back once more to plurality, is seen in all aspects of Nuer thought as a paradoxical opposition that is everywhere—in the psyche, interpersonally, politically, and cosmologically. Like twins, birds reflect this balance of polarity and duality, or unity in duality, being of both sky and land. The people see themselves as earthbound, their humbleness toward God balanced by their arrogance toward outsiders, for they are fiercely inhospitable.

There is no overriding theory or metaphysic that reconciles this divided cosmos for the Nuer. Duality is embedded not only in physical things but in the annual calendar, the yearly round, which is divided into a wet and dry cycle. The people live in corporate village horticulture in the dry season and pastoral fish camps in the rainy season.

From the communal life of the village they go to the dispersed camps, where political coalitions are formed against neighboring peoples. This rhythm of fission and fusion is anchored in the balanced stability of alternating seasons. Cattle symbolize this changeless rhythm and the divided but balanced world of the Nuer, while wild animals represent intrusion and disruption that disturbs the social order. Roy Willis says, "A repressed historical consciousness confronts the Nuer in the alienated form of social relations with wild beasts." In ceremonials of adjudication, the judge, standing outside the static bisymmetry of the descent groups and their cattle, wears a leopard skin.

Nuer society does not resolve this contrariety between man and nature, or the duality between the individual and society. The herd for them is the cattle equivalent of the human lineage, and the ox is related to the herd as the human individual is to society. The contradictions remain unresolved, symbolized by twinship. At the very most, the single cosmos is characterized by multiplicity.

The Nuer are truculent, aloof, isolationist, and aggressive. Their arrogant superiority is an outgrowth of the fixing of identity in opposition to outsiders. Their symbiotic cattle mirror human society: The wild is opposed to the bovine and the bull to the ox. Human groups are juxtaposed with wild species. The wild is external, accidental, inessential. Wild creatures are emblems of contingent events, unlike cattle, which are at the center of value, identity, and ambition.

In the distinction between bull and ox, the bull represents plurality, divisiveness, and transcience, the ox sociality, unity, and endurance. The herd is like the patrilineal clan, symbolizing identity and continuity of society. The Nuer are totally absorbed in oxness. In it they see the culmination of sets of contrasts having their origin in the primary distinction between wild and domestic. Reality is a vast hierarchy of such symmetrically opposed concepts. The ox at the peak is the transcendent individual.

This brief sketch of an African cattle people is typical in many ways of pastoralists around the world. While duality plays a fundamental role in the development of cognition in all human beings, the duality of wild and domestic does not exist for generic man, the hunter. For pastoralists, as for hunters, animals remain close to the center of existence. But the opposition of wild and domestic is associated with a jarring alteration in world view. Not only does wild nature come to represent the inchoate "outside," but its social equivalent appears—the social outsiders, other peoples, pseudospecies.

An anthropologist at this point would be quick to point out that no two livestock-keeping peoples are alike, but the similarities of such peoples are inescapable. Around the world common elements run through their cultures: an obsession with the goat, cow, horse, sheep, or camel so extreme that every aspect of life mediates or embellishes its image; aggressive hostility to outsiders, the armed family, feuding and raiding in a male-centered hierarchical organization, the substitution of war for hunting, elaborate arts of sacrifice, monomaniacal pride and suspicion. The great document of such attitudes in the tribes of the Near East is Charles Montagu Doughty's *Deserta Arabia*.

The endless jockeying and scheming of Arabian minions, in a land skinned and stripped by livestock, the jostling readiness to kill for one's beliefs reminds us that Western civilization has a heavy heritage of pastoral thought. From the Hun and Scythian horsemen, Mediterranean goat- and ass-keepers, Semitic cattle-breeders, Persian shepherds, and Arabian camel-lovers; from them and other animal-keepers the Western world obtained its premises of a world view.

Pastoralism is any combination of browsing or grazing animals as the economic center of a tribal or national culture. Since its inception among the archaic herdsmen of the upper Tigris Valley ten millennia ago, it has taken many local forms, its people always proud and independent. It came to the Americas in part from the powerful Spanish Mesta, laying waste the grasslands of the New World. From the first goat-tenders to the agri-business-ranchers of Arizona and Texas, it has been enormously destructive, in Asia as well as the West, and to it must be attached the doubtful title of arch-destroyer of soils, grasslands, and forests. Far more than farming, logging, or mining, pastoralism has been responsible for worldwide erosion, the decline of ecological diversity and economic productivity, the greater frequency and magnitude of dust- and sand-storms, drought and flood. The advance of deserts wherever hoofed animals have been herded is a fact of history. The exclusiveness and aggressiveness that are so much a part of stock-keeping are not only social but ecological. The extensive scale of this enterprise has doomed wildness and wilderness wherever it has appeared. Cause and effect are intertwined in this interplay of animal fixation and environmental impoverishment. The basic totemism antecedent to all economies exerts an irresistible pressure to attend to animals, and its binary analytic mode of consciousness persists, producing destructive effects in domestic societies.

Smaller domestic animals seldom become the sole basis of an economy and are usually integrated with plant crops as part of a plural agriculture. Yet even they can be the agency by which a society speaks its unspeakable thoughts. An example is the chicken—more precisely the fighting cock—among the Balinese, who are yet another example of the transition from the totemic.

The cockfight on Bali, says Clifford Geertz, is a "popular obsession of consuming power." The Balinese, who are largely agricultural villagers, see animality as that which is reprehensible in man. Their demons have animal shape. The Balinese in general are not kind to animals. The cockfight is an expiatory act acknowledging the dark side of human powers. Like the "give-away" game shows on American television in which our collective greed is enacted and projected upon participants, the cockfight is an atonement by public games and a mode of indirect agression by surrogates.

But the combat does not extinguish those personal strivings, it only exercises it. The envy, resentment, and competitive feelings are otherwise publicly hidden. Men become fanatic about their birds; they are "cock crazy" and identify individually with them. As a form of "deep play," it is full of irrational elements and the surfacing of otherwise repressed impulses and energies, and at the same time becomes an engrossing spectacle in its own right.

The loser in a cockfight literally tears his bird to pieces and gives it to the owner of the winning bird, who eats it. Not only has the loser lost whatever wager was made, he has lost face.

The cock is substituted for his personality and the fight drama-
tizes a status concern that is unremitting. Risking status in the
form of winning and losing prestige in a cockfight is one way
that an intelligent and mature people indicate their contempt for
the whole idea of status and its mean consequences, yet they can
no more disengage from these concerns than any other people—
or any other primate, for that matter.

Betting by the spectators is along kin-group or allied kin-group
lines, or expresses village loyalty against a bird from a nearby
village, although cocks from very distant places tend to be favor-
ites. The birds represent not only human animality, but different
individuals and different social groups. To wager at all is to
affirm one's loyalties and at the same time to trivialize that which
is irrational and unadmired by turning it into a contest between
animals.

The betting also may express animosity of the moment, the
turbulence of injured pride or resentment. The outcome allegori-
cally humiliates individuals or repairs squabbles by affirming
loyalties in a dramatic and emotional spectacle. Instead of these
emotions being escalated, they are temporarily exhausted and
presented as inconsequential to the self and others, personified
by animals, and so reducing their pressure. No actual status
changes occur through the cockfight. It is largely an aesthetic
experience giving structure to themes in the society, using fighting birds as language by which the element of chance is held as
a backdrop to human affairs.

The examples of the fighting cock in Bali and the symbolic
role of the ox among the Nuer are typical of the special relationships of chosen creatures in the thinking of domestic societies.
Village life is almost everywhere conducive to adulation and
cruelty of these kinds, using animals. The invasion of such cultures by morality and hygiene condemns all such animal contests
and animal connections as dirty and degrading. Keeping pigs,
goats, or fowl in some rooms of the family dwelling, perceiving
in them personality and individuality, their use as slaves or sex
objects, and pitting animals against one another in bloody shows
—all are denounced by educated urban peoples of northwestern
Europe and North America who have simultaneously discovered
germs and cruelty to animals. What all of these animal fixations
seem to have in common, besides their basis in the dark side of
man, however, is their utility as the means by which unacceptable

and potentially destructive human behavior can be spent, and the mode by which the innate intellectual and aesthetic attention to animal forms can be exercised in support of social and cultural institutions.

Animals in the Domesticated Society

These brief descriptions of salient aspects of Nuer, Balinese, and Thai relationships to animals are arbitrary excursions into domesticated as opposed to totemic culture, that is, derivatives of totemic thought which itself is universal in mankind, toward class instead of clan organization. Being Third World, or non-industrial peoples, their totemic momentum is great; they are still involved directly with animals and strongly attached to them. Each trails remnants of totemic culture, as the people still do some hunting and gathering and know wild animals. But each is an example in its own style of the perversion of totemic thought by the annexation of animals directly into the social and political framework. Just as they share with each other this restructuring of nature—shifting it from paradigm to subordination—and its replacement by the products of work as criteria for the subdivisions of society, they also share it with the agricultural philosophy of medieval Europe. And they share it with the modified class systems of the industrial state.

So it is fair to ask here what significance, other than technical or historical, these village societies can have for us. In a sense, Europe and North America left all that behind in the seventeenth century. There is no need to list the manifold ways in which life in our urban, centralized world differs from that of our own rural past or from present Third World societies. Since most of us no longer are engaged daily in the keeping or the hunting of animals and gathering of plants, we think of them mainly in terms of our recreation and amusement, or as the objects of a specialized business.

Yet the differences may not spring from the size and industrialization of our society, or its sense of cultural relativity, for there are tribal peoples who are even more like us than the Nuer, peoples who show that a limited number of changes, having little to do with the physical signs of modernization, can move a totemic tribe rapidly toward an outlook much like our own. The

Fipa of Tanzania are such a people. They are egalitarian farmers living in permanent villages in which the idea of the village is the head of human experience rather than an orderly arrangement of its houses. Nor are they much concerned with the cognitive boundaries formed by names. The Fipa are indifferent to social or natural taxonomy, even proper names.

For these planters of cotton and millet and workers of iron, field rotations and smelting require planning as much as three years ahead, with cooperative working parties anticipating change. Hard work is extolled by the mythology. The village is at the center of an open, expanding universe. Outsiders are expected and accommodated. Although there are hereditary chiefs, political power is provisional. There is little attention to lines of descent, clan, or kinship. The principal ceremonies concern passages of the individual—birth, marriage, and death— rather than initiation, dietary laws, or attention to any except the pragmatic use of animals. Nature is a repository of forces, the control of which is the business of human society.

Men are dominant. The household, like the society, is the outcome of the superiority of the purposive intellect over the feminine qualities signified by the house interior: heart, passion, privacy, loins, growth, and death. Thus the intellect is seen as the dominant member of a duality, arraigned against the manifold nonrational that it overcomes by emergence and change. Speech is the prototype expression of self-activation and rhetoric is valued as an end in itself.

"Any culture that insists on individuals committing themselves to one pole of duality," says Roy Willis, "exposes itself to the risk that some will find the forbidden option too attractive to be foregone." So, in contrast to the polished, public persona so praised by the Fipa is the savage, interior self, the dark enemy, the wild and wilderness, all that seems resistant to the growth of the known and the corporate village. Therefore sorcery and anti-sorcery occur as an expression of an attempt to control dark magic.

In this connection a few wild animals remain important, seeming almost to be vestigial elements in this African equivalent of the Western mentality. The eland, python, and elephant remain the focus of symbolic attention. Elephant-hunting has its rituals; the eland, too, is large and dangerous. The python embodies all the potential of the resources of nature, and the necessity of going forth from the village in order to encounter it, as one must to do business, bringing it back where it is tamed and controlled.

Economically the differences between industrialized peoples and the Fipa are great. Yet our middle class household has its animal subordinates and symbols. In addition to pets themselves —including the neighbor's pets—the various media are like jungle, oceanic, and forest paths into our homes. Zoos in their traditional as well as "wild animal park" form, public and private, are not only the homes of animals, but the sources of publications and manufactured gift-shop figures, fabrics, soft toys and dolls, mechanical animals, and imported carvings. As much as one tenth of the subject matter of serious art involves animal forms and about one fifth of the cartoon strips in daily newspapers are personified animals. Suburban life is a mix of kept animals and wild forms, bird feeders, birdhouses, animal preserves and nature-study areas, school projects, the county fair, the horse ring, the dog and cat show, and dozens of specialized animal protection and admiration organizations. The very abundance of animals and their images in affluent societies taints them with superfluity and prompts critics to observe that here pets grow fat while elsewhere people are malnourished or starve.

If the animal figure is ubiquitous as a kind of commodity, we may in haste condemn it as another of those excesses of wealth. No doubt the cheapening of life and the endless neighborhood tragedies attest to the careless ease with which a commercial culture caters to all desires. Where there is too much of everything, it is perhaps too easy to scorn all abundance and to see the pet industry and animal toy factory as sources of more of the same material subversion.

Once we have noticed this surprising abundance of the animal image in our electronic society, we realize how tenaciously we cling to it and resist the man-made world foreseen as our destiny. Indignation over our pet-keeping excesses may be a faulty judgment of a very small minority. Perhaps our commercial enterprise is not uniquely to blame for the abundance of animal figures. We may have overlooked similar abundance in our recording of the past and are ignorant of this aspect of other times because of the biases of history-keeping.

Projected into the role-and-rank system of the human group, an animal may become a surrogate child, parent, sibling, demigod, slave, coworker, or sexual partner. The necessary modifications of domesticated animals are bred not only for what they produce—milk, meat, fur, power—but for submissiveness and compliance, followership and docility. Since submissiveness is a trait of immaturity in all animals, the placidity sought by the breeder is characteristic of the young: inhibition of aggression and fear, simplicity of needs, flexibility, dependence, adaptability to novelty or to confinement in barren cages and corrals.

In the wild an elaborate sequence of interindividual signaling and response among animals stabilizes and integrates reproduction, establishes bonds and competitive position, adjusts populations according to the resources available, and disperses and distributes the species. These are all inconvenient in captivity; they interfere with the business of adding flesh or wool or eggs. They would disrupt the person-orientation of the pet. The ideal domestic animal is safe around the human family, tranquil though playful in spirit, oriented to follow people, and stripped down in habits of eating, mating, sleeping, and grooming, leaving the most elementary behaviors, suitable for the stripped-down habitat. Such captives should neither eat nor be eaten by each other and must be disengaged from those complex food chains that are the most compelling aspects of life in the wild. Only this physical deprivation makes keeping animals possible. The psychological stripping is less obvious, for we are relatively unaware of our uses of animals for thought and its relationship to the complex patterns of wild animal behaviors.

But the psychological effects are just as real as the practical. From this blunted effect on the kept forms, we have generally drawn the wrong conclusion that "natives" who spend much time watching animals must be simpletons. We cannot find enough mystery in such creatures to arouse curiosity or hold our attention for long. The impoverished relationships among domestic and caged animals cannot evoke that speculative attention which penetrates by parallels to the human condition, unless it is equally barren. On the contrary, the interrelationships among animals are seen as our responsibility. One does not permit one pet to tyrannize another; one protects and rescues the weak and abandoned; and love among the animals is removed from sight according to social mores. Since we do not believe in murder, the animals are prevented from killing one another. Where grooming is important to them, we become groomers of our "friends," who are extensions of our community.

For us the domestic animal is no longer a medium by which contemplation of the nonhuman is the access to the equipoise between unity and diversity, nature and culture, self and Other. These animals no longer test the limits of our acuity or observation and deduction, nor do they seem to suggest the possible ways of being from which our human customs can be seen as mythopoetically justified.

As surrogate humans, domestic animals do provide companionship, especially to urban people who no longer live family lives, and to the suburban middle class who seem to substitute captives and pets for the extended family of an earlier era. Solitude and loneliness in our time is seldom a function of physical isolation, but of the separation of the immediate family from its secondary kin and the old, the absence of community and the significant events and places by which purpose and identity are achieved by the maturing personality. Some psychiatrists see "pet therapy" as at least a meliorating treatment if not a means to recovery.

But people do not seek psychiatric approval to keep pets, which are said to be good for children, teaching them responsibility, respect for the nonhuman, and providing companionship. The stereotype of the boy and his dog is one of those images of nineteenth-century genre and twentieth-century media so commonplace that its premises are never questioned.

The idea that the pet is an ideal companion for lonely people and a lesson in social responsiveness seems to be at odds with what has been said above—that the domesticated animal is a creature so denuded as to mislead about the nature of animals and life in general, lacking integrity and the imponderable difference of the Other, an impoverished being, a pillow with few contours of its own. After all, everyone knows that individual dogs and cats have distinct personalities, and there are surely many people who can attest to the rich and unique characters of all other kinds of domestic animals, as well as tame or captive wild animals. The quirks and kinks, the crotchets and idiosyncrasies, capricious appetites or physical peculiarities are produced by the processes of breeding and selection or capture and captivity. Indeed, captivity increases variation and exaggerates personality. But it is not their distinctive personality so much as their indistinct membership that is in question. The mushy aspect of kept animals is their loss of species form, that firm outline which explicitly associates them with niche and kind, and their species traits with purpose. Wild fauna were mankind's objects of thought for more than a million years, each species an actor in a social drama, each the "individual" protagonist in myth. Individual animals were never personalized. Their species was already the "person." The radical consequence of bringing them into the human family was to discover personality in individuals and traits in breeds. The diversity impaired our sense of the unity within the species. The animal species then seemed separated from one another in the same way that we individually feel isolated from humanity. Put another way, the discovery of human individual personality is an integral part of human consciousness, but it is achieved at the risk of the loss of connectedness to the whole. Wild nature, translated as an independent society by myth and art, had been both reassuring and heuristic, a projection of the boundless possibilities of being human, while yet the stable structure of ecological webs symbolically reassured us that diversity was not disintegrating.

The two modes of animal symbolism—totemic and domestic—are each balanced internally. The clans to which members of totemic cultures are assigned are socially designated. Membership may seem inevitable to the individual, but it is actually a cultural choice. The individual is assigned a social role that corresponds by analogy to species role in nature, which is part of the *given* or ecological nature of things. The clan member is in no way expected to resemble the totem; he is not engaged in worshiping or imitating it, except in some poetic way, and even then the significance of his membership is not mainly concerned with resemblance.

But the domestic use of totemic thought arises from the reversed belief that people *naturally* belong to personality or ideological types which can be foreshadowed and caricatured in the behavior or visages of animals. The type itself is held to be fundamental. The similarity of behavior—such as man and bull —seems to permeate beneath their differences. This incorporates the animals into a single great system defined by human ends and ideas and denies their true otherness. Conversely, social differences among people take on some of the definition of species. In such a system animals become candidates for human social niches—animal lovers, friends, and slaves—and animal liberation is not far behind.

A modern example of totemic culture, or the opposite of the

domesticated culture as represented by George Orwell's *Animal Farm,* is D. H. Lawrence, whose animals embody slippery elements of the human heart. They are entries to states of mind or feelings, many of which lie at the border between the conscious and unconscious mind. Kenneth Inness has observed that Lawrence's sense of male/female duality underlies much of his thought and that animals signify alternatives in a whole series of oppositions that begin with sexuality: self and other, change and stagnation, innocence and corruption, blood knowledge and discursive intellect. True humanity, Lawrence thought, was "being all the animals in turn," being rational and yet open to the indestructible, creative mystery and divine power in which the self is grounded. His reverence for the cosmic order as perceived in the physical world centered on humility toward the other, the otherness that in most moderns is their estranged self, glimpsed only obliquely as in the intimations conveyed in Lawrence's "A Doe at Evening."

> *I looked at her*
> *and felt her watching;*
> *I became a strange being.*

In Lawrence's novels, says Inness, the characters define themselves in part by their relationship with nature. Animals provide moral examples and help characterize persons. There is a kind of Lawrencian bestiary, certain constant representations—lions, unicorns, lambs, foxes, stallions, dragons, rabbits, whales, elephants—and there are tropes in which they occur, repeated metaphorical scenes: the lion leaping at the father of the herd or the carrion eaters on the rotting social corpse. But these eccentric conventions are not like the homilies of Christian preachers or the embellishments of elegant writing. They are part, Inness says, of "a quest for connection with the dragon-wilderness so as to get life straight from the source."

Notice that Lawrence does not use these elemental animalisms as a foil for human values; nor does he beckon toward some primordial lost Paradise. What carries his imagery directly into a totemic philosophy is the revelation by animals of the most complex and elusive aspects of human life. The totemic fiction of a society of nature has its own purposes and values, however much we browse and pick among its details in order to compose myths. Its possibilities are worthy of the greatest genius and of lifelong scrutiny. Even then, nonhuman life will remain in part unknowable, a mystery that extends the meditation on the self. Subjective distance between men and animals is essential to such a vision.

This realization of the diversity within ourselves by means of animal species is the antithesis of using the animal image to type the members of a race, nation, or class and thereby reduce individuals to tokens. The first process is possible because the individuals of a wild species are very much alike. Their similarity is not due to our bias, but due to the working of natural selection, which hones and clarifies species traits at the expense of individuality. Members of a flock of birds or herd of antelopes know each other individually, but such recognition requires only a few subtle clues. Wild animals are genetically more diverse than appearance would indicate. Intelligence, the capacity for learned behavior, synchronizes behavior and thereby compensates for the hidden genetic polymorphism that keeps a species young and adaptable.

The similarity of the members of a species increases the number of species that a habitat can support. The number of species is the result of niches, the niche being a way of life. So, the more nearly identical the members of a species are, the greater the diversity of animals there can be. When we remember that the richness of wild species was one of the stimulants of the earliest human intelligence, we see that we have a stake in diversity. Among domesticated plants and animals the same underlying potential for variation has been broken out of its protective shell of external similarity, as though evolution were calling on all possible forms at once.

Among dogs the personality comes from two sources: that which it inherits from the ancestral wolf, largely directed to other wolves, and from selective breeding for a more generalized responsiveness, a detachable loyalty. We consider the dog a member of our group, and it behaves as a subordinate and imperfect human, often personable and intelligent, but with only fragments of its own habitat, family life, symbiotic ecology, or purposes. There is great attention to breed-making, which signifies our unconscious sense of the poverty of animal surroundings and yearning for diversity, and explains our keenness for breeds and varieties and our tendency to make pseudospecies of cultural groups. A contradiction arises out of the spectacle of animal breeds, one side of which is our aesthetic sense of fitness in keeping the breeds pure, a feeling that things are in their place, while the other side is the knowledge of the weaknesses, frailties, and neuroses that often accompanies inbreeding. We know that curs or mutts are really the hardiest and best all-round companions, with the fewest physical and psychological problems, yet we regard them as lowly mongrels.

Cats do not have the same kind of ancestral communality as dogs. They are in part solitary, especially when hunting. The cat is notorious (or famous) for its independence, for its ability to live a partly wild life. This is not entirely due to the cat's own choice. It is a result of the different ecological texture and spatial requirements in which the small, stalking predator and the large, pursuing predator, such as the dog, live. Our city alleys and yards and rural fields still provide "normal" prey for cats, such as small mammals, birds, lizards. The scale of these man-modified habitats is similar to that of its ancestors, while the equivalent for dogs would be vast open plains roamed by large hoofed animals. Except for hunting and herding, the modern dog has to make do with pseudohunting play with humans or other dogs or chasing cats and cars. Because it goes alone, the cat is a limited human companion and plays a different psychological role in the household. Generally speaking, in spite of its aloof independence, the cat is more pliant and cuddly as an adult than the dog, and seems to have a more subtle sense of finesse and greater tact.

Perhaps for these reasons, along with its tidier pelage, the cat is widely regarded as feminine, as opposed to the dog's masculinity. That these two most common household pets are perceived as paired species reminds us that the assignment of sex to a whole species and the pairing of different species is, according to André Leroi-Gourhan, seen in the arrangement of the animals in the cave art of prehistoric man, an archaic theme in human thought. From full-time pet companions without private lives to captive wild creatures, which are like transplants or tissue cultures, bits of livingness cut from the larger ecosystem, kept animals become pseudopeople who enter the household trailing unraveled ends of a tattered integrity. Their resistance to humanization and supportive roles vary. Their keepers and owners have a variety of psychological needs, matched only by chance or by trial and error with different breeds and species. Someday we may have a psychological roster, a kind of zoological pharmacology, matching pet or captive to the owner. Like antibiotics specific for different bacterial infections, finches, hamsters, snakes, or horses might be prescribed for obsessive-compulsives, infantile fixations, voyeurism, lonely old age, or schizophrenia— not necessarily in that order.

Certain patterns have already been observed: small children like big furry animals that look like good parents or protective adults; lonely adults like little mammals that remind them of infants. A conventional wisdom has it that people and their dogs tend to develop similar facial expression, though, more likely, there are personality factors that underlie the choices people make among dog breeds, whose peculiar features do indeed have expressive qualities.

Caricature

The notion of the facial expression of traits shared by animal species and human personality type is the basis of caricature. The cartoon reveals the animality in the face of a familiar person, usually contemptuously. Or, any face could be analyzed for its signs of telltale brutality. Such sketches show the transition from beast to man and identify different animals with their human counterparts, so that man and animal seem to form a graded series.

A prominent penologist, Cesare Lombroso, early in the century decided that he had discovered the true cause of crime. He wrote, "I seemed to see all at once standing out clearly illuminated as in a vast plain under a flaming sky, the problem of the nature of the criminal, who reproduces in civilized times characteristics, not only of primitive savages, but of still lower types as far back as the carnivora." This explains, he added, the criminal's similarity in skull and skeletal traits to predators, cannibals, and apes, even the hooked noses of the birds of prey or the supernumerary teeth of snakes, the eyebrows like those of satyrs, arms like apes, and absence of nipples in certain women as in the platypus or echidna. In man all such features, which he found typically among lawbreakers, were throwbacks. "All these characteristics pointed to one conclusion: the atavistic origin of the criminal, who reproduces physical, psychic, and functional qualities of remote ancestors."

The idea may have been new to penology, but it had occurred to satirists and artists early in the nineteenth century. The sketches by Daumier, Grandville, and others, depicting half-human visages with the recognizable muzzles of bears, weasels, bulls, and birds, remain today a compelling genre.

The intermediate forms seem both disgusting and fascinating, disturbingly ambiguous mixes. The drawings depict a man-animal linkage that is neither strictly evolutionary nor mythological, but based on the common correlation of traits of behavior and facial form. They do not leave us so much with a sense of a series, with animal at one extreme and human at the other, as with the suggestion that all human faces are themselves part of the intermediary series, not yet quite human.

E. H. Gombrich points out that caricature is very recent pictorial art. The combination of animal and human features is uncanny, he says, and only in recent centuries have people been secure enough in their own identities to cope with such figures and find funny the deformations by which a greedy man, for instance, could be depicted as half-pig. But one wonders whether we moderns are so mature and sure of who we are. If, on the contrary, we are more desperate for self-knowledge than peoples of the past, we might seek it in ways previously considered too frightening. There is a long history of man-animal combinations in art, virtually all of it supervised by religious authority, its subjective peril ritually controlled. When art broke away from religious control, it promptly set about exploring everything that produced emotional impact, seeking pleasurable or frightening knee jerks, of which the linking of man and animal bodies has been both for thousands of years.

This caricaturing of people by the use of animals is quite different from the childhood use of animals as the vehicles of feelings and behaviors in order to externalize and grasp them. The latter is a form of voluntary predication in order to isolate and integrate the elements of one's inner diversity. Caricaturing is a clever form of typing people or pseudospecies-making. It is further expression of the domesticated view that animals are people in disguise. It is the reverse of clan totemism, which insists on an uncrossable chasm between the natural community and the human society, related by metaphor, a vision of man as one kind of creature among many kinds which he watches in order to evoke points of similarity and contrast in the dual series of men and animals. The alternative, postulated by domestication and its expression in caricature, is that men are the end product of the whole of life, individually different in degree and sometimes resembling creatures who tend, unsuccessfully as it were, to be human. The representation of animals by Goya, the Spanish painter, is an example of the sliding of human and animal into one another. Goya's monsters are not conjoined figures like satyrs, but gruesomely ambivalent in form. His portraits of decadent aristocrats have the mindlessness of sheep or the monomania of mules, while his animals are as gross and deformed as the peasants they live with.

With this glissade between grotesque figures—human and animal—in mind, we can recall the basic distinctions between domestic and totemic societies. While both descend from totemic thought—the use of animals as codes—they have opposite consequences. Totemic thought refers to that process in all human development in which the child uses plants and animals to learn to categorize and abstract, a primordial and inescapable human activity. But domesticated cultures make very different use of this than hunting cultures. The latter use the species and ecological system to evoke contemplation and organization of human society by analogy. But caricature arises in domestic thought, which makes social groupings that include various animals and sees workers or castes and animals as sharing traits.

Totemic thought regards the species as an individual. We give ourselves and other creatures two names: We have a surname and a personal name; animals have a genus and species. Cognitively, the two sets are equivalent. Except for pets (who have special naming rules), animals do not have personal names because the species in our eyes is the individual. This is implicitly recognized in mythology and folktales where the frog or fox are allegorical persons, not species.*

This strange idea that the species is an individual is useful as long as the tale takes place in phenomenal distance, connected to us only by parallels, as in totemic cultures. But when the animals become part of our household and are given proper names, as in domestic cultures, the animal kingdom is shattered

---

* When individual wild animals are given personal names, as for the rabbits in *Watership Down* by Richard Adams, they become psychologically domesticated. But the reader, when he next encounters wild rabbits, will still be unable to distinguish one from another.

into opposing realms. "Friendly" animals are extensions of the human society and the remainder, or wild group, is remote and, by default, at odds with society. Between them numerous ambiguous species are differently qualified and recognized, seen as a mélange of shifting "loyalties" and other pseudopolitical images.

In domestic cultures the paradigm or animal model of an ordered world is irreparably broken, so that the concrete reality upon which social groupings are predicated shifts toward something else, usually made objects or categories of work. The structure shifts from clan to caste or class. In the new idiom of work the domestic forms are producers or products while the wild continue to have secret purposes. The barnyard forms obey man, as man does God, and have his best interests at heart. The wild threaten him or endanger his stock and shift only for themselves; they are to man what fallen angels are to God. Domestic animals are part of the orderly world, the others are denizens of the unorganized, unproductive, and immoral wilderness. If the induction of animals into human society does not entirely exclude wild things, it simply ranks them low on the scale. It no longer celebrates ecosystem structure as a poetic expression; what men do no longer reverberates harmoniously with what Nature does, but seems, rather, to be in conflict with it and at a distance from it.

Animals in Folktales

One form of animal art that we share with the past is the animal fable. The fable emerged as an oral art, then literary, one of the ways in which animals persisted in culture in spite of the destruction of tribal mythologies by the Hebrews, Muslims, and Christians. The fable remained an acceptable means of lesson-giving in those heavily spiritualistic, humanized earth-traducing religions. It is usually a simple story with a moral lesson. The creatures are conventional personifications. The species represent types of human behaviors or personalities or occupations. That fable comes from basic totemic thought is clear: a parallel universe in which different kinds of animals form a society and a dramatic episode takes place that can be interpreted analogically. The fable of "The Ant and the Grasshopper," for instance, is the story of the pleasure-seeking grasshopper who spends his summer singing while the ant works, lays up stores, and thereby survives the winter. Like most fables, the natural history is superficial and misleading, but such homilies do not depend for their didactic purpose on biological validity.

Beyond its foundation in totemism, the fable has its own way: It produces a dictum, a cautionary rule, a moral code. No observation of ants and grasshoppers is needed, no further speculation or theory. In a sense the animals to which it refers have no existence except to awaken and refresh the lesson. They have no purposes of their own, no magic and no myth. They are emblems. The fauna of fables has the same destiny as animals who provide food, clothing, power—they are made by God for one purpose only. The fable animals have joined the domestic culture.

A published collection of such fables is a kind of taxonomy. From Aesop and the *Physiologus*, through the medieval bestiaries, these rhetorical stories were once adult fare. Today the bestiaries and cautionary tales are collected as the curios of a past age by a society that has deliberately divested itself of traditional forms. Like much of the remaining paraphernalia of a past culture, such things have a kind of museum or aesthetic interest. Relegated to children, they became quaintly pointless episodes for listeners who no longer personally harvest or store food.

The fable establishes unambiguous choices or contrasts. In the story of "The Ant and the Grasshopper," work and play are attached to the two animals by a spurious natural history, as though they were parts of the anatomy. Work and play are made memorable and every chirping grasshopper and every column of ants from then on are "playing" and "working." They repeat everywhere the lesson, and that is the final purpose of "The Ant and the Grasshopper." At its best the fable helps us to recognize and clarify aspects of the expectations of society; at its worst it falsifies the behavior of animals, narrows each species to a trait, and by analogy formulates a cast of human stereotypes. The fable is a domesticated or civilized rendering of animal predication for the purposes of teaching virtue and conformity rather than awareness of inner emotional experiences and feelings.

The fable uses animals to isolate and clarify pieces of social experience, but the fairy tale makes a different use of animal images. Unlike the fable, which assigns types of public behavior to different species, the fairy tale deals with internal concerns.

As in fables, certain aspects of the personality are loaded onto animal figures because distance is needed to distinguish their character clearly. But where the fable is admonitory about greed, competition, work, devotion to family and God, envy, ambition, faith, integrity, security, the market, rank, planning, deceit, punishment, and reward, the fairy tale centers on the anxieties normal to small children in relation to oedipal feelings, ambivalent attitudes toward parents and siblings, physical limitations, oral aggression, the consequences of the pleasure principle, fears of dark, of abandonment, and anxieties about guilt.

The fairy tale differs from the cautionary tale in that it always has a happy ending and is always set in a distant time and place. The linking of animals to unconscious concerns is based on the spontaneous curiosity toward the nonhuman and the personifying of feelings as animals: the ferocious and royal lion, the meek and skittering mouse, the tenacious bulldog, the wily fox, and the trickster/jokester crow. But fairy tales equate different animals with inner- rather than intra-human events. The frog in the fairy tale represents the principle of transformation, the wolf, oral aggression—qualities associated with more infantile processes than the more public behaviors of the fable. The benefit of the fairy tale is acquired without conscious awareness of the symbolism; indeed, it is destructive to discuss its psychological meanings with children. The fable's lesson, on the other hand, is explicit.

Another body of medieval animal literature is the stories of beasts and saints. Christianity exploits its own negative attitude toward animals by allowing that *even* the beasts know holy men when they see them. Recognizing the saints' blessedness, the wild creatures, instead of attacking ferociously or fleeing, all bow down and become humble and pacific. They have that power of innocence to recognize purity, virtue, and spiritual beauty. Their meekness also recalls the original state of all animal life before the Fall, the time before death when no meat was eaten and lion and lamb crouched blissfully side by side, a paradisiacal state surrounding the saint in his spiritual exaltation.

The stories imply that there are vestiges of an animal wisdom in people to know what is hidden. When he sinned and gained rationality, man lost most of his ability to apprehend as the animals do, to see through external appearance to one's true nature. This notion of the innate sensitivity of the animal is symbolic of that subquality in man. The totemic thesis that creatures are a medium or language persists, but centuries of domesticated thought culminate in the animals all surrendering not only the wildness in themselves, but in us. The wisdom of the wild is no longer distant and half-hidden, but has been subordinated to the thesis that the Word is the reality and that flesh and blood merely enact it. The boundary between natural and cultural is broken. Not only do the domestic animals stand in mute respect, but so do the wild wherever the churchly minions represent authority. They are brought across into the concentric spheres and hierarchic ladders where each has its rank. These stories are a rebuke to the doubters. Among the many parables of saints and beasts, that of the Abbot Gerasimus and the lion is typical. Having had a thorn removed from its paw, the lion became a disciple of the holy man, worked for his keep by "taking charge" of the mule, was given the name Jordanes, and died from grief on the Abbot's grave.

Reynard

But there are other extensions of the animal fable from folk cultures in which few people could read. One is the cycle of stories of "Reynard the Fox." When it did appear in print, Reynard became one of the three most widely read books of its time. After seven hundred years in print, it is still going into new editions. While the characters in Reynard are clearly projections of human roles and types and the stories are, in a way, educational, they certainly do not show that truth, innocence, or goodness triumph. These are ribald tales of cunning and trickery, a peasant view of the conniving among the powerful, set at the level of village politics (or, among other tricksters in folk traditions, at the level of tribal conventions, chiefdoms, fiefdoms, and parochial mores of all kinds). His crafty intelligence and animal vitality keeps Reynard one jump ahead of the hypocrites, charlatans, chiselers, and dupes who are seen in the tales as members of court. That village society is translated into an animal caste bearing aristocratic titles is a kind of peasant's revenge. One rejoices with Reynard not so much in his cruelties and victories, but in his defeat of humorless and unimaginative enemies, the merely vulgar and greedy who have no style and no detachment.

The characters in the Reynard stories all seem hopelessly narrowed by their animal mien. The treatment of human situations by animal stereotypes may be taken as sarcasm or cynicism where the individual is bound to a life that is mean, ugly, and rigid. The events of the stories are recurring occasions in which the underlying and innate animality of secular man rises to the surface. At the same time, these are farces acted by animals who are the only creatures around to witness human folly. One may look upon the bear, wolf, cat, and fox as familiar beasts in their own right who have, for the moment, put on a little charade, a burlesque of human cupidity, only for the show, and who will return at the end to their own reality. One is led to consider that the difference between the child's understanding and the adult's is that the child takes the story as an account of events in animal-land and accepts the illusions of animals talking and wearing clothes for no conscious reason, while the adult sees the tale as a strictly human one, but accepts the illusion of animal figures for the almost conscious reason that one does not openly criticize one's fellow citizens to whom one is beholden.

Put another way, one might say that the lesson of Reynard is concealment and deceit. The events in the stories are, for the child, concealed expressions of his own inner processes, such as infantile acting-out and primary thought process—desire for omnipotence, impatience, and envy. Like those of Br'er Rabbit, the Reynard stories are vicarious outlets for these feelings. Reynard conceals from his own readers that he is there to give symbolic vent to frustrating desires that are socially unacceptable. But the adult knows that those asocial wishes are in fact exercised, that the rules can be used to protect the wicked, that the real game is to deceive both one's victim and his legal means of retaliation. Reynard confirms the adult suspicions. The bear and fox are but masks concealing known individuals, local bureaucrats, lickspittles, knaves, and thugs.

The child and adult perspectives are in tandem. For the first, the stories enable the individual to recognize wishes and feelings in himself that are disapproved of as behavior, while, for the second, the stories confirm the universality of wickedness so close to the seats of power that the evildoers cannot be identified by name. Further, it is made clear that kindness, trust, and affection are not rewarded, that society is held together and its members motivated more by their greed than their ideals. If the Reynard fable has any positive quality apart from its sublimating, revelatory, and entertaining excursion into the varieties of betrayal, it must be its admiration of intelligence. Reynard is crafty and cunning, for he sees beyond the social mask and honeyed words to the fabric of the caste society. It is not surprising that the first great century of Reynard's popularity, the thirteenth, was that century when secular values came into their own. The Church could find no use in Reynard for its own self; he is everything that the beast/saint fables are not, a celebration of the independent intelligence as an alternative to faith, for Reynard has faith in nothing and no one except himself.

Reynard is only one of many animal figures employed over the centuries to satirize contemporary personalities; that is, not to conceal them but to minimize the storyteller's and publisher's liability at the hands of particular princes and politicians. It is surely the continuing applicability of these tales to local reality generation after generation that accounts for their survival. Their lampooning of particular individuals is aimed anew in the mind of each reader or listener.

Why should Reynard himself be depicted as an animal? Why a fox? He is a proud trickster without morals or sentimentality, a courageous liar, never petty in his skulduggery, an articulate cynic who disposes of fools and small-timers, whose schemes enable him not only to escape from rules and boredom but, as the underdog, to rise triumphant. It is not because these are animal qualities that the hero is a fox, however. They are human traits, and Reynard's character could be as easily portrayed as a person. But if he were human, along with the thug cat, pompous bear, and greedy wolf, verbal explanations of their differences would be necessary. Their animality is a telescopic means of typing each character in great detail and setting off the hero and supporting cast with an economy of description.

That Reynard should be a fox and not something else is not only due to the familiar cleverness of foxes, but to his power as a marginal animal. He is cat-like but also dog-like, game yet not eaten, inhabitant of boundaries—fence rows, forest borders, barnyard, and field edges—and of both daylight and night. He is the breaker of our conventions and therefore the secret idol of those who feel trapped in dull, rigidified, predictable lives without the means of escape.

The characters are not delineated; they are simply hooked to symbols. By contrast, the bulky apparatus of the modern novel is partly a consequence of having to create personalities from their common human mold. Our fundamental totemism links species with individuality, and the folktale has only to widen or narrow the spaces that already exist between the members of the imaginary society of animals.

Occasionally the modern author takes the same shortcut to character as the folktale. *Animal Farm,* George Orwell's satire on revolutionary socialist ideology, is a tale of domestic farm animals who revolt and seize the farm: the means of production, the real wealth. The different animals may be interpreted as types of craftsmen and laborers whose stereotyped animal traits endow each with instant personality. Because this permits a great economy of language, the story has an oral quality, a style far older than the novel. At the end, the revolution successful, the similarity between the animal leaders and the old human bosses who were overthrown begins to break down. Orwell has reached far below caste-typing to our subjective demand for an ordered world for the climax. There, in Everyman's unconscious, is the alarm that jangles whenever ambiguities between species appear.

Just as Reynard could have a human, not-too-bright king, a nasty, slinking minister, or a brutal and aggressive politician instead of a lion, wolf, or bear, Orwell might have had the human cynic, loyal worker, bureaucrat, traitor, slothful and weak. But both used animals because the species are cultural blanks for making types. The characters are one-dimensional personalities. But represented as a person, they would be time- and place-bound. Every era has its hair styles, costumes, posture, movement, and even more subliminal means by which the human figure condenses its milieu. The human face and form are as much disguises as telltales. The more explicit the description of an evil sheriff, the more likely it excludes the wicked sheriff that *I* know. The seedy bureaucrat in a provincial office may be spoken of as though he were a species, but actual civil servants come in all sizes, shapes, and colors. Perhaps the ability to recognize the universal in the specific requires a more mature vision and has to wait until we succeed in learning to recognize in the particular an example of the universal. The idea of a universal comes initially by removing as much confusing detail as possible. The fundamental premise of totemic thought is that different species are characters in a social drama, and one learns very early that all chickadees look alike. As primates we are very keen at separating individuals by their faces, but as humans we have great difficulty telling one starling from another, and some difficulty recognizing individuality in human races other than our own. Thus there is an equivalence between different individuals in *our* group and different races or species in a larger context. The logic of using animals in learning a set of abstract types is built into our native perceptional apparatus.

The episodes of Reynard have some of the dimensions of myth: They are extended stories about an antiheroic figure, embodying social insight and communicating a model for perceiving the structure of the human community. Although the stories are "about" the human community and have a kind of validity that lifts them above any specific time and place, the hero is hardly a public ideal, and certainly not an ancestor. We are fascinated with Reynard more than we admire him; he honestly acknowledges that it is a lying world where selfish intelligence survives. Things come out "right" in the end for the opposite reason than they do in fairy tales, where goodness triumphs. But there are real human societies in which Reynard as myth would be inappropriate, for myth is a culture-bound paradigm, where fairy tales are not. However much they imply wisdom about "mankind," there are operational limits to myths. Reynard would be incomprehensible in small, non-hierarchic, communal groups of the kind found in totemic cultures in which power cannot be seized or accumulated and which have no alliances and betrayals hooked to money and concentric spheres of bureaucratic power. It is true that the trickster and social-dominance systems are widespread if not universal. But the context in which Reynard operates is part of a bureaucratic and commercial culture. Reynard is everywhere, but the target of his cunning varies. Totemic thought is everywhere, but the world of small craftsmen, village markets, petty nobility, rural countryside, and feudal politics is a very different setting from that in which totemic thought came into being or in which many of us now find ourselves.

The trickster in us all enjoys the spectacle of good timing and risk-taking, the practical joke, and the sight of dolts in high places exposed. In a world of niggardly cheaters, Reynard at least has pride in his art and is unencumbered by ideology. He is audacious and unsentimental. His exploitation of small-timers, his verbal wit, his self-discipline, his escape from tedious rules and boredom appeal to all of us; he is the ultimate triumphant underdog, struggling against the juggernauts of his own time.

Animal Farm has no hero. It supplements the Reynard tales by demonstrating that there is no alternative to individual acts of subversion. Revolution is futile. Even if it succeeds, the same old inequalities and concentration of power inevitably make their appearance. For Orwell's society there was no wilderness left from which the figure of freedom and individuality could arise. Both tales confirm that the only successful counterculture is a group of one. Redistributing the wealth can never change the underlying premises of caste structure. But the individual can always make his private rebellion against the domestic regime, provided he still has in him a "species" of thought beyond the barnyard.

The Secular Bestiaries

About the same time that the first written versions of Reynard appeared, another secular literary work became popular. This was *The Love Bestiary*, a special form of the traditional bestiary. It was the work of Richard de Fournival, a thirteenth-century physician and chancellor of the Cathedral of Amiens. Like the traditional bestiaries with their allegorical lessons based on the natural history of animals, the love bestiary used animals as concrete examples of human actions. But De Fournival replaced the lessons with the logic of the man in love, who, according to the rites of courtly love, was pleading for "mercy" from his lady. In *The Lady's Response*, the game is continued as she marshals her resistance, animal by animal, contradicting his arguments. In their respective chapters on the crow, for example, he argues that its habit of first plucking out the eyes of a dead man as the means of getting to the brain is like love that first grows from sight, to which she replies that since love springs from vision, plucking out the eyes and eating the brain signifies not love but hate.

This *jeu parti* was a debate. Like all debates, it was in danger of too much abstraction. Secular love, with its turmoil and moods and shifting meanings, was difficult to discuss and full of exasperating confusion. The love bestiary was a set of creatures to which slippery ideas could be attached. They were like bones for anchoring fatty verbal logic and extravagant tissue of thought. Like other games, the thrust and riposte of allegorical dialogue was carried on by analogies to known animals.

This quaint literature is but a small part of a stampede of animals crowding into human consciousness in the latter eleventh and early twelfth centuries. The popularity of the regular bestiary—the nearest thing to an encyclopedia of natural history—the new zoos in stained glass and stone in cathedral architecture, the animal little brothers of St. Francis, and the first works of a scientific spirit such as Frederick II's treatise on falconry, all mark a widespread intellectual excitement directed to the discovery of information hidden in nature, a shift to an allegorical form of thinking in which the inquiring individual could seek clues illuminating social complexity from the observation of animals. The optimism of that world, with its contagious attention to illumination, light, and vision, is very touching. It is no surprise that scholars become addicted to its history and its charm can be felt across seven hundred years of intervening time when one compares it to the centuries before it, with their grim and pessimistic disdain of this world as opposed to the next.

This outburst of excitement for natural things was preceded by illustrated manuscripts, verbal folktales, the bestiary itself, the continuing survival of pagan thought in the calendar and astrology. But in spite of all that tenacious feeling for plant and animal lore in older peasant custom, the new atmosphere and sensibility to what animals could mean in the twelfth century suggests a revolution in the perception of nature. It is generally regarded as a kind of bubbling to the surface of European spirit, fertilized by contact with the Orient and the recovery and translation of classical literature. The rich abundance of animals and plants in art and thought are looked upon as ebullient decorations. But history is written by literary scholars, that is, men (not women) in rooms looking at books, for whom history is the documentation of political change and mechanical invention in a panoply of treaties, policies, trade routes, genealogies, and markets. As the African politician Waltari in Romain Gary's *The Roots of Heaven* put it, Africa has been the world's zoo and will never have a history until it gets rid of its animals. Waltari was educated at Cambridge.

To such a view an abundance of plants and animals is merely

an intrusion. Animal images are but the doodlings of a peaceful and secure people or period. But the animals were closer to the center of this dramatic change in human sensibility than book-men realize. The peoples of Western Europe and the Mediterranean basin, aroused by an inexplicable cultural renewal, took up the instruments that men have always used to examine their own being, a means to articulate the kaleidoscopic effects of change on their consciousness. Human and world variety are inseparable. The "discovery" of a world more diverse and interesting had internal consequences on all the pronouns, especially "I" and "we." The twelfth century was exactly that sort of breakdown of the grooves of dark ages imagination. The recovery of Greek thought created anxieties and culture-shock as well as liberation, and animals were a tool by which multiplicity of human experience was externalized, making it available for screening and ordering.

Totemic thought is much broader than clanship systems utilizing animal figureheads. It is the process whereby abstract ideas are anchored to living images. For millennia the richness of natural forms beckoned to thought about human possibilities. The fauna are always far richer and more abundant than the culture-bound circumstances of tribal life. As the modern world came into being, that archaic process of zoologizing human diversity worked even in the precincts of the humanized landscape with its bland domestic beasts, even in the city with its rats, mice, roaches, fleas, sparrows, pigeons, ants, termites, spiders, bats, lice, bedbugs, and pets. The speculative, discursive breakout of ideas in a world of change and progress could not escape its own essential intellectual devices. If the fauna diminished, it seemed not to matter, as the world drew upon a fauna accumulated in the cultural baggage, bringing images into the daily experience in ecclesiastical architecture, poetry, and drama, in all the arts, and particularly in literature, not as a frivolity of artists, but because there was no alternative.

Literary Thought and Animals

Renaissance cultures abound with animals. Montaigne's theme was that man's follies were due to his reason and his pride. Animals are happy because they have not overvalued their intelligence: Each species is a lesson in the advantage of keeping close to nature. His opponents, Descartes and Pascal, found him vainly seeking authority for "living like beasts" or simply out of touch with science or the Divine distinction between instinct and reason.

Others sought anatomical analogies to character, the study of faces for interpreting human motives and the rise of "a consistent portrayal of individuals and groups." Animal nicknames became popular; even Queen Elizabeth wore jewels cut in the forms of nicknames. Evil was made blacker by being personified as an animal, says George Boas. Portraits were enhanced, generalities made more concrete, humorous characters made more ridiculous, satiric figures more censured, pathos increased in poignancy. "The fundamental essence of the abstraction in animal form" was this intensification.

Helen Hastings asks, "What is behind all this literature about brute souls, intelligence, virtue, and happiness?" A contest, she answers, between the *libertine* and the *theologian,* a means of using nature to analyze and criticize contemporary society. "In the process of discussing animals, many problems of general interest in the eighteenth century were touched upon"—final causes, the chain of being, the origin of language, the relationship of man and nature. The humanitarian movement arose early in the eighteenth century out of such philosophical and theological considerations, picking up sentimental and protectionist movements later in the century. For three hundred years the savants wrestled with these enigmas of feeling, intelligence, and souls in beasts with two results: It produced a growing sympathy for protecting animals from abuse; and the dialogue set the "champions of the beasts" against the defenders of the superiority of man for so long that the "man against animal" became a general and endemic theme in European thought.

The idea that animals and savages were embodiments of different traits went public with book-printing in the sixteenth century. That each species epitomized some human characteristic —temperance, chastity, foolishness—extended also to peoples, Chinese, Polynesians, or Indians, who represented steps up from savagery to civilization. This produced a convenient and conventional idiom for the description and analysis of character that was to become and remain a major tool of social criticism and of fiction. But in the other direction its implications with respect to animals themselves unleashed endless complications and argument.

Is a beast happy? Does it reason? Does it have a soul? A language? Are animals innocent, virtuous, close to God? Montaigne argued that animals are good and pure. Wolfgang Franzius, Boileau, Jacques Rousseau agreed. Pierre Chanet, René Descartes, Bossuet, A. Dilly and others said no. The issue in the minds of most was by no means a simple set of alternatives, but a tangle of qualifications, degrees, and semantic problems.

These currents in French thought were forerunners of a general contemporary set of related questions. Do animals think? Do they have an aesthetic sense, consciousness? Do primates have language? Do men have instinct? Are animals a proper study for psychology or men for ethology? What keeps these arguments alive is the philosophy of ranked series, the heritage of domesticated or caste thought. Totemically speaking, they are meaningless. Yet most of the study and reflection on animals for nearly four centuries is premised on the humorless and often bitter insistence that the wholeness of creation is political and must therefore be perceived as links in a chain, rather than poetic, that there is one set of qualities, all of which are owned by our species, but which are shared out differently or seen in their negative expression in other species. There is no room in this view for difference except in quantity. It is holistic in a superficial way, with its Enlightenment notion that the Earth can be easily understood. Man is the head of a kind of organism to which all other species are joined as appendages. One of the first and clearest statements of this view was by Francis Bacon, who wrote, "If men were taken away from the world, the rest would seem to be led astray, without aim or purpose. . . . For the whole world works together in the service of man; and there is nothing from which he does not derive use and fruit."

Recent scholarship has given us a review of the streams of this process: "Beasts and Politics in Elizabethan Literature," *The Happy Beast in French Thought of the Seventeenth Century*, *Man and Beast in French Thought of the Eighteenth Century*, and so on. All of these works of diligent, dull scholarship deal with the conventions of animal symbolism and a history of debates about the nature of man. All of them perceive animals as styles and motifs. Their authors are like exotic specimens in cages built to look like libraries, doomed to struggle with a subject according to the law of comparative literature, which says that reality is an example of literary truth. Their insoluble problem is created by caste thought, the view that animals and men exist in a social continuum and that coherence amounts to scaling the distances between each animal and man. Analogical thought, by which totemic cultures perceived animal and plant systems as a separate domain, was disenfranchised by the organ transplant of domestication in which animals were literally removed from their origins and spliced into human society. When we need them to be unlike us, they have a way of slipping about under the knife and becoming too familiar.

The dilemma was tightly focused in the furor for which René Descartes provided the most fuel, for he had a clear intuitive sense that we needed animals to be fundamentally *other* and that only then could the bisymmetry of culture and nature be sustained. Descartes argued that animals do not have souls and sentience, which plunged us into three hundred years of debate about souls and consciousness, about pain, love, instinct, social organization, and marriage among the animals. The Cartesian debate continues to this day, one group accusing the other of "reducing" man to animal, and the second accusing the first of blindness to the evolutionary principle.*

The intensity of these debates is due to a concern about the definition, not of animals, but of man. As geography revealed cultural diversity and urban, industrial culture deprived the individual of important clues to his personal identity, the meaning of the social pronouns became increasingly obscure. Progress enhanced social relativism and existential uncertainty. What do all men share beneath their differences? What part of myself is given and what chosen? On what basis are we to generate answers to the enigmas of "who and what we are" if such questions are the domain of the new philosophy and not of religious authority? Were creatures once happy living instinctively and should we therefore take the irrational beast as our

---

* It is no accident that Darwin's ideas on evolution and much of his evidence came from the study of domestic animals, where continuity through change would be actually documented. Domestication tremendously accelerates what otherwise is too dispersed or too slow to see. The modern obsession with linear time is given instant visual form with the merging of breeds and varieties seen in domestic forms but not normally visible in nature.

model, or are the beaver and the ant and the elephant examples of primitive foresight, social responsibility, and cognition, more perfected in man?

It is clear that three centuries of literary labors dealing with animals were not produced mainly because of an interest in animals. Nor were the concerns of thoughtful people ever such, even among the most archaic tribal societies or savage hunters. But the difference between archaic peoples and ourselves is in how this animal thinking is applied to the formation of society.

The difference between totemic and caste culture appears in fictions about animal characters: whether human groups are related among themselves by a poetic imitation of the relationships among the animals which they have chosen as emblems, or whether the groups include animals and represent them. To do charades of animals, as totemic cultures do in ceremony, is to play a game of analogues. But to pretend that animals are people carries the inverse notion that people are animals.

C. S. Lewis once asked, "Why are the characters in *The Wind in the Willows* animals?" His answer was that the characters live with adult freedom in a child's world, a contradiction that could be resolved only by making the subjects neither adult nor juvenile, but animals. It works because our culture presumes that adult animals are essentially immature people.

> For Jung, fairy tales liberate the archetypes which dwell in the collective unconscious, and when we read a good fairy tale we are obeying the old precept, "Know thyself." I would venture to add to this my own theory, not of the kind as a whole, but of one feature in it: I mean the presence of beings other than human which yet behave, in varying degrees, humanly: the giants and dwarfs and talking beasts. I believe these to be at least (for they may have many other sources of power and beauty) an admirable hieroglyphic which conveys psychology, types of character, more briefly than novelistic presentation and to readers whom novelistic presentation could not yet reach. Consider Mr. Badger in *The Wind in the Willows*—that extraordinary amalgam of high rank, coarse manners, gruffness, shyness, and goodness. The child who has once met Mr. Badger has ever afterwards, in his bones, a knowledge of humanity and of English social history which he could not get in any other way.

To imitate an animal, as children do in games, is to venture within its mask briefly, to put on the mask, seeking contact where likeness is embedded in unlikeness. The child can then retreat back to himself with it, a kind of conceptual prize. But when the person is caricatured as an animal, as Lewis describes, the animal comes to him and invades him. According to E. H. Gombrich, caricaturing of an individual is an act of aggression intended to deprive the victim of his individuality, even his humanity. It is an exaggerated portrait in which the like-in-unlike is used to dismantle the individual and reassemble him in a fixed category. How are we to reconcile this with C. S. Lewis's benign view of *The Wind in the Willows*?

Is the story an assault in a war between generations, unrecognized by Lewis? A semantic problem—a confusion of caricatured as against characterized? I think not. Caricature is what is meant. But can you really caricature a group of people? Gombrich was speaking of the lampooning of public figures—individuals. Lewis is speaking of a figure who is already an abstraction, the British "old boy."

The Wind in the Willows appeals to children on totemic grounds because of its empathy and its possibilities, as Lewis said, for self-knowledge, but not, as Lewis thinks, because it introduces us to types of people—that is added by domestic culture. Still, the reader may ask, limited as stereotypes are, if they help the child or foreigner to understand members of an English class, why object to them?

Mr. Badger may indeed clarify class lines, but the damage is between man and animal. The premises are very different between the domestic and totemic cultural uses of animals as instruments of thought. The totemic premise is that species are radically different from one another and from man, but that shimmering points of reflected order occur. The domestic view is that the different animals are conglomerates of human traits, somewhat simplified so as to represent variations in human personality.

A principle of balanced duality governs each of these definitions. In totemic thought animals are regarded as naturally diverse and, by culture (myths or stories), are made to talk to one another as though they were actually a social entity. Totemic cultures translate this view into social structures by initiating individuals into secret societies, or clans, which have plant or animal emblems. They seek to diversify the common flesh. Domestic cultures make the opposite use of their totemic thought: People are naturally diverse and are born into groups that are estranged by inanimate models—what they make or produce. Animals are simply nonhuman subordinates that accompany the basic divisions of humanity.

In domestic or caste as well as totemic societies, all things can be potentially significant to human understanding. But for the totemic culture the meaning of animals is contingent on a kind of arbitrary logic, whatever man can make of the situation. Thought is guided by myth and taboo, but any observation of cranes overhead, a three-legged she-elephant, or moles running about on the ground surface is pertinent, and his logic after all is intuitive and poetic.

But King Solomon and the patristic theologians show what happens to the variety of animal life when the thought, if not the animal, has been domesticated. To Solomon the animal kingdom was "a vast and many-volumed book on all phases and features of human nature in which the world of lower creatures was held up to a man as a moral mirror, in order that he might see therein the reflections of his own vices and virtue." In addition to being a duality of good and evil, the entire animal kingdom was "a mere collection of types and symbols of religious dogmas and Christian virtues." Such was the opinion of E. P. Evans after an exhaustive study of animals in the architecture of churches.

Some church fathers had asserted that God "created the lower animals after the likeness of heavenly prototypes," a good Platonic and supportable Christian view, at least after the thirteenth century. St. Bernard was offended by the number and variety of creatures in Romanesque and Gothic architecture. Each of those animals may reveal a divine thought to some, but Bernard recoiled in exasperation and horror. The tenth-century encyclopedia of nature, the *Key of Melito*, had pulled the old caste thought to a new level: Earthly creatures were not just symbolic of human types, but of human—or divine thoughts. When the new Gothic cathedral went up, creatures seem to flock to the stonework: denizens from the old *Physiologus* and the new bestiaries, bears from Burgundian brooches, and the fauna from Anglo-Saxon arabesques, Byzantine carpets, tapestries, even from nature. All became "sacred" symbols. But Bernard was not fooled. Aesopian parables and animal tropes were one thing, but he knew totemic insurgence when he saw it, and could see that the craftsmen threw in a lot for fun, to tease thought. Fun was the last thing anybody who was serious about vices and virtues wanted. Post hoc sermons would make moral sense of the beasts in limestone and colored glass, but Bernard would ignore them. Being symbolic, the purpose of such beings was fixed by authority, even if true lessons had to be newly invented.

Burdened with the caste notion of hierarchy and the animal as an imperfect human, the Christians found the world full of other peoples arranged on the ladder below themselves: inferior cultures and races came into being in the same intellectual framework that regimented castes within society and brought the animal into the household and made it subordinate. The otherness of people was predicated on the otherness of animals, and when the latter fell into contempt out of familiarity, being judged in "our" human terms, they became targets of prejudice and chauvinism.

The debates on whether animals had soul and reason, like today's arguments about whether they have language or love, are a means by which men seek information about themselves. But the dialogue can be handled two ways. Totemic cultures adopted animals as emblems in order to apply ecological wisdom and logic to human relationships, while domestic cultures postulated animals as other types of humans and discovered animality as a human trait. Since the French Revolution, the domestic form has been heavily political and economic. Orwell's *Animal Farm* satirizes the illusion of perfectibility through ideology. Beginning in egalitarian democracy after the farm animals kick out their human bosses and take over the farm themselves, it ends in the rise of new class distinctions—the greedy sycophants, the self-deluded, the weak deserters, the mindless workers, and the new bosses. In analyzing by animal figures, the story is totemic in conception, but is domestic in its sorting of people according to traits of animal species and linking the classes with types of work. Like those nineteenth-century French cartoons by Grand-ville and others, satirizing human types by making them half-human, half-animal figures, Orwell concedes the inevitability of human caste: associates work with characteristic personality. The same nineteenth-century cartoons today decorate the pages of elitist or intellectual newspapers and journals. The human life caricatured there is dominated by the scramble for status, class, and wealth by a horde of one-dimensional figures. In *The New*

York Review of Books, for example, such drawings are totemic chic, a sort of *reductio ad absurdum* of the biological realm to titillate the readers of inbred literary essays. It is one of those baroque phases of domestic thought in which the purpose of the natural realm is to decorate the margins of humanism and to confirm its presupposition that animal diversity is but a reflection, and a meager one at that, of human depth and diversity.

Adherents of this perspective can always be spotted from a simple clue: Their definitions of man or human begin by contrasting him to animals. This must be done because man and animal are perceived on a continuum. This intellectual reflex is the unfailing contribution of literary homocentrism to modern thought, though its foundations go back to the domestication of animals.

Machines as Animals

The confusion introduced into human self-consciousness by the creation of domestic breeds was due to their poorer species definition and more generalized behavior. From the time of their coming, an element was attached to thought that connected the human at one end elastically with the animal at the other. The more breeds and variations it produced, the more continuous the gradation seemed.

Animals used for power, like the ass going around to turn the millstone, became parts of the machines they pulled. Thus domestic animals lead to a related source of ambiguity, the machine. A million years or more of the scrutiny of large mammals has produced a template for thought, not far removed from the child's belief that things which move—clouds, for example—are therefore alive and have volition. That template is the large, active body. Like dogs yipping at the tires of automobiles, just where the Achilles tendon should be in the caribou, antelope, or deer, city men cross busy streets without hesitation, like hunters moving in a herd of hoofed animals. The template translates "animal" at levels of subconscious perception in spite of the conscious knowledge that they are "only" machines.

Machines are never only machines. It has been said that the Greeks could have had a mechanized civilization. Their mathematics, knowledge of mechanics, and intellectual skills were adequate, but they were stopped by the uncanniness of the machine. They knew that a mechanical device was "only" a collection of inanimate parts, and yet it was too congruent to the template of the living body. That ambiguity was intolerable. Just why those sophisticated and worldly people should have been more vulnerable to the notion of the "ghost in the machine" than ourselves is a complex question for which there seems to be no easy answer. The modern concept of the inanimate did not become part of the Western mind until the time of Isaac Newton. Before that, no object having parts and motion, man-made or not, could exist without life or spirit. While seventeenth-century physics and biology separated animate from inanimate, they did not completely replace the older, deeper assumption, evident in contemporary discussions about whether machines have feelings, consciousness, intelligence, memory, and thought.

The reciprocal of this idea was that animals are special kinds of machines. Bodies are built up from particles of the same substances as machines. The investigation of bodies as machines began as early as the sixteenth century, when anatomist-inventors Villard de Honnecourt, Giovanni Borelli, and Jacques de Vaucanson explained the ability of the bird to fly as the operation of levers and pulleys. Modern anatomical and physiological studies sustain a mechanical model. From muscle action it went to explanations of blood circulation, digestion, and so on to the Pavlovian conclusion that the basis of behavior was the nerve synapse and the reflex arc. The machine paradigm is the fundamental ordering concept of most modern biological science: organ systems, self-regulatory processes, behavior, metabolism, and human developmental events are all "mechanisms." The animal is a self-regulating and self-maintaining machine.

In general we seem to accept the identity of animals as machines but to resist the notion that machines are animals. That machines are alive appears primarily in fictional speculation, often in connection with the sensibilities of computers and other electronic apparatus, but it is still an intellectual game for an educated few.

These questions have important consequences in how we perceive industrial pollution. Thousands of years of living with animals has led us to accept their stink and our willingness to endure it as only a smell nuisance, like baby feces or vomit. If machines give off stink like animals, then we can endure that, too, telling ourselves it is a small price to pay for the advantages that mechanization brings. But in reality the stink of factory fumes and smog is its least important fault: Smell or not, the machine is insidiously poisonous. We accept the odors with a shrug of the farmer's indifference to the stench of dung, as merely the "smell of money."

Central to this book are the lifelong tasks of refining the idea of the self to the self. As a naturalist, I hold the resemblance of machines to animals to be a dangerous error. The making of automaton toys, so glibly played with by fictionists, has hazards, such as the mistaking of life-destroying gases from engines for the smell of animals. There are a whole series of developmental undertakings in human mental and emotional growth that depend on the availability and abundance of nonhuman life. Until we understand exactly how these work, we should follow what might be called "the principle of phylogenetic probity," which is simply that the healthy function of an organ is most assured under circumstances similar to those in which it evolved.

Just as the body can mistake some rare, dangerous elements for common, necessary ones (the metabolic substitution, for instance, of radioactive strontium 90 for calcium and its deposition in and destruction of bone tissue), the machine is a perceptual surrogate for animals.

The dream of creating pseudohumans or "androids" would be completed with the manufacture of theroids, or false animals, presumably run by "clean" power. Almost everyone must feel some of the old Greek revulsion for such slaves or toys. Somehow it does not seem right, but why? Are we just old-fashioned?

What bothers the literary and theological humanists is clear enough. Entering into social and sexual relationships with machines has given them the creeps for years, but that is because they love machines, not because they hate them.* The humanist alliance with the engineers to improve human life and to demonstrate man's superiority has been a flourishing marriage since the time of Leonardo da Vinci. What they object to in personal

---

* In his acceptance speech for the Nehru Award, Jonas Salk declared that the deteriorating quality of life was because of our tendency to become slaves of machines. But Salk's eminence would never have occurred without machines. Like Jacob Bronowski and Buckminster Fuller, he raises the specter of the danger of machines as any shaman calls attention to the perils of animal spirits, signifying his own priesthood.

relationships with machines is that they are humiliating. That is to say, the reason that many non-science academics and an intellectual priesthood of them and physicists, chemists, and physicians object is that these relationships confound the hierarchic order of the universe that was outlined by Aristotle and given its final twist by the despiritualizing of "mere" matter. Their objection to a society with machines is only slightly less than to one involving acting "like an animal." It is an offense to their pride.

The confusion in joining animals and machine is not an error of the uneducated. It is the outcome of detachment and hubris. The same arrogance that misinterpreted Alexander Pope's dictum that "the proper study of mankind is man" misunderstands the danger of machines. That they are "mere" animals and "mere" machines is beside the point.

It is not to argue whether animals have souls or whether machines can think, but to observe that self-knowledge, from infancy to old age, requires oblique views and detours for the very reason that man most admires himself: to understand the capacity for abstract, discursive thought. Ordering ideas, the integration of intuition and rational insight into a creative whole that can be remembered and communicated, the growth of a mature, conscious understanding of the nature of being human and of being a self—these all deal with elusive processes as tangible as smoke, moments of recognition, flashes of illumination, and nameless apprehensions. Ideas are as slippery as eels and can be held only when hooked to something.

That something seems arbitrary. In the mythic drama of the cosmos shall we call the sky Father or, with the ancient Egyptians, should we call it Mother? And what image shall we use for the Earth? For transformation? For the cycle of life? What for the many aspects of a personality, or of feelings? Cut off ourselves from the empirical traditions of tribal custom, we relegate the subject to comparative mythology or the history of art: The cross *stands for* the tree of life; the dove *represents* peace. It is a game of labels. Why not invest our acknowledgment of the mystery of otherness in a man-made object? In this game the animal figures are little more than verbal tokens or visual emblems, a form of shorthand.

But the symbol carries with it all kinds of qualities and hidden associations. If we project feelings outward onto something tangible in order to find them in ourselves and to give them

names and enter them into thought, we take for granted a compelling correspondence. The machine is not part of a silent otherness like a stone; it is a man-made non-livingness. What the
nursing infant finds in the feel of the glass nursing bottle instead
of the breast, or the small child discovers in a toy vehicle is not an
independent selfhood which is responsive and vital like himself.
Lacking even the independent being of stone or water, they are
messages of man-extension, of self-extension, like domesticated
animals, except that they encode non-feeling and non-life.

The infant is struggling with the emerging idea of livingness
itself, external and internal. Take away the mammalian embrace
of care and caring and the child dies or proceeds to an impaired
childhood, unsure even that he is alive and unable to continue
the search for social and individual self. As an animal substitute,
the machine is an affront to the inanimate as well as to life. The
otherness of stones and stars, like that of wild animals, is their
deepest mystery, for they are not our products and their purposes are their own. They are the models for thinking our humbleness in the universe, and they are the key to the strangeness of
ourselves.

Machines are little shadows of our own imaginings, the toys
of minds, mirrors of concocted sequences and manipulations. If
we treat them as animals, we play a game we cannot win of as-
signing symbolic meaning to them and we fail to attend to animals. Examining our products to understand ourselves is like
studying our own feces, and a machine is a turd of the mind
with wheels.

Because machines are mirrors, humanism has loved them.
But it is necessary to outdo humanism in its own enthusiasms,
to go farther, to acknowledge the arts as the only hope, in the
absence of cultural totemism, of recovering the mature benefits
of totemic culture. We are no longer hunter/gatherers in an
economic sense; we are no longer culture-bound, but aware of
the relative validity of multiple customs, no longer formally
committed to a single tradition. Every day we are reminded in
scores of ways of the difference between ourselves and preliterate, preagricultural peoples.

And yet our thought remains totemic in that we use the nonhuman in structuring our thought. Different cultures articulate
totemism differently. It may be perverted and shriveled, but it
is there in all human groups. For us the question is how, in the

absence of clan society and ceremonial affirmation, we can reconcile that archaic reality with modern life.

The Pet as Minimal Animal

In the preceding pages the subversion of these needs of the human spirit by domestication has been sketched. Despite its elaboration of breeds, the barnyard is an inadequate fauna. Its blurred demarcation between kinds, the poverty of behaviors, the intervention of agribusiness—all these make for better slavery and efficiency but are stultifying to the need of minds, man's as well as animals'.

Some of the domestic animals are kept for nonutilitarian needs. The pet is our effort to extend a hand to the poor, broken brutes of the barnyard or agribusiness shed, to compensate for the vanishing bucolic community, a gray mass of egg-laying, meat-growing, milk-secreting machines, closed in the sterile barns of the new industrial farm. If we look at pet-keeping from this perspective of totemic thought—a need for animals as urgent as good nutrition and good mothering—pets appear quite different from our usual careless association.

Generally "pet" means two groups: the domesticated forms, which usually have comparative freedom; and captive, often tamed, wild forms. "Tamed" merely means accustomed to human presence but not biological change by selective breeding. The two may serve rather different functions, for the keeping of wild animals is largely a hands-off relationship, with more delicate care and cages or aquariums.

People keep pets mostly for companionship. We are not surprised that animals freely accompany people or share their homes, but that is because we have grown up in those circumstances. The choice of pets varies according to the needs and whims of the owner. Desmond Morris observed that breed choice is often associated with size, that little children prefer big dogs with lots of hair, rounded contours, and a flat, expressive face. Adults are more likely to have small, cuddly breeds with baby-like voices and helpless demeanor. But children like babies, too, and they are fond of miniature worlds where they, for a change, are the giant "adults." Children who are attracted to captive lizards would be terrified by eleven-foot Komodo dragons, the biggest known lizard. These distinctions are only crude beginnings. The differences between adolescents and juveniles, males and females, city-dwellers and farmers as pet-keepers remain to be explored. Like the preference for friends, favorite breeds are in part a function of personality and of the immediate stresses and situations of life.

The boy and his dog and the girl and her horse are commonplace, at least as popular stereotypes. In each the psychological slot into which the animal fits differs. Many boys like horses, but three times as many girls than boys put the horse first in their list of desirable animals. Girls at the age of puberty may become virtually obsessed with horses. The horse for them is a male figure or their own maleness, as it has been in the human imagination for at least twenty thousand years, to judge from the cave art of ancient man. The young horsewomen are working through their "problems" with boys, or with masculinity, by attempting a mastery of the horse. Their surge of psychic-sexual energy away from its primary object sometimes gets fixated for life. Whether "horsey" women remain in some ways juvenile or have chronic sexual neuroses is not obvious because many such individuals develop a leathery toughness, almost a fierce strength, which seems anything but immature. Men develop obsessions with horses too (as in Peter Shaffer's play *Equus*), but seem in this not to be dealing with the "other" sex and therefore are possibly involved in a form of homosexuality or with extensions of their own masculinity. In either case, such people are but a small fraction of those attempting to deal with their psychosocial problems through animals. These attempts range from occasional fascinations or fixations to perversions. Their objects range from houseflies, which Freud said were often the first examples of copulation for the child, to bulls, whose sexual uses have been known to include special harnesses to suspend them over privileged nymphomaniacs.

The sexual relationships of people and animals, like their uses for power or types of food, is peripheral to this book, though in one respect it is pertinent. Kinsey and Pomeroy found in their 1950s studies that, even in America, where there is less rural isolation than in most of the world, up to 50 percent of farm and ranch boys had sexual connections with animals. In literature and mythology it is a theme as old as there are documents. In Robinson Jeffers' *Roan Stallion*, Balzac's *Une Passion dans le*

Desert, Grimm's "Frog Prince," Lucian's *Lucius, or the Ass,* and in scores of other works the subject is present. Around the world, pastoralists accept copulation with sheep, goats, llamas, asses, camels, pigs, chickens, heifers, and dogs as part of the way of life. All this sodomy, bestiality, or zoophilia is no more a surprise than the worldwide cruelty to animals with which it is psychologically connected. What makes it of interest here is the extent to which it signifies a breakdown in the order-making processes that give structure to the world and inwardly strengthen and affirm the self as individual. It is not sufficient to assess copulation with animals as degrading—a word suggesting that it is insulting to one's rank or class. All kinds of sexual activity are held degrading by somebody. What is far more debilitating operates at an unconscious level, in the way in which life is understood to have its own diverse integrity. That is, it damages the understanding.

In Greek mythology, that Freudian history book of the unconscious, animal-man combination creatures were often signified as cross breeding between people and animals. Monsters—god or devil—came from the unnatural union of human and beast. One of the most conspicuous crippling effects of domestication on animals is that the signals that work like lock and key to prevent crossbreeding among them are lost or overriden. In tribal societies the interbreeding between kind is the equivalent of human incest. In the farming idiom, purity of seed, breed, and genealogical lines are primary values. The readiness of farm animals to mate with the "wrong" partners is enhanced by selection for readiness to breed at the whim of the herdsman and the loss of its species courtship-signaling system. Non-seasonal sexuality and the collapse of appropriate sign-signals for partner lower the barriers to the crossing of horses and asses. Different species of fowl interbreed, masturbation increases, male dogs, goats, and bulls attempt to mount people while the females display and entice before men or become indiscriminately passive.

In addition to sexual relationships and friendly companionship, all other social relationships are transferable to animals. The ethologist Nikolaas Tinbergen pointed out thirty years ago the flat-faced, small-chinned, large-eyed, steep-foreheaded shape of all infant skulls, which evoke mothering and protective feelings in people. Baby animals are not only small and helpless, but also appealing because human adults respond innately to infantile traits and shapes. The case of "lost," injured, or stolen baby animals is not prompted only by sympathy, but also by their devastating emotional appeal that we transfer between species. Barbara Burn, coauthor of *A Practical Guide to Impractical Pets,* says that the determination to keep baby animals that come our way, often by chance, is a syndrome due in part to this release of human care-giving behavior in situations that are often inappropriate, when keeping the baby is not only impractical but impossible.

In totemic culture animals are discrete models for concepts, ideas, qualities, and other constituents of whole beings and human groupings. Insofar as the distinctions between kinds are now blurred, the system no longer holds and the animal models fail their totemic function. Perhaps it is partly in reaction to our deep discomfort with this failure that we keep wild forms and attend to exaggerated images of human types that can substitute for category-making. In advanced peasant societies, religious and folk images include a panoply of distorted faces and figures, sometimes trailing animal parts into their realization. These conventionalized figures have features that attempt to approximate the sensory distance between species. Look at the pantheon of Buddhist and Hindu gods and you see the humanoid equivalent of a faunal taxonomy: figures with distorted faces, multiple limbs, obese bodies, exaggerated muscles or breasts, all further idiosyncratized by costume, body paint, jewelry, mutilation, and coiffeur. The same is equally evident in Hebraic, Islamic, and Christian mythology, more so in the past than today. The range of humanoid models that externalizes our innermost experiences includes a host of demons, a heavenly hierarchy of angels, and the iconographic individual figures of Moses, Christ, and Muhammad in excessive physical peculiarity.

The vacuum left when caste and civilized societies replaced totemic-clan societies, oriented to a concrete reality model of plants and animals, was filled in two ways. One was the use of the products of class work as the tangible representations of group difference. The other was the creation of pseudofaunal varieties of fantastic humanoids. Intellectually, one model may be as good as another. Psychologically and empirically, however, the fallout from this transition has been that the "great world religions" disassociate themselves from the real nonhuman. No society has completed this process and become purely human in its imagery. Sacred monkeys, cows, and man/animal combinations continue. Christianity in the age of science has pruned away its faunal vestiges by reducing the animals to fables, parables, symbols, and other token-signs. From time to time some order or sect has energetically asceticized and humanized much of its sacred imagery, but when it approaches a threshold of intolerance and loses its connections to real plants and animals, it begins to lose its adherents.

Pets may fill some of this gap. Today's pet is a nonhuman companion kept for amusement. To us it seems like a normal part of everyday life, but actually pets are extremely rare in human history and, as we think of them in terms of fellow beings, rare around the world. In the past only a tiny fraction of wealthy and leisured people had pets. The very concept is unknown among most of the world's pre-industrial peoples, except as object and curiosity and status by an affluent minority. There are as many people who keep dogs to eat as those who keep them as pets. Only in this perspective of the rarity of the pet does the pet explosion in modern cities take on its full strangeness.

Pet-keeping has been described as an adjustment to the limitations of civilized life, a kind of compensation for our lack of animal contact, a form of mental hygiene or therapy, On this basis, not only with the seriously ill but as preventive therapy, the psychological literature supports pets. More than thirty years ago, J. S. Bussar wrote on "The Mental Hygiene of Owning a Dog," and Marcel Heiman, a decade later, defended the dog as an "aid in psychological equilibrium." They gave a new sanction to the nineteenth- and twentieth-century stereotype of the "boy and his dog," a part of the nostalgia of a society in the urban transition, when city-dwelling adults remembered their childhood on the farm through a sentimental screen of time. More recently, in a thoughtful book, Boris M. Levinson has attempted to identify the benefits and dangers of pet-keeping.

Levinson thinks that pets fill an elemental need for people to be associated with animals, which was part of everyday life across the millennia of human time and is a universal of the human psyche. With the authority of an experienced Manhattan analyst, he notes that group processes are alone inadequate to deal with the chronic sense of loneliness and alienation, which are ecological as well as social in origin. Pets, he says, remind us of our origins and thus give relief from the overdense human environment. The keeping of an animal opens an emotional channel that becomes occluded by the very nature of urban social barriers, channels even between parents and children. The family dog may be one of the few things they share.

But the pet, for Levinson, is far more than a restorative, a mental anodyne. The "pet-reared child" finds the environment more gratifying and therefore needs to demand less from his own body. The small child can exercise his imaginative understanding of behaviors and feelings by his mimicry, empathy, and analogy, by projecting parts of his undifferentiated self upon the animal until his ego is strong enough to integrate them.

As a child's companion, Levinson continues, the pet is a constant and devoted friend in a world in which most adults are indifferent. But it is a nonjudgmental friend, one that also must endure toilet-training and bowel discipline, one that doesn't always obey, which helps the child realize that his wishes are not magic commands and helps him to outgrow his infantile omniscience.

In a small urban family, the child spends much of his time in an adult world of giants whose motives and purposes are seldom clear, or among peers who rebuff him and among whom his social status is uncertain. In contrast, his pet has no secret motives or responses. Its needs and helplessness are evident. Small like himself, the pet is an "exercise ground for love."

It is not only a real, but a fantasy companion upon which the child's anxieties may be projected, making interpersonal adjustment problems more accessible. In a world of shifting residences, unfamiliar neighborhoods, and changing environments, the pet is a constant, a kindly intermediary being between the uncertain self and the sometimes overwhelming nonself. The pet is an introduction to knowledge of animal habits, to sex, birth, and death, even to elementary planning and money-management.

In his last chapters, Levinson points out the value of pets to the adult and to the old. Here the list is shorter. The pet serves as a hedge against loneliness or as a child substitute. It is less obviously or urgently needed by the young adult than the old person. Levinson sees the waning years of life as a time when the pet serves as a means of redirecting interest to the nonhuman, to an extended realm of life and being in general. For the old, the pet is a demonstration of loyalty and caring during times of disability or bereavement. Levinson tells of conspicuous changes in the morale of the house-bound and bedridden, occu-

pants of rest homes and hospitals by the simple addition of a
canary or parakeet.

In sum, many things can be said for the pet in the home life
of our "alienated society." It is a focus of common interest between parents and children; it helps restore the process of emotional concern; it is a protector and nonjudgmental friend; it
demonstrates independent behavior, showing that the small
child's wish is not magic; its care is a lesson in cause and effect;
it is a substitute authority and recipient of projected anxieties;
its care requires learning responsibility; by moving with the child
it reduces separation anxiety; it is an aid to learning about the
body, sex, death; it consoles in bereavement; it is a preparation
for parenthood, and a child substitute.

In addition to these homely virtues, the pet has been used
with success by various psychiatrists for diagnosis and for treating serious mental disease, from childhood autism to adult
schizophrenia. In the drawings by children in the psychiatric
ward of Bellevue Hospital, aggression and wildness are associated. Children with only mild behavioral problems tended to
draw tame animals, while those with psychopathology chose
wild species. Children fleeing from bad homes made pictures of
birds or horses. Those representing themselves in the home drew
cats and dogs instead. Those with depression and inferiority
problems represented themselves as tame animals with fierce
expressions on their faces. Other aggressive animals were associated with animal phobias in which the creature was threatening to the child, or attacking and vicious species with which the
child identified. The more severe the psychosis, according to
Lauretta Bender and Jack Rapoport, the more aggressive the
animal. Depressed, rejected, inferior-feeling children identified
with large, unaggressive animals. The projection of certain features onto the fantasized animals (particularly oral, genital, and
anal traits) were from themselves or their parents, confirming
that virtually all of these figures were substitutes for either a
parent or themselves.

Toward the end of latency and the start of adolescence, when
the oedipal father-fear is still present but the renewal of infantile
processes characteristic of puberty has begun, the youth experiences a deep yearning to return to the mother. This desire is redirected toward large "maternal" animals that become symbolically pleasure-laden and invested with libido, yet, because of the

oedipal threat, are also anxiety-producing. "Back to mother" is therefore transferred to appropriate animals and to some extent to nature in general. "Back to Nature" is a juvenile theme that may be extended into adolescence and adult life, depending on how well these normal "problems" are resolved. Metaphors on the blissful primal state supply social idealisms with imagery, including the myth of world creation, a Mother Earth, and warm, friendly animals.

In general there does not seem to be much difference in the function of the pet among seriously ill patients and among normal children. Whether one begins with the inchoate child or the psychopathological individual, the development of a mature and healthy sense of self is helped by the availability of a non-human nonself.

One of two possible generalizations seems likely from these observations. One is that the animal companion is a kind of universal human need, like good nutrition. The alternative is that the conditions of modern urban life make it an appropriate preventive or treatment. The latter would make it analogous to the substitution of vitamin pills for a balanced diet, a sign of modern society's loss of contact with a healthy setting for human life, a situation welcomed by the entrepreneurs who get rich from all such remedial and preventive medicine. The therapist sees the extreme cases, in which the objective is to get the patient up to some kind of level of independent, stable function. What we seem to aim for in modern health care has almost never been the quality of vigor based on whole-body, whole-society medicine, but rather pathological medicine aimed at restoring the sick. If the modern child needs a puppy in order to encounter birth and death, then that child is in serious jeopardy already and the welcome benefits of the puppy, however real, should perhaps be seen as the kind of catch-up measures that characterize most of modern medicine and shut the physician away from attention to the quality of healthful life by committing him entirely to the care of the disabled and ill.

It is unlikely that the limitations of the domestic pet or captive animal as a health tool can be seen from within the sick society— or, rather, from within the perspective of the sick society. The pet-reared child and pet therapy can be examined against deprived children or patients or against the human (species) developmental schedule in a setting without domestic organisms,

whose breeding for superficial or utilitarian traits has deprived
them of the subtle, delicate nuances of behavior and form of
the wild. The captive is a sick creature, the domesticated animal
a monster; that we find them remedial is a comment on the desperate status of our human ecology.

The difficulty of receiving this message in a society where only
a few naturalists study nonhuman life in its native habitat is
immense. What is at stake has little to do with "appreciation of
our wildlife heritage" or wild animals as "natural resources," as
an "intangible value," or even as irreplaceable genetic reserves.
Captive and domestic animals are ontologically different from
their wild relatives. They are inextricably annexed to the human
landscape—which is itself a product of an economic system, a
net cast across everything, defining everything.

It is noteworthy that a theory of the value of pets should be
put forth by psychiatrists rather than, say, educators or social
workers. It speaks well for psychiatry which, like the other sciences of man, was without a nonhuman gestalt for too long.

Sigmund Freud, the father of psychiatry, called attention to
the animals in children's dreams, fantasies, and phobias in
Totem and Taboo. They typically occurred, he said, where there
were family problems that were repressed as too threatening to
confront. Hence animals were construed in the psychic realm as
human representatives. Since totemic societies saw animals as a
fantastic reflection of human kin relations, he said, and their
myths and beliefs were similar to the fantasies of troubled children, Freud concluded that animal imagery signified stress and
pathology, whether individual or cultural. This view of savages
easily made them victims of terrible anxieties. Freud himself
was not dogmatic about this, being more tolerant, less certain,
and more inventive than many of his followers. The Freudian
heritage says, in effect, however, that totemic thought is a vast
array of projections upon animals originating in neurotic behavior or as a crutch against its crippling effects. Either way, the
development of the personality is seen as a completely human
process, other species appearing only where it gets untracked
and employs them as mild surrogates.

Karl Menninger and Marcel Heiman emphasize the dog's
"totemic" functions; that is, its substitution for parents, helping
to sublimate "pre-oedipal cannibal fantasies, oedipal and aggressive drives." Ernest Rappaport observes that dogs serve in a

variety of ways as sexual objects, unconsciously displaced from the normal expression. Menninger regards dislike of animals as a phobia, and he includes hunting and vivisection, all as "reaction formations" originating in conflicts between people.

The Freudian psychiatrists are totemists with a vengeance. They certainly see the animal as a constituent of the personality. But they are not totemic in culture, for they equate the animal almost entirely with irrationality. For them it more often represents the failure of control and integration than it does a source of strength. The beasts of the human heart or head are not very poetic: The nightmare is a terrifying ride into a dark, id-dominated world; vicious beasts symbolize aggression, fish the aquatic substrate of our existence, and others intolerable, unnameable, unfaceable realities, as though the figure of the animals was left over from some Paleolithic terror of animals when they were themselves the realities.

One gets the feeling that the unconscious, like the jungle itself, in this view, is a tumult of contending monsters and storming furies, mostly hidden id-insurgences. Like the forest, the unconscious may be lawful in the sense of the blind forces of the galaxy contemplated by Newton, but not of the order of daily life.

No doubt the evidence of Levinson, Menninger, Heiman, and many others is based on clinical fact. But virtually all the benefits of pets that they have documented are compensations for social and ecological shortcomings of the society at large. In effect, as Levinson says, we humans are cut off from one another and from Nature, and the pet is a form of mental hygiene. The point is not to challenge their diagnoses or prescriptions, but to raise a somewhat different question about the nature of the processes for which pets are balm, and whether the *origin* of the problem doesn't have animals in it somewhere. There is something too simple in the idea of destructive animal impulses as opposed to peaceful human reason. There are good people living in small groups in remote places around the world, now almost exterminated, who do not attack their neighbors, who attend very carefully to both ecological and unconscious events, and who deliberate on the actions of the creatures of dream and jungle which seem to them a kind of shadowgraph. Attending to these things, they are engaged in an endless healing. Neither manipulating animals nor treating psychopathology, they somehow produce a state of affairs in which both of the deep jungles seem to them friendly. Their thought seems closer to Geza Roheim's descriptions of dream animals than to those of the strict Freudians.

Roheim said that animals in dreams are ancestral beings. The landscapes in which they live are the introjected terrain of our genital anatomy. It is a world fashioned from our own interior. The dream is a tactile regression, emitting visual phantoms for the inner eye, which has been deprived of its contact with the outer world. The dream state reverses that progressive, oral, eye-dominated thrust of the conscious mind. Sleep is a reverse transformation, a shift toward the beginning, toward ancestors. That is why, he says, dreams are related to initiation and to totemism.

On the surface it would seem that urban and suburban people keep all these animals as substitutes for the extended family, now diminished by the loss of clanship and cohesion. The end of the extended or communal kin group, even the breakdown of the nuclear family, and the experience of loneliness and isolation among modern men have all been widely examined and published. One cannot argue with the person, alone except for his parrot, who tells us that he is less lonely than without it. Yet there is something too simple about this answer.

We have perhaps accepted without much question that it is the mechanics of the urban world—social custom, single family dwellings, apartment life, displacement from place to place— that causes a sense of isolation. But perhaps it is the other way around. The absence of a feeling of belonging prevents people from forming significant social bonds, whatever their housing and working conditions. While rootlessness may do little to help make for community, some keep the same job for years. Why shouldn't people who are willing to care for a pet in the awkward metropolitan, many-storied city not direct that energy instead into establishing friendships with neighbors, joining clubs, caring for an aged relative or crippled friend, or seeking those with common interests? There are no available statistics that tell us whether solitary individuals actually keep more pets than socially active or happy people. Certainly the stereotype of the "family pet" belies the alternative that friendless, single people have more pets.

Why, then, all these millions of captive creatures? A possible answer is that identity-forming processes in childhood and adolescence have deteriorated or failed and that alienation in mass society is not simply loneliness, though it may be experienced that way, but is symptomatic of the breakdown of a complex series of steps by which the mature person comes to have a confident sense of self. One cannot just belong to the living stream, or just to humankind; those are extremely elementary perceptions in personal awareness. One's belonging must be more precise and specific. If in some way this developing sense of roots and connections is time-critical, geared to particular events in childhood or adolescence, the failure of this produces lifelong regression and flailing attempts to reconstitute the necessary circumstances. Therapy for such an alienated adult can never cure but only help him to endure the frustrations and lack of fulfillment.

If this is indeed the situation in which large numbers of people find themselves, then we should not be surprised to find large-scale fumbling with the paraphernalia of totemic thought. Fundamental to that thought is a lively attention to the nonhuman, from which the child must shape order out of the diversity and otherness of the nonhuman. Without that start, the individual gropes thereafter with the raw materials of that process in the same sense that boys with insufficient oedipal experience are doomed to struggle on as adults with the nature of sex roles. Without folk traditions or religious commitment, there is little help, and the result is that quiet, desperate search backward and deeper for roots.

Adrift in a secular world in which he has no clan commitment, and no sense of self as a microcosm, or having a sense of being a microcosm in a chaotic universe, the person may grope for the tangible means by which children in less "advanced" societies master the art of differentiating and classifying: the world of plants and animals. But the mind, like the body, is an organ with multiple ripenings, and going back is a pathetic, exceedingly difficult undertaking. In going back for the animals that should have richly surrounded childhood and that should have been the instruments of poetic insight, the results can only be partly successful. The deprived adult is likely to have that querulous, bemused, erratic, attenuated quality of all biologically inappropriate timings, like eggs laid out of season, too-early emergings from hibernation, or unsynchronized mating behavior. The nature of his experience is not fully conscious or understood by the person trapped within it. What he knows is loneliness and inchoateness. Buying a pet seems arbitrary and mildly satisfying. Asked to explain it, he is likely to say, "Well, the goldfish keeps me company."

And it does, of course. But the loneliness is the outcome of a way of life lacking human connections *because* of deprivation within a larger field of groupings and interrelationships. The fullness of personal identity comes at the end of a long series of nested positions within an embracing structure, a series of early experiences related to the availability not only of goldfish, but of carp, bass, pike, sunfish, catfish, trout, tuna. . . .

And the goldfish pet, what does it do for its owner beside create another presence? What tortured vision of post-domesticated, post-adolescent worlds of unity, balanced by diversity, are shaped by this one poor fish? And his keeper, the alienated soul—would he be better off with a fifty-gallon aquarium containing twenty species of exotic coral-reef animals? It doesn't matter. The loneliness is irreparable for those people if it resulted from a lack of animals. Keeping pets is a hopeless attempt to resurrect crucial episodes of early growth that are lost forever.

But what about the education of children? Responsibility for a pet, it is argued, teaches care-giving and planning. The child gets companionship, a taste of nonhuman life, and, ideally, he is routinely obligated to provide its needs and clean up after it. Of course, much depends on what the parents require, but even so it is extremely difficult to know whether any of the benefits actually follow. Animals that are abused or neglected would teach carelessness and callousness by the same logic. We all know children who not only do not feed the family dog but also tease it; are we prepared to argue that they are coarsened?

Among children having parental guidance and a caring habit, pets may indeed train concern for others—at least for other animals. In those parts of the world where there are no pets, there are no animal protection societies or wild species preservation societies. One is tempted to see a kind of progression from caring for a pet to caring about all the "lost" pets, and all the neglected and maltreated animals in farms and farm-factories as well as households and city streets. It is only a small step from that to a protective feeling for all animals everywhere, especially those in danger, threatened with extinction, killed as pests or hunted.

There is a kind of generalizing process with the emerging symbolic capacity of adolescence by which elements of previous experience are seen in wider meanings. How else are we to explain that strange twist of the modern conscience that extends our responsibility to whales or whooping cranes or Siberian tigers by people who have never seen them and who have no mythological or economic interest in them? Given their record of blindness to cruelty to farm animals for centuries, it hardly seems that world religions can take credit for that peculiar and tenacious will to protect all animals. There are many national and international organizations, all springing from Western industrial culture, their publications directed to the care of the world's wildlife, which seem close in spirit to the kind of thoughtful accountability a proper parent hopes to see in the pet-owning child.

There are cynics who see in this concern for animal protection a displacement of selfish anxiety, a projection upon the species of one's own neurotic worry about death. This notion of totally selfish motivation for compassion, putting one's own soul as the beneficiary for all altruism, is not new, though it has only recently been directed toward the "animal lovers." But this cynical view is unsatisfying, even as explanatory theory, because most of us know examples of selfless concern. The meanness and smallness of such an accusation not only allows for no real generosity or love, but seems itself to be sicker than the gushing sentimentality and displaced maternal cuddling by which animal protectionists are parodied.

A distinction is not often made by the critics of "nature lovers" between the passionately intense observation of animals found in all totemic thought and these murky regressions that lock animals sentimentally into substitutions. The animal lover is an object of ridicule by self-styled realists, with their practical or properly humanistic, safe sense of human superiority.

But there are grounds for doubt about the psychology of animal protectionism. The possibility of arrogance on the part of self-assigned caretakers of all creation has a ring of validity. Perhaps a large part of the conservation movement has this same worm in the apple; the posters saying, "This Is Your Land—Take Care of It" are, at face value, responsible, forward-looking, and public-spirited. But can we really own the land, the planet, or the elephants? The poster subsumes everything under the master plan of our dominance. An early event in the novel about Morel —in Romain Gary's *The Roots of Heaven*—describes his liberation of the dogs from a pound and beating up the dogcatcher, so we are given to understand that the elephants that he goes to Africa to protect represent a simple widening of scope. When agriculture created a barnyard fauna, the means was created for perceiving all animals as the proper responsibility of man. Such was Noah's assignment in the Old Testament. For pre-agricultural peoples no such intermediary, dependent kingdom existed; there was no husbandry to suggest a planetary husbandry—nor were there maximizing economies that threatened the existence of large wild mammals. For urban man the barnyard bridge has largely ceased to exist, but the pet has taken its place: the model of his responsibility to animals.

If childhood pet care is a first step by which the maturing individual moves toward stewardship of all nonhuman life, it may be potentially valuable for man and beast in spite of the hubris it implies. We see that it is an adjustment to life in the modern world, not the recovery of an instrument from an authentic origin so much as grasping for ecological connections in a world where we seem buried under humanity and its products. Perhaps it is a sign of the desperate strength of the human loyalty to things larger than man, a silent thrust toward recovery of balance in a world overwhelmed with human weight and the noise of self-praise and self-denunciation.

In this sense pet-keeping may have social benefits that have nothing to do with the alleged character-building associated with steady dependability through routine caretaking. Whether such training would make people better parents or healthier adults may be less evident than its general effects of keeping otherness before us, in spite of the debilitated quality of the animal. But room for doubt remains.

In *The Roots of Heaven*, Morel, the obsessed protector of elephants, has no room in his life for family, friends, or pets. Like other true ideologists, he becomes impersonal and socially incompetent. Morel may be the end product of a whole series of man-animal relationships in which people take the lives of animals as their responsibility. What seems at one end to be simply generous and necessary is at the other shrill and arrogant. No totemic culture proclaims, as world religions have done, that man is God's viceroy, that he is the steward of the Earth. The historical model we have for being lieutenant of the planet is the shepherd and husbandman, who always destroy the wildness of the animals they seek to protect. The secular or professional form of this is "game management" or "wildlife management," in which the manipulations are simply more extensive. Surveillance, fencing, marking, trapping, controlled breeding or "game farming," sampling, harvesting are all the other metaphors from farming. Morel tried to avoid all these techniques and simply put himself between the animals and human encroachment, a mind-breaking task in the modern world.

Alone on a Domesticated Planet

In human societies of the Neolithic that first began to transform the environment on a large scale,* animals continued to be instruments of thought as they had been for thousands of years. They had served as a means of manipulating ideas by serving as concrete symbols of them and as a model of order. These uses were differentially adapted to phases of human development, one means by which the society coaxed forth the individual's self-awareness and intellectual activity by providing tangible references to which ideas could be linked.

The domestic animal must be seen in this same light, for men continued to use the nonhuman for purposes of discovering the self and group identity, creating a human analogy to the comity of creatures according to a logic of parallels and mythological explanations.

Domestic animals, however, do not exist in wild habitats. They are genetically adapted to environments made by themselves and people: the immediate environs of settlements, pastures whose characteristic plants are adapted to heavy trampling, overgrazing, erosion and soil impoverishment, and protection from predators. The domestic animal is inseparable from a landscape where the human shaping and the human smudge touches everything. The fiction by which myth converted animals to *dramatis per-*

* It has been argued, but not proven, that Paleolithic man modified his environment by massive exterminations and by the use of fire. Even if true, the use of this information against ecology is fraudulent. The small size of the human population in the Paleolithic, the vast time over which such changes took place, and the enormous areas of land not affected put this picture of the pre-agricultural impact of man on nature into proper perspective as a minor force in the world.

sonae incorporated, in tame societies, tame animals. Their inter-locking, humanized condition sometimes was represented by half-human monsters. But the stories, communicated verbally and by art, had the same end: to illuminate the nature of man and, to a more limited degree, of the world.

Men have always known that the medium of domesticated-animal images was insufficient. To minds honed on a million years of the natural riches of wild species, a few dozen domestic breeds would never do. Every society continued to shape the minds of its young on admixtures of wild and tame, even long after the particular wild species had disappeared from the nearby countryside.

Today, in contemporary versions of animal banners, coats of arms, scarabs, seals, emblems, the bestiary, biblical homilies, literary tropes, animated cartoons, stuffed-animal toys, puppets, illustrations for children's books, comic strips, motifs for fabrics, ceramic and glass designs, wallpaper, adventure movies, sculp-ture and painting and the decoration of objects, the wild remains mixed with the domestic. We cling to the need for ecumenical communication in which we see our human possibilities beyond the shaping by our own hand. Real quality in mankind cannot be imaged by the swaybacked cow, neurotic racehorse, bloated pig, flightless white duck, but only by the auroch, tarpan, boar, and snow goose; not the dog but the wolf.

The domesticated animals, like the wild, are a set of messages. Living in a world which, at the level of the senses, is heavily man-modified, congested, and polluted, the spavined horse, land-scalping goat, and pea-brained sheep are important signals. If we have made habitats of poor quality for all of life, we have also made bedtime stories of poor-quality animals. If our mastery of nature enables us to synthesize foods that are nutritionally in-adequate or poisonous, then, likewise, our mastery of animals gives us a vocabulary for revealing our plight to ourselves. The pathos of the over-fat pig, white rat stripped of nuance, and dog breeds with their congenital debilitations signals to us an aspect of the human condition. Animals have always been the agents of our self-knowledge. For most of human history we read that wis-dom in the flight of wild geese or the organs of the butchered bison. Now, our mastery of nature diminishes the goose or bison in our consciousness. We have laid hands on a few of the crea-tures and reshaped them according to the demands of productivity and slavery. They do not cease to be pieces of a reflecting mirror, for their good animal foundations and their very deformity are reports on our insides.

The fictional dramas that they enact are in the service of commerce. Their cutie exteriors and over-larded interiors are superficial parts of the message, side remarks on cosmetics and diet. Because of its truth, the heart of the message is, in a way, consoling. The monstrousness of progress, dominating nature and controlling the planet, as though its total life and physical processes were part of a beast-machine in human service, is built into the monstrous figures of animals that those ideals have produced. What we do to ourselves is there for us to read by analogy. In the beginning of the mastery obsession, as totemic culture was destroyed by class societies, the captive animals were the actual tools of control. Now they are ceasing to be such, replaced by machines. But they continue to be the most trustworthy readout on the quality of the planet.

As a part of the world's animal life, the domestic animals speak only to a part of us—a protected, unexercised, malnourished, psychopathic, socially fragmented, debauched part. As we are tradition-poor, our captive animals are instinct-poor; as we are confused in the meaning of our gender, they have been shorn of species recognition; as we gloat over the "great art" of a few geniuses, they produce prize-winning deformities; as they are free from want and predation, so we are free to vote; as they have acquired existential freedom from their species of origin, we have achieved ideological freedom.

In totemic culture the animal world was not a mirror, but a set of communications about a universe not made by man. Men have hung up some bits of scenery and proclaimed themselves makers of a world. A few animals were taken in as supporting cast in the playlet, but animals remain as the screen upon which some aspects of the drama are projected. For those aspects they are the only screen available.

Man's greatest fear, says Bruno Bettelheim, is being left alone, or "separation anxiety." This fear takes different expression as we grow older. In infancy it is the temporary loss of the mother; in childhood, of companions or parents; and in maturity, of spouse or friends. But is the modern loneliness only these? Is there some way in which we experience the loneliness of our species for other species? In Gary's *The Roots of Heaven,* Morel says, "Man on this planet has reached the point where really he needs all the friendship he can find, and in his loneliness he has need of all the elephants, all the dogs, and all the birds. . . ."

But apart from a kind of spurious friendship, or the master-slave relationship of domestication and pets, how can the individual experience anything for the species? Attempts to answer the question too often sound like a romantic dream for an imaginary Paradise. The answer may be that the loneliness is not social in the sense of a relationship in which man and beast consort, but a different mode, whereby the physical reality of animal difference and multiformity are in some way prior to the development of companionship among people, an experience of animals without which strictly human interactions give us crowding rather than fellowship. It is felt as a loss of harmony in the self or within society or among nations, but it has its source in a failure of the primitive sources of energy for bringing a disparate world together. Caste system, with its wrecking of our sensitivity to otherness, shifted to the production of types of goods by classes as the basis of society and now moves toward transforming the whole planet, making it over into an industrial farm. Modern technology makes everything a product of man. Order in nature, according to the philosophy of this view, offers no guiding wisdom, no heuristic design, no relationships with hidden analogies to culture. It offers only molecular order, to be rearranged for our consumption, species order to be tamed for our amusement, and stellar order to be the arcane playground of mathematical games and spectator rocket sports.

The image of religious man in peasant caste societies is that of the meditator whose aim is either stewardship or merger with an ultimate unity. Escape from the decline and disorder of this world is a reasonable goal in societies which, by dint of thousands of years of toil, have removed everything not serving man, thereby increasing ecological disorder amid the aimlessness of a consuming egoism. The intricate symbioses of wild ecosystems, the kingdoms of otherness half hidden in secret lives, the private purposes of migration, hibernation, and metamorphosis in the water or in the air come to an end and are unknown. That world cannot reveal hidden purposes of life where we have annexed and tamed its purposes. Deep in his heart each of us knows that the mystery of the self is as great as that of the universe—perhaps is the same mystery. Since men first began to think, to puzzle out their own self-consciousness, they found resonances of their inmost feelings in the world around them, creatures differing from one another as though to reflect the way their own ideas and emotions differed. The latter were fleeting and the former remained, as though the animals were a language speaking our own inner diversity, our own roaring and squeaking, our feathered thoughts and swimming emotions. When we excluded and exterminated that tangible empire, we lost the means of addressing the diversity of the self and of society. The wheat field, tree farm, and barnyard, the caged birds and pet cats are a few coarse phrases from that language.

We now try to puzzle out the meaning of our lives as best we can, by introspection, by being external mirrors to one another in group encounter, by fixating on the internal anatomy as the meditative points of departure. That language of which wild species formed the grammar always included internal reference points made visible in butchering. Lacking opportunity to witness dissection, we have substituted our own bodies for kinesthetic concentration. The seven anatomical centers associated with Buddhist meditation seem to be a final effort to continue the body plan as a kind of mental or spiritual tool, except that in Buddhist thought the mind leaps from that inner geography to an outer space eternal. We are, it seems to say, pure microcosms, without landscape, other animals, environment—no mesocosm. All of that is merely dross, a shambles, mere mortal forms, illusions, surfaces having imperfect worldly embodiment. Shintoists, Christians, Moslems, and Jews leap in their prayers from the inner self to the eternal sky gods. None of this tarrying with dumb beasts. And who can blame them, for the beasts are no longer worthy of holy attention. Christians screen icons from the temples and look down their noses at "superstitious" primitives who lack not only bathrooms and nuclear power plants, but who are still trying to puzzle out their existence by reference to other life—which we *know*, in our five thousand years of turning them into blobs, are neither interesting nor keys to spiritual grace.

Since sometime before the year 10,000 B.C., human groups have been undergoing the "agricultural revolution," of which the "industrial revolution" and "electronic revolution" are current modes. From worldwide totemic clan cultures to village caste systems—and from that to city-dominated principalities and urban industrial states—the transition is still taking place. All class societies turn away from plants and animals as a key to intellectual model-making. They are preoccupied with producing something and consuming much. The animals and plants that they find useful are turned into products or goods. All sorts of intermediate stages, mixing totemic culture with these production systems, occur today in tribal and village peoples. Over much of the world there is still an echo of that older system of binary oppositions and analogous realms. In a few remote places the wild still is seen as having an order of its own, like and yet unlike the domestic. That call of the wild lingers in the unconscious of people even in the most modernized societies, where it is commercialized as a media product in nature pictures, articles, or documentaries. Caste or hierarchic thought has yet to spread its net over everything on the planet. In its village or "third world" form, it incorporated domestic animals into the human group, lower than man, yet part of his society. Industrial agriculture is changing that alliance. Viewing the animals as machines, it is transforming them into rural factories. They are being replaced by breeds that are not producers or workers, but poor freaks of a different sort, kept on like the dwarfs, jugglers, and courtesans of the past, for their amusing performances or exotic personalities.

The remnants of the truly wild get smaller and less wild. What could be done by pastoralists with a flock of sheep can now be done with a herd of elephants in its park or reservation, with wildfowl in their refuges—their food, predators, and diseases more and more manipulated. The first step in domestication is taming, and around the world our representatives with notebooks, telescopes, drug-bearing darts, radios on collars, and endless cameras are making vicarious barnyards in the television tube. The zoo has become a halfway station and the industry supplying wild pets is beginning to rear rather than capture its stock. Stock is something on the shelf and livestock something on the hoof that will soon be on the shelf. The naturalists, cameramen, wildlife experts, tour guides, refuge bureaucrats, zoo representatives, and dealers in wild pets are out there in the outback, taking stock; counting, sorting, marking, shuffling, and sampling. Most of them are sympathetic to the plight of the wild and seem to personally enjoy their adventurous lives among the last of the wild. But they are as surely the forerunners of the juggernaut as ranching, planting, lumbering, pesticides, herbicides, roads, and fences.

6 THE AESOP ACCOUNT

There is an island in our collective mental landscape—or sea-scape—with a fauna all its own, not of exotic species, or endemic forms, as the biologist would say, but having its own unique mixture. The island is the huckster's sea-mount, a part of the archipelago of commerce, a coral strand of magazine ads where live the creatures of the adman's bestiary. All sorts of exploring parties keep putting in to the beaches, but they never pay much attention to the animals or plants. Yet the advertising business spends surprising amounts of energy and money to sway the consumer by way of animal pictures. There is no evidence that it knows why, but it works, and that's everything in the jungle of selling.

Advertising is a contemporary expression of a more general commercial theme; it must make connections with imagery and values shared by a large number of consumers or it will fail. It projects the popular mood more precisely than the fine arts, which have more lag and snobbery. When Marshall McLuhan used advertisements as both targets and instruments for social criticism, he became the foremost explorer of these islands and his *The Mechanical Bride* was a beachhead of skeptical forces amid the sweet talk and the whorling of images.

McLuhan wrote, "Ever since Burkhardt saw that the meaning of Machiavelli's method was to turn the state into a work of art by the rational manipulation of power, it has been an open possibility to apply the method of art analysis to the critical evaluation of society." David Potter, a historian of American character and its relationship to the land's abundance, estimated that advertising was at least as potent as the Church as an agency of social control, being founded on deeply rooted, common assumptions and reactions that can be exploited with symbols. He saw advertising as an institution with extreme sensitivity to its col-

lective membership and with facility in giving form to their beliefs by conventionalizing and projecting. Such institutions are
actually conservative rather than creative. They feed back to the
public what it already knows and manipulates them by imposing
those ideas as truths to which they hold the key. If Americans
no longer find the security of common conviction in church, they
seek it elsewhere. That advertising attempts to direct those ideas
to its own ends by linking them to the market is irrelevant to the
study of its power to disclose themes in the collective mind. The
misuse of its energy does not diminish its efficiency at social
reflection—what it asks the public to do is another matter. Potter
notes advertising's efficiency to pick the public mind and regrets
its institutional irresponsibility, a familiar enough lament, although the ethical shortcomings and greed may be just as much
a reflection of public mores as the content of the ads is of public
wants.

Anyway, the metaphor of an island in *our* heads is not quite
right. When we wade ashore to do our animal survey, instead of
arriving at the antipodes we may be skulking about in advertising's game farm. It is an enclave where media scows periodically
drop off the beasts snared from the dark forests of our collective
minds. Even if it is only a small sample and not the whole fauna,
it should tell us something about how we now think about
animals.

How seriously it is to be taken depends on your point of view.
But for the purpose of our tour, let us accept advertising's sensitivity with the friendly critics. It does not have to represent the
best of our cultural creativity, nor the mythology of our commercial culture to reveal what happened to creatures that have
surrounded us for thousands of years, when we and they become
denizens of the industrial state.

As we slosh ashore, a few words about the general geography.
What is reported here comes from a few hundred copies of *Life*,
Time, and *The Saturday Evening Post* (the island of Litisep?)
arbitrarily chosen from the mid-1950s—new enough to be pertinent but old enough to give us some sense of detachment. The
animal inhabitants are all the animals in a sample of ten thousand advertisements, big enough to provide data with some statistical reliability if you like that sort of thing, which most
naturalists (as opposed to biologists) don't. Excluded from the
analysis are those ads in which animals are the producers or the

recipients of the product, such as flea powder, dog food, saddles, milk, or sausage.

Of the total, 573 have animals. They roam through glossy landscapes that are exotic and yet familiar, a world not like another planet where everything is totally different, nor like the Galápagos, with its richness of half-familiar forms. The number of species is not great. Clearly it is not a tropical jungle with a vast diversity of creatures, but is more like a Pacific atoll or an Alaskan coastal island or one of the Hebrides. Less than 6 percent of the ten thousand ads have animals, and they are limited in diversity, yet the paper they cover probably cost several million dollars and the fauna are peculiar.

The Litisep animals are certainly not a random sample from nature. The animal kingdom of the natural world is commonly divided by biologists into twenty-eight phyla, each with its classes and orders. In the ads we find only two phyla: the Arthropoda, containing the insects, crustaceans, spiders, and centipedes; and the Vertebrata, the birds, mammals, fish, frogs, and reptiles. The flat plains and foggy air of our little island contain very few of the first group, which in nature constitutes three quarters of all the animals on Earth, and of the second group almost all but mammals and birds are excluded.

Still, what you see is what you get in the ads. The vertebrates are the conspicuous forms in our worlds, and we ourselves are vertebrates. Although only 6 percent of the animals on Earth are vertebrates, those include most of the large terrestrial forms. For the prowling naturalist almost anywhere, when he sees something move among the leaves or grasses, there is about one chance in sixteen it is a vertebrate. But we are not naturalists in remote jungles, and for us and the adman's bestiary, the crouching creature will be a vertebrate nine times out of ten. The perceptual exaggeration of vertebrates over "true zoology" is more than fourteenfold.

Among the vertebrates in nature's nature, the number of fish about equals that of mammals, and the fish and mammal species combined about equal the number of kinds of birds. The amphibians and reptiles, though numbering in the hundreds of species, are less than a third as numerous as mammals. The real planet is very rich in birds, with mammals and fish about even, relatively few frogs and salamanders, snakes and turtles. On the island, however, four fifths of the animals are those hairy milk-giving mammals, a seventh are birds, and the other 4 percent are fish, frogs, and arthropods.

It is a topsy-turvy world that cannot be entirely explained away as just a difference in what happens to be most easily seen, although that must be part of the explanation for the rarity of fish and insects. Man is a mammal and he undoubtedly has a special feeling for others with warm blood. All humans share in the suckling, cuddling, nesty parenthood invented by the mammals. Mammals have faces and move about in family groups. Hairiness may be beastly, but it is our kind of animality, while scales and feathers tend to leave us cold. Perhaps there is a universal bond linking all human mothers to all females who can lactate and connecting all of us who once nursed—or at least nuzzled—at a mother's breast.

Litisep Island is not a representative sampling even of mammals. The warmth of that feeling of fellowship is not democratically diffused. There are no weasels, pangolins, or bats, which are also Mammalia. If simple genetic relatedness were the whole answer, the timescape would be crowded with matronly apes and monkeys. Instead it is a swirl of dogs, cats, horses, and other hoofed animals, with a scattering of bears and elephants. It is a biogeographer's nightmare, reminiscent of the Walt Disney film based on the *Swiss Family Robinson,* set on a Pacific island teeming with elephants, lions, tigers, ostriches, and apes, few of which ever got east of Africa and none of which dwells on islands. Perhaps for the ad reader, as for the child, everything is possible, but the naturalist is likely at this point to sit for a moment while his vertigo subsides. It is in the same tradition of *Tarzan of the Apes* films, set deep in vined jungles, crawling with large animals, none of which actually lives in jungles.

In other ways, the ads are very unlike Tarzan films and more akin to the suburban and rural habitats of Northwestern Europe and North America. More than half the animals shown are domesticated forms, though not those of Asia or South America, no alpacas or water buffaloes to speak of. As we make our way through this terrain, every other animal we meet is a cat, horse, or dog, and the dogs are not those skulking, skinny scavengers that slip furtively around the villages in more than half the world, nor are the horses those lean, suffering skeletons wasted by heat and disease. This island may have a few bushy corners, but it is mainly a temperate climate, a man-centered community of domestics.

As good naturalists we will look more closely at just what dogs these are, and watch to see if what they do here is the same as at home. Thirty percent of all our animal sightings here are dogs. So many different dogs give an impression of different species, of different kinds rather than variations on a genetic theme. It seems unlikely that there would be as many dogs if they all looked pretty much alike. Biologically they don't actually diversify the fauna; put them all in one pen for a few scores of years and all the variety would be melted into one plain dog.

A spot check of more recent issues of these magazines shows the same range in types, but in different frequencies. The cocker, so popular in the Eisenhower years, has dropped down into the middle of the list. Fox terriers and bulldogs had their day before the spaniels, poodles, and cocker-poos, and fashion will undoubtedly continue to shuffle the breeds as part of the new-model or progress syndrome that envelops most of our commodities. Statistically they behave like species in a natural community: If the number of individuals is plotted on a graph with the breeds in order from most to least abundant, the points form a curve of the same kind commonly found among wild animals in real nature. A few kinds are very common and a large number of breeds are rare or very uncommon. There is no straight line of diminishing abundance. Whether or not we are aware of this kind of structure in nature, we seem to be collectively reconstituting it among dogs.

Next to dogs the hoofed animals are the most common, primarily horses. Before magazines and before recorded history, horses and men had a long rapport. Reindeer, caribou, rhinoceroses, and bears came and went in the diet of pre-Europeans, but for a hundred thousand years the horse was regularly hunted and eaten. Compared to that literal taste for horseflesh, riding and working them may be considered as having begun yesterday. Together with cattle, goats, and sheep, the horse-livestock group is about as abundant as dogs. While the purpose of the horse has shifted from food and power to riding and petship, it doesn't yet lie around on the hearth or go in the car, but it seems to be becoming just a bigger dog. Of the rest of the animals occupying these vistas, the cats and birds form a sizable portion.

Altogether there are a total of 124 species and more than 40 breeds. Of these, 56 species are mammals, 44 birds, 4 reptiles, 1 amphibian, 11 fish, and 8 arthropods, of which 6 are insects. Of the animals observed, 58 percent are domestic breeds: cattle, cats, horses, and a few birds and fish. The remaining 42 percent is a much more diverse group of 105 species of wild animals. Again the zoological rule of many uncommon forms in low numbers holds. Of these 105, 65 of them were seen only once. The adman clearly continues the tradition of the bestiary with his interest in the rare and strange. The fauna may be trite in some ways, but not in its fascination with the odd and unusual. Rarity has its place in the imagination, reflecting biology, a kind of reciprocal of the standardized brand name.

Like the bestiary, too, the Litisep fauna is not at all provincial. The explorer in Australia expects to see mostly marsupials, and in the Arctic, Arctic animals, but this island fauna belongs to no one part of the world. Cheek by jowl with 76 species native to North America are 35 foreign to that continent. About half of all the wild mammal species are exotic. This is less true of the birds, of which only a quarter are not American. Is it that birds are strange enough in themselves, or could it be that American mammals are insufficiently diverse or too poorly known? From the early days of discovery and settlement, American mammals failed to live up to expectations or comparison. Although Nicholas Le Challeux wrote of America in 1565, "The country is also rich in gold and in all sorts of animals, both tame and wild, which roam its large fair fields," it was wishful thinking. The streets of gold never materialized. Animals enough there were, the bison was passingly conspicuous to *some* white men later on, but many of the other mammals were smallish and prickly. Meanwhile, the fashionable ménage of Renaissance zoological parks included giraffes, rhinoceroses, zebras, and apes. The zoogeographic mythology of the times, coupled with new discovery, must have given the educated European a rich selection. The splendid reality of Africa put American faunas in the shade. Subjectively, perhaps it is still inadequate.

The magazine animals are drawn from worldwide habitats, but does the habitat come with them? Is the animal perceived in a white vacuum? Are there small but telltale signs of its appropriate environment, chunks of its native terrain, or whole landscapes? The answer varies depending on the kind of animal.

Three quarters of the domestic animals are standing on the earth, and there are signs of some kind of habitat or place. Of these, the dogs are nearly always seen as part of an environment. It is very different with tame and wild cats, the rabbits, elephants, the wild hoofed animals, and the birds, which appear more often to be dissected out of the tangible world and set amid a terrain of words.

Maybe the reason is that domestic animals are normally thought of as "part of the scenery" while wild forms are more often seen in zoos and museums (house cats are a special case to be discussed later). Or the knowledge that no animal is whole apart from its environment comes, for most of us, only from the experience of our pets. Fish, however, we all know to be dependent on their medium, so four swim in the ads for each one that floats in space. Three quarters of the bears also live in landscapes, though it is not apparent why. Not so the rabbit or the house cat. The familiar independence of the latter not only frees it from the necessity of human companionship, but of setting. Only 40 percent of them have so much as a blade of grass or wisp of carpet to walk on. It seems that there are fishy places and beary places, but few catty or rabbity places.

Part of the animal's environment is human. As one might expect, dogs and horses are nearly always encountered along with people. Many of the rodents live in yard, alley, or buildings, and there they are found most of the time. Yet, though they are fellow inhabitants with man of these places, they are only seen in his company about 15 percent of the time. The wild animals, in general, have about the same frequency of human accompaniment, except for elephants and bears, who appear with people four times as often. That is too much of a difference to be a chance variation and needs explanation.

That explanation will emerge as we look at the behavior of the creatures we encounter on Litisep Island. Behavior to a biologist usually means the animal's movements in space and time, including its interactions with others. Here its behavior means something more. One could record every moment of a bank president's day without ever acknowledging his role as an arbiter of lives or as an economic force in the community. The squirrel in the same town with the banker may be said to bury acorns, but it also plants forests. In nature, niches are specific to the kind of animal, and behavior is part of those niches. But they coalesce into broad categories. All green leaves, for instance, are "making sugar" and sustaining animals. Certain general categories of this kind seem to exist for the fauna of the ads. This, of course, is a naïve classification, an impressionistic grouping, awaiting its Darwin. The fauna looks like this:

Animalia Litiseps
"Adbeasts"

I Order *Hominis substitutis*
   Type 1: Allegorical
   Type 2: Analogical
   Type 3: Humanized

II Order *Hominis extendus*
    Type 4: Productive
    Type 5: Household
    Type 6: Social Status
    Type 7: Salacious

III Order *Trait fixe*
     Type 8:   Anatomical
     Type 9:   Physiological
     Type 10: Mechanical
     Type 11: Literary

IV Order *Tempus/locus*
    Type 12: Archaic
    Type 13: Mythic
    Type 14: Calendric
    Type 15: Habitat
    Type 16: Region
    Type 17: Circus

Type 1: Allegorical. The monkey with hands over its mouth is one of the three virtues. The slow turtle is dependability, as opposed to the skittering hare. Storks deliver newborn, geese lay golden eggs, and foxes look up at sour grapes. The allegorical animal is bent on giving us a lesson. It may be based on real or imagined behavior, but always has a second meaning, a traditional, instructive purpose, usually well known and needing no interpretation. The animals of Aesop and the bestiaries are, many of them, well-enough known that their precepts are evoked just by the image of the animal. In the ad world, this part of the fauna is predominantly wild animals, mostly birds.

Type 2: Analogical. Sometimes the explorer of strange places comes upon an animal caught in a situation that is strikingly parallel to a human event. It is not one of those customary lessons of the sort labored by bestiaries, but a transient posture or momentary problem that seems to mirror the human condition. An oasis in the desert with its camels is like a modern service station, while a rough-riding camel suggests an automobile in need of lubrication. Sheep in a herd remind us of the loss of individuality; big eyes are "insurance" for a tarsier; an alligator's "tail is dragging"; the mother kangaroo is a "long-distance mover"; and a fine horse speaks of purebreds in general.

Type 3: Humanized. Whatever else they may be doing, creatures wearing clothes, talking, or driving automobiles are included here. In presenting them as personified, less is left to the imagination than among the two previous types. They are usually caught up in human situations and behave like people, standing on their hind legs, smoking pipes, and rather more homely than their allegorical relatives in classic stories. Two thirds of these are wild animals. That is, domestic animals are more likely to remain only as we know them, while the wild, being strange and different, have less private character of their own. The type is heavily dominated by bears and rabbits which, on the adman's island, spend more than half their time being human—or is it people being bears and rabbits? Perhaps this helps to explain the frequency with which bears are accompanied by people.

Type 4: Productive. There is nothing subtle about this group. It exists for man's use, to carry his burdens, transport him, do his work, and serve him in other ways. One would expect that this would be a frequent type, since our culture is rooted in the man-animal partnership of historical Europe, and one finds mainly domesticated forms in this group. Surprisingly, of 332 encounters with domestic animals, only 10 percent were engaged in load-pulling, guarding, retrieving, carrying, and giving milk or wool. Social critics complain that we live in a materialistic society with a utilitarian sense of nature, and surely the existence of the adman's island where, indirectly, all the creatures are drafted into selling something, supports that view. Yet the animals are not often seen literally in human service.

Type 5: Household. An important "behavior" of pets is to complete an ideal family scene, to help give body to those idealized pictures of the stable and traditional family. As a complement of the human family group, these domestic animals (only 3 percent are wild) probably add a nostalgic feel. This is the second-largest type and is heavily dominated by dogs, not one of which is seen tied or penned. In the days of county and municipal restrictions, more fancy breeds and fewer children, the romping dog may be nearly as much a fantasy animal as the talking bear.

Type 6: Social Status. The family dog playing with children may still be a mongrel, but there is another realm dominated by dogs on Litisep where mixed breeds seldom appear, and that is as snob emblems. A few are merely indicators of economic status or social condition, like pigs in the yard of a hillbilly house. Most of these, however, appeal directly to the upward mobility and its signs of rank: expensive wild captives like parrots or lions, fine horses, and uppity dog breeds. Some of the setters and boxers in these pictures are so high class that they themselves are looking haughty. More often, they are just the innocent victims of the ghastly arts of the breeders and the ebb and flow of taste-making among the hoi polloi of dog fanciers. Generally hunting dogs are the elite, along with polo ponies, and all the other nineteen breeds of dogs in this never-never land arrange themselves in order, from poodles and terriers down to spaniels, dachshunds, shepherds, and to the bottom where hounds and mixed breeds attach themselves to scenes with kids and blue-collar workers and the inverse snobbery of plain folks.

Type 7: Salacious. Nobody needs to be told that sex is used to sell things. But when it takes the devious route of employing animals, it may seem unnecessarily complicated. Perhaps the arts of pseudosophistication are complicated, or the disguised perversions involving animals are thrilling enough to consumers to make a difference. Anyway, it is the familiar forms—dogs, horses, and cats—that predominate. The very association of women and large mammals is erotic, especially if the woman is fashionably dressed and the animals are high-spirited horses. Much depends on the elements of the picture as a whole, but French poodles with their little woolly wigs and intruding noses are part of a lap-dog tradition that does not have to be verbalized to be effective. Languorous women holding pussies attract the eye for similar reasons.

Type 8: Anatomical. Some animals are not only known for a

certain physical trait, but seem to be little else. Camels are humps, kittens are softness, kangaroos are pouches, ducks shed water, and zebras are stripes. This fixation on a single characteristic is not common among familiar animals of the household, but is a frequent "activity" of the large, hoofed wild mammals, or ungulates. It is as though the less well known the animal, the more narrowly conventionalized it is. Like the Cheshire cat, whose grin remains after all else has vanished, these creatures vanish behind a single bodily trait. There is evidence from field studies in Africa that the zebra's stripes actually help camouflage it, but on this island the stripes make it conspicuous, just as they do in the zoo. The whole series of wild forms seems to be a kind of storehouse in which each species is the guardian of some particular feature.

Type 9: Physiological. This group is essentially like the preceding one, except the point is what the animal does instead of how it looks. This is the largest group, with nearly one quarter of all the animals in the ads engaged in characteristic behavior. It may seem strange at first even to remark on an animal's behavior, since being itself is just what we should expect. But these animals are not doing all the things their natural equivalents do: They seldom sleep or eat and they never defecate or copulate, at least not in the presence of our exploring party. They are more rigidly typed than character actors in Hollywood. Just as the poor camel is condensed into a hump or two as an Anatomical type, here his brother mammal, the beaver, differs only in being distilled into his work—dam-building. There is no rest on Litisep for beavers or ants or bees. Mules only balk, turtles creep, bulldogs persist, bulls charge, and kittens play. It is a predictable world of specialists.

Type 10: Mechanical. Predictability of behavior is still short of pure mechanism, which is reached with animals composed of pistons, tubes, and valves. Here they are, not only Cartesian in theory, but in the public eye in forms made possible by two centuries of industrial technology to provide the anatomy. To imagine animals as machines, Descartes had only wheels and levers, and the whole idea still seemed exotic. But we have the vast array of familiar automobile parts, the popular mechanics imagery and electronic components of the insides of gadgets, which must surely be more familiar to us than the insides of pigs or sheep or anything else living. A typical example is an aviation engine called the Wasp and illustrated with the head and wings of a real wasp. The main alternative to this concept seems to be that animals are little people with furry coats on, and everyone worldly knows *that's* just for kids.

Type 11: Literary. This category does not allude to the written literature, but to verbal games. These creatures lend their names in wordplay, puns, alliterations, or onomatopoeic linkage to the adman's purpose. "From cranes to computers" or "from penguins to penicillin" are phrases from a whole series of examples. Most of them come from the folk phrases of metaphorical comparison: "to make a monkey out of," "to talk turkey," "to make a beeline for." Many are derived from natural history, like "Don't fish around" and "We perch our case" and durability of things that are "a bear for wear." This is the category in which animals without any logical association with a commercial product may be linked to it so that our attention is held. The intrinsic strangeness and beauty of the animal is enough. The diversity of the fauna is greatly increased by this linguistic connection.

Type 12: Archaic. While the preceding category tends to make Litisep Island exotic by pulling to it creatures from everywhere, the last six types all work in the opposite direction, associating the island with known places or times. The Archaic animal is an anachronism in this modern world. It is not only out of date itself, but disgraces anything associated with it in a world of progress. Horses pulling buggies and longhorn cattle on the range are obsolete, and the obsolescence, like a disease, attacks anything around it. Occasionally it enhances those things with historical virtue. For evoking a nostalgic past of nineteenth-century family farm, domestic animals in rustic stalls will do. It is even possible to combine that longing for a past that never was with the message that it was a lot of work and is not acceptable today. The real body-blows of the dead past are signaled by fossils, so we find dinosaurs and dodoes scattered among the merely old-fashioned forms. Any style of refrigerator or automobile on which falls the shadow of a dinosaur is too old or obsolete to work and should be replaced. It is a narrow line between gentility and decay, but the wizards of Litisep can walk it.

Type 13: Mythic. The remains of these creatures cannot be found in museums. They belong to an oral or artistic tradition, to folklore, magic, and myth. Some are not creatures of folklore in form, but in behavior or size, like Paul Bunyan's ox, or an Arctic mosquito that can carry a man, or an ordinary-looking goose that can lay a golden egg. Most of this type are birds, such as the phoenix or the roc. There are also reptiles, of which the most familiar is the dragon. But the climate of this island must be changing, for the mythical animals seem to be a tattered lot, especially the dragons, which are small, decrepit, and unobtrusive, even reduced to captivity, ridicule, and the role of comic.

Type 14: Calendric. Mainly birds and livestock, these forms are the symbols of a holiday or a season. There are not many left, but those that remain seem secure and abundant. They are St. Nick's reindeer, Independence Day eagles, the groundhogs and robins of Spring, Thanksgiving turkeys, and Easter rabbits. Like the folklore animals of the preceding type, they are survivors from a richer era, with bits of pagan celebration stuck to their fur, rather tolerated than encouraged in a Christian world. They seem like commercial captives doing stunts to enliven the human landscape and its gray creations. But their asinine yokes and banal looks may be simply signs of their reduced status—hiding, sleeping giants whose time could come again, bringing the rituals and ceremonies of a pre-industrial world.

Type 15: Habitat. Like the stuffed animals in museum "habitat groups," these animals represent types of environment. They are evocations of particular kinds of place. They are such powerful conventions of place that its aura seems to accompany them. Bighorn sheep bring us the upper mountain slopes, hippos the sluggish tropical rivers, the polar bear, penguin, or husky dog an ice field, and the frog a swamp. Especially noticeable in this activity are the birds, which seldom fly in a void but perch on appropriate vegetation. Like the birds on oceanic islands which lose the power of flight—such as the great auk, the dodo, the flightless rail, or the kiwi—the Litisep birds stay at rest where their plumage can be seen.

Type 16: Region. This suggests a larger piece of geography than just a habitat. Milk cows represent Wisconsin, pelicans mean Florida, and whooping cranes, Texas. The logic of these representations seems so evident that we are likely to forget that every state has its cows, the sea-bordering states their pelicans, and ten other states and Canada share the whooping crane. Yet even such widely distributed animals as horse and dog can play at this role, as among racehorses on a bluegrass farm in Kentucky and cart-pulling dogs in the Netherlands. Although dominated by wild birds and mammals, this type is surprisingly rich in the domestics. We now have behind us two full centuries of modern tourism, which takes its style from the romance of "the natives" in their milieu, a quaint world of milk goats, cargo camels, and fighting cocks.

Type 17: Circus. As the newcomer prowls Litisep Island, occasional vistas reveal seals balancing balls, lions sitting on high stools, elephants kneeling, and horses with plumes galloping around a small ring. Like much else that has largely vanished and left its fauna stranded, the circus itself is rarer than its animals. Zoos have taken over some of the acts, others have gone on television, and others have gone free on this island, where we find them performing for the vendors of things.

Like all taxonomies, this one of four orders and seventeen types is artificial. A large majority of the ad animals may be classified in two or more groups at once. This mixing of types does not occur equally throughout the kingdom. The wild animals have this plural connection more than twice as much as the domestic. This seems to say that livestock, cats, and dogs are seen more simply and narrowly. Although they are twice as numerous as the wild forms, they dominate only six of the seventeen types. They are more predictable and more singular. Among them, the most abundant group, the dogs, have the lowest valence of all. There is a playfulness about the meaning of wild animals, while the idea of what a dog should do appears to be strongly fixed.

The Zoological Groups

With 124 species, the island of Litisep is biogeographically about like Iceland or Tristan da Cunha. A large variety of bird life is typical of islands, and so is the limited variety of reptiles and amphibians. Some of the world's larger tropical islands, such as Sumatra and Madagascar, have many mammals, though none has many large forms or so large a proportion of mammals in the total fauna as this island. In short, the adman's island is zoologically much like a sub-Antarctic island on which a load of large mammals, wild and tame, has been shipwrecked.

INVERTEBRATES

To common sense, if not to the zoologist, the virtual absence of invertebrate animals is not surprising. Although the rich invertebrate life of oceanic islands suggests a treasure trove, for the magazine reader it is apparently remote and possibly dangerous. Most of them are either squishy or prickly, are radial in shape instead of bilateral, and seem more plant-like than animal. Insects are familiar enough, but are virtually banished from this island. Probably the world of the adman exaggerates our aversion to creatures without backbones, in spite of their enormous preponderance on earth.

FISH, AMPHIBIANS, AND REPTILES

The lack of amphibians and reptiles cannot be explained in exactly the same way, for they are not inconspicuous. Yet the biases against them are great; they are slippery and frightening and cold. In ads fish outnumber the rest; maybe they don't seem to be half one thing and half another, like frogs. Oddly enough, a third of the fish on this island have no species—that is, they are simply fish, as contrasted to the birds, which are identifiable by species 96 percent of the time. The lower the animal is on the tree of life, the less specificity it has.* The fish lacks personality, and in the ads nearly half were associated with geographic area. No doubt this is due to the geography of fishing, but it remains strange that an animal so invisible in the landscape should so often symbolize place.

BIRDS

In the adman's world there are forty-four kinds of birds. How many magazine readers can distinguish forty-four species? They occur in many of the types, but are most abundant in having a peculiar natural history (behavior, anatomy, geography) and of being punned on. They are seldom linked to man or machines and allegorical examples. In effect, they are the opposite of the dog, which is joined to man. The bird is the most complete embodiment of the animal, or that aspect of the animal, most

* Hence the joke about the grasshopper who, upon being told by a man that he had a drink named after him, replied, "What! You mean they've named a drink 'Howard'?"

distant from ourselves and yet significant in ways that other distant forms—frogs or worms—are not. Birds seem to serve the imagination so well that even its commercial dampers seem broken. The richness of bird lore seems to transcend the tawdry connections with selling.

WILD MAMMALS

Although there are more than twice as many sightings of wild mammals in a ramble on the island as wild birds, there are about the same number of kinds of each. Any given bird is "rarer" than any mammal (the mammals are better known). In increasing frequency, the mammals are elephants, rabbits, rodents, cats, bears, and hoofed forms. As you might guess, the elephants are best known for their anatomical and behavioral traits. The rabbits have a much more surprising existence. More than half the time they are talking or wearing clothes like people. One may ponder the influence of Peter Rabbit, Br'er Rabbit, Uncle Wiggley, Bugs Bunny, or *Watership Down,* but these may be only other examples, not causes. Why are bears and rabbits the anti-men of our society?

The rabbit is lively and social and dwells, like us, indoors as well as out. It has a secret and mysterious life as well as a public image. It occupies the domestic or humanized landscape, is vulnerable to predatory animals, almost has a face, sits or stands upright, and uses its front paws more like hands than most four-legged beasts. The rabbit has a prodigious sexual reputation and ancient mythical connections with the moon. As an inhabitant of the dooryard, it is visible to children as well as adults, a candidate for the parable or other homiletic.

The rodents are also dooryard, as well as in-house guests. While the rabbits and hares are seen as much alike, the rodents are much more varied. They include the repulsive rats and mice, but also the beaver, muskrat, porcupine, and squirrel. They are typed in the ads for their behaviors and natural history, and especially for situations analogous to those of men. Yet they are never depicted—Mickey Mouse notwithstanding—in the ads as little men with clothes on. More than any other mammal, they are shown without the company of humans, though often with environment. Though repeatedly seen in situations of human-like complexity, they are never complementary to the human household or status symbols or part of human history. It is odd, because in the real world they are all those things. They live in our homes and eat our food; by their presence they signify degrees of negligence and household sanitation; and, by implication, the householder's sense of pride, or lack of it. And they may have had more impact on human history than any other animal as the agents of plague and other disease, spoilers of stored grain and field crops.

Only slightly less numerous are the wild cats. They and the bears are the predominant carnivores of the island. But they also appear in the circus and are spread across all the categories. In heraldic form the lion and the captive cheetah indicate aristocracy, of which they are long-cherished symbols in spite of our egalitarian society. The lordly insouciance of the big cats seems to link them not only with nobility but virtue. Like the uppity breeds of house cats, panthers and cougars "have class" and therefore cast a classy reflection on the people around them.

Their relatives, the bears, are only half as numerous as cats in the adman's landscape, but they share typing in representing physical traits or certain places. The bear's dignity is a different kind. It is seldom depicted attached to a human household and does not radiate rank and privilege. The predominant function of bears is to be men in hairy overcoats, big brothers to the rabbit people. They suffer much punning on their name on Litisep Island. Their personification usually takes the form of a kind of gross, subhuman idiot, cuddly when small but lacking grace when grown. The zoo reinforces this image of the grotesque human caricaturization, perhaps touching our sympathy because of a melancholy or comic quality. The perception of bears as humanoid undoubtedly has a long history, predating Yogi Bear, teddy bears, Smokey the Bear, the Three Bears, and even the Russian bear, going far back into the bear cults of the last ice age. A vast amount of human thinking about bears lies deep beneath the surface of the trivial commercial pictures by which they are made to sell whiskey or tires. The great difficulty is that the bear is so easily perceived as a masked man in a fur coat that its true otherness is extremely difficult to see.

The wild hoofed animals far outnumber the rest. More than twelve species of wild ungulates roam this island: moose, yaks, reindeer, giraffes, llamas, camels, hippos, water buffaloes, bison, antelopes, wild sheep, and deer. Most of them simply display

some unique physical trait for the consumer, or represent stereotypes of behavior. They dominate the category of animals-as-
machines, three times as often as horses even, who have given
the term "horsepower" to the idea. The words "performance,"
"endurance," "mileage," and "storage" occur in phrases beside
them. Why should hoofed animals be associated with machines?
Why not just use machines to sell performance and mileage?
The large herbivores, with their barrel-like bodies and long, narrow (faceless) heads, are perhaps perceived by us as more
automatic than smaller animals, even more so than machines.
They rhythmically munch away; they lie still; they run along
like vehicles; stuff flows in and stuff flows out; they seem bound
to routines; and they seem interchangeable. Who can tell one
antelope from another?

DOMESTIC ANIMALS

Cattle are man-connected and serve frequently as symbols of
the past, special seasons, and holidays. Horses are an elite, living
in great abundance and subtle variety on this island. They do not
pretend to be people, nor do they have unusual physical traits,
mythical activities, celebrations, puns, or natural history. They
never represent a unique behavior. It would seem that to be a
horse is all that needs to be said of it.

Horses do signify the past sometimes, and are a utility, but
where they shine is in escalating human prestige. There are
some humble workhorses, just as there are mongrel puppies, but
there seems to be no animal as snob-making as a classy dog
unless it is a patrician horse. Little else can be said of them on
this island. Affinity for them seems not based on their otherness
but on a cherished image of a familiar, dependable beast—and
on their sexual fetishism.

Horses excite women erotically and represent male virility.
Riding and being ridden are interchangeable and widespread in
this connection. The symbolic ambiguity, as when a stylish
woman holds a stallion between her legs, triggers dreams and
fantasies so powerfully that it can be applied by increments in
the media by the placement and relative size of the images and
how close to the horses the women are.

The house cats are distinct from both wild and other domestic
forms. They seldom wear clothes, talk, or instruct by their na-

tural history or mythological, analogical behavior, and are never just machines. Like many wild forms, they are here because of their physical characteristics. They seem complementary to the human household, yet share the actual company of people in the ads only half as much, even less often than fish or bears. They are exceeded only by rabbits in existing without any environment at all. Like horses, cats associate with beautiful women, though the connection to them is by virtue of anatomical and behavioral traits rather than bestiality. The cats do indeed walk alone, a life divided on this island between the laps (or wild part) of exquisite women and the freedom of their wild relatives. Unlike many other animals, they seem to be very similar in adman's land to cats everywhere. Apparently they are strange enough in themselves that they do not need allusions and impersonations.

The dogs are by far the largest group, more numerous than all wild mammals together. Twenty breeds lope and yap across the Litisep landscape. On our visit the most abundant were spaniel and shepherd-like varieties, followed by mongrels, terriers, and poodles, with the least-common the wolfhound, Doberman, collie, and Chihuahua, but rearrangements of the order occur in cycles of about five years. The shifting around of breed abundance is about on the same tempo as women's clothing styles. As would be expected, the most frequent category for dogs was filling out the human scene. Three quarters of all such behavior on the island is done by dogs, giving them the nearest approach to a single-role monopoly. In this act of accompaniment they help signify the class and ambition of their owners. Bird dogs, fancy terriers, and poodles help make a success—especially economic and sexual—out of any bozo who can afford to have the dog's hair cut properly. Most kinds of dogs are very restricted in their typing while others, especially sled dogs, Great Danes, bird dogs, bulldogs, mongrels, and spaniels, are scattered across half the seventeen categories. The only type without dogs was mythology. Clearly the classical education is gone.

The Three Faunas

Throughout this chapter I have been pointing out the difference between this fauna of the advertisements and the animals known to science. Rebecca West once wrote, "The human animal is put in possession of material which inevitably provokes it to construct a hypothesis covering the whole of existence at an age when it is bound to fall into every sort of error about it. . . . Throughout the whole of his life the individual does nothing but match his fantasy with reality and try to establish, either by affirmation or alternation, an exact correspondence between them." That men must try all their lives without hope of success is because the two faunas are not reconcilable. "Every sort of error" is not simply a lack of information by which one of these kingdoms is corrected by the other.

Obviously there are truths about animals that are deeper than the details of their lives, truths that separate the wolf known to Little Red Riding Hood from the local race of *Canis lupus* of Northwestern Europe as studied by the mammalogist. The "correspondence" that is sought is not a matching or an attempt to make them the same, but a way of acknowledging different realities. The two faunas are not related by the way in which one verifies the other, but by the polarized field that connects them. If a "real" worm burrows into my brain and creates hallucinations of worms with men in their brains, and at the same time the worm is actually eating my brain, feeding his brain with my tissues, the question of real and unreal, inside and outside worms becomes difficult. The tangible worm and my imagined worm form a continuum or mutual interconnection. Parasitology and pathology are but two of the "ologies" that have become part of us all, which would like to limit themselves to the "real" worm, its consumption of my substance, secretion of substances, and effects on my blood chemistry. The "ologists" would not like to deal with those images of worms whose brains are burrowed into by men or, indeed my thoughts about the worm in my head.

Upon recovery from the acute stage of this infection, I could be obsessed with the notion that all worms are King Amenhotep and should be protected and worshiped in churches, or that all worms are friendly pork chops to be eaten on sight, and there would be consequences for a lot of "real" worms.

For the most part, the complicated relationships of fantasy and real faunas, worms of mind and mud, do not seem too confusing because we keep them separate. But there is a third reality to be considered. Of that "objective" world of our zoology, there are two parts; and the same is true of the "subjective" world of our fantasy. There are a complete zoology and a complete fantasy that include all the possibilities, but none of us is familiar with them all. Presumably there are still people deep in Australia or the Philippines who know nothing of penguins or of the penguin myths of Tierra del Fuego. The world we do know from experience is the *phenomenological* world. For each individual or each culture it is composed of a limited number and unique mixture of the real and imagined. It is a unique field of force by which the first two are related.

There are, then, three faunas. They fit the classical Greek notion of the tripartite nature of reality: a "real" or *ontological* world, the *ideal* world of the imagination, and the *phenomenological* world of encounter. Applied to Little Red Riding Hood, there is the wolf that we know about in nature, the wolf we know from the story, and the wolf that we have actually seen. Like all taxonomies, this one is artificial and does not need much searching to discover how poor its separations are, but it is useful, for it allows us to reflect on the kinds of comparisons we are making all the time, to see the animals of each of these realms as part of our true experience.

The Real world contains a million or more species, totaling billions of individuals, most of them seldom seen by people, either as individuals or kinds. The Ideal world is made up of the images and sounds of creatures, many of which embody the characteristics in some part of "real" animals and others not known from zoology. The Phenomenal world is a world of realized encounter, the outcome of probable meetings, a kind of sampling in which size, geography, chance, and cultural traditions play some part.

In a general sense the presence of animals in advertisements is no different from their presence in every other aspect of culture. Human attention to animals is not chosen by people, nor is it the result of a particular education or experience. It is spontaneous and innate, a part of being human. Even the use of animals as thinking instruments is part of our biology and not our sociology.

But which animals are seen and how they are seen is another matter, one that allows no such easy distinctions between Art and Nature. The animals in magazine advertisements are an example. Seen in a broader cultural context, they are in some degree representative of our time, a narrow, bizarre collection, twisted to fit commercial ends. For example, there are few ambiguous forms that are traditionally used for conscious-ness-raising experience or ritual acts. Western mythology is rich in these combination forms and anomalies from nature that seem to transgress the order of Creation. Among such figures are half-man, half-animal creatures, the primates, the in-and-out-of-water amphibians and legless snakes, monsters that seem to be put together from parts of creatures. If borderline forms, or mixed beings and creatures signifying transitional states are indeed tension-making because they symbolize disorder or the failure of a meaningful world to hold, it is not surprising that the hucksters would avoid them. The last thing the seller wants to do is alarm the customer. He wants no traumas of initiation or rebirth of the sort signified ceremonially by ambiguous animals or by the taboo of creatures that cannot be classified. The huck-ster may want comedy, but he plays a dangerous game, for laughter is a relief from the tensions created by conflict and ambiguity. The dragons and snakes, frogs and centaurs in the ads must be emasculated, portrayed with traits of immaturity and cuteness, and only then can they be admitted.

In the selling of automobiles, for instance, the attachment of an animal term to a model is commonplace: cougar, bronco, jeep,* or rabbit. But the favored terms are for animals that analysis of the advertisements shows to be least ambivalent in type. Oddly enough, automobile models are never named after those hoofed animals that the ads reveal are most often seen as machine-like. The metaphor breaks down if the animal is actually perceived as a machine. The advertisers themselves may not realize that the animal qualities suggested by these names are not necessarily perceived as part of the vehicle, but rather as vital sensations and feelings that the driver wants to experi-ence. The combination of sexuality and social status carried by horses may be the main reason for their frequent use for auto-mobile names, combined with their clarity of "meaning," or lack of other typing. In contrast, the centaur is part-horse, but its ambiguity is threatening. We want to share those thrilling qual-ities of horsiness, perhaps, but we do not want to become horses. The worst thing the manufacturers could do would be to call their new model the Centaur or Minotaur. Added to its basic

---

* A small, cuddly, innocuous monster that appeared as Eugene the Jeep in the comic strip "Popeye the Sailor" in 1936.

ambivalence of conjoined, unlike creatures, the Minotaur connected the human figure with the machine-like typing of cattle. Worse, the Minotaur (the monster represented as a bull-headed man from Minoan mythology) ate human beings, and the driver does not want to be reminded consciously or otherwise of death on the highway.

The seventeen categories of the adman's fauna are merely a kind of preliminary look at a bestiary of commerce. How, exactly, are the animals used to sell things? The animals are vessels. Each contains a quality that the seller wants to isolate and sometimes to project upon his product. He does not have to educate the reader; he assumes that the reader is already an expert at this activity, composed of three steps: identifying a characteristic in its best known or animal form; detaching it, so to speak, from pure language by representing its vessel; and then using it by assertion or analogy.

Why use images of animals instead of just using words? Why not illustrate the particular qualities by using images of people instead of animals? The use of the animal model is a child's game, derived from that time of life when meaning requires more than words and when people—including the self—are the object of the process, not its means. The animals are a set of bearers to which we as children learn to hook slippery concepts and thus create images for abstractions and feelings. Sometimes the quality is then transferred to the product itself, but the customer is not really so interested in the toughness of an automobile tire as suggested by a rhinoceros as he is in the authority with which he can go on the road. What he is buying is a change in his own state which the salesman claims will follow the purchase. That is, a shift in the quality space that he occupies as a person. The advertiser has taken a universal process that has always involved animals and modified it from one of understanding to one of acquisition and control. Fables and precautionary tales have carried animal symbols a step beyond recognition of the composite nature of individual experience by exhorting certain actions. The marketplace took the drama one step farther by inserting an object (for sale) which it claims will facilitate that doing or not doing.

Many advertisers have found that a certain animal image does this effectively, and they continue to use it for months or years. They associate commodity and animal to conscript the user into a mythical society of users, to develop special phrases and inside language, clichés like those that temporarily identify an adolescent as a member and give the illusion of belonging. In short, admen create a travesty of the totemic group with its emblematic animal. In a society where "belonging" and "identity" are felt to be in short supply, the buyer doesn't really have to believe deeply that his purchase makes him a member of an elite fraternity, but only to feel it for a moment, for the seller knows that he only needs a tiny advantage to gain a market where the products are very similar. The animals that best serve this purpose are few. A recent example of this is the use of the tiger by a breakfast cereal and a gasoline. The spring, aggressiveness, and good looks to be achieved by putting the tiger's fuel into machine or body virtually enlisted users in a fraternity led by a shaman in a tiger suit.

The impetus for cultural totemism may be looked upon in our society as somewhat vestigial. Wherever there are domestic animals, totemic society gave way to castes, which transformed our image of animals living in an independent, analogous society to one where they live as extremities of human society. Advertising reflects both forms of totemic thought by using wild and domestic animals. The predominant types of the wild are analogical or refer to abstract qualities. The tame—or domestic—are mainly members of the human community. The idea of an animal companion or slave is clearly reflected in huckstering, which implicates the animal directly in human social contexts. In totemic culture animals have neither duties nor rights, but in class society the prevailing political web envelops them, too. They can represent people, accompany them as subordinates, and stand in for them as though there were mutual understanding of purpose.

The mercenary motive behind an advertisement is no respecter of this distinction between totemic and domestic culture. In one series an insurance company used different wild animals with a natural history text, explaining how the creature protected itself, and then proceeded to isolate it from man by concluding that man, being unlike the animal, needed an insurance policy —a good example of totemic culture. At the other extreme is the dog seated next to his master in an automobile. From the animal's mouth comes a word-balloon, advising the man on the purchase of tires. Intuitively clever as he is in making the animal advertisement work, it's all one to the adman. He is only putting to his own purposes whatever streams of thought are available.

Advertising is only a little lump in the sea of human consciousness and its animal ads are a narrow mode of expression. Yet it reveals us to ourselves with unintended sensitivity. An intrinsic part of human self-consciousness requires animal images, and no amount of urban or technological glazing defeats it.

As we sail off into the sunset and think back over Litisep Island fauna as a whole, it seems a bizarre collection—biogeographically impossible, inconsistent, behaviorally outlandish, biologically disparate. It is an uneven shambles taxonomically and inexplicable ecologically. A naturalist might lament that it is a poor reflection of the real world, with its million species and infinite diversity of form, or even of our normal experience, with its lifetime accumulation of surprise and novelty.

But the surprise is that the fauna is there at all and is, indeed, as rich as a small island. As an adman's bestiary, it was created by people with a calculating eye for the main chance, symbols that will connect, common denominators. They may have skimmed off only flecks from the surface of a collective mental jungle. Why should they or their customers care at all about animals? The city is a world of men and microbes. Is it simply an anachronism, an old-fashioned sentiment for the past, or is it some hunger deeper than social conditioning? If the dog's duality of otherness and companionship, the toucan's and giraffe's touch of sunlight on the imagination are merely nostalgia or romantic images, then surely they must fade as such repining and illusion become too ridiculous or too expensive in the modern world.

Alternatively, the mind's demands are related to the whole of human experience, and to the generation of mind in Nature and the animality of Mind itself. Perhaps the rationalizations for liking animals, even the advertisements in which they momentarily give life and interest to some mundane object for sale, are but acceptable excuses. Thinking animals is as old as erect posture and good eyes, born in us like a hunger for love, as real as the necessity to communicate or make order and sense. We seem to live now in a philosophy of dispensable environment, where surroundings, like ideologies, are supposed to be arbitrary, where seeing, smelling, hearing, and knowing other creatures seems optional and frivolous. But the evidence is overwhelmingly against that narrow view of life. We surround ourselves with animals and then are surprised to see them. It seems to almost have a life of its own, this need for organic surroundings. It blooms or rises implacably to the surface, however we use it.

7 | WHAT GOOD ARE ANIMALS?

The land-use patterns that developed with Western culture are typically concentric around villages. As it spread north into Europe from the Mediterranean, agriculture repeated a design on the land. It was composed of zones around each human settlement. Close in, vegetables for the table were grown and milk animals housed. Near the village gate were field crops and, at a distance, pasture lands and the forest fringes where wood was gathered. Beyond was wilderness. The effect of these rings of land around each settlement was that wild and domestic creatures existed in a graded, reciprocal series: with few wild things in the village and few domestic ones in the forest between settlements. The same pattern was brought to North America and continued there until the opening of the Ohio frontier, the land survey, and the coming of farm machinery in the early nineteenth-century. In the new land the farmer lived at a distance from the village, each homestead becoming a domestic nucleus with its own concentric spheres of land-use intensity. As farmers in Europe became more mobile and new farms in North America filled the "empty" spaces, the habitat for most wild animals was greatly reduced, although the rough trim of most American farming and the casualness of field use and fencing allowed habitat for species like deer and rabbits, which require no un-disturbed wilderness.

An additional series of humanized nuclei in the wild lands began to appear with many dispersed industrial uses. Mining, logging, rail- and road-building camps, power-generating stations, research facilities did not produce the neat zones of modified space so much as intense impact with radiating lines of roads, rails, and wires. Now exclusions of wild things ran outward from them along the lines of transportation, so that a network of man-intensified, machine-occupied space added to the effects of agriculture and of towns themselves. This pattern is now repeating itself over the whole world. Until our industrial phases, the amount of wild land was closely related to the size of human population. But in industrialized nations the effects are multiplied. Affluence and manufacture raise the per-person demands on nature many times, reducing wild habitat accordingly. In peasant agricultural India, the lion and tiger continued to exist in spite of heavy human populations. Now, with extensive land manipulation of a network of energy and material mining, the lions of Gir and the Bengal tiger are diminished. Human population growth intensifies the whole process, but is not necessary to it.

The thrust of recent human history with respect to the reduction of the wild is beyond doubt. Extinction of species is only a small part of this pattern, though an important one. The concept of "endangered species" floats like some special curse over it all, but the massive reduction and local extirpation of animals and plants precedes the musical-chairs habitat game, in which they disappear forever, one by one.

In sum, there is less room for wild things larger than a mouse, and there will be less in the future. This includes domestic as well as wild. Wild creatures existed in the past apart from our design, part of a heritage. But our design has grown and will soon include the whole planetary surface. The deliberately designated wild places, the parks and refuges, are not sanctuaries for wild animals in the long run because the constant presence of man slowly warps the animals, which become tamer. The wildness is lost both by natural selection and behavioral adjustment. As more and more people come to see them, their management becomes more and more intense. Finally, they will become wild game farms.

Already the refuges are too small for wolves, grizzly bears, and condors. No matter how badly we want to preserve vestiges of those species, they are incompatible with the civilized mantle that covers all the land. As for the species not yet in jeopardy, false hopes encouraged the "game managers" in the early twentieth century, for they saw an increase in "edge species," coming from the mixed landscapes of field, brushland, crops, and woodland that had emerged from the rural, set element patterns of the nineteenth century. The deer, quail, muskrat, foxes, raccoons were said to have become more numerous than they had been. The cause of this was the small family farm, with its weedy fencerows, small fields, and rough harvest methods that left grains in the field. It was due to the casual and careless approach of the farmer to too-abundant land, and to the fertility that ten thousand years had stored in the virgin soil.

But the game managers knew that the clouds of waterfowl and shorebirds, pigeon and parakeet, elk, lion, bison, and sheep that had once nested and grazed across the whole interior of North America had by 1920 already been cut to a tiny part of what it had been. Scores of animals are gone from two thirds of the continent where they were formerly found. Millions of acres of marshes were drained and tile put under the surface in the Mississippi Valley. Forests that had never been cut ceased to exist, and with them went the diversity of primeval woods.

This story of America's reduced wildlife has been written many times. Always it has been discounted by those with vested interests in "civilizing" the land, or by those whose humanism and ideologies of progress outweighed their concern for the wild. The system produced its own wildlife experts who said that the game was increasing, and its vicarious arts, especially the photographic, which keep wildness before us on film. It is not just America's story, but one small chapter in the march of human population and the demands of the agriculture, machine, and electronic ages. At the leading edge of that history, the subsistence farm or family farm is now rapidly going; the bulldozer and chemistry have removed the living fence, and farms are swallowed by other farms. In Iowa today one farmer manages land that was three farms thirty years ago. The techniques are more efficient, the machines bigger, the fields vaster. All the small things— turtles, frogs, salamanders, moles, weasels, marmots, woodcocks, flying squirrels, bats, minnows, butterflies, snakes, dragonflies— can no longer get from one relic of habitat to another.

For a time the American landscape seemed enlivened. Animals abounded on the small farm. Bees, ducks, fish, cattle, horses, dogs, cats, poultry all seemed to be part of the environment, interspersed with those wild things that continued by the sheer momentum of wildness to be at the doorstep. The rabbit, grouse, raccoon, and the songbirds were part of that milieu, seemingly so stable and so rich. But that is all going. The farmer has become a specialist. If he has animals, it is only one kind, and they are hedged about and guarded and controlled to fit the constraints of machines, the market schedule, and veterinarians, and protected against a natural world to which they are no longer adapted.

Suburbia has prolonged the illusion of wild abundance. Middle-class urban people occupied what had been farmland and sustained for a time the texture of small farming, keeping song-birds and small mammals. But the spread of lawns, shopping districts, pipelines, powerlines, schools, highways, all the civic ensemble followed to the suburbs. Where farmhouses themselves had once been habitats, the suburban house was a desert. It won't last as a reprieve, and suburbia is too expensive anyway, a froth on the wave of superabundance that ends in America with the twentieth century. Scarcity is coming to stay.

In the long run, animals are competitive with man. They occupy his space, they eat what he eats. They use the planet's limited energy and materials. The evidence is overwhelmingly clear: Man has grown from a tiny population, perhaps half a million occupying some savannas in part of Africa, to the universal dominant creature, taking today more than half the energy that animals in all ecosystems use. To refuse to see this is to close one's eyes to the whole line of history and prehistory. In fifty years there will be eight or ten billion people on Earth, whose demands on it will increase many hundredfold more than the per-person requirements of the past. This is not romantic senti-mentality, not nostalgic longing for the past, or unconsidered accusations against machines and progress. The evidence could not be clearer or the facts more coldly realistic. The wild things must give way as the post-agricultural, human-centered system crowds them out.

This crunch is not experienced as a food or space conflict in developed states, but in terms of jobs and employment, economic stability, and regional or trade income. For example, when the federal courts upheld a law limiting the number of porpoises that tuna fishermen were allowed to kill and compelling the fishermen to cease fishing for the season, the mayor of San Diego, where part of the tuna fleet was berthed, argued that the local tax base, economic growth, and employment levels would all be diminished. When the problem is presented in this way, it does not seem to be a matter of replacing porpoises with people, but only a matter of imperfect fishing techniques. The death of por-poises seems like an inadvertent side effect. Even if no porpoises were entangled and drowned in the fishing nets, they would decline as the fishermen take more and more of the tuna. We have exterminated animals at an average of one species per year for the past two centuries, but only a few, such as the dodo or great auk, were directly slaughtered.

Even more crucial, from the standpoint of the individual, is the reduction and local extirpation of animals. For every species crowded into oblivion, hundreds have been splintered into scarcity and are no longer part of our personal experience.

In the late 1970s a reaction against the environmental movement of the 1960s began to reach its potential. The reactionary forces—brains, power, and money—were unleashed like a mighty tide. We can, the economists were confidently saying, have wealth for all and a clean environment. What the industrial magnates and their minions never understood was that the spirit of the environmental movement was concern for the brotherhood of life. They saw it instead as pollution, an "energy crisis," poor techniques. Dirty air and water, and the poisoning of the environment by wastes and fertilizers and pesticides pre-empted, for them, its real meaning. Political, economic, and ideological attention to the environment as an issue made pollution its cause, for that could be dealt with by the existing system.

The ecological revolution will come to a strange and peaceful plateau by the year 2000. There will be clean streams and air. There will be forests and lands free of crude, man-made poisons. Ecosystems will be intact but stripped, shorn of their end members, the last links in food chains. The microbes and insects and other invertebrates will be there, but what we think of as "animals" will exist only in parks, which are their refuge and their cages. Pets there will be, but the familiar farm animals will have completed their odyssey in the open air and will have gone indoors forever, to merge with the biochemistry of food production.

All will be well. Why should we preserve animals at all?

Animals will be a liability in the kind of world I have just described. Increasingly, what we do on the Earth will be done by design, and animals will not survive unless they are made to be part of that design. But why should we include them? We know that in *our* world nothing is free. In the future every animal on Earth will exist at some cost to humanity.

There are four arguments for preserving animals. Briefly, they are as follows.

Economics

Number *one,* the economic use. Animals are self-sustaining chemical factories. For all of human time they have provided us with their products and their meat. The whole animal side of agriculture takes up where hunting and gathering leave off, organizing the keeping of animals for their hides, oils, bones, eggs, milk, fur, tendons, feces, and scores of compounds and substances such as hormones and antibodies used in medicine. Their guts are microbe and fertilizer factories, making manure from crop residues and grass. Animals are important *instruments of power.* Not only do they pull, carry, guard, lift, and push, but their hooves and teeth have opened the world's forest lands to human settlement and sustained open land against the encroachment of woody plants. Far more than the ax and saw, the grazing and browsing animals have been the vanguard of civilization wherever there are forests. The care, feeding, breeding, and showing of animals is a growing domain. Much of this, except for the direct use of meat, bone, and skin, is relatively recent in human time, though ancient in human history, which is recorded for only a few thousand years. It is based on the fact that animals are available energy converters and chemical environments. Though the particular uses are different from culture to culture, the economic use of animals is worldwide.

Ecology

Number *two,* the ecological use. Naturalists and others have known intuitively for centuries that nature is an interlocking system, almost like an organism. Different kinds of animals play parts in it like the organs of a body, each related to and each dependent on the others. In 1864 a German biologist coined the word "ecology"* for the scientific study of these interrelationships. Such holistic thought was not congenial to the linear kind of point focus that dominated the use of science, however, and the application of simple cause-and-effect thought produced

* The German was Ernst Haeckel, the source, his *The History of Creation.* There is evidence that Henry Thoreau used the word in 1858, however, in a letter to George Thatcher.

many small disasters, which seemed to help prove the validity of ecological theory even before the details were understood.

In recent years every schoolchild is taught that things hang together and the ecological principle is accepted. It is common knowledge today that "even" the repugnant snakes and insects have a role to play and that the well-being of all depends on their existence. The popular image of the world biosphere divided into component ecosystems has gained authority over the more narrow view.

Ethics

Number *three*, the ethical argument. Since the rise of caste thinking, which extended subordinate membership in human society to animals, the life and death of animals has had an ethical dimension. Ideological thought, religious as well as political, therefore extends to animals and incorporates them. The value of life is subordinated to the belief system. One can believe with one faction that animals are without intrinsic value, or one can believe with another faction that they have souls and sentience. A society can place the survival of members of a class, such as slaves, solely with their master, or a society can decree that slaves have rights.

The world is rich in variations on this theme of animal rights. In all cases, however, the rights are part of the human ethical or moral system. In the Judeo-Christian European tradition, animals have had few rights. In the eighteenth century the "humane" movement began in England, which has since spread to the rest of Europe and North America. It first sought the protection of domestic animals from cruelty and the civil regulation of pets. In a sense the humane movement is an outcome of the American and French revolutions and the egalitarian ideologies of liberation.

The West has also been influenced by the Buddhist sects who venerate animals, who do not eat meat, and who consider it sinful to inflict unnecessary pain or death on any living thing. Arguments having to do with intrinsic rights to freedom of choice have been gradually extended from political choice and economic equality of opportunity among human races and contemporary forms of caste groups: religious, professional, and genealogical. Of course pets could never be liberated from human care, nor could domestic animals be given their freedom, but the extension of protectionist thought to wild animals is centered on their freedom.

Although the humane movement uses ecological arguments on occasion, its principal concern is moral. All animals in captivity and in the wild now come under its scrutiny, and the moral imperative against killing is enlarged to include the nonhuman. Albert Schweitzer wrote that all life is good and deserves to be protected wherever possible, that any unnecessary killing endangers the human soul.

Human torture and the vivisection of animals, human war and animal hunting, the neglect of the poor and the neglect of "helpless" animals are joined in the humane philosophy, and from it an ethical discourse is slowly emerging.

The Inadequacy of Economic, Ecological, and Ethical Arguments

Virtually all the motive and sentiment for the protection and preservation of animals has rested on one or more of the three foregoing arguments—economic, ecological, or ethical. But none, in the long run, will suffice to save the animals.

Economically, by industrial standards, animals are not very efficient. Only about 10 percent of the energy they consume is converted to tissue. The industrial discovery of fossil fuels and the technologies of atomic and solar power have made their use as pulling and lifting machines obsolete. Gradually, laboratory chemistry is synthesizing each of those substances which, in the past, came only from living bodies. Mock furs are possible in great variety, and leather is replaced by plastic. Whatever the merits or demerits of their synthetic nature, the substitution of factory-produced materials and power for the direct use of animals is inevitable. No doubt some now difficult secrets of protein structure will be learned slowly, some biochemical codes will be difficult and expensive to break, but in the meantime, tissue culture and cage-bound creatures will replace the free-ranging creatures, for whom there will cease to be space or food.

As machine substitutes and living laboratories, animals will soon have had their day, and the era of human predation on and tyranny over them will end. The reason will be simply that quicker, better controlled means will be found as alternatives for human labor and sources of the "animal products" we need.

Ecologically, all the creatures in ecosystems are not equally necessary to it. Some exist only because energy and space are abundant. Others (except their parasites) do not depend on them, although it cannot be proved that their presence does not add a little to the efficiency or the stability of the whole. These fringe inhabitants of the ecosystems are the larger mammals, not the multitude of small and seldom seen ones. In our present state of knowledge one cannot show that wolves, bears, tigers, eagles, green sea turtles, orioles, bullfrogs, monarch butterflies, olive baboons, red kangaroos, bottle-nosed dolphins, or a thousand other big species are really indispensable to their ecosystems. Indeed, the domino theory is just opposite the true metaphor of the web of nature. If one small strand goes, the whole does not fall, and in fact the survivors adjust to the break.

In the recent decade of acute environmental sensibility by the public, from about 1965 to 1975, many claims of potential disaster were made in the name of ecology. Arguments were put forward for the protection of rare species on the grounds that they are necessary to ecosystems for reasons we have yet to learn. But necessary and desirable are not the same. What is lost is not absolute for the ecosystem but relative. In spite of the dynamic balance of nature, "trade-offs" are possible. Animals could be extirpated from a locality without becoming extinct or the habitat dying. Elephants could be removed from the productive lands of Africa and bred in zoos. The buffalo disappeared from most of the American plains but the grassland communities went on, no doubt changed, perhaps lessened, but intact as communities of life.

To kill an ecosystem you must burn it up, plow it under, or poison it. Only at the level of its plant life, its microbes and its invertebrate fauna, is the natural system itself vulnerable. The capturing of energy and the flow of elements are its heart. To take away the elephant or bison may be to amputate a fingertip. As humans we depend on that deep structure, but we are not necessary to it any more than the elephant. And we may decide— we will inevitably decide—to put human protoplasms where elephants now are.

No large animal is necessary to an ecosystem. Ecology cannot prove that the whole requires any one, or any ten, species of large animals for its continuation. It proves, if anything, the opposite. Any mix of plant and animal species works out its reciprocities over time and adjusts to changes. Certain plant species, bacteria, or pollinating insects may be extremely important to the system's function, but the large animals are frosting on the cake, no more.

Ethically, there have been discourses against the enslavement, torture, and killing of people since civilization began without ending war, tyranny, or cruelty. There is no evidence that crime, brutality, or murder have diminished at all. If human behavior is not improved by the incorporation of such ethics into the dominant religions, what reason is there to suppose that such a new ethic can save animals? The very ideology that raises the importance of every individual and seeks the nobility in our species can be used to support the need to exploit animals, if need be, for the benefit of the most noble species. The avoidance of *unnecessary* cruelty, insofar as that is done, will make the moralists feel better and reduce pain, but it will not save animals.

The extension of the humane idea to the wild can only produce mischief, for it will see in the behaviors and interrelationships among animals infinite cruelties and seek to prevent them. The sucking of the host's blood by the parasite, the competition among scavengers to eat a carcass, the exclusion of the weak and sick, predation itself, the enormous mortality which removes the majority of the newborn every year from nearly every species —all these and more, humane action will try to prevent, just as it prevents dogs from eating cats and men from eating dogs.

Only in one sense is the ethical argument without the distortion of our human social model: that animals should be preserved because they are, as they are, because their existence itself is moral justification. But it is not a new idea and its application is ambiguous because such unlimited rights will always conflict with human interest, and there is no reason to think that people are so charitable or so good that they will yield in that conflict. The humane movement is marred by its faulty ecology and its unwillingness to accept death as the way of ecosystem life. And the ethical argument for saving animals can fare no better because of our human needs and imperfections.

A Fourth Argument:
Human Growth and Thought

The only defense of nonhuman life not dependent on a technology that may change or an ethic that is largely idealistic is one close to human well-being, regardless of the changes in science and philosophy. It might be called "minding animals." The purpose of this book has been to identify and explore the ways in which the human mind needs animals in order to develop and work. Human intelligence is bound to the presence of animals. They are the means by which cognition takes its first shape and they are the instruments for imagining abstract ideas and qualities, therefore giving us consciousness. They are the code images by which language retrieves ideas from memory at will. They are the means to self-identity and self-consciousness as our most human possession, for they enable us to objectify qualities and traits. By presenting us with related-otherness—that diversity of non-self with which we have various things in common—they further, throughout our lives, a refining and maturing knowledge of personal and human being.

This fourth argument for the preservation of animals is shamelessly selfish. It contains no pretense of ecological or ethical benevolence, though it must embrace both nature and charity. It is more closely related to the general utilitarian argument. But the utilitarian argument is improvisational. It makes do arbitrarily with animal fur or meat, and it can, as arbitrarily, dismiss their use. It is culturally based. But the argument for minding animals has no such option, and no chemical or electronic substitutes. Neither pets nor zoos, books nor films can replace it; indeed, they are threats to it.

By animals here is meant, I repeat, only the large and visible, the phenomenological fauna. Most of them are ecologically expendable, economically obsolete, and ethically disposable if it becomes expedient to replace their habitat with industrial parks and airports.

The conceptual uses of animals are an aspect of human biology, a part of "human ecology." They coincide with phases of personal growth. They are part of the *ontogeny*, or life cycle that each individual experiences in typically human fashion.

They are sequenced but not compartmentalized. Their tempo and intensity varies, like all the other traits of the growing human, from one person to another. Naming and grouping animals begins with language learning, peaks before age twelve, and continues throughout life, while personality trait and feeling-identification by mimicry and animal introjection appear in middle childhood and change to caricaturing in adults. The animal community as a social paradigm is associated with adolescence and poetic insight, continuing at lessened intensity in the adult.

Like other growth processes, these can prosper or wither. What the individual needs, as in nutrition, is not always what he gets. In all things essential to growth, men are flexible, so that the quality of parental care, social custom, or cultural provision can vary without necessarily crippling the individual. But human adaptability is more limited than it has been fashionable to admit. Like survival in dirty air, we seem to surmount a faulty environment because it does not kill us directly. But the truth to which medicine is awakening is that the illness takes strange forms and the symptoms may be mental or behavioral, regardless of the causes.

Much human psychosis is characterized by normal processes taken out of context or distorted. Minding animals also has its pathology. The most widespread is the yoking of non-human creatures into human society. It perverts the human yearning to find significance in other beings and misdirects it into social connection instead of ecological metaphor. It destroys the other behavior by hitching animals to our system. The distinction between animals as figurative people and as surrogate people may seem unnecessarily fine because we are not used to making it. But the difference is fundamental and it influences the way we see the animal world all our lives, and therefore the way we see ourselves.

That perversion was first unleashed by the keeping of animals in agriculture, but today is increasingly the result of keeping animals as objects of leisure or toys. Pets and captives do not appear distressed, and our pleasure in their company belies their poisoning of our understanding. They are like drugs that dull our hunger and pain, the semblance of what we need without the diversity, definition, or otherness. As the farm animal disappears, the pet population redoubles.

An even more difficult distinction occurs in animal image-making. Judging from archaeological evidence, the making of animal drawings, sculptures, and carved figures has been associated with reflection on animals for many thousands of years, and they are a universal feature of the poetic and mythological language of animal forms. Today those images are not made as symbolic objects, but instead as entertainment, for their beauty, or as substitutes for animals. Where in thought does the made image end and the real animal begin? Can we replace the non-human in our lives with films of them?

The traditional, ritual use of animal art is to provide for a group a shared image, part of collective thought. Its exact form has a dynamic relationship to the human experiencing of that animal, and it was never an end in itself. Only in recent centuries has this confusion arisen. Museum, academic, solipsistic, existential art is like the domestic animal, the pet. As Claude Lévi-Strauss has said, art has become the national park of the mind. But when we put a fence around the buffaloes of thought, we tried to amputate some part of ourselves. To what end do we scrutinize milk cows, Buicks, or old photographs of buffalo herds instead? Our need for animals is great, and that demand is met by the use of art in translating animals into the living language of ideas. So we spontaneously welcome those images, whether they be words or pictures. But nothing much follows. Someone says, "Enjoy!" But enjoyment is not our purpose or need. The animal curio in the zoo and the goldfish in the bowl at first delight and then baffle us, for they seem about to reveal themselves, to speak. We wait. In the end we turn from the zoo, thinking of prisoners and prisons, and we flush the irritating goldfish down the sewer. What we have discovered about ourselves is captivity and monotony.

It is no surprise that our Abrahamic, Faustian, Buckminster Fuller culture is furious with animals. They have failed us. We can obliterate them with the juggernauts of global development and planning with a clear sense of retribution, if not justice. We can now, as Eric Hoffer urges, put the world's youth to work domesticating the planet. The national park can become the art gallery of nature. We can there translate that flash of delight in the animal figure as the right combination to produce the pleasant nerve twitch of aesthetic value.

If our children, growing up with an inadequate otherness

from which to rebound the elements of self, are in danger of becoming less than human, we can get them less-than-human companions for their comfort. Measured on a scale of frogs and dogs, children will look fairly human, and that will comfort us, and we can all look at animal films and that will distract us.

For Parents and Teachers

How should we teach children about animals?

Apart from an introduction to survival ecology, this question has not been raised very often. Elementary classrooms are frequently speckled with natural things and art and reading programs often focus on plants and animals. Schools that can afford it take children on field trips and nature walks. An increasing number of schools have their own nature-study areas or use nearby woodlots, parks, or just vacant lots. But if you ask why we do this we tend to get one of two kinds of answers: either it is the learning of "ecology" or it is done for rather vague though often strongly felt convictions. Apart from a kind of "understanding" or "appreciation," there is no theory at all about why we feel that nature study is important. Are we satisfied to say that the child finds satisfaction in these experiences, or that a natural curiosity is satisfied.

No wonder nature study is considered a fringe benefit for rich children. It seems once removed from those things centering on creativity, social adjustment, study skills, or courses with content that seems closer to human needs. There is a long history of radical experiments in education that incorporate the "outdoors" in which the purposes are defined in broad, general terms but never in terms of the functional needs of the developing mind. The only difference in the kind of nature study given the child of seven and the one of seventeen is that the latter can go on more arduous trips and the work is more scientific. It is a fair enough distinction as far as it goes. Piaget has shown that the capacity for abstract rational thought is a function of age and that one cannot expect to make little scientists of second-graders. But Piaget sometimes gives the impression that the whole of the fascination with natural things is simply a precursor to the kind of detached observation that can be organized into science. Piaget has made, almost single-handedly, a breakthrough in the recognition of the importance of ontogenesis in childhood perception. But he has paid relatively little heed to those gene-schedule events that phase in and out at specific ages, and that do not bear directly on the growth of the calculating rationality.

What the teacher, like the parent, needs to remember is that all childhood nature study is fundamental to the child's competence as a person and to elements of the personality, especially with the formation of that network of attitudes, definitions, and attention structure that define consciousness uniquely for the individual. The point of this book is to assert that animals have a very large claim on the maturing of the individual and his capacity to think and feel.

Taxonomy and Cognition

The first of these claims on his mind is that of close visual observation and comparison. In a world rich in made things, this activity tends to be subverted, but its authentic and original object was plants and animals. In some ways plants and animals are its best and only means. One must learn to discover the external differences by which things are identified before they can be grouped, and they must be stored in and retrieved from memory, the basis for categorization, concept-formation, and binary order-making. This close scrutiny is a habit related to naming: of parts, details, of the kind of creature and of groups of kinds. This activity is so typically human that we can easily neglect it. That is, we can fail to strengthen and enlarge it. No teacher should ever be embarrassed to concentrate on the names of things, so long as he points out why something is this and not that.

It is easy to plan exercises, both indoors and out, that train this discriminatory ability. As much as possible should be done with real leaves or insects or seashells instead of pictures of them. It can also be done with external and internal parts of the anatomy as well as with whole creatures. No doubt there are parents who would be shocked to learn that their second-grader had participated in the bloody dissection of a rabbit (and second-grade teachers who would be reluctant to do it). Making a snail collection seems like a long way from disemboweling a warm mammal, but the two are similar in their use to the child.

The scrutiny of parts, names, kinds, and groups should continue throughout life, but should begin with language learning. Of course there are differences in the kinds of taxonomy appropriate for a ten-year-old as opposed to a sixteen-year-old. Attention span, accommodation, and other visual development, along with complexity of the task differ greatly, from the identification of things that must be held and closely examined to those that can be made only by waiting and watching, as in bird study. Nor are the sounds, smells, and feel of things omitted from this comparison and grouping.

Mimicry and Selfhood

A second of these animal claims on the growing psyche is the "swallowing" of behaviors. It is done by imitating animals in games or play. It, too, is a form of taxonomy. Instead of the names of kinds and parts, the objective is a repertoire of feelings. What an animal does is always similar to things that people do. The child can gain control over his feelings and actions only by knowing and recognizing them. To fear, threaten, surpass, envy, mother, submit, be lonely, curious, to work, wait, evade, incite— all the verbs and adjectives in our lives begin as unnamed, unrecognized experiences. As infants we are responding centers where emotions come and go. We reach, babble, and suck, but all without reflection. To make these things objective they must first be seen "out there."

Oddly enough, it does not help as much to see them in people as in nonhumans. Apparently it is easier to detach particular qualities from the more limited behavior of an animal. Then it can be introjected, or swallowed, and one becomes conscious of the experience of loneliness as a peculiar experience, an animal of our being. This necessary use of animals is available to education, in the playground and gymnasium as well as classroom. Games that deliberately evoke certain feelings can be played and then talked about.

From the recognition of certain feelings this mimicry grows toward their use for description. What do the expressions "to be dog-tired" or to "weasel out" or to "be chicken" mean to someone who has never seen a canine give himself up to instant sleep, watched a weasel slip between the stones of a rocky wall, or observed the tentative investigation of a strange object by chickens? These are metaphors to be idly used by some, but not by those who once had a teacher who said, "Now watch the dog. . . . Now, let's all *be* dogs." Simple dances incorporate the essence of certain behaviors in this way. The quality of certain experiences and the performance of certain acts can grow throughout our lives as our ability grows for sorting out the contents of our inner experience.

It may at first seem strange to the elementary teacher, who already thinks his pupils act too much like animals to be advised to invent games, dances, and individual scenes in imitation of animals. He is asked at the end of a trip to the zoo or a walk in the woods (or even a film or reading) to inquire not simply, "How does the spider differ from us?" but "How is the spider like us?" and "Can you imitate the spider?" Such playlets should include two or more animals in dramatic relationship, so that the actors can change parts. This way they "get into" as well as out of the qualities that different animals seem to represent. It is a kind of precursor to human roles and opens up in an indirect but vigorous way the idea of social niches and human differences as normal parts of a whole.

Note what this experience does not do. No thoughtful person, certainly no naturalist, imagines that one can get inside the skin of another creature, or even another person. One cannot truly know what being a fish or a spider is like, even though it might be argued that certain experiences, such as terror or hunger, have similarities in all sentient beings. But the purpose here is not really to understand animals. The mature reflection that one can never know the experience of another belongs much later in life, when one has achieved strength of self and firm identity. Natural scientists are incensed by anthropomorphism; nothing, they insist, could be more misleading to the young scientists they train. And they may be right about young adults. But children are anthropomorphic in their projections of human feelings onto animals for good and necessary reasons that have little to do with the factual knowledge of animals, though it does exercise their skill at watching.

Zoology, like other sciences, has a tendency to diffuse its concepts downward in the educational system. Young teachers carry the latest scientific concepts to their classrooms, and the writers of nature books and textbooks seem often to think that the objective is to make, in a simple way, hypotheses, design controlled experiments, learn detached observation and how to gather statistical data. This making of little replicas of scientists is given official sanction in the school science fair. But what is good for a high school senior may be bad for a first-year junior higher and disastrous for a third-grader.

One of the modes of talking about animals in the elementary classroom is economic. The teacher who says, "What is the robin good for?" is the dupe of a narrow materialism, even though the verdict on robins is good. It is as out of place as arguing the ethics of animal rights to children. Neither approach encourages the observation of animals. Each relegates the animals to the status of ciphers in ideological and economic games that are of little interest to children.

Analogy and Abstraction

A third educational application of the role of the animal in human growth is expressive and artistic. Literature is rich in animal simile, metaphor, allusion, allegory, and onomatopoeia. Some poets and artists make use of these figures more than others do, but the figure and reference to the organic nonhuman are so widespread that the artist must be able to assume that his audience understands this mode of thinking and seeing animals. Organic and animistic structure in the visual arts is also universal and clearly refers not only to shape but to affect, to the communication of feeling as well as form. It is not only a matter of art. The language of everyday life has thousands of figures of speech, phrases, colloquialisms, and neologisms that not only employ animal imagery but which assume a profound and fundamental habit of thought, relating consciousness to language.

Like any other usage, this animalizing of expression can be acute and fresh or merely idiomatic and stereotyped. The fineness of its distinctions depends on the diversity of animals in the mind, on the attention that the growing child has been encouraged to give the fine points of likeness and unlikeness in the natural world. For the high school student, exercises in writing, sculpting, and drawing, in which he is expressly asked to direct his work through the medium of the animal figure, have great advantage for the beginner. They allow him to tap the whole childhood realm of feeling through reference to the animal form. They dovetail with the discovery of qualities by projecting upon and introjecting from animals. They take the native childhood interest in the names and characteristics of things as a foundation on which to build. They say, in effect, "Not only do the different animals help you to sort out your own feelings, and others around you to do the same, but they enable you to use that habit to communicate your feelings to those same people, and even to use these more imaginatively." Out of this grew the more sophisticated arts of caricature, analogy, and recognition of the complex relationships between people and animals that exist because of language and imagination.

The mature artist, like the mature person, may seem arbitrarily to depart from such references. It would be interesting to know, however, how much abstraction people can stand without references to creature images. Do we really use colorful references to creatures only to embellish and decorate as we wish, or do they persist in some proportion in all our discourse? Do we all in some degree have an Antaean weakness? Is there a threshold of imaginative flight beyond which we must return to touch the earthly creatures? For every theorist who lives in the thin air of abstract nouns, perhaps we need twenty who can explain what he says by using the menagerie of familiar words.

No doubt there is a sense in which intelligence as the growth of mental agility carries us away from the creature reference. At the extreme, philosophy, theology, political theory, advanced mathematics and physics do not often find insects or birds to be useful images. It would seem that all striving to develop full individual potential must carry one thought further and further from flesh and blood. But even this remains open to question. There are philosophers, like Alfred North Whitehead, who believe that organic structure is the fundamental principle of reality, that solar systems, galaxies, "inorganic" molecules and atoms are all parts of wholes of which the organism is the prime example. To that extent, our thinking about ultimate things does not carry us away from the figure of the organism, in its form, structure, diversity, and behavior, but rather it escalates that figure to new levels. The homology may cease to use familiar species or anatomy, but yet remain unconsciously joined to the prototype with its life, metabolism, movement, reproduction, and sentience. Even non-Whiteheadians rely on some notion of order to hold the parts of their abstract creations together. There may be no models of coherence that do not depend on a childhood of think- ing bodies and thinking creatures.

Animals: Our Link with the Nonhuman Cosmos

Of all the unanswered questions of human evolution, there is one paradox whose seeming contradiction seems to me to tower hugely over the rest. The theme of our evolution has been to prolong youthfulness. Even in our adult lives we display capaci- ties for new growth, exploration, and unused potential. How do we reconcile the child-like qualities with the patience and wisdom of maturity? That we succeed even in part seems to be an ex- traordinary achievement, though perhaps we do not succeed as much as we should.

One of the characteristics of mind is its differentiating activity. In general, the world is rich enough to absorb all the separating and sorting and qualifying of which thought is capable, except in one respect: We find ourselves, our species, insufficiently di- verse. In fact, the fetalizing strategy by which our evolution proceeded made us less mature in appearance and more alike. From the standpoint of the questing brain accompanying the body, it was a disaster. The benefits of enhancing our plasticity and stretching the period of youth and learning into the third decade of life has cost us some of that external variation that the intelligent eye searches for.

We solved the problem by inventing culture. It may be de- fined as the capacity to acquire and transmit socially the symbols by which distinct groups of people define and differentiate themselves.

How this worked at first we can never know for sure. My guess is that the earliest of such differences were not so much every- day badges but formal and symbolic tokens employed on special occasions, like costumes worn in ritual dances.

Different species of animals were its model. These were con- veyed by stylized mimicry, by dancing a ceremonial expression of willed difference. Wearing parts of animals or emblems made to signify them further set off performers and memberships. Costume preceded clothing. Although their relative parts were divided, one formal and ritual, the other mundane, both arose, and continue to act as the outward marks, like plumage and pelage patterns, of group membership (or in our time, and to some extent, everywhere, in small differences) the private diversity.

For we humans there is danger in too much youth as there is in premature senility. Our hospitals are crammed with people whose mental problems frequently take the form of infantile behaviors. No less destructive is a kind of neurotic hardening of life, where rigidity and protective shells make a grotesque parody of true maturity. It is clear that a lifelong equilibrium exists between youthful openness and adult confidence. Many things may injure that steady interplay of Innocence and Judgment as they work together as partners all our lives. One is surely fear. It is in connection with fear that the constricting and deforming effects of our minding of animals may be important.

Perhaps fear underlines much of human conflict—the fear of those unlike us, other races, other ideologies, other nationalities, other cultures, despite homocentric insistence to the contrary. It is large enough to contain and predict analogies to all the human otherness we could ever meet.

This does not mean that each of us must learn to recognize every kind of animal as protection against all possible unknowns. The poetic notion that ecological relationships are a kind of society organizes nature's diversity. A new animal can be expected to fit into his community in a way that is already familiar to us. Having known a tiger is to fear the lion less, for we can assume that he too is limited, defined, a member of some group whose patterns are orderly in a generally familiar way.

Man did not evolve in a world of conscious cultural multiplicity, that is, awareness of belonging to a group whose idea of reality differed from others. He is not, therefore, a tolerant creature in that sense. He must learn to accept some relativity in human belief, even though the individual's convictions are strong. In the same sense, his geographical limitations as a hunter/gatherer restricted his familiarity to a single terrestrial ecosystem. Men who knew the tiger and his "friends" did not know the lion and his.

The diversity of natural communities does not threaten us. It just is. And, if the main tenets of this book are correct, it is our key to human tolerance. The compatibility of different ecosystems on the planet is our psychic model for strictly human peace.

It offers to the mind of the child just that combination of similarity and difference which the child as a totemic thinker wel-
comes. Even the boundaries between unlike natural systems, or
"ecotones," offer suggestive guides for cooling and integrating
the areas of contact between human groups.

But wait, you may say, we have known this variety of animal
and plant communities for a long time, and we still have war.
And before that, when people were still totally immersed in their
own culture and their own ecosystem, the knowledge of the
natural system did not prevent fear and aggression within the
human group. And before that, isn't there evidence that members
of a small group of hunters, who knew their natural environment
so well, sometimes fought among themselves? Doesn't the natural model suggest violence as well as peace? Nature may not be
all red in tooth and claw, but it certainly has its bloodshed. If
it is our model, when one creature eats another, does it not
symbolize one man's dominance over another or one nation's
swallowing another?

Historically these observations are correct. But they come from
an assumption about minding animals that is incorrect. It is not
a ready-made panacea for all human conflict. It may help reduce
the irrational fear of the other end of otherness. The eating of
one animal by another does not translate into obliteration in
analogic thought, but into marriage.

Living with domestic animals and class thought for so long,
we have fallen into the habit of seeing wild animals as a destitute
human society. Class culture perverts totemic thought by replacing metaphor with homonym. When totemic thought, with its
instinct for animal imagery, is carried forward into totemic culture, the wild animal groups are regarded as sets containing
necessary secrets for human conduct, translated by myth and
applied to actual human situations by speculative thought. When
it is carried forward into caste or class thought, on the other
hand, the wild animals are likely to be seen as atavisms ruled
by mysterious powers or mindless passions, while the domesticated animals represent puerile expressions of our civilized egos.

Thinking animals do not provide us with a literal model, but
a poetic one. In viewing the ecosystem as a mythic society, the
lion and zebra are not at war because one eats the other. Their
biological symbiotic need is mutual. The zebra watches the lion,

but it does not bolt except when chased. It does not fear the lion in the way in which I have used the word, in the sense of obsessive terror of the unknown. Zebra evolution does not lead to escape from lions, but to a more defined affiliation in which the moment of truth is directed through certain individuals at the appropriate stage in life. None of this is visible to non-totemic societies because they do not watch zebras—or, more correctly, it is apparent to any society to the degree that it watches wild zebras.

When the social Darwinists attempted to justify poverty and class conflict by pointing to the survival of the fittest in nature, they were not using nature as a symbolic model but as an extension of their theory. They were wrong not only because their natural history was inadequate (strength and pugnaciousness are only two of many factors influencing survival), but because they had misused analogy.

Much of the present dialogue among psychologists, ethologists, and others over the question of whether animals are good models for human behavior flounders for lack of this distinction. One side is right because of the validity of the poetic use of animals in the developmental program of the child's psyche. The other side is right because we know that people do not literally do things in the way or on the schedule that other species do them. All of the observations of wild animals made in the field are potentially useful to us if we allow that they provide unexpected forms of social and ecological texture. Most of them are useless or even harmful if we attempt to apply them directly to human society.

Except possibly his soul, man prizes his mind above all else. His mind is a product of his ecology as much as the rest of him. Every human mind is a product of its ecology—the same ecology. Nothing that evolves persists unless sustained by those same creative forces. Like a ball at the top of a fountain, the human head pivots on its animal backbone, the mind a turning knot of thought and dream on the end of a liquid spear of living animals.

The food and hides from animals are welcome but superfluous. Some animals support the cycles of the living biosphere, but those that whistle and howl and care for their young are minor ecologically, superfluous in the basic machinery of that sphere. They are vanishing one by one as proof of their own excess. We will not save them out of our goodness or their rights. They have no rights, any more than dinosaurs or trilobites had rights; they are not political.

We will save them, if at all, because without them we are lost. Though lost we may survive, but what we will then be cannot be foreseen. We will imagine we are all things and fear all things. The distance between us and the jellyfish and earthworms will increase, alienating us farther from the Earth. A "silent spring" will be nothing compared to the green prison of nature. The means of thinking through the difficult understanding of our humanity will be gone. We will be lost because wild mammals and birds are a magic monkey paw, a wishbone, a rabbit's foot that can enable us to love our own kind. From a once-pulsating knot of mind that gains something of its own recognition from each animal, our attention may be turned to slow cabbages or silent peas. Our thoughts will fly like pollen grains, spinning into the perfect freedom of thin, hot air.

NOTES AND REFERENCES

1. ON ANIMALS THINKING

p. 3 | Such a hierarchic, one-track approach is seen, for instance, in Bernard Rensch, "The Evolution of Brain Achievements," in Theodosius Dobzhansky *et al., Evolutionary Biology,* I, New York, Appleton-Century, 1967, and in Rensch's own book, *Evolution Above the Species Level,* New York, Columbia University, 1960, Chap. 10 on the evolution of consciousness.

p. 4 | E. E. Leppik, "Evolutionary Correlation Between Plants, Insects, Animals and Their Environments," *Advancing Frontiers of Plant Sciences* 25:1, New Delhi, 1970, and also "Evolutionary Correlation Between Plants, Insects, Animals and Soils," *Journal Paper J-4234,* Ames, Iowa Agriculture and Home Economics Experiment Station, 1963. The seminal statement of this is Loren Eiseley's "How Flowers Changed the World" in *The Immense Journey,* New York, Knopf, 1946.

p. 5 | To see a relationship between human cognition and the diversity of animals, see the following complementary papers: G. E. Hutchinson, "Homage to Santa Rosalia, or Why Are There So Many Kinds of Animals," *American Naturalist* 93:870, 1959; and Anthony Wallace, "On Being Just Complicated Enough," *Procedures of the National Academy of Science* 47:458, 1961. The role of diversity of environment in individual intelligence has also been studied by Burton L. White and his students at Harvard and documented in rat studies by Edward Bennet *et al.* in *Journal of Neurobiology* 3:47, 1972.

p. 8ff | Harry J. Jerison, *The Evolution of the Brain and Intelligence,* New York, Academic, 1973. This important book describes the evolutionary connection between ecological niche and style of intelligence. On the number of small-brained animals relative to the number of large, see Harry J. Jerison, "Brain Evolution: New Light on Old Principles," *Science* 170:1224, 1970.

p. 12 | For the basic biology of attention structure, see Monte Jay Feldman, *Diseases of Attention and Perception,* New York, Pergamon, 1970, especially Chap. 6, "The Mental Substrates of Attention."

p. 12 | The misconception of prey as victims and the confusion of history and natural history is examined in Richard Rabkin, *Inner and Outer Space,* New York, Morton, 1970, pp. 102–103.

pp. 14–15 | The mythical basis of the naming of animals is discussed in Elizabeth Sewell, *The Orphic Voice,* New Haven, Yale University, 1960.

p. 16 | On the evolution of the relationship of ear- and eye-brain in mammals, see Harry J. Jerison, *op. cit.,* 1973.

p. 19 | The intense preoccupation of primates with one another is described by M. R. A. Chance, "Attention Structure as the Basis of Primate Rank Order," *Man* 2:503, 1967.

263

p. 21 | The eclipse of the central valve of sound in modern culture is in Walter J. Ong, "World as View and World as Event," *American Anthropologist* 71:634, 1969; and Marshall McLuhan in *The Medium Is the Message,* New York, Random, 1967; and *Through the Vanishing Point,* New York, Harper, 1968.

p. 22 | Marie McDonald, "Transitional Tunes and Music Development," *The Psychological Study of the Child* 25:503, 1970.

p. 22 | See Carl Brown and S. L. Lahren, "More on Hunting Ability and Increased Brain Size," *Current Anthropology* 14:309, 1973.

p. 22 | Grover Krantz, *The Origin of Man,* Ph.D. thesis, University of Minnesota, 1971.

p. 23 | On the possibility that prehumans sang or spoke poetry before speaking, see F. B. Livingstone, "Did the Australopithecines Sing?," *Current Anthropology* 14:25, 1973. Livingstone's ideas are also discussed by Gerald Weiss in *Current Anthropology* 15:103, 1974.

p. 24 | There are many sources on the theory that language evolved as a code for recall. See, for example, Jacob Bronowski and Ursula Bellugi, "Language, Name and Concept," *Science* 168:669, 1970, or Allan Pavio, *Imagery and Verbal Processes,* New York, Holt, 1971.

p. 25 | Claude Lévi-Strauss calls the classification of anatomical parts "detotalization." See Chap. 5, "Categories, Elements, Species, Numbers," of his *The Savage Mind,* Chicago, University of Chicago, 1966.

p. 27 | Joseph D. Clark, *Beastly Folklore,* Metuchen, Scarecrow Press, 1968.

p. 30 | André Leroi-Gourhan, *Treasures of Paleolithic Art,* New York, Abrams, 1967. For criticism of his theory, see Peter Ucko and Andrée Rosenfeld, *Paleolithic Cave Art,* New York, McGraw-Hill, 1967.

p. 31 | The idea that cave art functioned to provide collective memory images is discussed in Bertram Lewin, *The Image and the Past,* New York, International Universities, 1968.

p. 32 | The concept of the transitional object is outlined in D. W. Winnicott, "Transitional Objects and Transitional Phenomena," *International Journal of Psycho-Analysis* 34:89, 1953. See also Arnold H. Modell, "The Transitional Object and the Creative Act," *Psychoanalytic Quarterly* 39:240, 1970, and his book, *Object Love and Reality,* New York, International Universities, 1968.

p. 32 | This approach to totemic thought is articulated in Claude Lévi-Strauss, *op. cit.,* Chaps. 2, 3, and 6.

pp. 33–34 | Marlene Dobkin de Rios, "Suggestive Hallucinogenic-derived Motifs from New World Monumental Earthworks," mss., n. d.

p. 35 | A good general history of gardens is Edward Hyams, *A History of Gardens and Gardening,* New York, Praeger, 1971.

p. 36 | Dewey Moore, in a personal communication.

2. THE MENTAL MENAGERIE

p. 40 | Charles F. Hockett and Robert Ascher, "The Human Revolution," *Current Anthropology* 5:3, 1964.

p. 40 | Stephen Potter, *The Theory and Practice of Gamesmanship,* London, Penguin, 1962.

p. 42 | On the cognitive function of the taxonomy of naming for children, see Frank Smith and George Miller, eds. *The Genesis of Language,* Cambridge, Massachusetts Institute of Technology, 1966.

p. 43 | Bruno Bettelheim, *The Uses of Enchantment,* New York, Knopf, 1976.

p. 46 | The developing sense of discrete locations for body parts is associated with the emergence of the concept of self. See Seymour Werner, *et al., The Body Percept,* New York, Random, 1965, and complementing it, from anthropology, William S. Laughlin's essay, "Acquisition of Anatomical Knowledge by Ancient Man," in S. L. Washburn, *Social Life of Early Man,* Chicago, Aldine, 1961, and Charles V. Lucier and James W. Van Stone, "Medical Practices and Human Anatomical Knowledge Among the Noatak Eskimos," *Ethnology* 10 (3), 1971.

p. 48 | The biology of language acquisition and its relationship to thought is a topic of widespread interest. Especially important is Eric H. Lenneberg's *The Biological Foundations of Language,* New York, Wiley, 1967. See also David Blok, "New Considerations of the Infantile Acquisition of Language and Symbolic Thought," *Psychoanalytic Review,* Spring 1976, and his article, "The Natural History of Language," in Smith and Miller, *op. cit.*

p. 48 | The developmental calendar of language as a species-specific event is widely recognized as a normal part of human ontogeny. See Lamar Roberts, "Central Brain Mechanisms in Speech," in C. Carterette, ed., *Brain Function III,* Berkeley, University of California, 1966, and Norman Gerschwind, "The Development of the Brain and the Evolution of Language," Monograph #17, *Language of Linguistics,* C. I. J. M. Stuart, ed., Washington, D.C., 1964.

p. 50 | Helen Keller, *Helen Keller's Journal, 1936–1937,* Garden City, Doubleday, 1938.

p. 52 | Roger Fry, "The Artist's Vision," in Chap. 1 of *Vision and Design,* London, Chatto & Windus, 1920.

p. 54 | Various anthropologists have called attention to the extensive taxonomic knowledge of many human groups. See, for example, Chap. 1 in Claude Lévi-Strauss, *op. cit.*

p. 55 | Gregory Bateson, *Steps to an Ecology of Mind,* New York, Chandler, 1972.

p. 57 | Morris Eagle *et al.,* "Imagery: Effect of a Concealed Figure in a Stimulus," *Science* 151:837, 1966.

p. 59 | See both Mary R. Haworth, *The CAT: Facts About Fantasy,* New York, Grune and Stratton, 1966, and Leopold Bellak, *The T.A.T., C.A.T. and S.A.T. in Clinical Use,* New York, Grune and Stratton, 1975.

p. 59 | For a discussion of the meaning of animals in the Rorschach see William Goldfarb, "The Animal Symbol in the Rorschach Test and an Animal Association Test," *Rorschach Research Exchange (Journal of Projective Techniques)* 9:8, 1945.

p. 60 | Margaret Blount, *Animal Land,* New York, Morrow, 1975.

p. 63 | The possibility that animal phobias are due to a failure of communication between left and right brain centers, see Earl Count, "On the Phylogenesis of Speech Formation," *Current Anthropology* 15:81, 1974. For a more Freudian explanation of animal phobias, see, for example, Ralph B. Little, "Spider Phobias," *The Psychoanalytic Quarterly* 36 (1) 1967.

p. 65 | Peter Michelson, *The Disney Version,* New York, Simon & Schuster, 1968.

p. 65 | Those who share the sense of nausea induced by *Jonathan Livingston Seagull,* but are not quite sure why, should see Philip Slater,

Earthwalk, Garden City, Doubleday, 1974, pp. 92–97. The story of "The Ugly Duckling" is disposed of by Bruno Bettelheim, *op. cit.*, p. 105.

pp. 72–73 | The literature on brain lateralization is now very large, but a good basic source is Stuart Diamond's *The Double Brain*, Baltimore, Williams & Wilkins, 1972.

p. 73 | Jerome H. Barkow, "Children's Tales and Information Transmission in *Homo sapiens*," unpublished ms., 1975.

p. 74 | The most comprehensive and philosophic discussion of birdsong is by Whiteheadian philosopher, Charles Hartshorne: *Born to Sing*, Bloomington, Indiana University, 1973.

3. AMBIGUOUS ANIMALS

pp. 78–79 | Two outstanding sources on the concept of taboo animals and words are Edmund Leach, "Anthropological Aspects of Language: Animal Categories and Verbal Abuse," in Eric H. Lenneberg, ed., *New Directions in the Study of Language*, New York, Wiley, 1967, and Mary Douglas, *Purity and Danger*, New York, Praeger, 1966.

p. 85 | Robert Graves, "What Is a Monster?", *Horizon* 10 (3), 1968.

p. 87 | Victor Turner, *The Forest of Symbols, Aspects of Ndembu Ritual*, Ithaca, Cornell University, 1967.

pp. 89–90 | On animal-headed prophets in general, see Zofia Ameisenova, "Animal-headed Gods, Evangelists, Saints and Righteous Men," *Journal of the Warburg and Courtald Institutes* 12, 1949. As for Moses, in particular, see Ruth Mellinkoff, *The Horned Moses in Medieval Art and Thought*, Berkeley, University of California, 1970.

p. 92 | "Caste" as opposed to "totemic" culture is an idea elaborated particularly by Claude Lévi-Strauss in Chap. 4, *op. cit.*, 1966.

p. 96 | The example given here is from Stuart A. Marks, *Large Mammals and a Brave People*, Seattle, University of Washington, 1976, pp. 132–45.

p. 99 | Two basic pieces on monsters are Wolfgang Born, "Monsters in Art," and Viktor Hamburger, "Monsters in Nature," both in *CIBA Symposium* 9 (5 and 6), Aug. and Sept., 1947.

p. 100 | Norman Cohn, "Monsters of Chaos," *Horizon* 14 (2), 1972.

p. 102 | Edward Deevey, "The Hare and the Haruspex," *The Yale Review*, Winter 1960.

p. 104 | William C. McDermott, *The Ape in Antiquity*, Baltimore, Johns Hopkins, 1938.

p. 107 | Walter Abell's theory is presented in Chap. 10 of *The Collective Dream in Art*, New York, Schocken, 1966.

p. 112 | The heuristic function of monsters for the education of neophytes is discussed by Victor Turner in *The Forest of Symbols, Aspects of Ndembu Ritual*, Ithaca, Cornell University, 1967, pp. 105–106.

4. IMITATING ANIMALS: THE CAST OF CHARACTERS

p. 117 | The quotation of Suzanne Langer is from p. 82 of Harold F. Searles, *The Nonhuman Environment*, New York, International Universities, 1960.

p. 121 | The prediction process is described by James Fernandez in his "Persuasions and Performances: The Beast in Every Body and the Metaphors of Everyman," *Daedalus* 101 (1), 1972, and "The Mission of Metaphor in Expressive Culture," *Current Anthropology* 15:119, 1974.

p. 125 | The adolescent's growing sense of the dual meaning of words is described in Norman Kiell, *The Universal Experience of Adolescence*, New York, International Universities, 1964, pp. 581–84. The way in which this characteristic is used in ritual initiation is the subject of Joseph Campbell's *The Masks of God: Primitive Mythology*, New York, Viking, 1955, Chap. 2, "The Imprints of Experience."

p. 129 | The importance of totemic thought for ourselves is the subject of Laurens Van Der Post's essay, "All Africa Within Us," *The Listener*, London, 13 Feb., 1975.

p. 131 | The Margaret Mead remark and the striptease theory are from Leszek Kolakowski, "Strip-Tease: a Dialectical Interpretation," *Atlas*, July 1967.

p. 133 | G. M. Sifakis, *Parabasis and Animal Choruses*, London, Athalone, 1971.

p. 135 | Hilda Kuper, "Costume and Identity," *Comparative Studies in Society and History* 15:348, 1973, and also "Costume and Cosmology: the Animal Symbolism of the Newala," *Man* 8:613, 1973.

p. 138 | Brooks Atkinson, *Natural History* 76:38, 1967.

p. 140 | Although mentioned in many ethnological works, the ritual sharing of game by hunters is the subject of a review paper by John H. Dowling, "Individual Ownership and the Sharing of Game in Hunting Societies," *American Anthropologist* 70:502, 1968.

p. 142 | Pages 142 to 144 are based on material from Roy Willis' *Man and Beast*, New York, Basic Books, 1974. Willis contrasts the ethos in three types of tribal-village economies, making the book extremely useful for comparisons.

p. 145 | The concept of pseudospecies is employed by Erik Erikson in "The Ontogeny of Ritualization in Man" in the *Philosophical Transactions of the Royal Society of London*, Series B, Vol. 251, 1956; in it he credits Konrad Lorenz as its originator, in *Das Sogenannte Boese*, Vienna, G. Borotha-Schoeler, 1964.

p. 146 | Among the outstanding essays on the integrated view of the human species are Robin Fox, "The Cultural Animal," in J. F. Eisenbert and Wilton S. Dillon, eds., *Man and Beast: Comparative Social Behavior*, Washington, Smithsonian, 1969; Robert Ardrey, "Four-Dimensional Man," *Encounter*, Feb., 1971; and Clifford Geertz, "The Impact of the Concept of Culture on the Concept of Man," in John R. Platt, ed., *New Views of the Nature of Man*, Chicago, University of Chicago, 1965.

5. PRETENDING THAT ANIMALS ARE PEOPLE: THE CHARACTER OF CASTE

p. 148 | G. B. Harrison, quoted in Peter Lowenberg, "Love and Hate in the Academy," *The Center Magazine* V:4, 1972.

pp. 150–51 | This description of Thai life is from S. J. Tambiah, "Animals Are Good to Think and Good to Prohibit," *Ethnology* 8:423, 1969.

pp. 151–55 | The synopsis of Nuer life is from Roy Willis, *op. cit.*

pp. 155–56 | The cockfight in Bali is based on Clifford Geertz, "Deep Play: Notes on the Balinese Cockfight," *Daedalus* 101:1, 1972.

pp. 158–59 | The Fipa synopsis is from Roy Willis, *op. cit.*

p. 163 | Kenneth Inness, *D. H. Lawrence's Bestiary*, The Hague, Moutan, 1971.

p. 165 | André Leroi-Gourhan, *op. cit.*

p. 166 | Cesare Lombroso, *Criminal Man*, New York, Putnam, 1911, p. 6.

p. 167 | E. H. Gombrich, *Caricature*, London, Penguin, 1940.

p. 168 | Richard Adams, *Watership Down*, New York, Macmillan, 1974.

p. 171 | See Helen Waddell, *Beasts and Saints*, New York, Holt, 1934.

p. 172 | See, for example, Henry J. Owens, *The Scandalous Adventures of Reynard the Fox*, New York, Knopf, 1945.

p. 177 | Carolyn Moburg, *The Love Bestiary*, a translation of the book by Richard de Fournival, ms., 1972.

p. 180 | Helen Hastings, *Man and Beast in French Thought of the Eighteenth Century*, Baltimore, Johns Hopkins, 1936; George Boas, *The Happy Beast in French Thought of the Seventeenth Century*, Baltimore, Johns Hopkins, 1933; Anthony G. Petti, "Beasts and Politics in Elizabethan Literature," in S. Gorley Putt, ed., *Essays and Studies Collected for the English Association*, Vol. 16, N.S., London, Murray, 1963.

p. 183 | C. S. Lewis, *Of Other Worlds*, London, Bles, 1966.

p. 185 | E. P. Evans, *Animal Symbols in Ecclesiastical Architecture*, London, 1896, (Detroit, Gale, 1969). See also Francis Klingender's splendid work, *Animals in Art and Thought to the End of the Middle Ages*, Cambridge, Massachusetts Institute of Technology, 1971.

p. 187 | Hans Sachs, "The Delay of the Machine Age," *Psychoanalytic Quarterly* 2:404, 1933.

p. 188 | C. S. Lewis describes the "discovery" of the inanimate in *The Discarded Image*, New York, Cambridge University, 1964. The emergence of the concept of the body as a machine is traced in Leonora Cohen Rosenfeld, *From Beast-Machine to Man-Machine*, New York, Oxford, 1940. See also Wallace Shugg, "The Cartesian Beast-Machine in English Literature (1663–1750)," *Journal of the History of Ideas* 29 (2), 1968.

p. 192 | Desmond Morris, *The Naked Ape*, New York, McGraw-Hill, 1967.

p. 193 | On the relationship of adolescent girls to horses, see Bruno Bettelheim, *op. cit.* pp. 56–57.

p. 196 | Marcel Heiman, "The Relationship Between Man and Dog," *Psychoanalytic Quarterly* 25:568, 1956.

p. 196 | Boris M. Levinson, Ph.D., *Pets and Human Development*, Springfield, Thomas, 1972.

p. 198 | Lauretta Bender and Jack Rapoport, "Animal Drawings of Children," *Journal of Orthopsychiatry* 14:521, 1944.

p. 200 | Karl A. Menninger, "Totemic Aspects of Contemporary Attitudes Toward Animals," in G. B. Wilbur and W. Muensterberger, eds., *Psychoanalysis and Culture*, New York, International Universities, 1951.

p. 202 | Gezo Roheim, *The Gates of the Dream*, New York, International Universities, 1953.

p. 203 | The developing sense of relatedness between the individual and the nonhuman environment is the subject of Harold F. Searles, *op. cit.* See particularly pp. 30, 329, 330, and 396.

p. 205 | A good example of the criticism of "nature lovers" is Alistair D. Graham, *The Gardeners of Eden*, London, Allen and Unwin, 1973.

pp. 209–10 | Romain Gary, *The Roots of Heaven*, p. 32.

6. THE AESOP ACCOUNT

p. 213 | David Potter, *People of Plenty, Economic Abundance and the American Character*, Chicago, University of Chicago, 1954.

7. WHAT GOOD ARE ANIMALS?

p. 244 | Of many treatises on the utility of animals, see Edward Hyams, *Animals in the Service of Man*, New York, Lippincott, 1972, and Herman Dembeck, *Animals and Men*, London, Nelson, 1966.

p. 244*n* | On Thoreau's use of "ecology," see letter by Paul H. Oehser, *Science*, April 17, 1959.

p. 245 | Although not new, John Storer's *The Web of Life*, New York, Devin-Adair, 1953, is a prototype. The ecological imperative for preserving animal life has been the subject of many articles and books. One of the most intelligent is David Ehrenfeld's *Conserving Life on Earth*, New York, Oxford, 1972.

p. 247 | The rights of animals has had much recent attention. Typical is Richard L. Means, *The Ethical Imperative*, Garden City, Doubleday, 1969.

INDEX